And Go Like This

This

stories

by

John Crowley

Small Beer Press
Easthampton, MA

And Go Like This: Stories copyright © 2019 by John Crowley (johncrowleyauthor.com). All rights reserved. Page 337 is an extension of the copyright page.

Small Beer Press
150 Pleasant Street #306
Easthampton, MA 01027
smallbeerpress.com
weightlessbooks.com
info@smallbeerpress.com

Distributed to the trade by Consortium.

Library of Congress Cataloging-in-Publication Data

Names: Crowley, John, 1942- author.
Title: And go like this : stories / by John Crowley.
Description: First edition. | Easthampton, MA : Small Beer Press, [2019]
Identifiers: LCCN 2019013499 (print) | LCCN 2019015563 (ebook) | ISBN 9781618731647 | ISBN 9781618731630 (alk. paper)
Classification: LCC PS3553.R597 (ebook) | LCC PS3553.R597 A6 2019 (print) |
  DDC 813/.54--dc23
LC record available at https://lccn.loc.gov/ 2019013499

First edition 1 2 3 4 5 6 7 8 9

Set in Centaur MT.

Printed on 30% PCR recycled paper in the USA.

Table of Contents

TO THE PROSPECTIVE READER,
UPON OPENING THIS BOOK

Books, unlike some other modes of communication, require no instructions for use. It's one of the reasons they've lasted so long. But a note as to why *this* book is perhaps worth a reader's attention might be welcome.

There are writers who form a style early on and apply it to what interests them. As their interests change or new ones develop, the style adapts but doesn't necessarily need to change; even radically different fictional situations and plots can be well served by the writer's refined and updated (but not necessarily reformed) style. Such writers can often be recognized in a single sentence: I think I could recognize any Thomas Pynchon sentence in the context of no context.

Then there are the chameleons of fiction writing, whose verbal and story-telling styles change with the subjects they alight on. Such writers are less likely to be identifiable in a single sentence extracted from their work; instead of the sturdy and dependable style, adaptable to any circumstance, there is a restless search for a proper coloration—that is, finding a way for the matter of the story to produce the language appropriate to it, as the mythical chameleon is colored by the background on which it rests and not the other way around.

You will already be thinking that I count myself in the second category, and I believe a reading of this collection will bear that out, even if the whole isn't read (though the whole will certainly demonstrate it). The chameleon mode doesn't involve just phrases or sentences; it can be seen in the deployment of time, how events are contained within the recounting of other events, past moments recalled that shape present moments and even endings—what might be called reader-writer relations, a form of diplomacy, in which readers are self-selected by the work if the work is inviting enough to them. Fiction doesn't need to be a conversation—most of Beckett can't be said to be—but the chameleon style almost has to be. In this collection readers may choose conversations that reflect the ordinary circumstances of ordinary lives in the approximate present ("Mount Auburn Street," in three parts) or the first-person—invented—memory story ("The Girlhood of Shakespeare's Heroines") or the fantasy-history couched in language flavored by the time-period ("Flint and Mirror") or the tenderly metafictional "This Is Our Town." Two or three brief joke stories that each require a language ("In the Tom Mix Museum," "The Million Monkeys of M. Borel," "And Go Like This") might form a tasting menu reflecting the chameleon method I am describing. In any case, I am confident (or vain) enough to think that almost any reader will find one or two things here that touch or amuse, and—the utmost hope—are remembered long after.

The Girlhood of Shakespeare's Heroines

In the late 1950s the state of Indiana had its own Shakespeare festival, though not much of the world knew about it. Far too little of the world, as it happened, to keep it in existence. But for a few summers it was there, a little Brigadoonish, or like the great Globe itself, that leaves not a rack behind.

That was a time for Shakespeare festivals. One had recently begun in Stratford, Ontario, directed at first by the great impresario Tyrone Guthrie. I used to pore over the pictures in my *Theater Arts* magazine. (I was surely one of the few boys my age who had a subscription; who asked for a subscription for Christmas.) It had begun as simply a big striped tent, then became a tentlike building; it had a clever all-purpose stage set on which Roman and Venetian and English plays could all be accommodated. The man who got the idea for a Shakespeare festival in this little town was a disabled war veteran, who liked the fact that his hometown was named for Shakespeare's. There was a picture of him, shy and good-looking, leaning on his cane.

Stratford, Connecticut, had a Shakespeare festival too, about as far from Indiana, where Harriet Ingram and I both lived, as Stratford, Ontario, was. On a summer trip to the sea—from which long ago her mother had been taken away by her father to sea-less Indiana—Harriet wangled a visit to the Connecticut Stratford. While her family picnicked on the great lawn waiting for the matinee to begin, Harriet walked up and entered the cool dark of the theater, whose smell is one of the few she can recall today from that time; she passed around a velvet rope and down into the empty auditorium. On stage an actor read lines to himself under a single rehearsal light hanging over the stage. Harriet walked down closer and closer, seeing up into the flies and inhaling the charged air, when the floor beneath her vanished and she fell into darkness.

The trap was only six or eight feet deep, and Harriet claimed to be all right, but the actor, who had heard her tumble down, made her lie still till help could be called; they got her out and took her backstage and bound up a nice long gash on her arm with yards of gauze, and she was made to call the theater's doctor on the phone, who put her through a series of movements to find out if any bones were broken. Then the young actor who had rescued her took her all over the theater, into the dressing rooms and the scene shop and the rehearsal rooms. When her mother finally found her, she was talking Shakespeare with her new friend and some others, like Jesus among the doctors, with probably something of a religious glow about her too.

Indiana had no town named Stratford, but there was one named Avon, an almost quaint little Brown County town through which a small river ran, where swans could be induced to reside. Not far from the town, a utopian sect had once owned several hundred acres of farmland, where they began building an ideal community before dying out or moving West; what remained of their community was a cheerless brick dormitory, a wooden meeting house, and a huge limestone and oak-frame circular barn: circular because of the founder's scientific dairying theories, and circular because of his belief in the circle's perfection. The barn was over a hundred feet in diameter, and lit like a church by a clerestory and a central windowed turret; when an ad-hoc preservation committee first went in, in 1955, it still smelled faintly of hay and dung. It was as sound as a Greek temple, though the roof was just beginning to leak.

So History wanted the place preserved; and Commerce wanted it to turn a profit and bring custom into the town; and Culture wanted whatever it was used for to be not vulgar or debased. A young man who had grown up in a big house nearby, who had made money in New York and then come home, conceived the festival plan. His money and enthusiasm brought in more, some of it, as we would learn, from unlikely places; and the process began to turn the great round barn into an Elizabethan theater. Among the methods the organizers used to publicize, and partly to underwrite, the Avon festival was to offer a number of apprentice positions to Indiana high-school students: these were a little more costly to the chosen students than a good summer camp would have been—I think there were scholarships for some—and provided the festival with some enthusiastic labor. When Harriet, that year a junior, heard about the program, she felt a tremendous grateful relief to learn that the world was not after all empty of such a possibility, and at the same time an awful anxiety that this one would escape from her before she could secure it for herself.

Harriet's mother used to explain Harriet by saying that she was stagestruck, but that wasn't so, and Harriet resented the silliness of the epithet; she connected it with a girlish longing for Broadway and stardom, glamour, her name in lights—Harriet's ambitions were at once more private and more extravagant. When one of her parent's friends asked her what she wanted to be when she grew up—she was about thirteen—Harriet answered that she wanted to be a trage*dee*an.

Harriet and I grew up on different sides of the state. Her parents taught (history and economics) at a little Quaker college in Richmond, in the east; my father was a lawyer in Williamsport. The Williamsport house was a big square Italianate place, almost a mansion, built by my mother's grandfather, who had been lieutenant governor of the state and Ambassador to Peru under Grant. A ten-foot ormolu mirror in the front hall came from Peru.

Harriet went to a smelly old public school—Garfield High—and after classes she took dance lessons and on weekends she rode horses; and she read, in that deep and obsessive way, with that high tolerance for boredom, that is (it seems to me) gone from the world: read books about Isadora Duncan and Mae West, read Shaw and Milton's *Comus* and the plays of Byron and Feydeau and Wilde's *Salome*. And Shakespeare: carrying the family's Complete Works around with her, its spine cracking and its fore-edge grimy from her fingers. She read the major plays, of course, though to this day she hasn't read *Lear*, but mostly she turned to the odd numbers, *Cymbeline* and *Measure for Measure* and *Troilus and Cressida*. She keeps surprising me with the odd things she read then and still remembers. I went to a little private school my family had an interest in, and spent a year home-schooled (as they call it now) because of my asthma, mostly better now. So we were both smart, sheltered, isolated kids, she isolated by being an only child, I surrounded by four sisters and a brother but miles from anything and dreaming about Theater, or Theatre, as I much preferred to spell it.

Mine was a kind of megalomania not so unusual in a kid with my statistics, so to speak; dreams of dominance and glory. Most of my ambitions, and most of my knowledge, came out of books; just like Harriet, I'd never seen many plays, though I tried to see as many as I could reach. They all seemed comically inadequate to me, shaming even, I bit my nails to the quick and squirmed in my seat till my mother took my shoulder to hush me.

I didn't quite understand then that the theater work I dreamed about mostly dated to a time thirty or forty years before, when the town library acquired the albums and monographs in the Theater section that I pored over. I was studying Max Rheinhardt's vast productions in Weimar Germany, the stage designs of Gordon Craig (he was Isadora Duncan's lover). Once, I found in that library a book about how to build your own Greek theater and put on pageants. I tried to convince my mother that a Greek theater like this would be perfect in our broad back yard, over in front of the tall poplars (the drawings in my books were full of poplars) and look, you could buy these Ionic columns from any building-supply house for ten dollars. The book, however (my mother showed me, laughing), had been published in 1912.

Harriet thought that was a sweet story. I told it to her in Avon, that summer we were both apprentices there, the summer that changed everything. We were sitting by the campfire the apprentices made most nights, far enough away not to be grilled, near enough so the smoke discouraged the mosquitoes. She listened and laughed and then told me about falling into the open trap in Stratford, Connecticut. By the end of her story everybody was listening.

It seemed then that Harriet had a better chance than I did of going on the way we were both headed. My visions all needed pots of money to realize, and the cooperation of many others, and the kind of tyrannical will and willingness to be boss that it would turn out I had none of. But everything Harriet needed came right out of Harriet; all she had to do was bring forth more, and there was more—that was clear. I knew it even then.

It's the middle of June in Harriet's thirty-eighth year, a brilliant day of high barometric pressure. Harriet gets up early to take her camera out and make some pictures.

The camera is a huge eight-by-ten plate camera of polished wood, cherry and ebony, with brass fittings and a leather bellows. Harriet thinks its the most beautiful and affecting object she owns; with its tripod of telescoping legs, also wood and brass, and its great glass eye, it seems to Harriet to be more a relative than a belonging, a gaunt beloved aunt, an invalid but still merry husband. *Did you ever ever ever in your long-legged life* (Harriet sings) *see a three-legged sailor and his four-legged wife.*

Harriet has been using not film in the camera but paper, ordinary panchromatic printing paper. When exposed, the paper becomes a negative, and it can be printed by contact with another sheet. The resulting image is exact and exquisitely detailed but softened and abstracted—both warmed and cooled—by the light's passing through a textured paper negative rather than through a transparent plastic one. The very first photographic negatives were made on paper.

So by the yellow safe-light in her bathroom Harriet on this morning removes from their box six sheets of paper, and slips them into her three plate-holders, front and back: six exposures, the most she would ever make on a single trip, even on such a day as this one. She slides each black Bakelite slide back over the face of the paper and locks them up, safe in total darkness till their moment of day has come.

Dismantled and shut up, the camera fits in the back of the Rabbit, though it takes Harriet three trips to bring it and its tripod and the bag of plate-holders out to the car. Harriet goes out of town early, driving up from the river into the old and largely abandoned farmlands above: hillside fields bordered by old woods are a thing she likes to photograph when the slanting sunlight seems to set fire to the tall sedges' heads and the shade is deep; another thing is dirt roads lined with old maples, the sun picking certain masses of leaves to illuminate like stained glass and the sun falling in tigerish stripes over the road's arched back.

Once Harriet and I were talking about what we would most like to have been if we weren't what we are. I said—I forget what I said, but Harriet said she had always thought it would be impossible to be a landscape painter and be unhappy; unhappy in your work anyway. She still believes it's so but only if you are better at it than she was or could expect ever to be. For a while when she was younger she did paint, and it made her not happy at all to work all day and then next day look at what you had done, which claimed to be what you had seen and felt but wasn't at all. The opposite of happy. But these photographs don't disappoint that way. The happiness they give is a little pale and fleeting—half an hour to set up the camera and make an exposure (hurry, hurry, the earth's turning, the light's changing) and an hour or two to make a true print: but it's real happiness. Since they're made from paper negatives rather than film, they seem to Harriet not to have that look of being stolen from the world rather than made from it that most landscape photographs have; they are shyer and more tentative somehow. Not painting, no, but satisfying in some of the same ways. And she says they are selling pretty well in her shop too.

By nine the sun has stopped making the effects that Harriet likes; she's made four exposures. She's more weary than she expected to be, getting in and out of the car, dealing with the camera's three legs, and her own four. The tripod lies on the back seat, her two steel crutches (enameled maroon) on top of it.

Coming back into town, Harriet's car pulls up next to mine at a stoplight. She calls over to me:

"Did you hear the news?"

"What news?"

"Somebody killed the Pope. I just heard on the radio."

"Yes. I heard that. But he's not dead. He's just hurt."

"Oh." She glances at the red light and scoots over in the seat to see me a little better. "I've been thinking about your question," she says. "I have."

"And?"

"And I have," she calls. "I have."

The month before, heart-turning May, I asked Harriet to marry me. She hasn't answered. The light changes, and we turn in different directions.

Those of us chosen for the Indiana Shakespeare Festival at Avon (it included almost all of those who applied that year, being a summer option unthinkable to most people in that state then or now) received a letter in May that showed a bust of plump Shakespeare, pen in hand—an etching of the monument over his grave in Stratford, I can see now—and instructions on what we were to bring that sounded like any summer camp's: raincoat and sweater, blanket and sneakers and writing materials for letters home. I watched my mother sew tapes with my name on them into every pair of shorts and socks.

We came from around the state by car or bus, pulling into town on the appointed day uncertain where anything was or how to get to the theater or the place we were to go, only to find that the town was so small that it was evident where everyone was gathered, on the little green by the riverside, where a Union soldier stood on a small granite plinth, the names of the town's dead carved on it.

She's almost the only one I can now remember seeing when we arrived, though I know she wasn't the one I looked at most, or took the greatest interest in. No. Harriet had her own way of dressing and looking, and it didn't fit with my received images of what I wanted to look at. The tough girls from northern Indiana, "the Region," favored beehive haircuts, mascara like kohl around their eyes, and pale lipstick; the country girls had blond flips and wore bobby socks over the stockings they'd put on for the trip. Harriet wore loose peasant blouses, and wide skirts in many colors, and flat shoes or sandals without backs; her haystack hair kept her busy pushing it from her face, and she drew strange orange-y eyebrows over her own, above the cat's-eye pink glasses. Her cheeks were flushed; I didn't know if that was makeup or not. She moved with overprecise grace, the studied manner of a dancer, though I didn't recognize that either. She was herself. She was a Free Spirit.

"Hi."

"Hi."

"Where've you come from?"

"Williamsport."

"Uh . . . ?"

"Near Lafayette."

"Oh right. Hi."

"Hi."

Why would she greet me? I didn't think of myself as particularly visible to others then, or possessing anything that would attract their attention; I don't remember my own clothes, but I'm sure they weren't designed to impress, as I wouldn't have known how to do that. I suppose *shy* is the obvious word, though like many shy people I only needed the right signs of acceptance and welcome—however I understood them—to offer myself more completely than the gladhanders.

By afternoon we were all gathered in the center of town, with our clumsy bags and suitcases—backpacks weren't common then; I remember Harriet had a couple of cases with poodles appliquéd on them, one of them round, like a pillbox. The festival director was to put in an appearance, and Robin, who would be directing the plays and managing the apprentices, was to welcome us and give instructions, but no one had seen them. Parents who'd brought their kids stood with them by their station wagons, the kids eager to slip away. We were about twenty in all, some of us full-grown, some still children. I don't remember perceiving that but it must be so.

Then—making an entrance, at which he was skilled—Robin was among us, going from one to another with a look on his face as though he had just discovered astonishing and unsuspected treasure. *Oh brave new world, that has such people in it!*

He was particularly attentive to the parents. Sandy, his wife, was with him, doing as he did but at the same time watching his performance appreciatively. They were the most beautiful people I'd ever stood near. Sandy with the collar of her soft white shirt up, her hands in the pockets of her capris, looked to me like Kim Novak: the same hooded grey eyes, the same softness; like Novak she would wear, sometimes, no bra. Robin was lean and hawklike, with piercing eyes and deep-drawn brachiators. They were both remarkably small—not small at all, really, but remarkably so for the persons they were, for the size of the persons they projected.

We apprentices were housed in a nearby summer camp that hadn't been used for a year, the cabins dusty and the mattresses musty; I can still smell them sometimes. An assistant stage manager and his wife were our counselors or chaperones. There was an old bus that each morning drove the twenty of us the five miles to the Swan—that's what they called their theater, their barn-becoming-a-theater—and back again at day's end to the camp, where we were fed huge dinners of children's food, tuna casseroles and spaghetti and Spam. The kitchen help made leftovers into sandwiches and gave them to us in boxes for lunch.

All day we worked in the Swan, cleaning and painting and building seating. That's what we were there for, free labor, but we didn't mind that, there was nothing we wouldn't do, and anyone who complained or refused immediately had his place taken by a volunteer. I'd never played sports unless dragooned into them, as at school; had never made the team or been to camp or done any group task at all—none except the pageants and plays I organized my siblings into, and the senior play—and I had a near-mystical experience being included in this gang. All the same I would often find ways to escape them, sneak out of the horseplay, hide. It wasn't hard. The funny fat little bus that carried us to and fro went through the town center as well, to pick up the actors and others who were staying in Tourist Homes or with proud citizens, and I would take it into town and sit on the Methodist church steps, or go into the cool book-odorous little library, or just stand in the street feeling this nameless, wondrous feeling that inhabited me, that was freedom, or something even better. Somehow without my even asking I had been passed through the membrane of common reality into another space, where things were not as they were where I came from; where Shakespeare was important, and everything else less so, and what I knew about mattered, and what I didn't know about was inconsequential, and it was midsummer.

I've always had difficulty associating with actors, and these actors (most of them wanted to be actors) were just embarking on their careers of self-display; there were sullen James Dean and Brando imitators smoking in silence and reading Rimbaud and Kerouac; there were extravagant hearts-on-their-sleeves personalities who had found out that by defining themselves as actors they could pretend to be only pretending to be the people they actually were, and get away with it; there were the narcissists-in-training, both the secret and the patent kind, jealous of their self-assigned centrality. The dramas they improvised all summer were wondrous and repellent to me; I saw more tears, male and female, than anywhere else in the whole of that decade. I'm given to nervous laughter, not the best response.

Harriet was different; she seemed at once avid for the blowups and collisions the others created and gently mocking of them—with me, whom she chose to take part in her study of them. I didn't know why.

Harriet was different. Harriet would seek me out at the campfires, take cigarettes from my pack (that was how I was becoming an adult) and let me light them, and then almost immediately discard them into the fire. Harriet called me *dear boy* because an aged, absurdly courtly actor in the company called every male that. Harriet would get up late each morning, sail out past the surly woman handing out the box lunches, skip onto the bus with a smile back at me. Sometimes I caught her looking at me in the rear-view mirror of the bus too. I didn't know why. I don't know why. But I looked frankly back at her in that mirror, and not away; and maybe that was enough.

At the end of a workday soon after we got there, Robin called us together from our jobs and herded us out to the field—it had once been farmyard and was to be the parking lot when the heavy equipment arrived, if it ever did—to the enormous oak that grew all alone there: an oak just like Stratford's, we'd all been told, and warned to carve no initials in it.

By the oak, Robin was hunkered down next to someone we'd never seen before, who sat hands on his knees in a chair that had been brought out for him from the dormitory building where the festival's offices were, or would be. The man wore a seersucker suit and a pale bow tie, the only tie in evidence there, the only jacket too. Beside his chair an old belted leather briefcase sat drooping like a weary dog.

When all of us had gathered (a few late arrivals wandering from faraway parts of the grounds), Robin stood, dusted his hands on the back of his pants, and looked us over. We apprentices were immediately silent. The actors, some at least, immune to his authority or his portrayal of authority, went on talking until Robin at last hushed them with raised hands. Then he paused before he spoke.

"I've asked you to come out and meet a man who has been very important to the progress of this festival theater," he said, "someone without whose help there would very likely be no season this year." He looked down at the man in the chair, who was smiling at once eagerly and apologetically. "It's a great honor to have him here today, he's come a very long way to be here, to see the progress we've made, and he's asked for a little time today to talk to you about something very important, something you may not have thought about."

Then he held out his hand to the man, and said his name, which I have never been able to remember; nor do I recognize it now among the names of those who were of his party, or shared his beliefs, though surely it is there amid all their privately printed publications and pamphlets and books. We applauded politely, and he held up a hand to us but didn't rise. He was an academic-looking man, long-necked and pale, with ginger hair so long and fine it floated in the faint breezes that came and went as he spoke.

"Oh now, thank you, Robin," he said, in the warmest and kindest sort of voice, one of those voices so unassuming and good that you almost have to smile in response to it, even before it says anything of consequence. "I won't take up very much of your time at all, I promise; I know how little you have in order to be ready, and I don't want Robin angry at me. But I thought I might bring up something for you to think about in the weeks ahead as you work and study here."

I suppose it was his not standing that made us, or me, study him a little more closely. He wore wing-tip brown shoes that seemed as though they had never been walked in, and around the middle of each, like a stirrup, a band of metal went, and up beneath the cuffs of his wrinkled pants. And in the grass behind his chair a pair of canes. I've thought of those canes, since then, and those braces. I've wished I could ask about them. There are things in your past, preserved in memory almost by chance, that only later on, because of the course your own life takes, come to seem proleptic, or significant, or fascinating, when other things don't.

"All of you," he began, "boys and girls, men and women, are so wonderfully fortunate to be here, in this beautiful place, immersed all day long in the works of the greatest author who ever wrote in English. I envy you very much. I wonder though how many of you have ever given thought to just who the man was who wrote these wise and witty and passionate works. Who was he? Well, we can look at that picture that accompanied the First Folio, the first complete printing of a number of plays ascribed to this fellow, and try to learn something of him, but we can't learn much, and in fact that picture doesn't actually seem to be a picture of anyone, does it? There's something wholly unreal about it, I think, that gets more unreal the longer you look. In the book a little poem is printed opposite the picture that says it's him to the life, exactly as he lived, but the picture's so odd that you wonder if the poem is a joke, an 'in' joke maybe. And in the end the poem tells us to 'look not on his picture, but his book.' Which takes us back where we started.

"Well then we might consult the histories, and look for the contemporary accounts of his life, how he lived, how he struck his friends and admirers, what he said. And of course there is next to nothing. Of the man credited with having written this vast body of deathless writing, we know very, very little. There is not a single letter from him in existence. We know that a man of his name was listed as an actor in the company that produced the plays; we have a few shaky signatures on a few legal documents; we know that the actor retired to Stratford, where he came from, and sued a few people and signed a will and died. That's about it. In his will there is no mention of plays or manuscripts, indeed no mention of books at all; perhaps he had none. He certainly was unconcerned with his own writings."

He pulled a large handkerchief from his pocket and wiped his face. From where I stood beneath the oak, I could see Harriet sitting on the ground near the speaker, elbows on her knees and her cheeks on her fists like a gargoyle, fascinated or seeming to be.

"Very well then," he said. "Suppose we confess that we know just about nothing that we would like to know about the author of these poems and plays, not a thing at all about the mind or opinions of the actor whose name was the same or similar to the author's—I say 'similar' because on none of the documents we have is his name spelled as it's spelled on the first major edition of his works, the First Folio as it's called.

"We have to turn around, then, I think, and see if within the works themselves we can learn something of the man who wrote them. Most of them, of course, are plays, and not personal opinions or lyric self-expression, but not all; there's a large body of personal, very personal, writing, the Sonnets, and even in the plays the mind of the man comes through in the allusions he makes, the things he seems to know about and uses for poetic comparison and so on. And what appears when we study the work with this in mind?

"Well, I've made a list," he said, and grinned somewhat self-deprecatingly. "I'm not the first to have made one, and I think that many of you may have a mental list of your own, a list of what you think the man was like." He flapped open the briefcase and after a brief search pulled out some typewritten sheets.

"First of all, he was apparently a man." He looked up, and we laughed dutifully.

"He seems to have had a classical education." He consulted his paper, though it was evident he had no need to. "All his writing is full of allusions to the Greek and Latin classics. He seems to have been very familiar with Italy, with certain other European places, such as Navarre in France. He also read Italian: some of the plays are based on Italian stories that had not been translated when he wrote. What else? Well, the Sonnets picture a man who was at one time poor, in disgrace, in exile. I say exile because sonnets which complain of his separation from his beloved make it sound so enforced. 'When in disgrace with fortune and men's eyes,' he says, 'I all alone beweep my outcast state.'

He looked up at us. "He says, not once but several times in the sonnets, that he's lame," he said. "Interesting. 'I, made lame by Fortune's dearest spite.' Could that be a metaphorical lameness? Well, maybe; but he says it more than once. 'Speak of my lameness, and I straight will halt,' meaning stumble.

"So.

"A few more things. His knowledge of the law is so extensive, and his use of legal terms in all sorts of situations so constant, that it's hard to believe he wasn't trained for the law. And another thing we can guess at, that some critics are more certain of than others. The sonnets suggest that at least some time in his life he was what the learned of the time described as *paiderastes*, or in our modern language, a sexual invert."

He folded up his paper then and put it away with care, as though to give us time to ponder all this, which we did, I did anyway. I was beginning to feel very odd, as though a trick or a trap were being constructed for me, a *gin* Will would say, and that the man's self-effacement and reasonableness and sweetness were part of it.

"So." He removed his jacket, still without standing, and there were dark sweat-circles under his arms. "What if you were to suppose that you *didn't* know the name of the man who wrote these plays. Suppose you knew *when* they were written, and knew a lot about the people living in England then, and any one of them could have been the author, and not just the one actor fellow with the similar name. Who would you suspect? How would you narrow the search? Where, if you were a detective or a private eye, would you turn your magnifying glass, or your flashlight?

"Well, you probably already know, or many of you do, certainly Robin here knows, that this search has in fact been going on for a very long time, ever since people began to suspect that the man Shakespear, or Shaxper, or Shagsberd, made a very poor match with the writings.

"If the author was someone else, he kept his identity secret. That's all we know to start with. He kept his identity secret, and must have had a reason. Well. I can tell you some of the people who have been suspected at one time or another, who various detectives have guessed might fit the particulars we worked out, and other ones too.

"There are educated poets, like Christopher Marlowe and Edward Dyer. Now, Marlowe was certainly a pederast. Of course Marlowe was murdered before the Shakespeare plays began to appear, but, well, maybe he wasn't really. There's the Earl of Oxford, who loved plays and players but maybe wouldn't have wanted to associate himself with the common theater. Unfortunately he died before several of the greatest plays were written. One candidate isn't even a man: someone's claimed that Queen Elizabeth herself was the author."

He paused a moment, waiting for us to join him in marveling at this. Then he wiped his face again. There is nowhere hotter than Indiana on a July afternoon.

"There is one name, though," he said, "that has been consistently proposed by students for nearly a hundred years as the most likely. He was an educated man, a man who was familiar with courts and the nobility, trained as a lawyer, a major character in the political realm who may well have had reasons for keeping his playwriting a secret. He may have left his signature in the writings, because he was interested in codes and ciphers, and made up his own. He was certainly *paiderastes*; that's well attested. His name was Francis Bacon."

There was a sort of movement among us then, as the name went around, some nodding or crossing their arms or grinning, perhaps because they agreed, or because it was the name they expected to hear, or *not* the one they expected to hear, or simply in acknowledgment that the little speech had reached a climax.

He went on to lay out, I'm sure, the Baconian case that day, and I could recreate it as I've recreated his speech to us; I don't remember it in detail. But I remember what he said at the end.

"I haven't come here to make a convert of anyone," he said. "I'm just fortunate to've been able to help get this wonderful project under way, and these plays produced here, no matter whose name is attached to them. Or why they're here rather than someplace else."

He reached behind him, groping to find the canes in the grass where he had dropped them, and Robin quickly got them and handed them to him. He stood, and we watched him accomplish it.

"Please remember this, though," he said. "Remember that nothing needs to be the way you've always thought it has to be. Even if everyone with the power to say so insists it must. Francis Bacon said, '*The monuments of wit survive the monuments of power.*' Well, I think that in his case it's true. The monuments of his wit have survived under another's name, where he hid them himself from the machinations of power. I believe that's so. I don't ask you to do so. I just want to wish you all the very best of luck in this coming season."

He seemed to have moved himself; we were all very quiet, sensing that, and maybe he sensed our stillness. Anyway he laughed, and put out his left hand to Robin, who took it with his right, and we all applauded, rather wildly actually, the whole thing had been so startling and unexpected, and here was the end of it; and then we dispersed.

I knew that this controversy existed, of course; it was the kind of thing I would read about in my mother's *Saturday Review* or see on *Odyssey* on Sunday morning television. I thought Bacon was the old-fashioned choice, and had been passed over in favor of some more convincing others. I didn't really care. I was as interested in these theories as I was in flying saucers, or the guilt of the Rosenbergs, or the miracles at Lourdes. I thought the world was one way, and it was obvious what that way was, and people who struggled to alter it had reasons particular to them, a kind of sublime dissatisfaction that had nothing to do with what is in fact the case. I still think so, most of the time. Between the enthusiasts and the hardheads who dismiss them, I love the enthusiasts and stand with the hardheads. I don't think Harriet likes this about me, all in all. She thinks that nothing needs to be the way that power insists it is. It's part of being a Free Spirit.

The next day we found screwed into the wood of the Stratford Oak a small and elegant brass plaque.

Placed in Memory of the British Polymath and Genius
Francis Bacon
And in honor of his deathless contributions to our literature & language
July 10, 1959
The Monuments of Wit Survive the Monuments of Power

"But it's ridiculous," Harriet said to me. We walked together from the Oak to the theater. "You can't go around talking about *bacon*. 'I've got to study my bacon. So much wisdom can be found in bacon. We can all get smarter by studying bacon. Oops, I've misplaced my bacon. I mean come on."

"'Shakespeare' is a kind of odd name," I said. "It's just that we're used to it."

Harriet looked at me in contempt. "It's a beautiful name," she said. "Maybe the best name ever. The best."

We trudged along, raising dust. In my crowded family the way to go on from here would be to insist on opposition, take a position, tease and deride, all to keep up the connection, maybe even win a victory, of wit or force if not of reason. I knew better not to now. But not what I might do instead, or otherwise.

"What are you doing today?" I asked at last.

"Making armor," she said.

Maybe it was because the company was just beginning, was mostly young and fleet but not so impressive in stature, or maybe it was just that all the available money was going into the theater and the road out to it and the parking lots and offices: but the first production of the Indiana Shakespeare Festival was minimal, radically minimal for the times, and was meant to appear so: that was Robin's conception.

The play was *Henry V*. The company, divided into French and English, were to be dressed only in jeans and sweatshirts, rehearsal clothes; but those of the French were white, and the English dark blue. Their banners were too, just plain rectangles on poles. The play would begin with the Chorus, alone, sitting on the apron of the stage, also in rehearsal clothes of black, with the script in his hands. He was, in effect, the director of the play, and his anxiety about its effectiveness was the director's.

> *But pardon, gentles all,*
> *The flat unraiséd spirits that have dared*
> *On this unworthy scaffold to bring forth*
> *So great an object . . .*

There would be a big wooden box on stage, and from it the actors would take out the "four or five most vile and ragged foils," a mismatched collection of prop sabers and swords, as well as pieces of buckram armor for the nobles. There were four kids recruited from the high school band, two trumpets, a French horn and a kettledrum, who stayed just off the open stage and visible the whole time, playing the alarums and flourishes. Robin himself played the Chorus. I'd wondered why this play had been chosen, certainly not one of the top ten, a patriotic pageant for a country not ours: but in Robin's version it was about theater itself, and making do, and four boards and a passion. In all my grandiose thinking about theater I couldn't have come up with such a gimmick. I think now that he was good; I wonder what became of him.

There were more women in the company than you'd think would be needed, since there are only four female characters in the play (though one gets the best speech). We found out how two older women would be used when they came to rehearsals one day with hair cut short, almost cut off: they were to be the priests who begin the play, who justify Henry's war. And do no fighting themselves.

"That would be hard," Harriet said to me; we watched the women self-consciously touch their gray hair with their hands.

But that wasn't all.

Robin called us all together to see something he'd been working on.

All the plainness, he said, and the bareness, it was all fine, he loved it and it was working, working really well he thought, but it wasn't completely satisfying, was it? Did we think so? I thought whatever he thought, of course, but I nodded with the others and assented that maybe it wasn't enough. Robin said that in Elizabethan theaters they made up for the plain bare stage with brilliant costumes—most of them the cast-off clothes of noble patrons—but we didn't have them here. So he'd developed another idea, and he wanted to show us.

I don't know now if Robin had worked out the new idea long before, if he only wanted to produce in us the same surprise he aimed to achieve in audiences by saying he'd just thought of it. I know it made him seem all the more a magician to me.

He said: "Think, when we talk of horses, that you see them, printing their proud hooves i'the receiving earth." Harriet, next to me, glanced at me for just the briefest second as though it were all the time she could spare me from her attention to what was happening. And Robin lifted his arm and brought forth a horse: from the rear draped chamber it, she, stepped forth.

It was Sandy. She was the horse. She was in a leotard, I suppose, though I probably didn't know that word then; her feet shod in some kind of high shoe, a tall long-nosed mask on her head that seemed to lift her almost to a horse's height. She took slow steps and pawed delicately: printed her proud hoof in the receiving earth. Looked around herself with haughty animal unconcern; tossed her high head as though tugging at her reins.

I felt Harriet stir beside me.

Robin came close to Sandy as though to take her reins, or put his hand on her. "I will not change my horse for any that treads but on four pasterns," he said. "When I bestride him I soar, I am a hawk. He trots the air, the earth sings when he touches it."

They were the Dauphin's lines, from the night before the battle of Agincourt. Sandy tossed her head as though the steed heard these compliments.

"It is a beast for Perseus," Robin said. "He is pure air and fire, and the dull elements of earth and water never appear in him but only in patient stillness while his rider mounts him."

He took her shoulder. She was still, obedient. We were all still and silent, witnessing what it almost seemed we shouldn't. Then suddenly he dropped the character, laughed, turned Sandy to face us, who lifted off her mask; Robin lifted his hands to say, well, that's all.

We applauded.

"There won't be many," Robin said, coming downstage. "Six or eight. If any of you have experience in dance or gymnastics—I know some of you do—I hope you'll come see me and make a time to try out for these parts." He laughed. "Parts. Well. I promise you'll be on stage more than some parts with lines."

"Maybe you should," I said to Harriet, and she turned her head my way as though she had heard a small, unintelligible noise of no interest; then slowly back to the stage, where Sandy was slipping off the high shoes and holding out the mask to the costume people to take away.

Of course she tried out, and was selected. She would be the Duke of Bedford's horse, caparisoned in his arms; the actor playing the Duke was a thick hirsute man with wrestler's wrists and a low, winning voice he seemed to have invented. Steeds and riders practiced together, extra rehearsals with Sandy and the fight captain, as he was called. I could watch, if I wanted.

There's a lot about horses in the play, enough to account for a lot of action. Harriet was one of the exhausted starving English horses the French made fun of:

> . . . *Their poor jades*
> *Lob down their heads, dropping the hides and hips,*
> *The gum down-roping from their pale-dead eyes*

And in their pale dull mouths the gimmal bit
Lies foul with chew'd grass, still and motionless.

The Duke rose, weary, sword heavy in his hand; and Harriet his mount arose, in brute pain, her head lobbed down, her shanks trembling, but still willing, still proud, lifting and shaking her high head when the dresser cast her colors over her.

"I learned some more about Bacon," I said to Harriet. She'd come off the stage glistening with sweat, a huge pair of dungarees and a white shirt pulled on over her dance leotard. She laughed that laugh, and I saw what I'd said, and I laughed too. "No. Listen. At the library. I learned a lot."

"Well, where else? No, what."

"Do you know who first thought that Bacon might have written Shakespeare?"

"Of course I don't."

"It was a woman. Her name was Delia Bacon."

"Oh no."

"She was no relation though. She said so herself."

"Yeah, sure."

"I can show you her book," I said. "If you want. There's a lot of books about this."

"Okay." And her smile of frank complicity.

When the bus came by the theater on its endless round we took it into town, which seemed stunned into motionless silence in the noonday heat, drooping like the grieving Union soldier on his plinth.

"She came from near here," I said. "Western Ohio. A hundred years ago. Her father was a missionary, and they came from Connecticut. She made a living as a teacher, then she wrote books, then she became a public lecturer. She never married."

"Hm."

"She did have an affair, though, or a romance, with this guy in New Haven. She came back to Connecticut to do this lecturing. He was a minister."

"Weren't they all."

"He lived in this hotel where she lived. She sent him a note saying to come visit her, and he told his friends. But he started seeing her."

"Did she tell him about Shakespeare?"

"Yes. He thought she was right."

"How do you know all this?"

"It's in a book." Going into the dim library I shivered dramatically, and Harriet looked at me with interest. Maybe it was the sudden cool air; or a kind of intimacy, as startling as a touch, to take her here.

"There was a scandal," I said. "Delia's family claimed that this guy—his name was McWhorter—had asked Delia to marry him, and now was breaking his promise; but *he* said it was Delia who'd asked him."

"Ha," said Harriet. "She asked him."

"She said."

"Maybe," Harriet said, "she was a Free Spirit."

I led her down the stacks. "What's that? I mean how do you mean?"

"A Free Spirit. Is somebody who does what they want. Like a Victorian lady who asks a man to marry her. Or just be lovers."

The stacks were on two levels, green-painted iron, the second level reached by a circular stair. We climbed up.

"My mother says what I want to be is a Free Spirit," Harriet said. "She says she was one too. So I get it from her."

"Can you want to be one?" I asked. I didn't know what I was talking about. "Isn't wanting to be one the same as being one?"

"No," Harriet said.

The Shakespeare section was three or four shelves, plays in old editions, commentaries, lives, and a dozen books on who else might have been Shakespeare.

"Here," I said. It was *The Philosophy of the Plays of Shakspere Unfolded*, by Delia Bacon. There was photograph of her inside: a bonneted dark lady of indeterminate age, smiling a knowing smile, a smile of frankness and good humor.

"I like her." She riffled the pages but read nothing.

"Look at this one," I said. "It's crazy."

A huge volume in moldering leather called *The Great Cryptogram*, by Ignatius Donnelly. Thousands of pages of methods for finding the secret words planted in the texts of the plays to reveal the true author. Who was Francis Bacon.

"He liked Delia. He thought she got a bad deal."

We were squatting close together to get at the books on the bottom shelf. I could smell Harriet's perfume and sweat. She drew out a small blue volume from the shelf.

"'The Girlhood of Shakespeare's Heroines,'" she read, and sat to open it, slipping off her laceless sneakers. I pulled out other books: *Bacon is Shake-speare. Shakespeare, Bacon and the Great Unknown. "Shakespeare" Identified in Edward De Vere, Seventeenth Earl of Oxford. Shake-speare: The Mystery.*

"Look," I said. "Here's the one that says Queen Elizabeth wrote the plays. Listen: '"The psychic urge that made Elizabeth place Portia, Rosalind and Viola in men's clothing might explain her disguising her own authorship in masculine raiment. For every strong and mature Shakespeare heroine we have a weak, vacillating, impetuous hero."'

"Well sure." She was involved in the small book she'd found.

"What is it?"

"It is," she said, "a book about the girlhoods of Shakespeare's heroines. Just as though they were real people who had girlhoods you could tell about." She glanced at the front of the book. "Eighteen ninety-one. Here's one about Beatrice."

"Which one is she?" I hadn't read many of the comedies.

"*Much Ado About Nothing*," she said, shooting me a school-marmish glance. "You know, dear boy. Beatrice and Benedick."

"Oh right. She's a Free Spirit."

The floor of the level we sat on was of glass: a milky glass that let the light, I guess, fall down to the darker level below. I'd never been anywhere like this cast-iron structure, on this glass floor.

"I want to take this out," Harriet said. "Do you think they'd let me?"

"Sure. I bet."

I don't know how long we sat. Harriet probably looked at her little wristwatch on a gold band and made us leave. I remember that I went down the ringing spiral stair before her, and that she held her hand out to me to be helped: and that afterward I smelled her perfume on that hand. For years after I would be caught by whiffs of that scent on the street, at parties, and finally I somehow learned its name: Ambush.

Delia Bacon didn't, in fact, at least at first, decide who the real author of the Shakespeare plays was. Her original insight, and it wasn't entirely original with her though maybe she thought it was, was simply that the lowly mummer from Stratford could never have created so lofty, so vast, so moral a work as the plays seemed to her to be. And she did see them as a single work, growing over time as the Author matured, but enfolding a single unified philosophy, humane, radical, even subversive— a philosophy that she, Delia Bacon, was the first to articulate.

One writer has pointed out that Delia's obsessive denigration of the actor fellow, which appears in her thinking rather suddenly, might be a displacement of her anger at the despicable McWhorter and his falsity, and her replacement of him by a more suitable love-object, who had her own name (and her stern beloved father's) to boot: a neat piece of psychologizing, though it doesn't fit with the Free Spirit conception. A Free Spirit would never take someone like him so much to heart, or allow herself to be so caught and mishandled. Never.

But there's no doubt she's different from all those who follow her, different in what mattered to her. They all regard the plays with a standard sort of awe, works of genius and so on, couldn't have been written by any lowborn player, but beyond that they have little to say about them: they only search them for clues and codes and secret messages.

Delia's argument was different. The reason she suspected that the true author of the plays—or authors, for she thought it likely that there were several—had hidden behind the Shakespeare name was that the philosophy they enunciated would have been dangerous, even fatal, to espouse. The plays of Shakespeare, she thought, promote a thoroughgoing anti-royalist republicanism, a view of all men as created equal in their needs and desires and sufferings. From the endless, repellent broils of York and Lancaster down to the awful compassion of *Lear*, the plays show kings as mere men, flawed, sinful, guilty, overreaching, without claim to divine right or men's allegiance.

And who, she then asked, would have conceived such a philosophy; who would scheme to hide it in a series of popular entertainments whose secret goal was to educate and uplift and even incite the people who stood to listen, or sat to read? Who would then need to hide his own identity behind the globous face of the faker from Stratford? Bacon, father of science and the New Learning, court official, intimate of monarchs, himself ennobled, makes perfect sense to be this person, this fair mind bent on an unimaginable future, the end of kings and nobles and the beginning of equality and a common humanity; of "pity, like a naked new-born babe"; free men and women freely choosing one another in love and fraternity.

What would the Queen his mistress have said to that?

Actually Delia conceived an entire cabal within the Queen's court, aristocrats risking their heads to reach England's people with their message—which maybe they heard too, since the Englishmen who began in those years to come to America (though admittedly most of them, at least at first, were theater-hating Puritans) eventually *did* found a nation with those ideals; and then the secret of their transmission was uncovered at length by a woman born in that Republic, even named for the transmitter, and a Free Spirit maybe too, certainly with a mind and heart of her own.

Which is why—this just occurs to me—it was right and proper that in the United States we should have sat before his plays, by limelight and lamplight, so persistently; and why it makes perfect sense that in the state of Indiana just a hundred years after Delia Bacon enunciated her, or Shakespeare's, philosophy we democrats should have gathered in a Utopian's barn to read and study and perform his plays. In fact *Henry V* was one of Delia's examples of Shakespeare (considered collectively) working on the people's souls to show what kings are, and what their wars amount to:

> *I think the king is but a man as I am, the violet smells to him as it does to me; all his senses have but human conditions. His ceremonies laid by, in his nakedness, he appears but a man . . .*

Of course that's Harry himself speaking, while disguised as a commoner, so the irony is multiple, nearly impenetrable, but Delia knew that; she's actually most sorry for the king— unfitted, as any mere man must be, for the vast responsibilities placed on him; a man who needs as much or more than anyone to be freed.

There was a party at the camp for the actors, the crew, the apprentices, end of a work week, or dress rehearsal, I don't remember. They liked to have parties, they brought in cases of beer and everybody got some: impossible to imagine now.

Harriet in the big dining hall was reading aloud to some kids out of *The Girlhood of Shakespeare's Heroines.* June bugs banged against the screens. I talked to Robin.

"It just can't be true," I said. "You should read some of this stuff I found. These people are nuts."

"Well, what's truth," he said, as though he'd just thought of this big question. "Maybe truth is multiple. I mean how can we ever know? How can we know anything for sure? We don't even know for sure that you and I are here talking, and not just figments."

Considered as a profession, theater people aren't much given to analysis and logic. In the theater somebody who seems to be Lear *is* Lear; maybe it's the same with thought, and to the average actor something that seems like a reasoned argument doesn't differ importantly from an actual one.

Robin looked down at the unopened bottle of Drewrys beer in his lap. He had what we called a church key in his hand. "You know," he said. "I've never been exactly sure he believes this theory." He apparently meant the Bacon advocate who'd talked to us. "He may not be completely convinced the plays were written by Francis Bacon."

He was an actor too in how he "telegraphed"—let you know when a stunner was coming, bad practice in a boxer, skillful in a raconteur.

"Oh?" I said my line.

"No," Robin said. "He thinks its maybe more likely to have been his smarter brother, Anthony."

He popped off the cap of the bottle, his own rimshot.

"So here little Beatrice gets captured by outlaws," I heard Harriet say. "She's so sharp. 'Corpo di Bellona! A spirited young devil she is! I'll drink your health, young lady!' That's the robber chief. He wants to marry her. 'Fill me a cup, and I'll pledge you all, good gentlemen, said Beatrice. But I have no ambition to be your queen. I should soon be an unpopular monarch among you, for I should begin my rule by reforming your ways.' Oh God."

"I've known him a long time," Robin said. "I know him to be a completely sweet, completely sincere and very smart man. And. He's nowhere near as mad as his mother."

"'A little gray-eyed, red-lipped thing, that looks too bright and fearless to know what tears mean,'" Harriet read. 'She speaks up so open, and looks so straight into your face, that you feel as if she must be right, and you wrong . . .'"

"His mother," Robin said, with vast seriousness, "has discovered that within the plays of Shakespeare there is a code, or a cipher. There's a difference, but I can't remember what it is. And the code, when you break it, tells a story."

I held my tongue.

"A long story."

I waited.

"It turns out," he said, "that hidden in the plays is the story of how Francis Bacon is actually the son of Queen Elizabeth and Robert of Leicester, her lover."

I started to laugh, that nervous laughter: in too deep, resisting.

"They made a secret marriage," Robin said. Still deadpan. "So Francis Bacon was in fact *rightfully heir to the throne.* Francis I. But if he ever let that be known—" And here Robin drew his hand suddenly across his throat, executing himself. "So he hid the story for this amazing woman to discover, three hundred, three hundred . . ."

Then at last he laughed.

"But," I said, in trouble.

"Listen." He had lost all urgency, dropped the part he'd been playing. I saw that Harriet had come near and stood listening. "It doesn't matter. The fact is that the son has spent most of his life not thinking about Bacon, ha ha, or his mother, but in making money. Quite a lot of it, as I understand. In the commodities market. And whatever else he may have been or is, he is a good son and a generous man. And we wouldn't be here without him. And that's enough. And that's that."

He looked from me to Harriet to me. Harriet, hands behind her back and her finger in the book's pages, looked like an illustration for something. She was smiling with sweet acceptance, and her smile moved from me to Robin. They were both looking at me, both smiling. I felt very odd.

Others came and claimed Robin's attention.

"He's right, dear boy," Harriet said to me.

"But."

"Come on," she said. "I'd like to walk."

Night came on with such solemn slowness those summers, the birds falling silent and the frogs and bugs awaking, the sky turning green and yellow, the trees and low poplars black. Talking nonsense and making dance spins she led me as though by chance up the way that led from the camp buildings to a knoll where low shrubs grew, and tall grasses; from the little fastness or hideaway they made you could glimpse the road back down to the camp, and look outward over the meadows to the river, an onyx meander in the darkening green.

"You like this?" she said, and she sat, floated with practiced grace to the soft ground.

Harriet had chosen me. It was as simple as that. Try as I might I can't remember how she let me know this. Maybe she didn't. I only remember being there in the growing dark, already knowing.

"Clipping," she said, and took off her pink-framed glasses. "That's what Shakespeare says. I like that word. Clipping and kissing."

I was profoundly alarmed. This thing that I had thought so constantly about was before me, and I'm sure I looked like an apprehended criminal, like a shy wild thing transfixed by the explorer who's first discovered it. I didn't say anything or do anything of all the many things I could have done, that I knew could and ought now to be done; and Harriet stopped and looked at me cautiously.

I didn't answer.

"Okay?" she said.

I said nothing.

"You aren't whatchamacallit, are you?"

"What?"

"That thing Francis Bacon was. Philorumpties."

"*Paiderastes*. No. No no."

"Are you sure?"

"I'm sure."

"Okay then." The only obstacle out of the way. We began. Grass and fields were at any rate my medium; all the little clipping I'd done had been outdoors, like a swain, or a rabbit, though I'd never got even this far anywhere else.

Her peasant blouse was easy to get off, seemed made to come off easily, and then there were the underpinnings, like grappling with a time-bomb in the dark, decoupling the wires; she helped out frankly.

"They're liddlies," she said.

Almost all I knew about the act that was to follow, all of it theoretical, I had learned from a book called *Ideal Marriage*, which said that it involves all of the senses, taste, touch, smell, sight, but not hearing, which should, the book said, be notable by its absence. No talking. Harriet talked. It was the strangest thing of all.

There were other features of the act that with delicate care *Ideal Marriage* had described. Those we did or had. One's Shakespearean name I had thought about and said over often to myself, like a charm, or a promise, sometimes with an actual shiver, anticipation mixed with some apprehensive revulsion: *the velvet clasp.*

"Oops you weren't supposed to," she panted in my ear.

As well remind the deer not to start away. Not supposed to: I hardly knew I had.

"I think it's all right," she said. "I think."

It turned out it was all right. God knows what we would have done: I think of that sometimes. And the next time I didn't, nor the next.

I was awed, bewildered, filled with weird guilt—not guilt for any religious reason, I've never had any of that, but because I wasn't in love with Harriet, or she with me; what she had invited me to obviously wasn't the commencement of always-ever-after in my life; I felt like a Shakespearean virgin who's been played the Bed Trick. I couldn't have said any of this then, only felt it. *Dint know whether to shit or go blind* they said then in Indiana. It was part of the Free Spirit effect, but I didn't know that then either.

I finally got less tongue-tied. My strangulated silence ought to have been outrageously insulting to Harriet, but in fact she didn't change her attitude toward me through the days, only her voice sometimes had a throaty kind of quality when we talked about nothing or about Shakespeare or the work, as though she might start laughing any second from some kind of warmth or pleasure, at my discomfiture only maybe.

"You know something?" she said to me, this time in a counselor's cabin we'd found a way into, a bedstead, a stained mattress. "You know something? You have a nice penis."

O wonderful, wonderful, and most wonderful wonderful, and yet again wonderful, and after that, out of all whooping! In this world into which I had come this happened, this too; everything. Of course I didn't know it happened also in the world I came from, at summer theaters and summer conferences and summer gatherings all over, that it was for this that they foregathered (not entirely or always, no, but still). I sensed, smelled as it were, the hot life all around me, as I never could have done before I became part of it, the clippings and couplings, the satyr-play in the buggy woods and weeds. *Paiderastes* too among them certainly. And she and I. And she and at least one other. She told me later, but I suspected it even then, though "suspected" sounds too cunning; I didn't know what I was supposed to feel or do about that, and so I felt nothing about it in particular, nothing but more.

Henry V opened on the July Fourth weekend. It began just as it had the first day of rehearsals, with Robin in jeans and a sweater dragging the big wooden box of swords and armor out to the middle of the stage. The house lights weren't down, and the audience of course thought he was a stagehand or a stage manager, which he was, and would be. And then the stage lights started to come up, but only a little, and the house darkened, and Robin came and sat on the apron with his script, as he had on the day he began rehearsing. And almost before anyone knew it, he'd begun to speak—not orate, just speak, wistfully almost, about how only a muse of fire and princes to act could bring forth Harry. As he talked the actors playing Harry and the Dauphin and the rest came out of the shadows in their jeans and sweatshirts and chose weapons from the box, and Harry put on his crown. And when he said *Think when we talk of horses that you see them, printing their proud hooves i'the receiving earth*, then a light lit one of the horses, center stage, Henry's, in its bright caparison; she printed her proud hoof, and another horse—Harriet—appeared behind, and another. There was a little gasp or sound from the audience, a titter here and there too, and I felt a sharp deep shudder as though I'd been seized, and tears filled my eyes.

———

It's good, so good that the play was produced, that she was able to be in it, and that its short run was up.

It was a Sunday. A lot of the actors had gone home, some of them not to return, others arriving to be in the second play of the year, *The Tempest*. Some of the apprentices too, gone home with bags of dirty laundry and blisters on their hands, to return next week.

I stayed. Harriet stayed too.

That little camp where we'd been put surrounded a small lake, a green torpid body of water reverting to swamp. Some of us swam there sometimes, urging each other in, rowing a foul-bottomed boat to the middle and diving into the duck-weed. Harriet wouldn't go in, and neither would I.

But it was hot, insufferably hot. And not far from the town of Avon, along the little river, was a public beach, a crowded place but clean and sandy. On the day before, one of the few of us who'd come in his own car took Harriet and me and a couple of others out there.

It too was still, its water brownish and thick. There were crowds of small children, diapers dangling, chased by their mothers; and children older than that, and dogs. No one understands to this day what it was about places like this, public beaches in the summer, if there really was anything about them, or if that was only a kind of leftover medieval fear of plague or cholera. I don't know. We'd been warned so much, every year, threat hanging like the heat over the days.

I see that beach still, I swear, in dreams, every detail the same, only darkened, as though seen through dark glasses, or with sunblind eyes. Soundless. Dreadful. It might not be that place at all I see, of course; and the place itself might be wholly innocent, harmless. I wake up in a sweat.

Next day was Sunday.

The library was open that day. Why open Sunday? Maybe I have something wrong about the days. The library was open. I know it was.

In the library I went to the Shakespeare section, climbed the spiral stair again. I was going to do research. I was going to take some notes, and show them they were wrong, make them admit it. Get this snake out of Paradise: no, I didn't think that, surely. But if they had to admit it, then—then what? They'd stop, I suppose. No longer soil the best name in the world.

I don't know what I thought. I was beginning to feel very odd, to feel cluster around me a being, a *soma*, that wasn't my own but that I recognized. I got Ignatius Donnelly and the others in my arms and came down the stairs to sit.

There was a photograph of Donnelly—*Senator* Donnelly—in the front of his book. I realized, looking at it, how old this thing was, how long ago.

> *If the reader will turn to page 76 of the fac-similes, being page 76 of the original Folio, and the third page of the second part of King Henry IV., and commence to count at the bottom of the scene, to-wit, scene second, and count upward, he will find that there are just 448 words (exclusive of the bracketed words, and counting the hyphenated words as single words) in that fragment of scene second in that column. Now, then, if we deduct 448 from 55, the remainder is 57, and if he will count down the next column, forward, (second of page 76), the reader will find that the 57th word is the word* her.

Folded up inside the book was a copy of one of Donnelly's worksheets, showing his method. I unfolded it. A page of *Henry IV*, the Folio, with red and blue pencil lines, line numbers, arrows drawn to other lines and words, lists of words from other places in black, blue, and red.

Now let us go a step farther.

My hand was shaking: I lifted it before my eyes and watched the tremors.

There's a sensation that all my life I have hated profoundly, dreaded, even though it hasn't happened to me often (multiplied, though, by my memories of those few times). It's the sensation that all intentionality and will is being drained from the world, all consciousness, that there is nothing in earthly activity but malign blind indifference; that even the willed behavior of persons, speaking, thinking, doing, is only mechanical ticks and tocks. Finally that they cannot even be heard or seen, because all eyes are blind, all ears are stopped. My own consciousness the only one existent to know this.

I wonder if it's like the onset of schizophrenia: the sense of living in a world of automata. It's often been associated for me with the onset of some illness; I wonder if I didn't first experience it before an asthma attack. Or was that time in the Avon library the first? And is that why I fear it so much?

Donnelly's huge screed, so full of wishing, so human a thing. I looked down at the pages and felt him, the froggy man in the picture at the front, lose his him- or he-ness, sadly wink out into unaliveness, only these endless numbers and words multiplying. I wanted to look away, and couldn't.

Voiceless. And all other books, and Shakespeare too, and all those who thought about him: they lost their voices, couldn't make sound, lost consciousness. The air itself lost mobility. I couldn't move.

The librarian, the only other person there, was looking at me, making the gestures of seeing me, of taking off her glasses, rising from her desk, coming to where I sat. She seemed to say what's wrong, is something wrong.

I think I have a fever, I said without sound.

She touched my head, her cool hand suddenly real and scorching.

Oh my goodness you do.

It's a summer cold.

Where do you belong, she mouthed.

I answered.

She spoke.

I tried to get up from the desk and fell down.

What happened then was that she sent someone—a passing someone in the street—to go out to the offices of the Festival and get Robin, out of bed actually, and he drove into town in his Ford convertible; and by the time he got there the librarian had got me outside, and I was sitting on the steps of the library; and then they got me to the office of a doctor, which was just around the corner, and we waited on his step for him. And even before he got there Robin saw that he would have to drive me to the hospital, an hour away, and when the doctor did come that's what they decided.

I didn't know or understand anything of this, and don't remember it now. I was told it all in the days to come, and in a letter from Robin to my parents.

He drove me to the hospital, and I do remember that fact: his car and the smell of its upholstery. I was in back with

Sandy, who held me wrapped in a scratchy Army blanket that I also remember. Robin said that all the way there he recited Shakespeare, to keep anxiety down; he said I asked him to, but I don't believe it. He recited most of *The Tempest*, which he was to begin rehearsing the next day:

> *The cloud-capped towers, the gorgeous palaces,*
> *The solemn temples, the great globe itself*
> *Yea, all which it inherit, shall dissolve,*
> *And, like this insubstantial pageant faded,*
> *Leave not a rack behind.*

What I remember is waking in that hospital when the fever broke. I remember the white sheets and a smell of soured milk and disinfectant. And I wondered why I had been strapped down to the bed so that I couldn't move my legs at all. Why had they done that? The nurse came in and pulled the sheet aside, and I could see my legs were not strapped down: they just wouldn't move.

Harriet says it was the same for her, strangely. Why have I been strapped to the bed? What good does that do? Why has that been done to me?

They say that in the old days almost everybody got it, but if you were very young when you got infected then it had no lasting effect, it was just like a cold, or like nothing, you didn't even know, and then of course you were immune ever after. The older you were the more likely you were to have damage.

But then they had the vaccine, and somehow it vanished overnight, except that it didn't if you had been missed, if you were at home with asthma when the nurses came to your school, if you didn't go to a school, if your mother was a Free Spirit and didn't altogether believe in medications and wanted to wait and see a while in spite of what everybody told her. I don't know. I really still don't.

It was the last major national outbreak. There were seven cases in Brown County alone: most of them were kids under twelve, and then me, and Harriet. Over a thousand of us nationwide.

They didn't tell me that Harriet was there, in that hospital, in another ward nearby. She'd been brought by the stage manager and his wife, a couple of hours after me. Why didn't they tell me? Because they didn't tell things then. What they knew might kill you, they thought, if you knew it too.

We lost each other for a long time then, or better say I lost her; I'm not sure how much Harriet thought about me. At first we were in specialized hospitals far apart, and then home. I didn't have her address—we never got to the point of swapping them, or phone numbers; making long-distance calls, even across the state, seemed momentous still in those days. Well, that might not have been why it took me so long to call. In any case, when I did at last find her number and talked to her father for a moment, I learned she'd gone to still another hospital, somewhere in the East, for more treatment. It was obvious he didn't want to talk about it; he sounded remote and frightened, as though I'd roused him from a cave.

And that's really what kept us apart: that we had both, each alone, gone off into this disaster, and now were separated, along with our blighted families, from everyone else. It was a secret, what had become of us, but a secret that had to be exposed in every new circumstance you entered, explained, confessed to.

Well, he's not as strong as other boys in some ways. To coaches, teachers, bosses. My family nearly died of shame and bravery.

And I was one of the ones who came back, too. I came back nearly all the way. You can see me now and know right away that something's wrong, but I've walked without aids for most of my life. I was a loner anyway, without much sense that the world was waiting for me to make an entrance on its stage. There were times I was actually relieved—and ashamed, of course, to be relieved—to have a reason, such a profound and unchallengeable one, for non-participation.

I can't think Harriet ever felt that way. But I didn't know. I didn't know anything about what had become of her, whether she came back, or not. We were sundered. I got a Christmas card from her that first year. Then nothing.

Harriet calls me at my office in the Liberal Arts building, the afternoon after we met on the road.

"You were right about the Pope," she says. "He's not dead."

"No. Hurt."

"Tough bastard."

When this pope's accession was announced, and it was made known that he'd be taking the name John Paul II after John Paul I, his predecessor, Harriet said *No, no, not John Paul again! George Ringo!*

"I heard them say it was a vulgarian who did it . . ."

"Not a vulgarian, Harriet."

"And I thought that was an odd snap judgment to make."

"A Bulgarian. A spy."

"Yes. I figured it out." I heard her sip tea. "You want to come over tonight?"

"Okay."

"Air-conditioning's still busted."

"Okay."

"Bring a bottle of that wine you think is so good. Brook-wood. Woodbridge. Bridgewater."

"Waterbrook. My last class is over at five."

"Good. Okay."

I still have that Christmas card. It isn't different from anyone's—snow, dark pines, star. Inside it says *May your every Christmas wish come true.* And it's signed with her full name, as though I might not remember her. I knew even then, though maybe I couldn't have said, that it wasn't a greeting.

Oh, you don't know, you can't: our parents knew it instantly, probably, though my mom with her sense of privilege and being welcome everywhere maybe took longer to understand. The way it was then. You were obliged, for everyone's sake (it seemed) to check out of the world; you found out that after all you had only been a temporary guest there, on sufferance. It was no longer for you, and you were under an obligation not to make others uncomfortable by your presence. Maybe that's why we all shunned one another; two of us at once, outside of a hospital, would have been a shocking solecism. Just think about it: There were a lot of us, and when do you ever remember, if you're old enough to remember, seeing two of us hanging out together? On the street, at the malt shop, the movies? Never.

When I said that once to Harriet she said it was silly: the reason people never saw us was because in those days you couldn't get out of the house, off the front porch, up on the curb, up the stairs. That's all.

"They never saw us together?" Harriet said, and laughed. "*They never saw us at all.* We weren't there to see."

46

———

By the time I leave school the day has turned dramatically lowering, hot and heavy. I walk across campus with a younger colleague, a woman in American Studies. She's careful to walk slowly to accommodate me, but not quite tactful enough to conceal that she's doing so.

"Tell me something," I ask. "If you heard someone—a woman, say about your age, maybe older—described as a 'Free Spirit,' what would you think was being said about her?"

"Oh," she says. "That she sleeps around a lot. I knew a lot of them."

"Knew?"

"Well, it was kind of a thing to be, wasn't it? A Free Spirit. Barefoot, living on the earth, sleeping around wherever. You know."

"Don't you mean daisy pickers? Or is there not a difference?"

She shrugs. "Someone without much sense of reality, I guess. About men or life. Some of them got away with it"—and here she makes an airy gesture of escape or detachment—"but not always."

She slows so I can catch up. "Why do you ask?" she says.

"Cultural anthropology," I say.

"I'd worry for her," she says.

I see her logic. But I think that there are—speaking anthropologically—several varieties. There are the ones that anyone could recognize, untrammeled, living in worlds of their own; but then there are the secret ones whom you wouldn't know about unless you know. The librarian and the mailman (curls put up beneath her gray cap) and the dental hygienist. Not soft, not unwise; knowing the costs, and the benefits. Free

Spirits free even of the label, choosing more carefully than Delia Bacon did.

And Harriet: Who's going to guess it about her? Sex is something not expected of us. That's the secret part: and I know it's astonished more than one person. But Harriet's had lovers, dozens of them (*tens,* she says, *not dozens; lovers by the tens*). Maybe she hasn't in her life had all those she wanted; maybe she's been turned down a lot. But being a true Free Spirit—as I conceive it—means she chose lovers when she wanted them, and didn't when she didn't: could have sex with whoever whenever, but knew when to eschew it too.

"Eschew?" Harriet said to me, in mock wonderment, when I made this case. "*Eschew?*"

That was the night of the first day we met again. The early morning of the following day, actually. In her little apartment here in this New England town on a wide river not named Avon, nowhere either of us would have guessed we'd come to, much less both of us, but have, for altogether different reasons. Mine the mundane one of a job offer; hers something to do with those tens of lovers, though the story's obscure to me still. She loves it here: the shop she's built, the Federal house she owns where both it and she reside, where she has the solitudes she needs as much as she needs company. I've actually wondered if they're entirely different, for her, solitude and company; and if that's sad, or not sad.

"You know something?" she said to me that night or morning. "You have a nice penis." And I remembered, hadn't of course ever forgotten, when she'd said it to me first; wondered too if it was something she said often, just a nice thing to say.

"Yes," I said. "It's a Pendaflex."

"Really. Wow. The rotomatic?"

"No. I'm saving up for one of those."

It was June, June again. She rested her hot face in the crook of my shoulder.

"It'll stand you in good stead," she said. "A nice penis like that."

I thought it ought to be strange to me, even eerie, to have gone so far from where I started and to find her here, and somehow to take up where we were when we parted so completely, but all different: she so altered, in ways I'd long wondered about. Like dreams you might have, dreams I've had. But it didn't seem that way at all. It doesn't now.

Harriet's shop is called As You Like It. Under these words on the painted sign over the door is a sort of scroll or banner that reads *Wonderful wonderful and most wonderful wonderful.* There's a tinkle bell that sounds when the door is opened, though it's hardly needed.

"Hi."

She was waiting on a customer, wrapping something small and precious with wasteless motions, tissue, box, ribbon, label. One of her hands is different from the other, and the work seems to pass from one to the other as needed, as between two friends, one the stronger.

You'd think that the worst thing was how all that physical grace and power was blasted and reft from her, and it's true that that was the loss; but what's just as true is that all Harriet's grace, all her strength and physical precision, lay in a more central part of her than that, a place from which she draws all the time now making her way in the world, and everybody who sees her knows it. I watch her in the absurdly crowded shop turn and move, put out a hand to touch, just touch a wall to keep her balance, reach to take something from a high shelf, turn again and put it before you, without a wasted gesture or effort: she's still that steed.

"I brought you something," I say.

"The wine."

"That too."

I took it from the grocery bag that held the bottle.

"Oh my God."

"It was in the college library."

A small octavo volume, as they used to say, silk-bound, the gold lettering dim but plain. *The Girlhood of Shakespeare's Heroines*.

"You know something?" I say. "All the others are there too."

"Yes?"

"All of them are. Still. Ignatius Donnelly and Delia Bacon and *Shake-speare: The Mystery*. In the same places they always were." As though library time universally stopped that afternoon, at least in that range of Dewey decimals, all those books growing more useless and foolish every year, never changing their minds or hearts.

"Delia Bacon," Harriet says. "The Free Spirit."

"Well, so you thought."

"Did you look in them?"

"I did." I didn't say it had taken me a long time to open one. Of course I'd always known they were there. Volumes that I use in classes and research are nearby them. But I'd never opened one; that was true.

I help Harriet close the shop. Harriet studies *The Girlhood of Shakespeare's Heroines*. White ink numbers on its spine.

"You know," she said. "I never took it back. That one from the library in Avon. I never took it back. It's probably still there, in that cabin, today."

———

Delia Bacon went to England in 1853, perhaps largely to escape the McWhorter mess, but also because people she knew in Boston and New Haven told her she ought to go and find the facts that would prove her conception. Once there, though, she only went on thinking and studying the plays, growing ever more certain she was right. Bostonian bluestocking that she was, she had letters of introduction from Emerson to Carlyle, who was shocked by her heresies (he shrieked, she says, turned black in the face). She would do no research, though; she wrote essays about her idea, as though all by itself it ought to convince; she ran out of money and was practically destitute when she was taken up by Nathaniel Hawthorne, who was then the American cultural attache. Hawthorne took her part, generously, and stood by her, and helped her prepare her huge book (*The Philosophy of the Plays of Shakspere Unfolded*) for publication, and paid for it too: but he didn't believe either.

I don't know how she got the idea that the proof she needed—or rather that the world needed—could be found in a grave. First she supposed that it was buried with Bacon at St. Albans, and when she was refused permission to open that tomb, she went to Stratford-upon-Avon. Hawthorne says that Delia told him she had "definite and minute instructions" about how to find, beneath Shakespeare's gravestone in Stratford church, the documents that the cabal had caused to be put there.

She got to Stratford sick and shabby, and could find no room at the inn. She wandered the town, and finding a rose-covered cottage whose door stood open (all this is true) she went in, and sat down. And when the ancient woman who lived there alone came in, and saw her there, she couldn't bear to send her away; and there she stayed, looking out at the river Avon and the spire of the church where Shakespeare lay.

You know the doggerel curse that's posted on that grave: *Good friend for Jesus' sake forebear To dig the dust enclosèd here; Blessed be the man that spares these stones And curst be he that moves my bones.* It could have been this that kept her away—she wouldn't have been the only one. And of course there was already a huge Stratford Shakespeare industry, and no one was about to let her dig that dust. But she didn't even ask; for months she did nothing at all.

Then one night, she went to the church. Why night? She brought a dark lantern, and some other articles for "the examination I proposed to make," she wrote to Hawthorne: though what they were, or it was, she didn't say. She stayed there for some hours. The bust of Shakespeare on his memorial was above her, but it was too dark to see him; she couldn't see the ceiling at all, it was as though she looked into a midnight sky. After a long time she left, and soon went back to London.

Her book was published the year after that, and she underwent some kind of mental breakdown. She had no money to eat, and so she didn't; she ceased to leave her room. A relative in the Navy happened to be on leave in London, and called on her; he was shocked by her condition, and brought her home with him. She withdrew entirely into silence and inaction. Her relatives committed her to an asylum in New Haven, and she died there two years later. *History rest in me a clue* she wrote not long before her death, but what she meant by that no one knows.

———

"She died of Shakespeare," Harriet says. She's made omelettes for us with herbs from the pots on her windowsill, and I've opened the wine.

"The Shakespeare curse?"

"Not that. Just Shakespeare. It happens. People like you, sunk in Shakespeare. It's not good."

"I'm sunk in Shakespeare?"

"You make a living from Shakespeare."

"Elizabethan Drama," I say. "Not Shakespeare really."

"Look what Shakespeare did to us."

"What?"

"We were so caught up with Shakespeare. Shakespeare, Shakespeare. Just like Delia Bacon."

"Oh Harriet. Come on."

"We got sick from Shakespeare," Harriet says.

"Harriet," I say. "It wasn't Shakespeare."

"Oh no?" she says, with vast conviction. "Oh no? Well."

I say no more. Her challenge, or joke, evanesces. She drinks, looking out at the evening. The flush on her cheeks actually brightens when she gets extravagant that way, like a Victorian heroine's. Still, to this day.

"You should write that story," Harriet says. "In a book."

"What story?"

"Delia Bacon. Killed by Shakespeare."

"Oh, I don't know. A whole book?"

"Well, aren't you supposed to write books? Publish or perish?"

"The only book I want to write," I say, "is the history of the Free Spirits."

That draws her eyes to me again. "It's a secret history," she says.

"I know."

"Isn't it already written?"

"Some. Not all."

"Maybe it is though. Maybe it's all written down someplace. In code."

"Well. If Queen Elizabeth wrote the plays of Shakespeare, maybe it's in there."

"Now *she* was a Free Spirit," Harriet says. "Don't you think?"

"Yep. Whatever Delia thought."

"Secret marriages. Illegitimate children."

"'And the imperial votaress passed on/In maiden meditation, fancy-free.'"

She holds out a hand to me, and I get up to help her rise. In her tiny apartment behind the store, she can get around without her braces if she's careful, moving like a gibbon from handhold to handhold to the big low bed. It's where she socializes.

"I'm listing," she says, pausing in the door frame. "Two glasses of wine and I'm listing."

So I take her up, remarkably light, and lay her down on the bed.

Harriet's body isn't like other bodies you're likely to have encountered in this way. Her shoulders are broad and strong and flat, like anvils, and her upper arms look plump and soft till you take hold of them and find them to be iron. Harriet says her orthopedic surgeon could never figure out exactly how Harriet walks; she shouldn't have the muscle strength to do it. However she does it, it's given her washboard abs that any high-school boy would envy, and they look like a boy's, finely cut and tender somehow in spite of being so hard. Her butt is a boy's too: slight and soft and hollowed in the flanks. That's where the nerve damage starts, and goes down her legs.

It's like making love to a marionette, I said to her once, lifting and propping apart her stick-thin legs, and she started laughing and had a hard time stopping and going on. But it had taken her a long time to uncover them when we were in bed, let them be part of our lovemaking.

Two crips like us Harriet says sometimes, but that's only a funny kind of politeness, to include me with her in a commonality, not to make me feel excluded.

"So you've been thinking," I say. It's late in the night.

"Yep."

"And?"

"Let me pull this sheet up over me."

"That doesn't sound good."

"Reach me the bottle, will you?" she says. Still a lot of Hoosier in her language. I struggle up to get the bottle and glasses, which leaves me outside the underside of the sheet with her, and posted on the bed's edge.

"So how come you asked me this, by the way?" she says. "Just so I know."

"Because I love you."

"You do?"

"Harriet," I say. "I love you. I've always loved you, even when I didn't know it. I'll love you till the day I die." The wine is sweet and still cold. "That's how come."

She drinks, and thinks; or maybe she already knows what she thinks, but not whether to say it.

"So you're not afraid?"

"Of what?"

"My history. I mean it's not like I've been waiting for Mr. Right. There's reasons I'm alone."

"I know."

"Not lonely. Alone."

"I know. I'm not afraid. Maybe I should be, but I'm not."

"Okay then."

She isn't done. Far-off there's a borborygmic rumble of thunder, the uneasy sky heaving.

"So, have you heard about this new thing we get?" she says.

"What thing we get?"

"They've just started to discover it. A *syndrome*. Us old polios. My doctor told me about it last week."

"You were at the doctor?"

"I started getting tired," she says. "Or not tired, exactly. More like weaker. I wondered. And he told me. He'd just been reading about it himself. Post-polio syndrome."

"Explain," I say. I say it double-calm. That's a word Harriet invented for how actors say certain things in movies.

She hands me her glass, so she can hike herself up with both hands. "It seems," she says, like a joke's opening, "it seems there's this thing about the nerves you use. I mean everybody. The nerves that get used all the time to do things, in your hands and your arms and so on, they have like redundancies. Backups. As you live your life, the nerves wear out. Their coverings get worn away. Used up. So by late in life you're using the backup ones."

"Ah."

"But in polio, the nerves get damaged. The ones you'd normally use, and even the backups in some places, so you've got nothing. And in the places where you've still got something, you're using the backups, you're using the surplus. Even if it's nerves you think have always been fine: sometimes it's really the backups you're going on. So."

"So you wear them out sooner."

"It's how you come back," she says. "You somehow discover these backup nerves, and how to use them. Or you find other muscles, maybe without so much backup, because they're like minor for most people, and you use them like nobody else. It's how you get better. I got better. Even some of the iron-lung kids got way better. Now they're old, and the surplus is gone. So we start to lose."

I wonder if I've noticed any of this, in myself. I can't tell. Maybe I'm more tired, have a harder time with the long walks across campus. Maybe.

"You know what's sad, though," Harriet says. "It's the ones who worked the hardest to come back, get function back, that are going to be losing it soonest. All those exercises, all that grit. The ones who weren't going to be beat."

I put my hand on her leg. She puts her hand on mine.

"So," she says, double-calm. "Get it?"

I get it. I do. It's my answer: Harriet's got a lot less function than I do, and if she knows she's going to start to lose what she has, she can't say yes to me: can't, because it wouldn't seem like a free choice, would seem to have a reason, an urgent reason; it would seem like a way to get the help she knows she's going to need. Would seem, even if it isn't. We'll talk more, talk into the night, and I'll say *Don't fall for that, Harriet, don't fall for that no-pity stuff*; I'll say *What about me, Harriet, what about the fact that I want to be with you no matter what, for better or for worse*. But it won't matter.

"I think it's rotten," she says.

She's crying now. Only a little.

"I don't usually feel sorry for myself," she says. "Wouldn't you say that's so? Have you seen me being sorry for myself much?"

"Never," I say. And it's so.

"I wish it would rain," Harriet says.

It does, toward midnight, wild nearly continuous lightning and hellacious thunder, almost Midwestern in its intensity, and Harriet clings to me whooping and laughing as though on a carnival ride; and when at last it's gone, and quiet, and we've lain a long time listening to the gutters running softly, she sends me home.

The next day she gets up early again, though not quite so early, to go out and make pictures. The day is terribly beautiful, sun-shot, raindrop-spattered, mist-hung. She loads her film holders, planning her moves from house to car with all the things needed, hoping she won't miss the light, knowing she can't hurry. Hurry is slow; hurry costs time. *Festina lente.*

By midmorning she reaches the place she set out for, that she had imagined in advance. But a vast wind has come up, moving through the leaves of the huge trees, passing amid them, and then going around again. The trees are moving too much for Harriet's slow exposures. She stands by her tall patient camera and watches. The wind stirring the heavy masses of new leaves lends the trees one by one a momentary animal life different from their usual vegetable one, a free will, or the illusion of one; and they seem to be glad of it, to delight in it even, raising and shaking their arms and shivering in glee.

On her way back to town she cruises the tag sales. The families have just put out their stacks of mismatched dishes and white elephants and *National Geographics,* the pole lamps and tiered end-tables unaccustomed to the outdoor air and looking as though they feel uncomfortably conspicuous on the dewy grass. Harriet is an Early Bird and picks up a few "smalls" for the shop—a set of twelve silver "apostle" spoons and a nice set of wartime tumblers with decals on them of pinup girls in scanty uniforms. At one place she finds a game of Shakespeare, a board game which she has known existed and seen around but never played. The box is shut with a bit of masking tape, and is going for a quarter. Something touches her, and she puts her hand on it.

"It's all there," the householder tells her. "Complete."

Harriet gives her a quarter.

Back home again, she unloads her camera and brings in the shoulder bag she carries for purchases. The game of Shakespeare in its box. She thinks a while there, poised on her crutches like Chaplin on his stick. Then she goes to her closets—Harriet has no basement or attic, wouldn't need or use them, but she has many closets—and after some searching she pulls out a small blue suitcase, one of a matched set that once included a round hatbox; there's a poodle appliquéd on it. She humps the suitcase—it's heavy—to the dining table, which she uses more for laying out and mounting pictures than for dining, and snaps open its clasps. Inside she has yearbooks and photographs and mimeographed programs from long-ago recitals, awards, blue ribbons. Scrapbooks too. She takes out a ragged manila envelope, addressed to her old house in Indiana, and from it the journals she kept and the letters she wrote home that summer, the program of *Henry V*, the 8x10 of Robin she took from the bulletin board in the theater.

She has all that piled on her dining table, now in the summer of 1980. She adds the book I brought her, *The Girlhood of Shakespeare's Heroines*. The game of Shakespeare too. She picks that up, hefting it in her hand—heavy, heavier than she expected, or is it some new weakness in that hand, which is not her good hand? Gripping tighter, she picks at the tape holding it shut, and maybe because she's holding it too tight, she loses control of it and the box opens and spills its contents before she can recover. Among the contents are a dozen tiny busts of Shakespeare, the counters in the game, and they go bouncing over the table and onto the floor, rattling into corners and under things in that purposeful way that small dropped things have, as though trying to escape.

Plastic Shakespeares red and white, black and brown. Two or three roll—Harriet catches them in the corner of her eye—under the tall armoire that holds more of her stuff. Now that's a drag. Box still in hand, Harriet stares unmoving. She'll have to get her braces off, lie full length on the floor, grope around in the narrow dark space under there maybe with a broom or some such implement, and knock them out from where they're stuck. And she won't be able to reach them, and she'll have to get someone to shift the wardrobe and reach down the back to extricate them. Someone. Unless she chooses just to leave them there forever.

In the Tom Mix Museum

1958, and we are going to the Museum of Tom Mix. It is in a place called Dewey. "Dewy" is what my father calls my sister. A dewy girl. She lowers her eyes to not see him looking at her. I have my guns on, I buckle them on every morning when I put on my jeans. They have ivory handles with rearing horses carved on them that look like Tony, Tom Mix's horse. My father's name is Tony too. There is a horse on the hood of the car, and my father said we follow the horse wherever it goes. I used to watch for the horse to turn right or left, to see if the car went that way, and every time it did. But I am older now and I get it. Tony was a trick pony. My mother says that my father is a one-trick pony. Tony can think and talk almost like a person (Tony the horse).

The Museum of Tom Mix is Tom Mix, but Tom Mix is much larger than you would think, taller than the statue of Paul Bunyan in that other town. We go around to the back of his left boot, which has a heel as high as I am, with a door in it. We go in one by one. There is a stairway up to the top of Tom Mix, and it is dark at the top. Tony is there, halfway up; then above Tony is the other Tony, after Tony died, and above him another. Far, far up are Tom Mix's narrowed eyes, letting in the light. We are standing together, I love them all, and we wait to see who will start to climb.

And Go Like This

There is room enough indoors in New York City for the whole 1963 world's population to enter, with room enough inside for all hands to dance the twist in average nightclub proximity.
—Buckminster Fuller

Day and night the jetliners come in to Idlewild fully packed, and fly out again empty. Then the arrivals have to get into the city from the airports—special trains and busses have been laid on, of course, day and night crossing into the city limits and returning, empty bean cans whose beans have been poured out, but the waits are long. The army of organizers and dispatchers, who have been recruited from around the world for this job—selfless, patient as saints, minds like adding machines, yet still liable to fainting fits or outbursts of rage, God bless them, only human after all—meet and meet and sort and sort the incomers into neighborhoods, into streets in those neighborhoods, addresses, floors, rooms. They have huge atlases and records supplied by the city government, exploded plans of every building. They pencil each room and then mark it in red when fully occupied.

Still there are far too many arriving to be funneled into town by that process, and thousands, maybe tens of thousands finally, set out walking from the airport. It's easy enough to see which way to go. Especially people are walking who walk anyway in their home places, bare or sandaled feet on dusty roads, with children in colorful slings at their breasts or bundles on their heads—those are the pictures you see in the special editions of *Life* and *Look,* tall Watusis and small people from Indochina and Peru. Just walking, and the sunset towers they go toward. How beautiful they are, patient, unsmiling, in their native dress, the Family of Man.

We have set out walking too, but from the west. We've calculated how long it will take from our home, and we've decided that it can't take longer than the endless waits for trains and planes and buses, to say nothing of the trip by car. No matter how often we've all been warned not to do it, forbidden to do it (but who can turn them back once they've set out?), people have been piling into their station wagons and sedans, loading the trunk with coolers full of sandwiches and pop, a couple of extra jerry-cans of gas—about a dollar a gallon most places!—and setting out as though on some happy expedition to the National Parks. Now those millions are coming to a halt, from New Jersey north as far as Albany and south to Philadelphia, a solid mass of them, like the white particles of precipitate forming in the beaker in chemistry class, drifting downward to solidify. Then you have to get out and walk anyway, the sandwiches long gone and the trucks with food and water far between.

No, we've left the Valiant in the carport and we're walking, just our knapsacks and identification, living off the land and the kindness of strangers.

There was a story in my childhood, a paradox or a joke, which went like this: Suppose all the Chinamen have been ordered to commit suicide by jumping off a particular cliff into the sea. They are to line up single file and each take his or her turn, every man, woman, and child jumping off, one after the other. And the joke was that the line would never end. For the jumping-off of so many would take so long, even at ten minutes a person, that at the back of the line lives would have to be led by those waiting their turn, and children would be born, and more children, and children of those children even, so that the line would go on and people would keep jumping forever.

This, no, this wouldn't take forever. There was an end and a terminus and a conclusion, there was a finite number to accommodate in a finite space—that was the *point*—though of course there would be additions to the number of us along the way, that was understood and accounted for, the hospital spaces of the city have been specially set aside for mothers-to-be nearing term, and anyway how much additional space can a tiny newborn use up? In those hospitals too are the old and the sick and yes the dying, it's appalling how many will die in this city in this time, the entire mortality of earth, a number not larger than in any comparable period of course, maybe less for that matter, because this city has some of the best medical care on earth and doctors and nurses from around the world have also been assigned to spaces in clinics, hospitals, asylums, overwhelmed as they might be looking over the sea of incapacity, as though every patient who ever suffered there has been resurrected and brought back, hollow-eyed, gasping, unable to ambulate.

But they are there! That's what we're not to forget, they are all there with us, taking up their allotted spaces—or maybe a little more, because of having to lie down, but never mind, they'll all be back home soon enough, they need to hang on just a little longer. And every one who passes away before the termination, the all-clear, whatever it's to be called, will be replaced, very likely, by a newborn in the ward next door.

And what about the great ones of the world, the leaders and the Presidents for Life and the Field Marshals and the Members of Parliaments and Presidiums, have they really all come? If they have, we haven't been informed of it—of course there are some coming with their nations, but the chance of being swallowed up amid their subjects or constituents, suffering who knows what indignities and maybe worse, has perhaps pushed a lot of them to slip into the city unobserved on special flights of unmarked helicopters and so on, to be put up at their embassies or at the Plaza or the Americana or in the vast apartments of bankers and arms dealers on Park Avenue. Surely they have left behind cohorts of devoted followers, henchmen, whatever, men who can keep their fingers on the red button or their eyes on the skies, just in case it has all been a trap, but we have to be realistic: not every goat-herd in Macedonia, every bushman in the Kalahari is going to be rounded up, and they don't need to be for this to work—you can call your floor thoroughly swept even if a few twists of dust persist under the couch, a lost button beneath the radiator. The best is the enemy of the good. He's an engineer, he must know that.

And it is working. They are filling, from top to bottom, all the great buildings, the Graybar Building, the Pan Am Building, Cyanamid, American Metal Climax, the Empire State—a crowd of Dutch men and women and children fill the souvenir shop at the top of the Empire State Building, milling, handling the small models, glass, metal, plastic, of the building they are in. The Metropolitan Museum is filling as though for a smash hit opening, Van Gogh, Rembrandt, the Modern as for a Pollack retrospective or Op Art show, there is even champagne! How is it that certain people have managed to gather with people like themselves, as on Fifth Avenue, at the Diocesan headquarters, Scribner's bookshop, the University Club, whereas old St. Patrick's is crowded with just everybodies, as though they had all come together to pray for rain in a drought, or to be safe from an invading army? They *are* the invading army!

We know so little really, plodding along footsore and amazed and yet strangely elated among the millions, the *river of humanity* as Ed Sullivan said in his last column in the *Daily News* before publishing was suspended for the duration. The broad streets (Broadway!) just filled all the way across with persons, a river breaking against the fronts of the dispatcher stations, streams diverted, uptown, which is north more or less, downtown, which is south. And now the flood is at last beginning to lessen, to loosen, a vortex draining away into the shops and the apartments, the theaters and the restaurants.

She and I have received our assignment. The building is in Manhattan, below Houston Street, which we have learned divides the newer parts of the city from the older parts. Though old Greenwich Village is mostly above it and all of Wall Street is below it. We would like to have been ushered down that far, to find a space for ourselves in one of those titans of steel and glass, where perhaps we could look out at the Statue of Liberty and the emptied world. We were surprised to find we both wished for that! I'd have thought she'd want a small "brownstone" townhouse on a shady street. Anyway it's neither of those, it's a little loft on the corner of Spring Street and Lafayette Street, an old triangular building just five stories tall. Looking down on us from the windows on the east side of the street as we walk that way are Italian men and women, not people just arrived from Italy but the families who live in those places, for that's Little Italy there, and the plump women in house dresses, black hair severely pulled back, and the young men with razor-cut hair and big wristwatches are the tenants there. They're waving and shouting comments down to the crowd endlessly passing, friendly comments or maybe not so friendly, hostile even maybe, their turf invaded, not the right attitude for now.

But here we are, number 370, we wait our turn to go in and up. Stairs to the third floor. It seems artists now live in the building, they are allowed to, painters, we smell linseed oil and canvas sizing. Our artist is lean, scrawny almost, his space nearly empty, canvases leaning against the wall, their faces turned away. We look down—maybe shy—and can see in the cracks of the old floorboards what she says are metal snaps, snaps for clothing, from the days when clothes were made here by immigrants. Our artist is either happy to see us or not happy, excited and irritated, that's probably universal, we are all cautious about saying anything much to him or to one another, after all he didn't invite us. *Okay okay* he keeps saying. Is that dark brooding resentful girl in the black leotard and Capezios his girlfriend?

Well, better here than in some vast factory floor in the borough of Queens or train shed in Long Island City, or out on Staten Island not much different from where we come from. The ferries are leaving from Manhattan's tip for Staten Island every few minutes, packed with people to the gunwales or the scuppers or whatever those outside edges are called.

World's cheapest ocean voyage, they say, just a nickel to cross the whitecapped bay, Lady Liberty, Ellis Island deserted and derelict over that way, where once before the millions came into New York City to be processed and checked and sent out into the streets. The teeming streets. I lift my lamp beside the golden door. For a moment, thinking of that, looking down at those little metal snaps that slipped from women's fingers fifty, sixty years ago, it all seems to make sense, a human experiment, a proof of something finally and deeply good about us and about this city, though we don't know what, not exactly.

It's the last day, the last evening: we're lucky to have arrived so late, there won't be problems with food supplies or sleeping arrangements that others are having. The plan has worked so smoothly! All the populations are being accommodated, there are fights and resistance reported in various locations, but these are being handled by the large corps of specially trained minimally armed persons—not police, not soldiers, for the police forces and the armies were the first to arrive and be distributed, for obvious reasons—because they could be ordered to, and because of what they might do if left behind till last. And now it's done: everywhere, in every land, palm and pine, the planners and directors and their staffs have taken off their headsets, shut down their huge computers and telephone banks and telex machines—a world-wide web of information tools whose only goal has been this, this night. They have boarded the last 707s to leave Bombay, Leningrad, Johannesburg, and been taken just like all the others to the airports in New Jersey and Long Island, and when they have deplaned, the crews too leave the airplanes parked and take the last buses into the city, checking their assignments with one another, joking—pilots and stewies, they're used to bunking in strange cities. When the buses have been emptied the drivers turn them off and leave them in the streets, head for the distribution centers for assignments. Last of all the dispatchers, all done: they can hardly believe it, not an hour's sleep in twenty-four, their ad-hoc areas littered with coffee cups, telexes, phone slips, fan-fold paper, cartons from the last Chinese restaurants: they gather themselves and go out into the bright streets—the grid is holding!—and they take themselves to wherever they have assigned themselves, not far because they're walking, all the trains and taxis have stopped, no one left to ride or drive them; they mount the stairs or take the elevators up to where they are to go.

It's done. The streets now empty and silent. *The city holds its breath* they will say later.

In our loft space we have been given our drinks and our canapés. It's not silent here: we allow ourselves to joke about it, about our being here, we demand fancy cocktails or a floor show, but in a just-kidding way—actually it's strangely hard to mingle. She and I stick together, but we often do that at parties. We stand at the windows; we think they look toward the southeast, in the direction of most of the world's population, though we can't see anything, not even the night sky. Every window everywhere is lit.

But think of the darkness now over all the nightside of earth. The primeval darkness. For all the lights out there have been turned off, or not turned on, perhaps not all but so many. The quiet of all that world, around the earth and back again almost to here where we stand, this little group of islands, these buildings alight and humming, you can almost hear the murmur and the milling of the people.

He was right. It could be done, he knew it could be and it has been, we've done it. There's a kind of giddy pride. Overpopulation is a myth! There are so few of us compared to Spaceship Earth's vastness, we can feel it now for certain in our hearts, we hear it with our senses.

But—many, many others must just now be thinking it too—there's more. For now the whole process must be reversed, and they, we, have to go home again. To our home places, spacious or crowded. And won't we all remember this, won't we think of how for a moment we were all together, so close, a brief walk or a taxi ride all that separates any one of us from any other? And won't that change us, in ways we can't predict?

Did he expect that, did he think of it? Did he know it would happen? Moon-faced little man in his black horn-rims, had he known this from the start?

One final test, one final proof only remains. We've received our second drink. At the turntable our host places the 45 on the spindle and lets it drop. In every space in the city just at this moment, the same: on every record player, over every loudspeaker. The needle rasps in the groove—maybe there's a universal silence for a moment, an *expectant* silence, maybe not—and then the startlement of music. That voice crying out, strangely urgent, almost pleading, to take his little hand, and go like this.

Alone together in the quiet world, the nations begin to twist.

Spring Break

So the last proj I did junior year at Spectrum Cumulus College was with my bud Seymour Chin, who was in Singapore—I was in Podunk, OH. It was a proj in Equality Engineering, required, tough but not so. We picked Toiletry and had scads fun and then did the CGIs, and we thought if the world had these johns and janes it would be equal more, definitely. Remembering now the probs we thought up.

"Transgen women can't go in the women's jane, hey," Seymour said. "They're men actually, they might abuse."

"Nah," I said. "They got no interest, yah? What you got to do is keep the lesbians out. They could abuse. They got an interest."

"Obvi."

"Ident," I said. "Run a kit. Ten thousand self-ID'd lesbians amalgamed in half-length pix. Surveillance cams can scan and match in .9 seconds. Match, they get sent to the john."

"Harsh."

"Gentle it. Just a few words." I flashed him words: *Please use the adjoining facility.*

"I see a problem."

"Yah?"

"Yah. No one in the john knows you're a les."

I pondered. "So if they go in the john men could abuse."

"Yah."

So all that was actually utter dumb and from old, but I was on propanolol and Seymour was drooping, four AM Singapore, which is 5 PM mytime the day before. Next meet we switched the thinking to unigender, made progress. Can't remember how we scaled it, but we got PASS on it and that's what counts.

Then: Spring Break! My first spring break, because costs. Fam decided this time to go in on it for me, because PASS. Max lucks!

All over the world, Spring Break time.

Received welcome package in gmail, unzipped it. Nice oldtime fonts. *Heyjoe! Great year, yah? Now's for rest-n-rec, yah? As a fulltime student of "Spectrum Cumulus" you hereby receive a special invitation to Spring Break at our Grandparent College, "Yale"!*

Went on a bit about Yale, this place, the oldness, the motto—"Luxe y Vanitas," same as ours—and the many years that SCU.edu/sg and Yale had worked together, and-cetera. Pix and vids, leafy, stony, grassy. This was to be so fun.

Then Seymour Chin checked in. Seymour hates-hates to type like words, so what I got back was a string of emojoes to express. I got the meaning right away.

"Heyjoe, we not on?" I flash.

Seymour has affluenza—nose running, coughing, sick like a dog. (Do dogs get specially sick? Don't know. Never had one.) Not going to make it, not on day one anyway.

I'm on my own at Yale.

So it used to be I guess that Spring Break was in the you know spring, like March. Everybody left Campus and went to crazy-hot places to party—not like now. But who wants to go to New Haven in March? If not snow, rain, ice, and-cetera. So they do it in June, which was when back then a student would get their diploma. And since there's nothing else going on there then these days, good time. But they still call it "Spring" Break. Know what? You can actually get a train ride (*take a train* they say) from New York up to New Haven, get off. There's a Shuffle that meets this train and takes you to Campus. Town is wastrel, but then you drive through this stone portal—like in a fantasy RPG—and there you like are.

Wow. The place is old. The buildings look like castles. Old corroding I guess granite. Pointy windows. Pointy tops. Pointy everything. And what happened just as we drove in and down this avenue? Bells started ringing. They were playing songs, but with bells, somewhere up in a tower. Ancient songs I remember from as a kid. I sort of teared up a little it was so amazing.

We were led through another portal into this big square of lawn, a quad it was called—four sides, get it?—where there were long tables and these young guys and women were waiting to hand us stuff, all of them waving and saying Welcome and Hi and Get in Any Line. The spring-breakers were some of them zonkered with sleeplessness, come from around the world like Seymour Chin did or actually didn't, others up for it and giving high fives and whatnot. The woman I came up to checked my name/pic on their pad, and started piling things in front of me, calling out the names as they did it. Sheets and stuff! Orientation materials! One six-pack beer! One swechirt (with huge white "Y" on it)! Goody bag! Hat!

It was a blue flat cap—blue for Yale, Old Blue—and it had a number on the front, 2016. "What's that?" I asked them.

"What's what?" they said.

"The number."

"Heyjoe, that's your class!" They took it and put it on my head and tugged it down, laughing, really white teeth. "Class of twenty-sixteen!" they said, and shook my hand. "Welcome to Yale, Yalie!"

So the hat and the number were for the old-time scenics too. I laughed with them—they were sort of actually quite hot. "2016!" I told them. "That's like my dad's year!"

"Yeah!" they said.

Actually my dad didn't go. Because army. But if he had.

I loaded all this stuff up plus my kit and started off. A whole bunch were headed for the dorm we were assigned, only it wasn't called a dorm, it was called a college, which they said in this special way, a College. Why a college in a college? Who knew. My orientation pack explained, probs. And it was a castle too. It had a fucking coat of arms over the archway. All of us pouring in through the iron gate yelling, like overthrowing peasants, minus torches.

I have seen actually a lot of dorms, the boys and women in their little rooms, bunk beds, the stuff that happens. Squeeing and flaming on, the micro cutoffs and docked T's, pizza-boxes, selfies. Actually, now I think of, a lot of that was in porn. Vintage porn, but it gave you the scenics. The room I actually got was not like a dorm room. It was more fantasy RPG. The monk's lair or hmmever. A marble fireplace. Like wood walls made of oak. Dropped my stuff and sat down on a futon couch and felt a little—you know—I don't know.

But you know what? The john/jane was also like from another age. Urinals? Yes. Had to try one. Everything we designed out in our Toiletry proj. Flashed Seymour Chin but no emojoes in response. Then seven guys and a woman poured in and it was sorting out the rooms and the beds (the wood room with the vampire-castle fireplace was just to hang in) and we cracked the comp six-packs and the night began. Hoo-hooting and woo-wooing from all around the quad.

I put on my droops and the gimme swechirt and 2016 cap and went out with my class into the quad. There was plenty of light there but most of the buildings, classrooms and such, were all dark inside. Way up far-off on a hill was a regular type building, part of the science center I think we got told, lit up normally but looking so far away. These old parts had been left behind years ago.

I'm not that great in crowds—always have this impulse to say things, right, like actual things and not just tags. The Meaning of Life. Sometimes I guess I put people off. Anyway thinking like this I got away from the quads where the spring-breakers were. Thinking of all these buildings being full long ago, now when it's all collabs across the world, actually better for sure but still there was a kind of sadness to feel, just wondering what it would have been to go to classes in those buildings and throng around the quad all day hugging books, talking to professors like f2f. Maybe I was born too late.

Tomorrow was going to be utter. We go to class. We hear a lecture by some heyjoe about some subject. Like we walk all together into one of these lecture halls with seats that have these paddle arms where you put your notebook and take notes with a pencil. I got a pencil in my goodie bag. No paper. Maybe the note stuff was like for kidding.

By now I was somewhere that was pretty empty of spring-breakers. The buildings felt like they were sort of looking down on me, like looming. Up in the corners of buildings and on the edges and gutters were these faces—little heads, of monsters or like demons. Staring, grinning, showing teeth. Not for kidding: they were there.

Freaking out a bit. What happened to everybody? Was this still Yale? I went past a building that was like a giant white cube, with squares on each face, sort of like a ginormous Rubik's cube without the colors. Not old. Not old but cold. And then when I hooked a left and a right there was the most, the tallest, the most looking-at-me building ever. It had to be a church. I've seen churches. This was the churchiest church I'd ever seen. The steps that led up to the churchy-pointy door were worn away, by a million feet going up and down a million times. I stood in sort of shock. Ancientness.

Then I saw that the door was open. A little. I could tell that if you went up and pushed on it it would open more.

So I did.

See, what I learned: that you can be born too late, and really old things can seem, like, familiar to you. There's a sadness. What it is, it's more of an entrancement. Which is on the whole not a good thing, because you can just wander on and never come back. Not that knowing this was any help, as it turned out.

The church was just like in this VR tour of somewhere I did once. It was huge and empty and gray. The pillars of it ran together into arches high up. There were little windows made of colored glass, pictures in glass made long ago, or looking like it. What wasn't there were all the rows of seats to sit in and like worship. It was empty, it was the emptiest place I've ever been in. It made you gulp. The VR tour not so much.

I went over to one of the pillars and put my hand on it, the stone, worn by the ages. Cold and rough. Not even VR can give you feels. I was liking this when a weird feeling came over me, like somebody was nearby.

Somebody was. I don't know how he came up to me that close without making a sound, but when I turned I saw him and I did the guh-guh-guh! thing.

"Looking for something?" he said. I didn't know then how long I was going to be listening to that voice, or how much I would want to not hear it. He was a little guy with a round head, almost bald, and this farcey moustache. Smiling.

"Is this," I said, "a church?"

"No indeed," he said. "Or in a way, yes, a church. A Cathedral of Thought. It is in fact a Library."

"Wow."

"Yes."

"And who are you?"

"I am," he said, "the Librarian."

"Wow, so a Library." I took a few steps further in, and he kept close to me. "And you're a Librarian."

"I am *the* Librarian. There are no others. Not anymore."

What's that ancient movie, Seymour sent me snips once, a Cathedral, and this ugly messed-up heyjoe who loves the bells and climbs up the tower to ring them? For some reason I thought of it now.

"Why," he asked, "does your hat have the number two-thousand sixteen on it?"

"Oh, 'cause I'm a student, and that's my class." I could tell he didn't quite get it. "I don't really know why I'm here, I just . . ."

"Oh, I know why you've come here," he said, getting a little too close.

"You do?

"Because you're a Student. You're drawn to books."

"Actually not so much."

"You love books."

"Um." I made that look—eyes sort of closed, shoulders up, hands out to show they're empty. Like hmmever.

"You don't. You don't. Like books. You hate them."

I laughed. "Well, they're sort of heavy, you know? A whole lot of them together especially."

He laughed at that, kind of wildly, which made me think I was making a like good impression. Poor guy. His eyes were sort of bulge-y, that condition, you know? And they sort of vibrated. Not his fault, but.

"So books?" I said. "Where are they?"

"In the stacks."

"Stacks? You mean all piled up?"

"Well, 'stacks,'" he said with the double finger-waggle. "Called stacks. All neatly placed on shelves. You went up, up . . ." —he pointed up, like to heaven, to the ceiling—"and got the one you wanted. If you were allowed."

"Uh," I said. "Who's not allowed?"

"Students," he said. "Haha, too bad for you. Haha, not true, you could, But long ago, no."

"So . . ."

"We-ell," he said, as though I was little kid, "what you did was, you looked up the book in the card catalogue. You see those cabinets over there? They're all that's left of the system, and they're now actually empty. But once there were hundreds of cabinets, and each drawer in each cabinet held hundreds of cards, all in alphabetical order" (here he stared at me with his goggle eyes vibrating, like to make sure I understood what that is, which I do, sort of) "and the card told you what the book's call number was, and then you looked at that sign over there, which told you where in the Library that range of numbers was."

"You called the number?" I dialed with a finger, another finger to my ear, like in oldtime cartoons means call me.

"No no. You'd write it on a paper. And ask a clerk to go find it."

"Every book had a different number?"

"Every book. Every. Single. Book."

"Of like how many?"

He bent over so close to me, with this creepy suspishy smile, that now I was thinking that he, or well they, was maybe gay or bi. "Millions," he said.

That sort of staggered, yah? Millions?

"You want to see them," he said. It wasn't a question.

"Don't know," I said. "Do I?" I looked away and up and around, the darkness was like solid, there was no sound. Place was entirely soundproof, with all these books—like a million pounds of insulation.

"Jeez. They must be unbelievably valuable. I mean worth a lot."

"Not really so much," the Librarian said coldly. "Not one by one. All the really valuable ones—they've been taken out, they've been put with all the most valuable ones in that big marble cube—you saw it, right?—the Beinecke. And locked up so no one can steal them or handle them or even *see* them except the big shots, who don't care much anymore anyway."

He looked up to the spaces overhead, as though he could see the books up there, in stacks. "What's here are the ones they don't care about. Oh, they aren't valuable, no. They're just here. Abandoned. This building's kept safe and locked and a few lights on until they can decide what to do with them. Ha. Pretty clear what they'll decide."

I thought: Place had not been locked when I arrived.

"Listen to me," he said. "I'll tell you something no one knows but me. There is one book in this library that is unique. If they knew it was here they'd take it and put it in with the Audubon Elephant Folio and the Gutenberg Bible and all the rest over there. Because you know why?"

"Why."

"Because there is only one copy of this book in all the world." His nose was almost touching mine, far back as I pulled, and he whispered, like somebody might hear. "It's one thousand years old. It's covered in gems. The pages are made of the skin of goats, pounded so thin you can almost see through it." He smiled this mad smile. "Only one copy. It's never been kindled. It's not on the Internet Archive. It can't be accessed on line. It is fabulously valuable." He goggled at me. "This book is mine."

"Okay," I said. Mostly I was trying to picture jewels stuck on a goat's skin, and getting nowhere.

"You want to see it."

"Yes. Maybe. Sure."

He let out this strange sigh, as though deflating, like after you've held tension a long time. "Yes," he said. "You do." He jumped up, dusted off his core-droys, and set off, wagging his hand for me to follow.

I followed.

He took me down the hall to this place that would have been an altar, if it was a church, and then around and through a little door.

"Up," he said.

This was a different space, narrow not big, closed not open, low-ceilinged, tight.

"The stacks," he said. Slowly by slowly we went up the zigzag stairs. They made this ringing noise in all that silence. His steps, my steps. Now and then we go through a padded door and then up again. There was an elevator, but a lock bar was bolted over it. He'd look back at me grinning, like a dad taking a kid for a treat.

There were so many books. Endless. Lonely. Fearsome. Looking at me, like those demon faces. Thinking their words, reading themselves to themselves.

I knew we were high up now, but it didn't feel like it; it felt like being down in a mine. There was only a light now and then, and it was just an emergency or like a nite-lite. "What's that smell?"

"Books."

It was a strange smell, musty or mildewy but dry and not ick, sort of appealing actually, like I don't know what, a nice cave or a grandma's bedroom or. It smelled . . . old.

He turned down a narrow passage and ran his hand gently across some books looking no different to me than the others. "Poe," he said. "You've read Poe, of course."

This suspishy look in his eye made it clear I was supposed to say Of course, but of course I couldn't. "A little, maybe," I said. "I think I played the game a few times."

He took one out, opened it, and spoke words, not like he was reading them, like he was remembering them or making them up. "There was a discordant hum of human voices!" he whisper-yelled. "There was a loud blast as of many trumpets! There was a harsh grating as of a thousand thunders! The fiery walls rushed back! An outstretched arm caught my own as I fell, fainting, into the abyss. It was that of General Lasalle. The French army had entered Toledo. The Inquisition was in the hands of its enemies."

The Pit and the Pendulum. Didn't know then. Sure do now.

He closed the book gently, like it might be hurt if he smacked it shut, and put it in its place like putting a baby to bed. Patted it.

"Up," he said. He pushed me along to the next stair up.

Then another smell, almost not there at first, then more. Not nice, bad. Something dead, dead rat like we once had in the basement.

"Books," he said.

"Not books," I said.

"Up," he said. "It's up this way." He pushed me ahead of him through another padded door and up another metal stair. It was starting to feel a little close-to-phobic. "Where's this book?" I said. "I gotta go. There's a party. There's a class."

"Here!"

There was an empty space in the ranks of shelves, where they'd been sort of dismantled somehow. He grabbed my shoulders and turned me toward it. I was done here, hey, I wanted out, and wondered if I knew how to get out. "Okay," I said, "just a peek, then we go, yah?"

"Shut up," he said. He gave me a shove in the back, he growl-shrieked, and then that's all I knew. I guess a minute or two, or seconds, and things appeared again, like coming into focus. I'd got hit on the head. Hit on my fucking head with something by this fucking heyjoe.

I reached out to smack him, and I couldn't. Fucker laughed.

I was stuck to the metal shelving. With zipties.

"What the fuck," I said, calmly. I even tried a little laugh.

"What indeed," he said.

"Heyjoe," I said. "Come undo. I can't."

"I see that you can't."

Getting so weird. He was looking at me like I was a big goodie bar.

Then. This happened. No shit. He turned and from the shelves across the walkway he started pulling out handfuls of books and plopping them down around me. Then more. "You'll be happy here," he said. "Right here with the other book lovers, ha ha. Yes. One on each side of you. Kyra I think was the name. And Ira. Or something. Tweedledum and Twee-dledee. You'll be right in the middle, like Alice."

"Shut up," I said. "Get me out."

"You won't have much," he said. "And soon you won't need much. Oh but you'll have what no one else does. You'll have books!"

He was piling up the books any which way, pressing them against me. Working like a madman. I almost couldn't see over them now. I could hear the Librarian breathing, almost pant-ing, like—well, like panting.

"For shit's sake!" I cried. "For the love of Mike!"

"Yes," said the Librarian, calm-cold, still piling books. "For the love of Mike."

There was no more light now. I was behind the wall of books. It was black dark. I couldn't even read the titles.

I started yelling. I knew it was no good, but I did it anyway. Actually it wasn't a plan. I just did it.

"Calling for help?" the Librarian said, and I could hear the sneer. "Who do you think will come to your rescue here? Pip? Holmes? Allan Quatermain?"

85

I didn't know those guys. Or any guys. My wrists were bleeding from fighting with the zipties, you can't break a ziptie, this I knew but still.

"If you need me," he whispered into the cracks in the bookpile, "I will be downstairs. In Reference." And he laughed like a maniac, which he actually was. I could hear his feet go down the metal stairs.

"No!" I yelled. "I love books! *Books!* BOOKS!"

Nothing. No sound. Probs I gave another scream. I don't actually remember. In a Library no one can hear you scream.

How long was I in there, behind the books? A day? Days? I blacked out, then came back, and there were books. I believe I peed my pants. When I was alert I could only see books; also when I was passed out. Once I thought I'd got free and was reading one, but that wasn't factual. It seemed all the time that the books were actually coming closer to me, like pressing in, the stacks squirmishing forward to crush me.

He came back once. I heard his feet. I thought he'd had a change of heart. I sort of moaned-pleaded, I could hardly speak; he nosed around like some rat sniffing for what he could get.

"Help," I whispered. "Oh help." Then I wandered away again into nowheres, and when I came to he was gone again.

I was done for. Like Kyra and Ira. I could see them in my mind, skeletons hung up with zipties like corpse pirates, behind their books. I was just in the act of passing out again, for good this time, the books smothering me in revenge—and at that exact second I heard footsteps, foot-dings, on the stairs, not one person's but two or three's, coming up from below. Then came this wild kungfu yell and the books were pushed away, this side, that side, and a little light came in. An outstretched hand caught my arm.

It was the hand of Seymour Chin. The Singaporean had reached New Haven. The Library was in the hands of its enemies.

What I remember after that is not much. Seymour Chin looking at me like his face was going to pop—I'd never seen the man in the body. Behind him this very large diversity person in body armor, Yale blue, their hand on their gun, looking like they'd seen a well you know.

Then I fainted.

So what it was that happened, which I learned later in the Yale hospital, where they checked me out: Seymour'd followed a thumbnail microtag we worked on freshman year—our first proj! I installed it on myself way then, and forgot! Amazing he could trace his way up through the stacks, but that was what the tag was supposed to do, and damn it did.

Seymour explained about the rumors. Hadn't I heard them? The Old Campus Vampire. No I hadn't. Heyjoe, everybody tells them for giggles, just. But some people really had disappeared over the years, maybe just wandering in the empty buildings or like looter-ish. Never found. Seymour was very into stories like that in gaming and such. But not kidding? Not one kid, he said. The Library Ghoul. The Book Fiend. We had to laugh, but it wasn't actually funny. Because it wasn't just Kyra and Ira. It was others. They're still looking.

"Heyjoe," he said to me when we'd left the hospital and got out from around the media collected there. "Still time. Let's go to the College, get a beer. Wet T contest! So I heard. Rock out!"

Seymour too loves old things.

"Not for me, Seymour, sorry to say." I checked my watch, saw messages and-cetera. Relief. "Love you, heyjoe, but you know what?" I said. "Spring Break's over. I need to get back to the real world."

Then I see it's the Library Fiend. Like looking at me out of my watch. Startled, very. Then I see it's like Foxnews, it's his what, arraignment? In this dim New Haven courtroom. He seemed so small. When the public defender person said something about a psych-eval he piped right up, and his weird eyes started revolving. "True!—nervous—very, very dreadfully nervous I had been and am; but why will you say that I am mad?" He tried to get to his feet but a cop shoved him back. "The disease had sharpened my senses—not destroyed—not dulled them. Above all was the sense of hearing acute. I heard all things in the heaven and in the earth. I heard many things in hell. How, then, am I mad?"

Well, fuck yes you are, heyjoe.

"Poe," I said. "I bet."

"Hmmever," Seymour said. He was guiding me along the street through the crowd. They were going in and out of the tech stores and the clothes and shoes and such. But not into one store, on a corner, that seemed closed. We got closer and it looked closeder. But it wasn't. There were lights on inside, and on the window was written BOOKS.

I stopped.

"I wonder," I said. "Poe."

"Oh no, heyjoe. Step away from the door."

"Just books, Seymour."

"Heyjoe," he said, tugging. "You can't be too careful."

The Million Monkeys of M. Borel

In the uncomfortably warm months of December and January in the year 19—, I found myself with little occupation and therefore much time for idle thought. Reading had become difficult for me owing to a progressive deterioration of my eyes, and if there was no one interested in reading to me from that small collection of volumes which I could still count on to give me pleasure, then I did not read, or rather I did not hear the voices of authors. Plato, as is well known, said that when we read a book we believe that we hear the voice of a person, and yet when we try put a question to it, it does not answer us.

What occupied my thoughts in those somnolent days were certain metaphysical or logical propositions that had been argued or at least passed around a great deal in the time of my youth. I was considering the million monkeys of Émile Borel, as described in his 1913 essay *La mécanique statique et l'irréversibilité. J. Phys. Theor. Appl.*, 1913, 3 (1), pp.189-196. As is well known, Borel posited that a million monkeys randomly hitting a typewriter keyboard for ten hours a day will in time almost surely type all the words in all the books of the Bibliothèque nationale in many combinations, including the order in which they actually occur in those million volumes. In the restatement of the theorem most popular among English speakers, the monkeys eventually type out the collected works of William Shakespeare. The crux of the argument, as enunciated by Borel and those who took up his proposition, was that the term *almost surely* has a precise definition in the language of the mathematics of probability, a definition rather unlike the one we use: *Almost surely my mother loves me above her other children; almost surely my ancestor was a hero in the battle in which he died.* These statements differ from Borel's.

In later years the million monkeys of M. Borel were replaced in the theory by an infinite number of monkeys, or by a single monkey typing all the time forever. In the latter formulation, all of Shakespeare must eventually be produced; in the former, all of Shakespeare (and every other written work) is produced instantaneously as soon as the typing begins. Neither of these refinements seemed to me to be as worth pondering as M. Borel's million monkeys who could only almost surely produce the soliloquies of Hamlet, the madness of Lear, and the love of Antony and Cleopatra—who indeed could almost surely produce them even if Shakespeare had never written them, and likewise all other books both already written and never written before.

At this juncture, a visitor arrived with a piece of machinery he had brought to see if it could assist me in the dilemmas both banal and esoteric which a loss of eyesight entails. He had come to be devoted to certain works of mine, published in obscure journals long ago but apparently ubiquitous now. The machine was a computer of a kind not yet available to the general public, which he could set up in such a way as to cause it to read aloud whatever text it was given, or which it was directed to ask for from its memory. My young friend assured me that the memory of the computer—no bigger than a lady's vanity case—contained the entire works of several of my beloved authors, as well as Shakespeare, the Bible in several languages, and other works of science and philosophy. If manipulated in the right way it could also reach into libraries around the world, where other bodies of miniaturized and encoded texts were kept.

My wonder at this was somewhat dampened when, after working an afternoon, he directed the machine to read a text I had selected (a story of Chesterton's). The voice proceeding from the machine was neither the voice that the story had spoken in when my eyes had used to pass over it, nor the voice of a human reader sitting beside me. It was the voice that the dead gods of Egypt might have spoken in when summoned by Agrippa or Trithemius: a corpse's voice. My shock and grief (for I had greatly anticipated the riches awaiting me) at this inhuman parroting of human words saddened my friend, and not wishing to seem to spurn his good intentions toward me, I began to question him about the machine and its powers.

"There are puzzles in metaphysics," he said, "and thought experiments in physics, that can now be carried out in actual fact. The long-standing problem of how few colors a map-maker would need to construct a map where no two contiguous countries or regions would be the same color, no matter what the shape of the regions: a computer (more powerful by far than this one) has proven that three colors are in fact enough, which before there was no way to demonstrate. The only drawback is that the proof resides in the computer, and is so complex that only another computer as powerful as the first can certify it.

"And there is the problem of the million monkeys who sit down to type all the works of Shakespeare," he continued, astonishing me with the workings of Coincidence, whose laws might also be known only to computers, and provable only by other computers. He said that computers were easily able to produce random series of letters according to any rule the maker imposed. Suppose for instance a rule was set that the computer should generate a text exactly as long as the First Folio of Shakespeare, all letters, punctuation and spaces being counted. In a matter of seconds the computer could generate a text wherein, as in the Cabala of Abulafia, the letters of the Shakespeare text were replaced en bloc by others produced at random. It could be shown that if the computer were to produce these false folios at the rate of one per second, it was estimated that the universe would end, the suns burn out, and all would be reduced to aimless atoms and cold, before so much as a single play, perhaps a single entire line, was produced in its proper place.

One rule, however, would hasten the process. (He called it an *algorithm,* a word of the Arab arithmeticians who in their texts had liked to write out their endless equations in words made of letters, and not in the number forms they had themselves invented.) The computer could easily, in its comparisons, determine if so much as a single letter of any false text fell by chance where the same letter fell in the Folio text. Preserving that letter in its position, the computer would examine the next, and the next, discarding everything in each one except the letters—it might be two, or ten, or none—that fell where the same letters fell in the text.

"If that little rule is followed," said my young friend— eager and smiling, it was hard not to see him as the herald of a triumphant army, come joyfully to demand the instant surrender of an ancient town—"then the entire works of

Shakespeare can be re-created in a very short time. All that's needed is for the computer to save the accumulated coincidences of all the false texts with the real text."

All that was needed, then, was for the text to exist in advance of the attempt to produce it. It was, as he said, a simple matter. Yet it would never satisfy those who contemplate, in the shadows of ancient libraries, the million monkeys of M. Borel. For the secret longing of those dreamers is not for the books of ours they might reproduce, but for those texts of their own, unknown to us, unknown even to themselves, that they might create. The great computer my young friend contemplated, examining the texts that its blind mechanical monkeys produced at inconceivable speed, retaining only what they shared with an Elizabethan whose works we know by heart—what other works, unknown to us, works we have needed and sought for and dreamed of existing, would it, every day, every instant, discard forever?

When the young engineer had gone—somewhat downcast, it seemed to me, yet promising to return to give me further instruction—I placed my hand upon the box he had brought; as silent now as the statue from which the god has departed. The fact that it—unlike those fatuous and impossible monkeys—actually could generate such things could break the hearts of those who, in another day, were able to smile at the thought of an endless library composed of all possible combinations of all the letters that we know. "We think, when we read, that we hear the voice of a person; but if we question it, it will not reply."

This Is Our Town

When I was young I lived in a place called Timber Town. It can be found in a book called *This Is Our Town,* which is part of the "Faith and Freedom" series of readers, and was written by Sister Mary Marguerite, S.N.D (which stands for Seours de Notre-Dame), and published by Ginn and Company, copyright 1953. Catholic children read it in the fourth and fifth grades.

Timber Town was a small river town, where exactly the book never said, but it would have to be somewhere in the Northeast, maybe in Pennsylvania. Upriver from Timber Town was a place called Coalsburg, which was where the trains from the mines came down to load their coal onto barges. Downriver from Timber Town was a city of mills called Twin City, because a part of the city was on one side of the river and another, poorer part was on the other side. These names were easy to remember and understand, even for young children. River ferries and trains ran from town to town and farther, down somewhere to the sea, I suppose. In the double title page you can see us kids high on a hillside, looking over the river valley and the mills and the church; we wear the saddle shoes and the striped shirts and flaring flowered skirts we did wear then, and in the pale sky are pillowy clouds and the black check-marks of flying birds. I can still feel the wind.

The book tells stories of then and now, of the flood that hurt so many houses in Timber Town and nearly washed away Coalsburg: I saw all that, I was there. The book has stories of long-before, when miracles happened to children like us in other lands, and stories of saints like St. John Bosco, the saint after whom our school was named. But most of the stories are about our town, and the nuns in our school, and the priests in the church, and the feast days and holidays of the months one after another. The stories are all true and of course they happened to us or we caused them to happen, or they wouldn't be in the book; but the book never told everything about us, nor all that we could do and did.

May, 1953:
It has been a long time now since I last saw my guardian angel. Of course I know she's here with me all the time whether I can see her or not, and I can hear myself tell myself the words she would once say to me to guide me and keep me from harm, but I haven't seen her as herself, the way I guess all kids can.

I remember how she stood behind me at my First Communion, her hand on my shoulder, and how it was the same for all of us in white kneeling at the rail as the priest came closer to us, going from one to the next. We never talked about when or how we saw our guardian angels, but we all knew. My brother Thad walked along beside the priest, in his cassock, with his hand on his breast, carrying the little tray on a stick (the *paten*, he told me it's called) to hold under our chins as Father Paine placed the Host on our tongues, in case some tiny fragment of the Body of Christ fell off and to the purple rug: because every fragment of the Host is God, at least for a while. Perhaps because it was the first time, we didn't feel—at least I didn't—the wondrous warmth and sweetness, the dark power too, that comes with swallowing God. It would come gradually, and we would long for it.

After Mass was done we all went out into the sun and the trees in flower and marched—or went in procession anyway—around the church to the white statue of Mary, crowned the previous Sunday with pink roses that had shed petals all around the statue's base. I never much liked this statue, white as the plaster casts in the library, her eyes unable to see. And there we sang.

My white dress and my little white missal and my white kid gloves were all put away and I was sitting on the back steps wearing dungarees, my feet bare, and she said (my guardian angel) that a sad thing about being an angel is that you can never partake of Communion like living people can. Angels know that it is a wonderful thing and they can know what their person feels, because they know their person and they know God. But they can never have it themselves.

I asked: Does that make an angel sad?

Well, my angel said, nothing *really* makes an angel sad.

And then she clutched her knee in her linked hands, just the way you do when you're sitting with crossed legs, and said There are angels for other things than people. Every animal in the world has a kind of angel, a little one or a big one, who's born with the animal and vanishes away when the animal dies.

Will you vanish away? I asked, but she laughed the way she does and said I am yours forever and will always be with you.

She doesn't have wings, and a long time ago when we were younger I asked her why. I don't need wings to come and go, she said. The pictures only show us with wings because that's the only way people can think of us, able to ascend and descend, bring messages, see to the whole wide world. But big feathery wings or little wings stuck to their backs—who could ever fly with those?

I thought about that and about how birds' wings are their arms, really.

Does Cousin Winnie have a guardian angel? I asked. Cousin Winnie wasn't a Catholic and didn't say prayers or go to any church.

Of course he does.

What is Cousin Winnie's guardian angel like?

Just like me. But older and . . . quieter. Actually I don't know what he's really like.

He can't see his guardian angel, I said. Can he?

Well, you know what? my angel said. Grown-ups can't, mostly. Can't see or hear them.

They can't?

Not mostly.

I thought then that that was the saddest thing I had ever learned. And now I know it's so.

June:

My mother wasn't born a Catholic. She went to many different churches, she said, and in school she learned to play the organ, and sometimes played in the churches her family went to. They moved a lot from town to town until she came to Timber Town and met Dad. Sometimes I think she was the only person in Timber Town who wasn't Catholic; but when she married Dad of course she had to become a Catholic, and she did, and she was glad about everything we did and the holidays and the feast days coming like chapters in their turn. But the one thing she went on loving were the hymns and the music in the churches she'd grown up in. And because she sang them in her soft voice as she worked or cooked, we learned them too; at least I did. She sang *Abide with me, fast falls the eventide* and she sang *Jesu, joy of man's desiring* and *Praise God from whom all blessings flow* and I sat in silence and listened, and the words and the music entered my heart and still remain there.

She had a way of talking about things like saints and hymns and Bible quotes that made it seem she thought they were not serious or important to her, that they were like funny old poems or Bing Crosby songs, but I think that was because she actually loved them and wanted to protect them. She called the Thursday of Holy Week Maundy Thursday (we pretended she'd said Monday Thursday, and laughed every time, every year), and she knew of saints we hadn't heard of. Like St. Swithin. If it rains on St. Swithin's Day in June, she said, it will rain for forty days; and if the sun shines it will shine for forty days. He was also the patron saint of apples. She would sing:

> *High in the Heavenly Places*
> *I see Saint Swithin stand.*
> *His garments smell of apples*
> *And rain-wet English land.*

Mom's cousin Winnie came to stay with us now and then—when he had to rest, she said. We were told to call him Cousin Winnie as she did, even though he was older than Mom and I don't know whose cousin he really was. I also didn't know what he did in the world or what he had to rest from, but I do now.

He would arrive weak and thin and shaking and be put into the little room at the top of the house and my mother would take care of him, though I was never sure she really liked him that much. He was a dim sort of person, at least when he was resting. When he got stronger he would help around the house. One thing he was good at was card tricks. He told us the Devil had taught him, and that's why we could never see through his tricks, but I don't think he believed in the Devil any more than he believed in God.

When he came to rest in our house for the last time he did none of those things. He didn't get up at all. When I brought him coffee in the morning it seemed he had been crying. He was gray-white like the worn old sheets he lay on.

I told Mom he was dying. I was sure of it, and my guardian angel was sure of it too. And I said she should call Father Michaels to come. Father Michaels is the Parochial Vicar and helps Father Paine. Cousin Winnie's not a Catholic, she said. But I knew what I knew and I just looked at her and looked at her until she went to the telephone.

Father Michaels came and talked with him a long time with the door of the little room shut. We waited in our rooms or in the kitchen and didn't make a sound. Cousin Winnie died a little while later.

I asked Mom: Did Father Michaels win his soul?

Well, I don't know, my mother said. Winnie said a prayer at the end. And crossed himself. So I don't know.

Did he make a good Act of Contrition? I asked, because no sin can be forgiven without that.

Well, my mother said. He had a lot of sins to recount, and I doubt he got to all of them.

Then he would only go to Purgatory.

Uh-huh, my mother said, and even though she was crying she was laughing too. You bet. For a good long time too.

July:

In the book *This Is Our Town* there are more chapters about the great flood than about anything else. It nearly washed away my house and other houses, and did wash away houses of miners and other people in Coalsburg; their houses came down the river in parts and pieces, roofs and fences and once a doghouse with a little goat riding on top of it. My brother Thad went out with his friends in the fireman's rescue boat and rescued the goat. Along Second Street, which runs along the river, the water reached the windows of the first floors and kept rising. The gas and electricity stopped and we lived by lamps and candles and ate from cans. There is a chapter about how Mr. Popkin refused to take his ferry out for fear it would be swamped and lost. There is a chapter about how Father Michaels went up the river with an old man in a little motorboat to bring the Blessed Sacrament to the man's friend, who was dying. It's very dangerous, the man warns Father Michaels. *We will not think about danger,* Father Michaels replies. *My life would be worth nothing if I am afraid to save others for Christ.*

And then the Church of Saints Peter and Paul, our church, began to sag to one side as the earth and stones were washed away along the bank where it stood. It was decided that the school children should be taken to Twin City and stay in shelters made in the big school and the parish hall, sleep on cots, and go to Mass in the huge dark church there. We were among strangers.

The sisters who taught at St. John Bosco had come too and shared rooms with the Sisters of St. Joseph in their convent, and they came to the big church to Mass and to the special services held to pray for an end to the flood. It was like a big engine had doubled its power. Not all nuns are smart, and not all nuns are good; I knew that even then. But all of them have the power that God grants to all of us to bring about what we desire and need, and that power is greater in them. It's like the difference between the Twin City ball team and the Yankees.

This was for us to know: Prayer is how the world is managed. The Epistle to the Thessalonians says *Rejoice always, and pray without ceasing.* I prayed at night before I went to sleep and in school before classes. I prayed when I walked and when I waited. I prayed in prayers I knew as well as my own name, and I prayed in my own words: that Dad could keep his job in Twin City in the machine shop where he cut gears—I didn't know what that meant but Dad loved his job and though it seemed the shop would fail I prayed as hard as I ever had and it didn't fail. I prayed that Mom would stop smoking Old Golds because they aren't good for your lungs, and though I never told her I was praying for it there came a day when she stopped. She never said a thing about it, just stopped forever; later on when cleaning the living room she came upon an old pack half-empty and looked at it a long time as though she couldn't remember what it was.

Prayer isn't for things, Sister Rose of Lima told us. Prayer is attention: to God, to the soul, to the Virgin, to our hearts. Praying is for help to those in need, strength and courage for ourselves, honor and thanks to God. But I knew, and I knew she knew, that it was for things too: you had only to pray for something and receive it to know that. *Ask and it shall be given you:*

seek, and you shall find: knock, and it shall be opened to you. God made that promise to His Church, and He can't take it back. Father Paine said that if we pray for what will harm us or harm others God must give us that to—though it may come in a form we don't recognize, and won't like. There must be a whole bureaucracy in heaven that is managing these things, putting everyone's prayers together with everyone else's and assigning the work of carrying to God the prayers made to all the varied saints who are patrons of this and that, of health and work and the soil and the sufferings of people.

I have prayed for what might harm me, and I have prayed that others might be harmed, or at least obstructed. I have wondered if those prayers were answered in ways I can't know.

The rain stopped at last and the water receded, leaving everything filthy and covered in mud. We returned to our beloved Timber Town, but we kids decided it ought to be called Mud Pie Town now. The church hadn't fallen into the river, but it would take a Capital Campaign to raise the money to fix it. Father Michaels said we should pray that the Capital Campaign would succeed, though he knew that many, many people were badly off now because of the flood, and the bishop doubted the money could be raised. But by July the money had been raised and the men of the parish were volunteering to help fix the church.

August:
It was the day before the Feast of the Assumption of the Virgin, which is a Holy Day of Obligation, which means you must go to church just as if it were Sunday. There were extra confessions to go to on this afternoon, which I could now

go to and had to do, if I wanted to go to Communion in the morning, which I did. In the pew I did my Examination of Conscience and I couldn't find anything except the time I told my brothers to shut up because I was doing my homework, which was a lie because I was just reading a book.

There was a line for confessions. Waiting in my pew I read my Instructions for a Good Confession. What is a sin? A cruelty to others; a false representation of ourselves; a failure to honor God and the Saints in all the times and places we can, in all the ways we can, as often as ever we can.

I had falsely represented myself to Thad and Willy and so I guess I had sinned. I hadn't been sure.

In the dark of the booth I confessed to Father Michaels. I asked him himself to forgive me, because the priest has the power to do that. *Father, forgive me for I have sinned.* When I was done with my one sin he spoke in Latin and blessed me (I could see the faint motion of his hand through the screen) and he told me to say a decket of the Rosary and he was shutting the grate when I said Father, can I ask you something? And he said Certainly.

Is it true that older people can't see their guardian angels and talk right to them and hear them?

He paused for a little and then said: They hear them in a different way. They see them in a different way.

But I knew from the little pause that it was a priest's way of saying Yes, it is true. And he said: Our Lord tells us that faith is the evidence of things not seen, that what we believe but can't see has substance.

I said Oh. Thank you, Father. And he shut the grate.

I went to kneel in the pew in front of the Mary altar, where Mary is holding the baby and also holding out a rosary, which makes her look a little like a busy mom doing two things at once; but her face was as serene as always. I said my penance, the beads passing through my fingers as I murmured the prayers one by one, and with the saying of it my sin went away from me and my heart was cleansed. That's a nice feeling, your sin going away like dirty water down the drain. It would probably be a sin in itself to go out and sin just to feel that feeling. But I thought of it.

I went out of the church and sat on the steps and took my Brownie cap off (it was the only hat I could find that afternoon) and a group of nuns from the convent next to the church were going by together, their habits sweeping up the dry leaves that lay on the pavement. The beauty of them moving all together, the airs lifting their veils, their smiles and voices—they sang together, the younger ones, out of simple good cheer. I thought of being a nun, singing and never sinning again. Yet maybe the beauty of it was that it was something to see and not something to be, like geese you see in the autumn sky following the leader, all the same but each itself, and you want to join them. I *felt* I was among the nuns even though I wasn't, and wouldn't want to be, not really.

It's so nice, I said to my guardian angel. The voices. Singing.

It is, she said. It's the only way we angels ever talk to one another.

September:

One night at dinner Dad told a joke. It was because of the new (or rather old) school bus that the parish had just got for the grade school, given to them by the Twin City Bible Camp because it was so broken down and shabby they wouldn't use it anymore and had got another. The bus was needed to bring the children who lived out on the Timber Town road to Coalsburg to school and back again. It said Twin City Bible Camp on the side but Sister Fausta the art teacher said she would get some yellow paint and paint that out and put St. John Bosco School on it. On Monday the priest was going to bless the bus.

The joke Dad told was this: A little public school had got a brand-new bus and wanted it to be blessed by the different clergy of the town. So the Protestant minister came and read some verses out of King James's Bible. And the priest came and said some Latin and dashed the bus with holy water. And then the rabbi came up and instead of any of that he cut two inches off the tailpipe.

My mother blushed and smacked my father's hand. But nobody would tell us why the joke was funny. I thought maybe it was just funny because rabbis do funny things.

When we got to school on Monday the side of the bus was painted and the new name lettered on very carefully. But it was really pretty old and battered. I looked at the tail pipe for no good reason and it was very rusty at the end and sort of decayed. After school was done Sister told us all to go out into the yard and those who were going to Timber Town road and Coalsburg should get on the bus and everyone else gather round. When we all got on and found a seat—there was a lot of arguing about that, and pretty soon Mr. Kowalski the groundskeeper, who was now going to be the bus driver too, got up and yelled that we should all pipe down— we could see that Father Paine was coming, and he was wearing his stole and his biretta and an altar boy came after him with the bucket of holy water and the thing the priest uses to sprinkle people and things with. Yes, I know what they are really: the bucket is the *aspersorium* and the sprinkler is called the *aspergillum*. Thad told me that, and he is studying Latin and will maybe be a priest. He thought I would forget as soon as he told me but of course I didn't. I cannot ever be a priest.

Father Paine had a look of patient suffering, but he always does; it makes me think his name is the right name for him. He is so very kind and gentle and isn't suffering really, I don't think, any more than anybody. He crossed himself and said the *In nomine Domini* and we all did too, even we on the bus. And then the priest said *Aspergo te omnibus* and more and he splashed the water on us, and drops hit the windows and I thought of rain falling in the months of school still ahead even though this day was sunny and warm.

Then Mr. Kowalski started the bus, but it didn't start. It sort of shrieked or groaned, but nothing more. We all waited. He tried again, and this time the bus tried to start; it shook and made noise and then a loud bang came out the back and black smoke. Then it stopped. "It died," Mr. Kowalski called out the door to Father Paine. Father Paine thought a moment, and then he turned to the students and the nuns and the lunch lady and with his hands he told them to kneel. When they had knelt he crossed himself and prayed. We on the bus couldn't kneel but we folded our hands, except some boys. Mr. Kowalski turned the key again and the engine started. It was as if it didn't want to but it had to, like Dad getting up in the morning. The bus rocked and coughed and made small bangs out its rear end and a boy said a bad word about that and got shushed. Then as the priest stopped speaking and the people waited, the bus ceased to suffer, and began to breathe easy. The bad smoke smell went away and a good smell of September air came in the windows. The bus seemed to be happier, not so tense. And cleaner. It purred.

Father Paine smiled, and he waved to Mr. Kowalski to go ahead, and Mr. Kowalski very slowly moved the bus away from the school, as though he still wasn't sure it wanted to. But it picked up speed, and we all took a deep breath, and somebody laughed and somebody else cheered, and the bus was happy now. The seats seemed less stained and shabby, and the windows fit better in their frames. We turned onto the road that goes along by the school and then onto the road that goes along the river and then we couldn't any longer hear the kids and the nuns cheering from the lawn of the school beneath the pale statue of Our Lady. And after a time we on the bus were quiet and felt the shadows of leaves pass over us.

October:

On the day of Hallowe'en, Sister Rose of Lima, our principal, told us in school meeting to be careful how we dressed up that night. She reminded us that this night is the Eve of All Saints, and in the morning tomorrow we will go to church and honor all the saints, not only the ones we know but those many, many saints in heaven whose names are not known except to God and to those who have been visited by them, their families or their friends or their enemies. The night before the day of a great feast can be a risky time, she said, and this feast more than any other. We should be careful of how we dress up and what costumes and masks we pick, she said, because to dress up in costumes as ghosts or demons or figures of Death like skeletons or corpses might draw those very figures to walk with us. On this night they are allowed to walk abroad, and though the Church knows very well how they can be prevented from doing the harm they may wish to do, children out and about in the streets might not know that what seem to be other kids following them in costumes like theirs really aren't, and careless children can be threatened and their souls drawn out from the houses of their bodies unwitting and into the world to come.

A word to the wise is sufficient, Sister Rose of Lima said. She said this once every day more or less.

I was pretty safe because I wore a Brown Scapular (scapulars are sort of itchy and always get tangled around your neck but everyone puts up with that) and Our Lady of Mount Carmel has promised that no one who dies wearing it will die in a state of mortal sin. I had a Miraculous Medal as well, which my favorite teacher in first grade gave to me. Because of these things I wasn't afraid to walk in the night on All Hallows' Eve, at least not more than a little. But because of what Sister said I dressed up as Snow White.

Kids in my neighborhood of Timber Town would go to the houses in better neighborhoods, where you can knock on doors and say Trick or Treat and get better treats (not that I knew how to play tricks on anyone who gave me nothing). The way to get to those houses was to go up the street away from my neighborhood and cross the bridge over the old canal that runs to the river, which in the book has no name. I had heard—we all knew—that down under this bridge hoboes had their camp, and there were remains there of fires and cardboard shelters and tin cans. Kids told stories about the hoboes, that they could rob you or even kill you, but I didn't believe them; I said *I don't believe that story* but in that way you poo-poo stories you don't want to worry about. My brothers and their friends told the stories when we crossed the bridge, and they made claws of their hands and tried to be scary.

We knocked on the doors of the houses that had Jack-o'-lanterns on their porches fearsome or silly, with their fiery smiles and eyes, and my bag was full of treats to bring home, and so we started back. Then the boys got the idea to run to the bridge and across and leave me alone on the street. That was very mean of them and stupid and I called after them and said I would tell when I got home. I was more angry than afraid, and I walked on toward the bridge in my Snow White dress as though nothing was amiss. I set out on the bridge over the hobo camp, where maybe once a child had been killed though probably not. I could see a kid ahead of me on the bridge, in a white sheet like a ghost. When I looked again he wasn't there, but I thought he wasn't actually gone. And then again he was there, but only sort of. He was dawdling, as though he wanted me to catch up with him and maybe be with him, and he'd take me with him as Sister Rose of Lima had said; but he didn't seem dangerous or evil to me, just lonely and sad. I spoke an Ejaculation under my breath: *Lord Jesus Christ have mercy on me and on all the living and the dead.* I felt the Miraculous Medal grow warm against my chest and I knew that I was safe. And after I got across the bridge I could no longer see the little ghost child. He had remained behind.

November:

On the Feast of All Souls, the second day of November, I went to church after school to pray for the release of souls from their sufferings in Purgatory. On this day alone prayers of the living faithful can absolve them of their sins and admit them to heaven. The church was pretty full and smelled of damp wool and candle smoke and people, a smell I always liked and didn't like at the same time. On the cards that were placed in every pew was printed the Prayer of St. Gertrude, in white script across a colored picture of a gravestone and a praying child. *Eternal Father, I offer Thee the Most Precious Blood of Thy Divine Son, Jesus, in union with the masses said throughout the world today, for all the holy souls in purgatory, for sinners everywhere, for sinners in the universal church, those in my own home and within my family. Amen.*

Sister Rose of Lima said that God had promised St. Gertrude that when her prayer was said on this day with a righteous heart, a thousand souls would be freed from their sufferings in Purgatory. I looked around me at the others gathered there also praying for the dead, and some of them wept, perhaps for someone once in their own home and within their family, and I thought of Cousin Winnie. I didn't know if it was allowed to pray for one soul in particular, but I thought of the kid I had seen on the bridge in the night and I asked in my prayer that if he was a soul in Purgatory he might be one among my thousand. I prayed also that if Cousin Winnie was in Purgatory he might be one too. And I said the prayer for the dead: *Eternal rest grant unto them, O Lord, and let perpetual light shine upon them.* I felt the rush of the thousands of escaping souls winging upward into perpetual light. I was happy and sad as well.

December:
I wanted snow for Christmas very much. The last Christmas it had only rained, a small gray ceaseless rain that made the town's decorations look miserable and hopeless, like a birthday party no one has come to; and then the floods had come and

turned Timber Town into Mud Pie Town. Empty buildings on Second Street along the river still had dark shadows showing where the river had risen to.

My guardian angel didn't know how to ask for snow on my behalf, because though there are saints to pray to for rain, and saints for fine weather, there aren't any saints to pray to for snow. But I thought I could get a hearing. That's what Dad would say when he went to talk to the union shop steward: I'll get a hearing. God will do what we ask, I knew, if we ask in the right way; but it's not always easy to know the right way.

I took down the *Book of Saints* from the shelf and started from the beginning, but there are a lot of saints (about twenty St. Johns) and it was hard to pay attention. In due time I found that there are certain saints who are called Ice Saints in far Northern countries, where they need to know when cold weather will come. One was St. Servetus, and there was St. Agnes and St. Priscia, St. Mamertus and St. Boniface. If their feast days are cold it will stay cold a long time after. So maybe they could bring snow as well.

When Dad asked me what I was doing—making lists of saints' names, drawing charts and birthdates, writing prayers—I told him I was praying for snow. He said he didn't think God would answer such a prayer. Snow or no snow happens because of big weather patterns, which they show in the newspapers and describe in the short-wave radio broadcasts he liked to listen to. If God wanted to bring snow on a certain day—even His own Birthday—He'd have to start up the right weather patterns a long way back, long before you asked Him for snow. It can't just be Ta-da, here it is.

I said *If you abide in me, and my words abide in you, you shall ask whatever you will, and it shall be done unto you.* That's the Gospel of

John. And Dad looked down at me sitting on the floor with the crayons and I knew he loved me even if he didn't think you could pray for snow and have your prayer answered.

No snow fell that week; the weather was cold but clear, day after day. I wore leather gaiters under my wool plaid skirt and watched the breath come from my mouth as though to tell me I was alive and warm inside; and I kept up my prayers to the Ice Saints.

On the Third Sunday of Advent Father Paine gave a sermon about prayer, and about asking for things in prayer. As though he knew about me and my plan. Dad looked at me beside him and winked.

What Father Paine wanted to explain to us was a question that he said many had. If God knows all that has befallen the world, and has known since before the beginning all that would befall the world, why should we pray that things will come out well for us and for everyone? Hasn't it all been decided already, the good and the bad?

And he said that time for God is different from the way it is for us, that to God everything that was or will be is happening in . . . well, you could say in one moment, but moments are parts of time, and there is no name for what God sees. And when God sees a thing that by chance the world in its progress is bringing about, and the thing doesn't conform to His will, He can easily reset the conditions in the past, even at the beginning of the universe, so that the thing won't happen after all: because there is no "after all" for God.

That is the power given by God to our Holy Church, and by delegation to each of us, Father Paine said, and his sad pained face was alight. If we petition Him correctly, and if what we ask doesn't conflict with His larger purposes, He can't refuse us. At each moment He can reform the whole history of the world again from its beginning so that it will come to be. We may ask what we will.

And we call those things miracles, and answered prayers, and sins.

I thought then, sitting with the others in the newly rebuilt church that still smelled sweetly of wood and tartly of plaster: *It's like a movie.*

It's like a movie, where you know that the good guys will win in the end, no matter how often they lose and lose, how much they suffer: you just know they'll win. And even so, through the movie you are afraid for them every minute, and cry out to them to watch for the bad guys sneaking up on them, and your heart races and you get tears in your eyes *just as though you didn't know*: but you do know.

And the reason is that those who wrote and made the movie know you want the good guys to win, and so do they; and whenever in the story they are writing it looks like they can't win, the writers change the story of the movie so that in the nick of time it happens that they can, and they do. Just as we watching hoped and prayed they would.

When we went out of the church on that Third Sunday in Advent so long ago we found that it had begun softly to snow. By the end of the day it had worked up to a pretty good blizzard. That night with the wild flakes flying in the street lights and the sound of tire chains in the street I knelt beside my bed and said my prayers and gave thanks to St. Mamertus, St. Pancras, St. Servatus, St. Agnes, St. Boniface, and I seemed to see them high in the heavenly places, like great snowmen striding above Timber Town and Twin City and the high hills beyond, the snow falling like seed from their hands.

———

The boys and girls I knew in St. John Bosco School, and my brothers, and Sister Rose of Lima and Father Paine and Father Michaels and the mill workers and the men who helped to build the new church, all still live in Timber Town, and so do I. But in another way I left a long time ago. I lived in many places, and things happened to me that I could not even have known were possible in the world, and some of them were not good and were my fault and some of them were dreadful and the fault of many people or everyone; and yet even as I grew up I thought that whatever bad things happened, however we *stumbled* as Father Paine used to say, overall in the world things were getting better, and old bad things were going away. And it has grown harder and harder to think that way.

I knew, when I was a child and thought as a child, that in the world I lived in the good guys would win in the end even when it seemed impossible, because even if they went wrong and lost their way and made mistakes, God and His angels could always change the beginning of the world so that in some unexpected way it would come out right, even if it could only be made right after death; and because of what Father Paine said about time, I knew *how* God and His angels could change such things even though they couldn't know before-hand what wrong way the world would take, because we are God's creatures and we are endowed with free will. Because nothing is over in a book that's being written or in God's world being made, not until everything is over and the book is fin-ished and closed.

I still know now in the deepest part of me that it's so, and that all will be well, all will be well, all manner of thing will be well, no matter how long and sad and scary the story gets. I just wish that once again, just once more, I could believe that the ways of changing things are mine too, that I am a writer of the world: and that as we did in the Timber Town flood I could reach my hands into the world, into the story of our town and all our towns, and change things so that the good guys would not be defeated forever.

MOUNT AUBURN STREET

1. Little Yeses, Little Nos

Harry Watroba had gradually become unable to remember his dreams. It seemed to him the most painful thing about growing old, though he was only just past sixty and was in good health and could suppose that many distressing things, worse ones too, lay ahead. It wasn't that he awoke with no sense of having dreamed, as he had often done all his life; he awoke knowing he had dreamed, the events and images still as it were floating within his waking; and then he felt them slide away from him and turn to nothing even as he grasped for them. That was the new and painful part. It was though the picaresque sagas he had once upon a time inhabited, and woke in delighted or horrified possession of, still occupied his sleeping mind, only they were now erased like computer files just as he awoke.

"Why anyway," he asked Dr. Macilhenny, "do we dream? Any progress on that line of inquiry? Last I heard they didn't know."

"They still don't know," said Dr. Macilhenny. "They have some guesses. But nobody knows. In my opinion we're getting closer, but answers, even good likely possibilities that can be tested, might be farther off than they seem." He hadn't lifted his eyes from the columns of figures, Harry's own Pay

Attention! scores for today, which he was adding. A good Divided Attention man. Harry had tested okay for Selective Attention, poor on Divided and Alternating. No surprise.

Harry had asked other men his age (when it seemed appropriate; it was an odd question) if it wasn't a shame how advancing age took away dreams, and found that many of them didn't suffer from what he supposed was a natural, maybe a universal, concomitant of the aging brain. One of his friends, a long-time alcoholic (after drinking nowadays Harry himself neither dreamed nor slept), told him that his dreams were if anything longer, more vivid and memorable, than ever; often, he said, he went off to sleep in pleasant anticipation of the weird adventures that lay ahead for him.

"Maybe the effect is irreversible," Harry said.

"To tell you the truth, it's not something I've heard about," said Dr. Macilhenny. "It's not my area."

Harry watched Dr. Macilhenny total up the day's results, and then asked how he'd done.

"Oh, better and better," Dr. Macilhenny said mildly, as though it was a good thing but not necessarily all that significant. When they had first begun on the seemingly meaningless tasks that Harry did as part of his Cognitive Rehab Program, Dr. Macilhenny was unwilling to tell Harry how he'd done, but upon considering it he'd decided that there could be no reason not to tell, and maybe after all knowing you did well would spur you on to greater efforts. "It works in every other area of life," he'd said. The program was new, though, even groundbreaking, and Harry suspected that Dr. Macilhenny was sort of making it up as he went along.

Not, he told himself, that there was anything wrong with that.

———

Harry drove back from the city where Dr. Macilhenny's office was to the town where his daughter Hope lived, in whose house he was staying, just temporarily; he had been there for a month now, in a little bedroom under the upstairs eaves. As he drove he tried to Pay Attention! and make his right and left turns with care. He'd visited Hope here often enough in the past, but his wife had always been the navigator then, and he had (of course) no mental map of the area to check his guesses against. (Which direction would a right turn here take him? Toward or away? West or east? Harry wouldn't know, and might never know.) He put his car in the narrow driveway, and as he climbed out he looked at his watch and saw that he ought to go right on to pick up his granddaughter at her school a couple of blocks away. Harry locked the car, zipped his jacket, turned left to go down the street, and then at the next inter-section he paused, pointed (mentally) one way, then the other, and chose his turn.

Hope had astonished her parents (her father, Harry, anyway) with her choice of a name for her first, so far her only child.

"Muriel?" Harry said. "You're going to name your daugh-ter Muriel?"

"Not Muriel," said Hope. "Mur*iel.*"

"Muriel is a cigar," Harry said. "A well-known cheap cigar. My father smoked them. There was a famous ad on TV long ago. A cigar, a female cigar, animated you know, dressed like Mae West. And the cigar would say 'Why dontcha pick me up and smoke me some time.'"

"Oh my God, Dad," Hope said, not really much scandalized.

"Edie Adams did the voice," Harry said. It was like probing an old wound, he knew, the way he went on piling up these references that could ring no bell with her or anybody younger than himself, Mae West, Edie Adams, cheap cigars. Probing old wounds was something he was prone to, not always metaphorically either.

It was a sunny day. Harry walked on the brighter side of the street, liking the warmth on his back from the heating of the dark fabric of his jacket. His shadow went out before him, its feet stepped on left and right by his actual feet. It seemed to Harry that it was the same shadow that had gone before him since he was no more than ten; maybe it was the boy's shoes he wore, black and white Keds, but it was the outgrowing crewcut too and the skinny neck and the wide ear-wings, the slight build and long-wristed hands swinging beside, which were all just as they had been. He knew what age the shadowed boy had really reached, and he measured himself against time's onrushing effects, counting against them the head of hair still pretty full and dark, weight though not shape unchanged for years, mouth of mostly his own teeth, normal-limits blood pressure, firm though not often pertinent erections. He had read a study (he liked to read—was compelled to read—studies) that men who as adolescents masturbated every day had a significantly lower incidence of prostate cancer. So he was good there.

Tied at halftime. That wouldn't continue.

The school was a dark brick old Catholic one, where Hope paid a high fee for a kindergarten run by nuns, all now in mufti. Once when they were kids Harry and his sister had cut out a hairdo from a picture of a middle-aged lady in a magazine, and then set it over the pictures of the fully habited nuns in the high-school yearbook; it was hilarious to see them with hair, transformed into ordinary matrons. No need for that any more. Muriel sat on the low wall before the school, and she smiled to see her grandfather coming, but she didn't jump up; she propped her elbows on the plastic backpack in her lap and cupped her smiling face in her hands, watching his approach with interest as though he were a movie. They got along well, Harry thought. Hope at her age had been a little dour and fearful, and Harry's heart had sometimes been plunged in doubt for her; the sight of Muriel almost always filled him with, well, with hope.

"Hi, Grampa."

"Hi. How was school?"

She lifted one shoulder, still smiling: a measured response. She jumped off the wall and slung her backpack on; he took her hand and they started for home.

"Grampa, did they give you tests?"

"Yes. Dr. Macilhenny."

"Give me the test."

"Okay. Say this backwards. 1-2-3-4."

She leaned down as she walked as though were going to heave something weighty into the air. "4-3-2-1," she groaned.

"How about this. Say this backwards: C-B-A-D."

More titanic effort. "D."

"Yes."

"A."

"Yes."

"B."

"Yes? Actually I forget."

"Grampa!"

"I do. But I bet you're right."

"C!"

"Yes! You're a genius."

She took his hand again. "I hope you did all right," she said.

"I think I did." He pointed ahead, to Hope's little brown house on a leafy street. "And here we are home."

It was October when Harry had knocked on his daughter's door, like Frost's hired man, with nowhere else to go. Deciding to leave the motel where he had been living since the fire had been a major positive step, actually, and Hope was always trying to get him to take major positive steps, so he thought that his coming to stay with her might be seen as one. Most of the little he was left with was in the back of the huge old station wagon he'd driven for nearly twenty years.

"Dad."

"Hi. Did you get my letter?"

"What letter?"

"Mind if I come in?"

"Of course I don't mind. I have to go to work pretty soon." She looked doubtfully at the wagon and the things inside it.

The letter was in there too, unmailed, though Harry didn't know it; he'd been racking his much-racked brains to see if he couldn't draw forth a memory of himself stopping at the post office, taking the letter (which his mind's eye could see) from his inside jacket pocket, or from whatever pocket, and putting it into the right or the even the wrong slot, and hadn't quite been able to, which didn't (he thought) mean for sure it hadn't happened. But after all it hadn't, and Hope hadn't expected him. She took him in, and sat him at the kitchen table, and poured him coffee from the vacuum pot she'd have had to empty later anyway. He really had no place to go.

"Have you heard from Mom?"

"I talk to her now and then," Harry said, as though he spoke of a somewhat distant acquaintance. "There's a lot to get straight. Legally. I mean you know that even though the house is gone, or mostly gone, the land is still ours. The ground around. Hers and mine."

"Does she still mean it, about the divorce?"

"She means it."

"You know she says things when she's angry."

"I know." Atrocious things, hurtful things, conceivably true but not actually true things; and then later when he would try to respond, or charge her with what she'd said, she'd be *Oh I was just angry when I said that.* Amazing woman. "I believe she means it. I've got a lawyer's letter."

Hope slowly lowered her eyes and her heavy head; her shoulders sank toward the table on which her elbows rested as though resolution, possibility, good prospects, all leaked away from her. "Stupid," she said, and Harry supposed she meant more than the lawyer, more than her mother, more than himself, an ultimate stupidness that blanketed and smothered the living and hoping world.

On August 30th the house that Harry and Mila Watroba lived in, the house Hope was born to and grew up in, had burned to the ground, as it's said. Actually there was still quite a bit left above the ground, including one whole unit that seemed almost untouched, only its roof bitten off from behind like a cookie, though inside it there was nothing but blackness and filth. Harry was supposed to see to the leveling or razing of the remainder, and was making some progress toward the appropriate decisions. He thought. Mila didn't. The house had burned down when neither of them was in it; Mila far away on business, Harry not so far away but out late where no one was going to be able to find him and tell him, so that he learned it in the most unforgettable way, by driving up the hill and into the awful sour smell of wetted burnt wood and building components, wondering what on earth, then almost passing by the already incinerated house still surrounded by trucks and cars all alight, unable for a moment to recognize it as his own.

"That paint," said Hope. "So stupid."

Harry had to admit (to himself; his womenfolk had no reluctance in saying it) that it had been his job to dispose of the paint in the basement. It had been on his to-do list for a long time. For years, he had to admit. Decades. The job was daunting: Harry loved colors, and discriminated with assurance between closely similar shades; whenever there was some part of the house that needed repainting, he liked to try out a lot of possibilities, colors with the names of food or weather conditions or unlikely vegetation or foreign places, or combinations of these (Persian Violet or Arizona Chile or Cotton Candy Cloud). It was, of course, the decisions that were hard. The colors not finally chosen, many of them nearly full cans, mounted up in the basement like unforgiven sins, waiting to be dealt with, finally running to the dozens. Harry—and he believed there was at least a shadow of the exculpatory in this— was the one who said it was a fire hazard, who noted how often in newspaper or TV accounts of fires the neglected paint cans and "oily rags" were named as the cause, and though Harry couldn't actually picture the physics of it (oily rags or cans of paint suddenly beginning to smolder, then bursting vividly into flame) he at least acknowledged the possibility. Now and then when down in the basement he had touched the dripped and spattered cans, to see if any were getting warm.

The problem was that there was nothing you could do with them. It used to be that they could be taken to specially designated spots miles away on designated Toxic Waste Days, when they would be received and bound up in fifty-gallon drums and done somehow away with; now that no longer happened. At the town dump—now the Recycling Center—certain Toxic Wastes could be brought in and taken off the possessors' hands on the first Saturday of alternate months, and oil paint was one of these. Harry tried to remember when these alternate first Saturdays were, and on one he did bring in a certain number of very old and rusting cans, but he was ashamed to bring in all he had at once, and then the months went by, and so on. Even more intractable as a problem was the latex paint. The aged guardian of the Recycling Center told him that latex paint could not be recycled, thrown away, dumped, drummed, landfilled, or disposed of in any way; and he tugged the bill of his cap with finality.

What then was Harry to do with it?

Well, he could open the cans, the old fellow averred, and let the remaining paint just dry out; wholly and completely dried-out paint cans could be tossed into the compactor. But Harry's cans were almost all nearly full, or half full anyway; they would take months, years, to dry out, their tops off, in the damp basement. He could take one or two up to the attic, and let them sit there and dry out, and each year on some given day throw those two out, and open a couple more. Mila grew impatient, then caustic: the problem was unsolved, and Harry's brain had ground to a halt over it, and he could see in his wife's expression whenever he considered it aloud in her presence that she had had it with him and with it, and with his inability to make a move regarding it. He gave it more thought. And on the hot night of the thirtieth of August it did what the pamphlets and the PSAs said it would. It most likely began, the fire inspectors later said, with a leaky can of thinner, which rested on a pile of old newspaper; and then the gallon jug of shellac next to it, which went off like a Molotov cocktail—Harry would come to learn that shellac was actually not toxic at all and could have just been thrown away; and then the ten or fifteen years of paint, can after can, all the Sidewalk Café, Fringed Gentian, Mocha Frappé, Periwinkle, Chinese Jade, Leather Leaf, Aquarium, Comet, White Asparagus, Desert Rose, Creme Fraiche, Raspberry Sundae, Italian Straw, Cotton Field, Cape Sunset, heated and popping and finally exploding all at once in a blast that blew out the upstairs windows and brought all the neighbors out.

Among the vast inventory of what was destroyed—months later Harry continued to remember things that he no longer possessed—was Mila's home office and all its Rolodexes and bulletin boards and files, which Harry had intended to look into that very night to see if he could find the name of the hotel where Mila was staying, which she had mentioned to him but which he couldn't remember. (His recent brain researches suggested that in a brain like Harry's, terms for similar things might be gathered in clusters rather than each being firmly and purposefully attached to Harry's reason for needing to recall it, so that a call of "Mila's hotel in Ottawa" brought forth Holiday Inn and Ramada and Hilton and Travelodge and Best Western and Marriott all in a slurry. It was chemical, apparently.) Harry looking at the vastation of his house from the window of his car (for a long time he was unable to get out) had no idea how to reach her and tell her. Not that anything was going to get any better or worse by the time she got back, or until she figured out how to reach him after learning their phone was dead (it was quite dead); but Harry had a premonition that those couple of days of ignorance on her part and inanition on his were going to matter, and the fact that Harry had forgotten it was the York Ramada *outside* Ottawa that she had been staying in, and that he hadn't been able figure out how to find this out, was going to be unforgivable. He ascribed her decision to divorce him (made, or at least voiced, the very night she returned) to this. *You asshole*, she screamed. It was way past midnight. Her scream was like a nail in the head. He had always wondered how loud it could get, whether it would really keep on rising limitlessly with the gravity of the offense; it couldn't really, but it was penetrating. *Oh you stupid stupid fuck. This is it, this is it, this is really really it.*

"It wasn't that," Hope said, her eyes still on the table, watching her finger draw spirals in the fine breadcrumbs scattered there. "She told me she just couldn't go on making all your decisions as well as all her own. She's done it all your life together and she just wasn't going to anymore. She said the risk was just too great. She said she'd have done this even without the fire."

"I don't believe it," said Harry. But he remembered, just then, that he had, under pressure of her rage, suggested that after all they both knew the paint was there and she too could have tried to solve the problem; and it was then that her voice started to rise to unearthly volume. "You know, your mother sometimes suffers from Chanticleer syndrome."

"She suffers from what?"

"Chanticleer syndrome. Chanticleer is a rooster, the rooster in Chaucer. He's convinced that his crowing is what causes the sun to rise every morning. And of course he's got good evidence, because every morning after he does his crowing the sun does come up."

"And?"

Your mother, Harry thought. Ascription used by a parent in speaking with *gravitas* to a child about the other parent. He ought to make a note, for his book. His burned book. "People with the syndrome believe they have to keep prodding and reminding everybody and pressing decisions on them. And when people do do the things, then they, I mean the sufferers from the syndrome, they think it wouldn't have happened without their prompting. But they might be wrong."

"Aha."

"Yes. Chanticleer syndrome sufferers can exaggerate their own importance. Or they can experience anxiety. Or anger at all the responsibility they have to bear."

"Where did you learn about this?"

"I made it up," Harry said. "Or better, I named it. It's real."

Hope knew; he knew she knew. She rested her chin on her hand and regarded him as though he needed study. "Well, actually, I don't understand what kept you together anyway so long," she said with some bitterness. "I really don't."

"Love," Harry said.

"Oh yeah right," said Hope.

"Pheromones," said Harry.

"Dad," said Hope, a warning. "So what are you going to do? Like split the insurance?"

"It seems so. And sell the land. It's almost as valuable as the house. It got to be, over time." He lowered his eyes. It was like talking about someone who had died: it was evident Hope felt so, though it might be someone she had ceased to have a lot of contact with in recent years.

"So you'll get money for the stuff."

"Well. Yes. The things that can be replaced." Harry wouldn't name those that couldn't be; they included the family archive of photographs and letters, his side's at least, going back a hundred years and more. *Who's this?* Hope used to ask him, poring over dim sepia snapshots of a man in uniform, a woman in a fox fur-piece. Sometimes Harry could remember. And of course in the blackened and floorless second floor there was, or rather was not, the only manuscript of his book, almost done, a revision and expansion of his modest bestseller, *A Rhetoric for Everybody*. For nobody now.

"Listen, I've got to go to work," Hope said.

"Right, sure." Hope was a medical technician in a tall and ramifying medical center in the city. "You can stay. Of course. I've got the extra bedroom."

"Where we stayed before. Mila and I."

"No, that's Muriel's room now. The little one."

"Okay. Fine, that's fine."

"It's small."

"It's fine. Small is beautiful. I'm small."

"Okay."

Harry had to pull his car out of the driveway beside the house so she could remove hers, which he had driven up behind (their cars would go on being in each other's way for the length of time he lived there), and then when she had left he sat on the steps of her house amid a scatter of yellow ginkgo leaves remembering many things.

When he and Mila had met she was eighteen and he was twenty-five. She was on the run from immurement in middle-class family ambitions and duties, or thought she was; a lot of people were then. He picked her up on St. Mark's Place, took her to his old-law apartment; they danced together in that tiny space to "Down Along the Cove," and got together into his bed. Pheromones he actually knew nothing about then, but— whatever destiny each of them was out to avoid—they opted without a question for the one that had suddenly appeared before them, and for months, for a year, they hardly left that bed; it was possible in those days to live with minimum of hustle, and they needed nothing much. When they seemed momentarily to cool she decided to go on, get back to the path away that she'd first chosen. Went West. Harry stayed. He was still there when she circled back a half-dozen years later. Like an extinguished candlewick relighting by mere proximity to a lit one, their present selves caught fire from their past ones. But they didn't understand how differently they had each unfolded meantime.

How she had, anyway. Whatever it had been that had driven her from the standard life choices, she was ready for them now; she turned out to be endlessly resourceful and quick in the making of them; maybe she always had been, and maybe Harry had always been as forgetful and indecisive as in their shared life he would prove to be, only there had never been much to be decisive about earlier, so it wasn't apparent. It was true that Mila had made the decisions in their life together, but he considered himself actually the more thoughtful of the two, and even sometimes believed the decisions he would eventually have come to would have been better, all things considered, than her sudden ones, if she'd only given them time to evolve.

He should have married someone else, he thought, immobile on Hope's stoop. Someone as incapable as himself, or maybe more so. How tender he would have been to such faults, exasperated, sure, and blowing up in harmless gales sometimes, marveling at her incompetencies, she laughing at herself as though she had every right to. How many times, a thousand times, he'd forgive her, let go by her witless, her what, her fertile no flaccid no fecal no flocked feckle feckless her feckless fecklessness, because he loved her, because she was at heart not responsible really, no worse than anybody, because at bottom it didn't really matter at all. Rarely mattered that much. Very rarely mattered a whole whole lot.

Harry moved in that week. Hope took him and his stuff up to the room under the eaves that looked out onto the garden and the backyards beyond. Harry stood gazing at the bed she'd made up for him, a single bed narrow as a boy's and clothed with blankets and coverlets she had probably brought with her from the house when she went away to school—a cotton Indian blanket with faint images of rodeo cowboys and sheriff's stars; an old quilt made of strips taken from even older men's suits, herringbone and pinstripe. The white sheet folded down. Muriel had put a brown bear on the pillow; it bore a grave and yet welcoming expression. The longing Harry felt to lie down there, to wrap himself in those covers, the long-lost delight in safety and solitude he knew he'd find there, was almost painful.

He did a lot around the house to earn his keep. He and Mila had both been self-employed for years, and Harry found it impossible to imagine how a single mom with an eight-hour workday ever found time for any household business at all. He cleaned the house after she'd rushed out, ran the errands with the list that he would always conscientiously make lying on the passenger's seat where he could check it often (and even then speaking out loud to himself to keep his duties straight—"first to the store, and then to there to get that, and then there and there," he would say as pictures of the various destinations rose in his mind). And he walked Muriel to school and home again.

"Here we are home," Muriel echoed. She had the most amazing facility for mimicking the words and attitudes of grown-ups, shrugging elaborately to express ignorance or indifference, groaning and smacking her brow to show exasperation. It was a little spooky. Harry found graham crackers and milk for her.

"We had a sad day," she said.

"Oh yes."

"Noemi's nanny died."

"She died?"

"Yes. Noemi said. She told everybody."

"That is sad."

Muriel sighed deeply, and tenderly bent her head to one side, eyebrows lifted. Then she returned to her snack. "I hope I never die."

"I hope that too," Harry said.

"It would be terrible."

"Yes," Harry said. "Terrible."

"Grampa," she said. "Are you still sad because your house burned down?"

"I'm less sad," Harry said, and she gave him a toothy grin in payment.

"Is it cause you go to the doctor?"

"No," said Harry. "It's just time."

Muriel nodded solemnly, ah how well we all know.

It was Hope who got Harry together with Dr. Macilhenny. She came home one day when Harry had been living with her for a month and told him about a Lunch Hour Lecture she'd gone to at the medical center. A neuropsychologist talked about missed signs of early onset dementia like Alzheimer's, or head injuries that show no physical trauma but are still effectively TBI. The doc had said that very often the signs that nurses or PCPs are looking for have to do with memory loss. But there can be earlier or subtler signs than that. Harry listened and nodded, wondering if he ought to know what TBI was, or PCPs, and how much further he could follow the conversation without knowing. The signs were often a new hesitation about decision-making, a loss of incentive, a willingness or need to be cued continuously about what ought to be done next. Executive Function, Hope said. That's the thing that goes. And during the question period she'd asked if it was possible that a person's executive function could deteriorate even if there wasn't TBI or dementia.

TBI, Harry thought: Traumatic Brain Injury.

The lecturer said that he thought that was possible. Many learning disabilities, including ADD, were now seen as executive function disorders, diagnosable through neuropsychological assessment. A PCP might be able to refer if he perceived problems in this area, even without other symptoms.

PCP: Primary Care Physician. Harry now understood what Hope was going to say next, but he was not going to let on that he knew. If she couldn't bring herself to make a suggestion, a cue, then Harry was going to let the whole conversation slide on past. Hope said she thought Harry ought to go see this guy, if he could get a referral, and just. Well, just go see. And Harry said maybe he would. It was four in the afternoon of that day, she'd been on the early shift, and the day was November gray. Now it was December, and the weather had turned clear and cold, the sun bright.

"The doctor is curing you though," Muriel said.

"Well, I'm not really sick."

Muriel eyed him sidelong. "Very mistuvious," she said.

Dr. Macilhenny had turned out to be younger than Harry, though he was getting used to that, most of his doctors and lawyers and the last two presidents as well, younger than himself by years. A lean sleek man with a button-down shirt and tie but Calvin Klein black jeans and sneakers. They chatted for a while, went over the insurance situation. Then Dr. Macilhenny, after carefully describing what he was going to do, administered a series of tests that would, he said, give him a baseline as well as possibly identify any problem areas. It took a long time. Harry took the Category test, the Tactual Performance test, the Seashore Rhythm test, the Finger Tapping test, and Trail Making. Only after the doctor decided that there was nothing to indicate dementia was Harry told the names of these tests, which he would remember ever after. He took the Stroop test: in this one, he was shown words on a computer; they were all color names, and the letters were colored too, but not colored the color of the name: "blue" was colored red, "green" was colored yellow. Harry had to say what color the word was, rather than reading the color name. It was hard. He took the Wisconsin Card Sorting test, in which he sorted cards that showed a trio of simple items, a blue star, a black square, a black circle, without being told what criteria he should use, only if he was right or wrong.

A card with a blue star. A card with a black star. Harry sorted the stars together. Right. He went on sorting the cards that had similar shapes. Then Dr. Macilhenny said Wrong.

"Why?"

Dr. Macilhenny said nothing. Harry tried again. Two squares and a circle. He sorted it into the similar-shapes pile. Wrong again. Harry tried again, guessing that something had changed. He sorted a card of three blue things with another card of three different blue things. Right.

"You're changing the rules."

Dr. Macilhenny said nothing. Harry went on sorting. He tried to count how many cards he went through before Dr. Macilhenny changed the rules, but he couldn't do that and sort too. Sometimes he forgot what criteria he had been using, or which new one he had chosen. Dr. Macilhenny started chatting with him about nothing, making it all the harder, and Harry tried to shut out his sweet and pleasant voice. He got bored and irritated. Dr. Macilhenny kept score with a pencil in his left hand. When Harry was all done, he was cagey about what it had all meant; next meeting they could go over the results. Harry went back to Hope's house rattled and weary.

There was no discernible pathology in Harry's brain, no organicity that Dr. Macilhenny had been able to discover. Harry went back to the doctor's office, which was in the same medical complex where Hope worked at other times of day, to listen to him say so. And yet taken all together it was easy to see, he said, that Harry Watroba's Executive Function was compromised in measurable ways.

"Executive function is largely about response to novelty," he said. Harry found he enjoyed listening to Dr. Macilhenny talk, calmly and with a pleasant uninsistent certainty, about things Harry had not realized it was possible to know. "Most of what we do all day is practiced, automatic. But novel situations require decision-making strategies. We have to be able to both initiate appropriate strategies, and inhibit inappropriate ones." The Stroop test was about that, Harry learned: seeing if you could inhibit your first response, which was to read the word, and choose a novel one, name the color. Harry had failed that one, though Dr. Macilhenny laughed gently when Harry said it that way. Attention meant selectivity, choosing among inputs, what was important, what was distraction, yet being open to new unexpected information. Harry's attention was compromised.

"So now I know," Harry said. He almost laughed; it was hardly a surprise. He almost thought he perceived an answering smile on the doctor's face. "Is that it?"

"Well," said Dr. Macilhenny. "I don't want to overstate this, but there are rehabilitative programs. Cognitive retraining for people who have limitations in this area."

Harry said nothing.

"The brain's an amazing thing," Dr. Macilhenny said. "Do you remember when they used to say that after you leave adolescence the brain ceases to grow? Well, not so. It's plastic. It continues to make new connections. You can actually see them with magnetic resonance imaging, CAT scans and PET scans, people with damaged brains developing new pathways and circuits."

"The more specific CAT scan," Harry joked, "the more general PET scan."

"If you'd like to try to work on some of these things," Dr. Macilhenny said, "there's a program being used now successfully called CRT, Cognitive Rehabilitation Training."

"I thought you said I was undamaged."

"Well, that's the interesting part. It might work for anyone with a similar problem."

"One thing I've noticed," Harry said, not having known he was about to. "I have a very hard time with directions. I mean left and right, north and west."

"Uh-huh," said Dr. Macilhenny patiently.

"I can't find my way back to a place I've come from."

"Until it's been practiced."

"Well, yes."

Dr. Macilhenny nodded.

"My sister's the same way," Harry said. "She always said, though, that we could probably do it fine really, as good as other people; we just weren't paying attention."

Dr. Macilhenny nodded again, and went on nodding and smiling very slightly, as though Harry had proved something that Dr. Macilhenny had already known about him, and all others like him; and Harry felt a flush of something between hope and fear.

On her day off Hope took Harry and Muriel to look at a new condo building in the town next down the valley.

"It's not like I want you out," she said. She'd said it more than once, and Harry believed her; she was, he thought, glad enough of his company, and he was helping with Muriel, which surely made things easier for her; but she would eventually want to date, wanted to already probably, and he'd have to be far away for that to be easy. Mainly though he thought it was the strain of decisiveness she inherited from Mila, a restless dissatisfaction that no firm move was being made or even worked toward, that led her to propose things, make suggestions it was hard to turn down. And why would he want to turn them down?

It was a nineteenth-century mill building where something plain and useful had once been made, kitchen knives or horn buttons or brushes, Hope couldn't remember, all those had once been produced around here. It was right near the middle of the pleasant gentrified and prosperous downtown, and was quite small. Hope put her car in the newly striped parking lot and showed the place to Harry with a gesture that seemed to him faintly disparaging, though he thought this was just Hope's way; she never liked to invest in things too soon, so as not to be disappointed. The brick walls of the place had been cleaned somehow and restored to what must have been their original warm rose pink. Nice.

It went on being nice. Harry liked the matte-black metal of the new door-frames and window-frames, which he touched as they passed. He liked the honey-colored wide planking of the halls, ancient and "distressed" as the antique dealers said by labor and use in another time. Muriel watched her feet in their multicolored sneakers fall on it, absorbed. Harry wondered if she was now placing in those unexpungable files this exact color, to be reminded of it—and of this unimportant, this unremarkable and unrecoverable moment in her life, with all its ramifying proprioception, its gestalt—by some new car's or jet's or time-machine's brilliant hue in time to come.

"Here," said Hope, and pushed open the door of the Sample One-Bedroom, enough like all the others that a choice could be made or at least embarked on through study of it. It was nice too. Muriel went to run the water and flush the toilet (she had come to enjoy strange bathrooms, and could go nowhere new that offered one without visiting it), and Harry and Hope examined the features and ran their hands over the Formica and the stainless steel.

"Nice," said Hope.

Harry was entranced. Not a thing here had a history, even though it was placed within this shell of history. It was so clean: he had never lived in a new house or apartment, only old ones where decades of private grime had to be overlooked and dynasties of mice secretly resided. He could smell glue and sealant, as though the job had just been finished this morning. "I'd need everything," he said.

"Ikea," said Hope. "One day. Buy everything, have it delivered. See the built-in desk? You could work."

He could work. He could have new Ikea furniture in blond beech or pine. He could have a narrow bed with new bedsheets in clear colors, covers of virgin fleece made from who knew what. An armchair, one that looked fifty years old (like his velvet one that had burned) but was new, the nap of its plush crisp and tall; or dark cool leather. Books, but no more than dozen or two, all as yet unread.

"I wouldn't need all that much," he said softly.

"No," said Hope.

"One cup," Muriel said at his side. "One plate. One fork and one knife. One glass and one spoon."

"Two," Harry said. "Two of those things." He smiled down at her, and she shrugged elaborately, lifting shoulders and turning her hands palm up by her cheeks, smiling too to say *Whatever*.

Harry turned and looked out his windows. Every day he could go down to town, to the *pasticceria* they had passed, and have coffee and biscotti, and buy a loaf for his dinner. Every week he could go to early Mass at that church, as he had for a while in one bad year, he didn't know why he'd stopped. Every month he could sit at that desk and pay his bills: only three or four. And afterwards sit to read, or nothing. There would be nothing else required.

"What do you think?" Hope asked. "Any thoughts?

Harry had long used to think that he wouldn't live much past his sixtieth year. It was a statistical thing more than a sense of fate: his father, both his grandfathers, and a grand-mother had died at sixty, or sixty-two, or fifty-nine. Now it appeared that the statistical approach wasn't any longer valid, and modern accounting suggested that Harry was more likely to be looking at seventy-five or eighty. Mila always told him he had to prepare for this, mentally or spiritually, but he never knew what such preparations would entail; it was like the way she said *Be careful* when he embarked on some journey in bad weather or tricky business negotiation: he would, indeed he would, but what command did it actually give? His to know.

Well, maybe this was it. Check out at sixty-three and at the same time still remain. It seemed almost like bliss, like a pleas-ant and undemanding afterlife. "It's great," he said.

"I think they're great," Hope said.

"I think they're great," said Muriel, with exactly Hope's permanent shadow of dissatisfaction or doubt.

"They won't last long," Hope said. "These are going to get snapped up."

"Oh, I believe it," said Harry.

"They'll get snapped up," said Muriel.

"Should I snap one up?" Harry asked her

"Snap one up, Grampa!" she commanded. "You snap one up!" And she snapped the fingers of both her hands at him fiercely, like a flamenco dancer, though no sound came forth.

———

Harry drove to Dr. Macilhenny's office in the city for the tenth session of his Pay Attention! program. Two sorts of day seemed to be occurring at once in the broad valley he passed through, a warm and damp one and a colder, clearer one, each with its own array of cloud and wind and light, you passed out of one and on into the other and yet could see the first lying still ahead the way you went. On the highway south, Harry's old station wagon was passed by a great bulging SUV in an intense shade of blue-green, teal or peacock—Harry wasn't sure what name applied to it—and as it hovered in his side-view mirror and then went heaving past him Harry experienced a momentary memory trace. That's what he called the experience, a memory trace, though whether that was an accurate term or not he didn't know: it was an instant sensation that somewhere in his far past, in childhood, in infancy maybe even, something of that color had filled his consciousness for a long or a short time. He could feel, taste, know, re-experience intensely the bit of past time, yet couldn't say what it had been, what had been colored like that or what or when it was that he was reminded of.

There it is, Harry thought, damn there it is again. For this peculiar *temps retrouvée* thing had once been rare, so rare he could hardly have identified it as a kind of thing at all, and now it was suddenly common. It was now most often started by the vivid colors of new cars. He felt it go on, this sensation, as the SUV pulled away, at the same rate as the sensation faded.

What, Harry asked his brain, what, what is it, what did I see once or have or hold?

Gone.

Reds most often caused the sensation, scarlets and crimsons from tomato to fire-engine to blood, but also metallic golds and bronzes and one or another shade of the sudden startling yellow that sports cars and trucks now sometimes came in, so saturated as to be unreal, more shining and deep even than the shining circle within a newly opened can of paint. None did it consistently, but when his brain was in receptive mode (or whatever it was) they produced around Harry's head and in Harry's heart and in the world an aura like the aura that's said to precede an epileptic seizure, yet each one different, because each was drawn from the life of his body in his real past. And yet he couldn't reach that past, or it couldn't reach him. Like the dreams he lost, but rather than slipping from consciousness they struggled to arise into it, or didn't struggle but only smiled blandly and faded as Harry strove and failed to draw them up.

"It's like those experiments thirty years ago," he told Dr. Macilhenny. "The ones where they showed that no memories are ever lost, and you could excite a single neuron, or was it an axon, with a fine probe, and the patient, the subject, would suddenly have a vivid memory of her long-dead dog. Or smell her childhood house."

"I remember the stories."

"Isn't that right? Memories are all stored forever somewhere in the brain, if only you could access them?"

"Well. We don't use that model any longer."

"Oh no? There were those experiments."

"They turned out to be non-repeatable."

"Oh." Harry realized he hadn't taken his jacket off, and that the room was warm. "Too bad. I always hoped I could volunteer."

Dr. Macilhenny broke out the practice materials, and he and Harry sat opposite one another and began to work. Harry had already decided that the weird and pointless tasks he was made to do here were ineffectual, amateurish, like quack nostrums of some other medical era. That he got better at them seemed to matter not at all. But he did as he was asked, and at the end of every session went over with the doctor when he should come back again. He had nothing better to do.

That day he drove back from the city along the valley roads to the town where his daughter lived. At a wide sweeping turning of the highway, between the mass of a mountain on the left and the drop down to the river on the right, Harry felt himself understand for the first time that the landmarks he was noting—that junkyard, that stand of pines, that playground—and the stretches of road between them, were the same as the ones he saw going the other way, only in reverse order and seen from the other side. Of course it was something he knew, but just then he knew he knew it. The experience of going and the experience of coming back had been unrelated, somehow, but now the two ways, the way there and the way back, merged smoothly and wholly together in his mind, his poor mind, into one way. He felt it happen, and wondered if it was an experience only someone like him would ever note; if anyone not like him, like him or his dead sister, would even understand it if he spoke of it.

A mild winter rolled on. There seemed to be no particular programmed end to the Cognitive Rehab Program, and Harry found that he didn't want it to end. There were no tests to tell him that his Executive Function was improving outside the office where he sorted cards and recited lists of words backwards with greater and greater accuracy. Dr. Macilhenny said that children with ADD could be shown to have been measurably helped by their Pay Attention! work. But—Harry wondered—what if your shortfall or limit or however it was to be described had gone on all your life unattended to?

"Well." Dr. Macilhenny had been about to begin Harry's workout, but instead folded his hands carefully before him. "That's what we're trying to learn."

There is always this oddness with doctors, Harry thought, that they are something more than intimates, and yet less than friends; no matter how desperately you need what they can give, the giving of it is, for them, a job.

"So you don't really know."

"This is a very new area, Harry," said Dr. Macilhenny. He leaned forward on the table that separated him from Harry and regarded him with a look of tender interest, almost compassion. "But suppose you're a person who's limited dispositionally in his ability to make decisions—just the necessary small decisions that others make more easily and quickly every day, the little yeses and little nos that we have to say, in response to many situations and challenges. It seems reasonable to think that without intervention such a person might never develop strong decision-making capabilities."

"Little yeses," Harry said. "Little nos."

"And such a person might, yes, actually come to have difficulty making big life decisions, necessary ones, as well as the littler ones. He would have learned over a lifetime to depend on the cuing of others. Overseers."

"Overseers?"

"Parents, perhaps. Or anyone who took an interest, wanted to help, or had a reason to put some pressure on him. Teachers. Not that he'd like it, necessarily. Just because you have this difficulty with decision-making doesn't mean you can easily recognize it. You might refuse the overseer. Go your own damn way. Become habitually oppositional. We see this."

For years Harry had heard the voice of his father in his head, assessing his, Harry's, choices, suggesting other and better ones, a guide Harry never followed, or opposed even when he did follow. He used to marvel at its persistence, despite absence, beyond death; the man only ceased talking when Harry married Mila. "And," Harry said, "I guess, you could be passively oppositional too. You could learn that. You could learn that from life."

"Yes, sure."

"So that instead of doing the opposite of what these overseer people wanted, you could just do nothing."

"Yes."

"A strategy."

"Well yes. Not maybe a good one."

Harry knew it was so. He was sure that he could tell the doctor with absolute certainty that it *was* so, because it was what had happened to him. He had grown up with a deficit that no one could see or know about, not a funny quirk of personality or an eccentricity he could alter if he wanted to, but something in the shape or functioning of his physical forebrain where his deepest self took place. He could only function completely at the behest or command of others, and he would forever depend on them and resist them, actively or not, and when one died or passed from the scene he would adopt another, or if none appeared he would build one in his brain out of the ones he had before depended on. It wasn't because he was stupid or incompetent or lazy or unwilling to do the work. It was what he had been given, and all his life it had only got worse, because he hadn't known, and neither had anybody else, how to work to make it better.

Little yeses, little nos. Which way do you want to turn, Harry? Do you want to go to college, join the Army, get a job? Do you want to sign up for this? What color should this be, Harry? Do you need one of these, or one of these? If they raise your rent, should you move or pay? How do you feel about it, Harry, do you want to go to bed, have a child, buy a house? A terrible pity came over him for that child, that boy and man.

Mila, he thought. Oh I am so sorry.

On a January day Harry was Dr. Macilhenny's last patient. Harry wrote a check for the amount he owed, the part that the insurance wouldn't cover. "The paypal," he said. "The copal. Capo. Copay." Dr. Macilhenny tidied his office, put away the games Harry had played with as though he kept a day-care center, and when Harry put on his coat to go, Dr. Macilhenny put on his, and they left the office together. When they got to the street level they found that the temperature had fallen, and the slight rain that had been coming down most of the day had turned to ice. Even as they stood at the door of the building assessing this, they saw a passing car brake too suddenly, slide balletically left then right and narrowly miss sideswiping a line of parked cars glistening with frozen rain. Far down the straight avenue in the other direction they could see the behemoth of a sand-truck, already on its rounds. Harry proposed a novel strategy: next door was a bar. Best to wait a while till the situation had been dealt with. Somewhat to Harry's surprise, and after a long moment's consideration—thought moving from forebrain to remoter parts where perhaps feelings and fears were stored—Dr. Macilhenny agreed.

The bar was dark and smelled of the previous night; Harry wondered if he'd made a mistake. They ordered. So this neuropsychologist walks into a bar, Harry thought of saying.

"There's something I have to say," said Dr. Macilhenny after a time, sliding the base of his glass around slowly in its satiny puddle on the bar, and then for a long moment said nothing as Harry held still waiting to hear. "I've just recently been forced to make a decision."

"Yes?"

"It hasn't been easy, and perhaps I've put off acknowledging what has to be done for too long. I find that I have too many commitments, and I am going to have to limit my practice."

"Ah," said Harry.

Dr. Macilhenny took a sip of beer and continued, looking not at Harry but out the window as though he were speaking to himself, or into his mini-recorder. "I've come to the conclusion that I will have to sever my relationship with the center. I won't be seeing people there any longer."

"Where will you be seeing them?"

"Well, for a time I won't be." Sip. "I'm going to be taking a leave of absence, I guess that's what to call it. I have . . . I have a lot of personal things to attend to. Absolutely consuming. My parents. Decisions to make. I just don't feel I can devote the time that I feel I must to people. I don't want to do things half-assed. It's not fair to them. But to do it right is just a huge burden."

Harry for the first time wondered what kind of a person Dr. Macilhenny was, weak or strong, quick or slow. What if he had problems too with mentation? It seemed very important, now, that Harry know; as though the doctor should have told him before they began. "Where are we going to continue?" he said.

"Well, I'm afraid we're not."

"I don't think I'm done," Harry said. A kind of frightening looseness seemed to have come over the bar, the day outside, the surface of the table, his own hands before him. "I'm not done."

Dr. Macilhenny checked his watch. "Well, you see, the training is a sort of ad-hoc thing, really," he said. "There are lots of ways you can practice on your own. Play chess. Chess is nothing but strategic decision-making. Video games. There's evidence that kids who play them show measurable improvement ."

"When will you be returning, I mean taking up this, this—"

"I don't know. I can't say. I really can't." He contemplated the beer remaining in his glass with what seemed a melancholy fascination; then he looked up at the gray window and the weather, and said, "I think I'll take a chance on it. I really have to go."

In an hour Harry himself started home. The Oldsmobile he drove needed a road as free of danger and irregularity as possible. Harry hadn't been particularly proud that he'd kept the same car for twenty years, though he'd marveled at it sometimes, and now he saw that keeping it was only another symptom, an inability to decide on another, to see there was a better way, a thing to do, a thing to avoid.

What was he to do, what now? Get a grip on himself, make a firm decision to be less indecisive? It occurred to Harry that Dr. Macilhenny hadn't tried to figure out with Harry an alternative, another doctor, a plan. He hadn't even said he was sorry. What kind of behavior was that? Unprofessional. Weird, to say the least. There sure was something the matter with him. Burnt out, maybe, overstretched, unsuited to the work? Guy ought to have his head examined, Harry thought, and just then the Olds skidded, just for a fraction of a second, as though giggling at Harry's thought, and Harry laughed at it too. Ought to have his head examined. Giddy with detachment and helplessness Harry drove laughing away from the city along the road that went both there and back.

When Harry got home he found Hope hadn't gone to work, afraid of the ice.

"It wasn't too bad," Harry said to her. "Except on the side streets. What are you doing?"

Hope had spread out before her a glossy brochure of paint samples, the kind that shows you the named oblongs of paint and also photographs of elegant rooms painted in some of the colors.

"I'm thinking of painting upstairs. Now that I've been going up there more I see how shabby it is."

"It's not bad." Harry saw that the brochure described something called the Calm Collection: variations on neutral, basically, warmer or cooler, blue-gray to taupe to buff.

"I'm torn between bone and ash," said Hope.

"Ah yes," Harry said. "Ah yes." He thought for a moment of volunteering to paint, even to help choose a color, but from his frontal lobes there issued an Inhibition just in time.

"Listen," Hope said, and put down the brochure. "You ought to make a decision about the knife works."

"The what?"

"The condos we looked at, in the old knife factory. Come on."

"Right. Of course."

"You've got papers to fill out. Even to start the process. You just have to do it." She had the calm but watchful face of a man in a Western waiting to see if the other man was going to draw.

"Yes," said Harry. "I have made a decision. I'm not going to do it."

For a moment Hope said nothing; then she said *okay* with a wary hesitancy.

"I can't do it. I have to talk to Mila. I have to."

"You don't need her permission, Dad."

"That's not it. The fire ruined her life."

"It ruined yours."

This seemed certain, yet Harry couldn't feel it that way. His life seemed not to have been ruined but to have vanished, as though it had hardly been there anyway. "I never told her I was sorry. When we talked. I just stood there." He realized he was gripping Hope's hand where it lay on the table, and this was probably why she was looking at him with a regard he couldn't quite read, maybe tender or concerned, or just puzzled, or none of these, something else entirely. "I can't remember," he said. "Do you play chess?"

That night, toward dawn in his small bed under the eaves, Harry dreamed.

He dreamed that he walked in New York City where he and Mila had first known one another, the city they had left to find a space in the country for a family and a little ease and gentility. It was dark and splendid in his dream; he went from place to place within it on various errands, entering into vast interiors, one a place where many scholars sat throned in Victorian carved chairs, kind people laughing and self-effacing, and one for Harry, which he wouldn't take; and a subway line where crowds avoided a peremptory dead body wrapped in burlap and laid up against the tiled wall; and other places, like and unlike places he had once known there, through which he walked and walked. At length the adventures had gone on so long that Harry wearied of them, and yet found himself still asleep. What to do? Well, as long as I'm asleep and dreaming, he thought, maybe I ought to try flying. It had been a long time since he had flown in dreams. He was then standing in Grand Central Station, looking upward into its night-blue sky, the people passing around him, and though a little self-conscious amid them (they took no notice of him, actually) he got a running start and then arms and legs milling he got off the ground, always the hard part, and went upward. In the thinner upper air, staying aloft was pretty easy, a matter of attention and will, he thought, and the night city (he had come to be outside under the sky) turned below him in beautiful geometries of steeple and avenue and tall bright-windowed buildings as he swooped and sailed. He tired of that too after a while, and let himself down into a vertiginous but fairly graceful running landing, like paratrooper or a pelican, and found himself on streets he thought he knew. Still asleep, and who knew for how much longer; tired of endless alteration and scene-shifting; ready for a stable waking world. What should he do? Harry knew: this street wasn't far from his own neighborhood; he needed only (he plotted it in his mind, taking care) to turn left, then right, uptown, and keep going a couple blocks, and he'd be at his own apartment building; he could go up there to his apartment and sit, just sit in his old armchair, and go no farther, and wait till he woke up. Good: Harry set off walking, and turned the corner onto the familiar avenue; but it wasn't the familiar avenue; no a long wide esplanade lay before him lit with antique lamps, beflagged yachts drawn up to moorings, the black sea and buoys and harbor lights: and Harry thought, laughing in dismay, Oh no, this isn't going to work, I'll never reach the old apartment, of course I won't, this'll just go on: and laughing he woke. Harry woke. Snow was falling brilliantly outside the rumpled window of his room. And his heart was full and rich with gratitude, because he remembered this dream, he remembered it all, all: all.

2. Glow Little Glow-Worm

Spring can really hang you up the most, Stan found himself sing-humming as he turned off the highway and started up into the hills, but actually it wasn't a sentiment he could say he felt. It was certainly spring, and fully so, nothing missing to make a late April day: the willows were green, tossing their long hair in the light airs like teenage girls just shampooed and proud of their tresses; and the sky had adopted that new blue; and the rushing brook by the roadside undercut tussocks of new grass, where tiny flowers white and blue sparkled as he wheeled by; and birds, and all that. Robins building nests from coast to coast. Beautiful and gratifying it was, but Stan didn't feel the overwhelming relief and thanksgiving he once would have, that sense that what was happening to Mother Nature was happening at the same time in his own breast. It seemed to answer no deep need, lift no particular burden. Just another nice day, better than a bad day. A very nice day. Like so many demanding delights and pains, victories and defeats of past times, springs were coming and passing too quickly to engage him full force. Like a film on fast-forward. Hadn't it just been Christmas? Stan was, he pointed out again to himself, getting old.

Also it was still bright day, Daylight Savings Time, when he turned in to his own driveway at workday's end. Terry, his wife, stood as though stoned or stunned amid the flowerbeds, holding a rake; around her other tools, a hoe, a grubber, dirty white gloves, like an allegory of the season. She lifted a slow hand to Stanley as he got out of the truck, seeming as full of the day as he was not, a mild grin on her face: but she was ten years younger .

"So how did that house look?" she asked as they went inside together.

"The strangest thing," Stan said. Terry washed her hands, letting tepid water cascade over her fingers for a long time. "It looks fine from the outside. Appealing, actually. Three stories, nice porch, though it's wrapped in plastic sheeting just now, you know, for winter. Original shutters on all the windows. Big garage with an upstairs room I haven't seen yet."

"Marketable?" Terry asked. Stan sold real estate, mostly houses, all through the Hills, and had since he took an early retirement package from his recently downsized plant.

"Well, I don't know." He looked in the refrigerator for last night's bottle of Muscadet, still half full, and pulled the squealing cork. "I told you it was lived in by these two brothers, right? For like forty years. Just the two of them. Neither ever married. It had been their parents' house. But over time—this is what the present owner says, he's a cousin who inherited the place, the only relative left—they became estranged, or I don't know, fell into some kind of enmity"—he laughed, and filled glasses with gurgling wine—"and it got I guess worse and worse over time, but neither was willing to move out, and so what they did was to divide the house in half. Not horizontally, you know, by floor—vertically. They put up walls to divide the space, divide even the rooms, the kitchen, into two spaces, so they would never have to see each other. They divided the staircase in two."

"The staircase?"

"With a sort of flimsy two-by-four-framed Celotex wall, right up the middle of the central staircase, so each one could get to his own half without seeing the other."

"Oh God. How sad."

"In the kitchen," Stan said, "you could see that one brother had put down a fresh layer of linoleum—but only on his half."

"It sounds awful."

"It is. I mean it wouldn't take much to at least get rid of the dividing walls, but the whole place still isn't going to be particularly aesthetically pleasing. As you can imagine."

"And one of them couldn't just leave? Or both, and leave it all behind?"

Stan shrugged elaborately, how would he know. "Solitaries," he said. "Apparently."

"Doubletaries," Terry said. "Alone together."

Stan looking at his wife holding her glass of wine thought he was right, spring was doing her good. Some sort of dry gray quality that had been in her face much of the winter had been wiped away; she looked moist, bright, like a. Well, like a flower or new leaf. He laughed again, this time at himself. "Strange," he said.

Terry was Stan's second wife. His first had been a years-long puzzle and grief to him, consuming him and then building him up again like a bonfire only to consume him again, even long after they divorced. He still dreamed of her sometimes, dreamed of her turning away from him in contempt or boredom, naked or malformed or not herself. He was Terry's second too, her first a fine attentive guy who just one day silently decamped, leaving her with two kids, eight and eleven. They got divorced by mail. Stan in certain clearheaded moments saw that it was the two kids—both brown-eyed, both witty and wise, self-sufficient but still somehow empathetic to an old fart like himself—that he had fallen in love with, childless himself, and his firm love for them had won him Terry: no surprise. He and she had been married fifteen years. Both the kids still lived in the Hills, not too far away.

"So how was the doc?" he asked her.

"The doc was fine," she said, her slow smile that seemed more teasing than it usually was. "Has a new receptionist."

"I meant," Stan said, "how did it go. Did she, you know. Have anything to say."

"Not really. Have to see how it goes. She thinks it's going fine so far but if there are side effects or whatever then you adjust. Up or down."

Terry had begun a regimen (as the doc called it) of hormone replacement therapy. Not as old as many women who began on it, she'd been suffering from menopausal symptoms since before fifty, and lately they'd got insupportable; she was continually uncomfortable, constant hot flashes, her tender parts dried like an apple (she said), and her moods black or violent. She hadn't been on it long, and said she already felt better. Remarkably better.

"Did you ask your question?"

"Which one?"

"You said you were going to ask if you were just supposed to go on taking these things for the rest of your life. Put off menopause till the grave."

"I wasn't going to say that."

"Well."

"No," said Terry. "I didn't ask. But I do wonder."

Days were getting longer, but so nowadays for Stan were nights. Not that they took any more clock-time, but that he experienced more of their passing than he used to. No more now the closing of the eyes on the darkened scene and then opening them again on a brightening one. Now night came in parts, or acts: first, grateful slumber coming easily and right off; then a muffled ballet of shifting positions vis-a-vis partner, doing her own dance to find comfort. Realization that he is in fact wide awake, as though it's day. Lying then on his back, arms under his head, looking into the night sky of the ceiling; speculation on the day passed and the one to come; sleeping again, but soon startled awake by strange groans of pain or anguish—just his own snores, or Terry's, who never used to snore. Awake again, though his Indiglo watch seems to assert (hard to read without reaching for his glasses) that night's got hours left to go. So: one half-hour, examination of conscience; one half-hour, political debate with wicked fools; random memory shopping, listening to Terry's soft steady passage between dream states, lucky her; then sudden blinking off without noticing. Dreams, which when he awakens seem to him the point of the whole exercise, like a boring novel's finally getting under way. Tonight featuring a gripping story of adultery, not his own but a woman's, whom he encounters in her huge drab crowded house; she making it clear he is to come to her. Her husband or consort just leaving her bedroom as Stan approaches, catching Stan's eye meaningfully or threateningly as he departs; then Stan wafted will-lessly in to where she kneels on the bed, and without preamble embracing her, madly reckless, in that certainty of wild desire that filled his wet dreams back when he had had such.

He woke erect and astonished.

Terry was restless beside him, which was probably (along with that dream embrace, he felt its force again) why he'd awakened. She rolled his way. Her skin was hot. Day was growing blue. She moaned softly.

"Hot flash?" Stan murmured. His hand against her told him she'd pulled off her pajamas in the night.

"No," she said. "No. The meds stop them."

"Oh right."

No panties even. She rolled away from him again and Stan turned toward her, his nakedness (he never wore nightclothes) against hers, inserting his knees in the hollows of her knees but tucking that weirdly persistent boner out of the way so as not to prod her rudely. She drew his arm around her and slept again.

These last years they'd mostly given up on sex; it had too often ended in nothing but her discomfort and his discouragement, and they'd rarely felt the compulsion to set the whole float in motion. Stan thought that she'd mostly risen to it out of a willingness to meet his need, but if that were chiefly Stan's reason too—to meet what he thought was her need—then it didn't have much of a basis. That was sad, but in a way seemed less dreadful than a younger Stan would have felt it should be. It was a lack. Sometimes Stan felt guilty that he didn't feel as bad about it as he should have; felt guilty when he found himself believing that there were more important things in a marriage, in their marriage. He wondered if Terry felt the same way. It was hard to bring up.

It was also true, and seemed sweet but strange, that since this unspoken truce or abatement, they had come to lie more often in one another's arms: front to back, as now; or her head on his breast, leg over his, warm breath on him. More kisses too. He slept sometimes wrapped around her; in former days he'd never believed he could sleep in such a way, like some god and nymph in a painting, but it turned out he could. As now he did, dreaming.

"Pheromones," Harry Watroba told him the next day.

Stan had been trying to remember the name for those chemicals that aren't smells but come in through your nose, or your sense of smell, that cause emotional reactions. Aggression. Arousal. Harry knew the word: words were, as he said, his business.

"That's it," said Stan. "Pheromones."

Stan was selling Harry's house lot, which was not far from Stan's house in the hills. Harry's house had recently burned beyond salvation, a sudden fire that was due (the fire chief told Stan, for his information, since he might in his business have occasion to warn homeowners) to old paint cans and thinner collected in the basement. The land should be worth quite a bit, but even after the remains of the house were removed there hung over it a sad and maybe repellent air of ruination and loss that kept even cool-hearted bargain-hunters from making an offer that Harry and his wife—now ex-wife, Stan was given to know—could accept. Now and then Stan ran into Harry in town, as he had this afternoon at the ice-cream shop, and caught him up on progress, if any, or just talked. Harry knew a lot of odd things, not just words, and Stan enjoyed listening.

"In India," Harry said, "there's a kind of firefly that fills the trees at a certain season. Of course you know that fireflies flash in order to attract females."

"Glow little glow-worm," Stan said.

"These fireflies all flashing on and off. Then as the phero-mones connect, this is hard to believe, they begin to synchro-nize. More and more, until all the fireflies in one tree, in two trees, a line of trees, all flash at once, like caution lights. On. Off. On. Off."

"Insects," Stan said. The hairy antennae of moths are for picking up pheromones: he remembered that.

"Well how about this. Did you know—it's a well-attested fact—that women in a girl's dormitory, say at college, crowded in together, will gradually synchronize their periods?"

"Really."

"What could it be but pheromones, chemical triggers?"

Harry dabbed his moustache with a paper napkin. He'd ordered a root-beer float and was addressing it with a kind of complex interaction that took into account its impressive size and his own slight one, wielding spoon, straw, and napkin in turn like a matador with cape and sword. Around them the kids from the local high school swarmed from table to table, in a pattern like the dancing of bees, expressive probably of impulses and hierarchies Stan would never know. Even when he'd been one himself he hadn't been aware much of such things, and these anyway were beings of a different order than those he'd known then. This one, young breasts hiked up by a bra that maybe was like one from his youth but quite clearly on show, straps visible on her brown shoulders; her tummy already brown too, and the bones of her hips rising out of her low-slung pants. Life's a beach, the bumper stickers said; he guessed they were dressing for it. He looked away. Harry hadn't.

"Harry," said Stan. "Don't do that. They'll catch you."

"Right," said Harry, and returned to his float. He appeared not to feel reprimanded. "But really. She's chosen to dress that way. What's she expect?"

"Well, they're not dressing that way for *you*," Stan said laughing. "Not for some dirty old man."

"You're right," said Harry mildly. "Somehow I can't help it. I feel compelled. I feel a sense of loss if I turn to look at one passing me in the street and find she's gone, got away, turned a corner or whatever. One gone forever."

"One? One what?"

"Oh, you know. A missed opportunity to mount."

Stan laughed.

"Just doing my job," Harry said.

"Your job?"

"As a male. Listen, if we male mammals didn't think about sex almost all the time, and if our senses weren't preternaturally attuned to the nubiles, well, think about it. We wouldn't be here at all. We humans."

"But Harry, you're not mounting them," Stan said. Harry was a man of Stan's own age, or older. "Are you?"

"Of course not. I don't even dream of trying. Still." He drank, the straw rattling the last of the creamy liquid at the bottom of the glass. "I feel compelled to assess. Add them up. I don't know—I think it's like counting coup."

"What's that?"

"The Plains Indians," said Harry, adopting the manner of a kindly teacher, "thought the height of bravery was to encounter an enemy, and instead of killing him to ride up close enough to give him a little tap with this special stick. The other guy was out then, out like in a game, humiliated, defeated. But no harm done. He was counted. See?"

Stan sort of didn't. He didn't think as Harry did, though Harry wasn't the only man among his acquaintance whose eyes tracked the passing scene that way. Yet just now, today, here in this shop, he felt moved: moved not in the sense of touched or affected but in the sense of being transported or carried. Carried along. He remembered what it had felt like when he was a boy, chivvied and pushed around by ardent feeling—"remembered" it in the somatic way of feeling it newly here and now. Maybe it was the pheromones, the massed phero-mones of all these nubiles. Harry'd told him that "nubile"only meant "of marriageable age," but wouldn't that mean "putting out pheromones" too?

Why today so strongly? Just spring, he guessed.

That night Terry wanted to have the bedroom window open, though Stan thought it would be too cold by the wee hours; she insisted. When he woke later on in the usual way, he lay a long time and felt and listened: all those night noises, birds and animals and cars passing and the little river rushing through the town, that hadn't been heard in here for a long time.

Terry moved beside him in wakefulness too. He took her hand, turned his head toward hers on her pillow; she turned to him, her face too dark to read.

"The isle is full of noises," she said. "Sounds and sweet airs, that give delight and hurt not."

Stan at first heard "the aisle is full of noises," and ruminated a while to make it come out right. "What's that? Shakespeare?"

She didn't answer, only swept aside the blankets and rolled herself against his cool flesh. She kissed him, he her. Then in sudden wondrous certainty he enfolded her, and she opened her legs to admit him. It was so easy and unimpeded that he might have thought of it as dreamlike, like his dream of the night before, except that it was entirely actual, and Stan wasn't thinking; within minutes they were both crying aloud, barking almost, clinging to each other as to a life-preserver, or two drowners each mistaking the other for a life-saver. It didn't last long.

For a time they lay damp and embracing, panting a little. Stan laughed. He hadn't laughed after sex in years.

"God," Terry breathed. "God, I thought you'd never."

"What. What."

"I just thought you'd never, never get." She swallowed, overwhelmed, full of liquid—he could hear it. Never get it? Never get over it? Around to it? Never get it up? How long had she been waiting, knowing that she was waiting and knowing he didn't know? For a long while she wouldn't release him. Outside the bugs and beasts seemed to have fallen silent, shocked, but Stan could hear—returning him to the world—the far-off rattle and wail, far down in the valley, of the only night train.

When morning came they awoke and almost without a word started again, as though it was a thing they did, night and day, morning and evening.

"Is it these medications?" Stan asked her afterward.

"Well," she said. She looked . . . he wouldn't have said "radiant" because that was just too, too what. But still. "It's what she said, the doctor, that it would help with, you know, the lubrication."

"A well-oiled machine," Stan ventured.

"Well, not just that though," she said. "More than that."

"You mean, they're doing more than that?"

"I guess."

"Pheromones," Stan said. "I think you're putting out like clouds of pheromones."

"What," she said, raising herself on an elbow. "You mean you wouldn't want to just on your own?"

"Well, it's part of wanting to. Isn't it? Putting out the signals. Why people do and don't. If you want to, I want to, and vice versa at the same time." That, Stan thought, if true, was what Harry Watroba had left out: how men too put out the signals, and how theirs work or don't work on the women. If true. "A feedback loop," he said.

Terry laughed a little, indulgently, seeming to be of a mind to dispute all that but not caring to make the effort, not important, and lay back on the pillow. "Stan, if pheromones could do it, I'm awash in them all day at school. Ninth graders. Industrial strength. You can actually smell them."

"You can't, really." Stan had looked them up on Ask Jeeves. "They come in through your nose, but you can't really smell them as a smell."

"You go into my lunchroom," Terry said. "The gym when there's a dance. Or a game. It's like a wall." She put her hands behind her head. "I have to get up," she said, and fell asleep.

163

That night, again. And though he warned her laughing not to expect much, they managed, three in a row she said, gleeful, triumphant even, something he hadn't done for thirty years: lying loose-limbed grinning and feeling that hot strain of fine exertion as in days gone by, maybe he ought to watch it though at his age. His father had once told him that every orgasm shortened your life. He'd died at ninety.

That triple play was never repeated, but the medical miracle, if that's what it was, ran on unabated, May into June. If they bustled out of bed in the morning without locking gazes, embarrassed or confused at the new abundance, they'd find themselves at cocktail hour grappling on the couch and talking dirty. His dreams were filled with lush gardens where dewy infants played, glamorous hotels full of sophisticates who swapped teasing jokes with him in grand salons. After some more tests Terry was switched by the doctor to a patch-and-creme combo, lessening the dose, and they waited to see what effect this would have, but it seemed to have none, to subtract nothing. They laughed about her youthful re-blooming, like a nature film run backward. She cried a lot too, "tears, idle tears," she didn't know why, she smiled while she cried, as though leaking more than weeping.

It was exciting and challenging, all he could say clearly about it, reaching for words he might have used at his old job to describe the prospects of a position to a new hire. Hilarious even, to be thrust again into the ninth-grade can't-wait mode, holding hands at the supermarket and making out in the car parked in front of a house awaiting them as dinner guests. But while Terry re-bloomed, Stan remained what he was. It began to happen that they'd begin all right, but then get somehow out of synch, moving at odds like two cars in a thriller trying to shunt each other off the nighttime road; or he'd find himself at a loss, straining and tense, a tug struggling to turn a barge. Surely he had once known how to please her, he thought she'd liked what he did, what they did, was grateful even he seemed to remember, as grateful as he was to her. He could remember that she'd liked it, but maybe he couldn't remember now what *it* was. Certain nights or mornings he was made to re-experience another part of the old days: the engine failing, the movie stuttering to a stop and going dark, the silence in the balled-up sheets.

"I guess I just can't do it that often," he said to her. He remembered the rule for these moments, you never said I'm sorry. He was breathing a bit hard, was that okay? He put his hand to his heart. She was smiling, not altogether kindly. Hot and humid today, it looked like.

"What's the problem?" she asked. Another thing you weren't supposed to say.

"It's my age, Terry. It's nothing about you. Nothing about wanting to or not wanting to."

"You should just relax. You get upright, I mean uptight." She yawned.

"I'm not uptight. I'm an antique."

"Oh, you're not an antique yet, Stan," Terry said. "You're still just a Collectible."

"Anyway I don't have the whatever," Stan said. "Or anyway not as much of it."

"Well," she said. "Come here a minute." And patted the place beside her on the messy bed.

———

Since so much of his work had to be done on Sundays, Stan had elected to give himself Wednesdays, or at least Wednesday afternoons, off. By Wednesday most people have stopped their Sunday-paper dreaming about houses, and not yet started on the new weekend's possibilities. It didn't always work out for him, but on this Wednesday nobody called that he wasn't able to put off. By three he was able to toss his old and rather disreputable canvas bag of clubs in the truck and go out to the country club, as free as a retiree or a dentist to hit the fairways on a weekday afternoon.

Though he had gone away for some years in the long search to find or build a life that would please his first wife, Stan had been born and grown up in the Hills and along the rivers that ran among them. At the little country club, not so much club now as public amenity open to all, Stan had learned to play by caddying for his father, watching and learning, and the game of golf had retained from those days a kind of educational quality, involving the passing on of skills and the continuance of rituals; even now Stan, when reaching the bubbler on the eighth tee and swallowing water gratefully, couldn't help wiping his chin with the back of his hand and saying Ah! Adam's ale!—as his father always had done just there.

He'd just as soon have played nine holes by himself, but as he was teeing up at the first, his doctor appeared beside him, having finished nine and lost his partner, and he joined Stan for a second nine. Stan liked doing well at games but was profoundly uncompetitive; he usually went for Personal Best, which in practice meant not paying a lot of attention to the score. Today, though, an unusual intensity of feeling about the game grew up in him by the third hole, a flame of need to win. Gripping his driver, his chin out, he eyed the girt doctor, bald dome already tanned (Florida, no doubt) at the tee, impatient for his own turn to dig fiercely into the ball. Freshly angry at his irremediable slice. Dr. Beha won handily. The day stayed glorious.

"So can you explain something to me?" Stan asked with a little laugh as they sat in the empty clubhouse bar.

"Sure. Unless it's a medical question. For that you'd have to see a doctor."

Stan ignored that. "My wife, you know, Terry, has started this hormone-replacement therapy. She's sort of early menopause, and it seemed like, well anyway the gynecologist recommended it for her, and it seems to do her a lot of good."

"Uh-huh." The doctor seemed to be aware of what was coming next.

"It's improved her, well, her hot flashes and whatnot."

"Uh-huh." Dr. Beha sipped his drink, unwilling to be helpful, Stan thought. "And your question is?"

"Well. It's certainly changed the. Well, the family dynamic." He laughed, swallowed beer for cover, wiped the foam from his lip with a cocktail napkin.

"It does do that," Dr. Beha said. "Surprises people. Spring awakening sort of thing. Is that what you mean?"

"I guess."

"Young again in all respects."

"Well, that's I guess the problem."

"Aha."

"I mean she's young again, but I've stayed the same."

"How old are you, Stan?"

"I'm sixty-three," Stan said; as usual it felt like a lie. He looked around the bar and not at the doctor. "This has all taken me a little by surprise, to tell the truth, and at some times I haven't risen to the occasion."

"It happens," said the doctor. "Just advancing age, I'm afraid. But you get concerned, naturally. Which doesn't help. It gets so you can't think about it even for a second or it fails. Everything okay down there? And woop." He illustrated with a drooping forefinger.

"Not that you can't get it up," Stan said. "You just can't count on it."

"It's common. Would you like me to refer you for counseling? Sometimes a change in attitude."

"Hm." In the tiles of the bar floor a comic stick-figure golfer was inlaid, his legs tangled, wild swing gone wrong, club bent, divot flying. It had been there for decades.

"Are you interested in trying an erectile-dysfunction therapy?"

"Well I hadn't. I mean."

"You know about Viagra."

"Well, of course. It's unavoidable. Bob Dole on TV. Jokes everywhere."

"It is," the doc said, folding his hands together somewhat medically or professionally, "a really quite remarkable breakthrough. Actually does what it claims to do, safely, few or no side effects even, for most men. It's like an elixir of life, the thing the Chinese sought for centuries, drinking gold or eating mummified tiger's hearts. Old men are taking young wives off to Niagara Falls, knowing they can perform. Stan, I've prescribed it for paraplegics, and it's worked for them."

Stan, looking within, as people tend to do in the course of conversations like this one, sensed an odd vacuity or absence down there where the old tripartite unit ought to be felt. Maybe he really was getting superannuated. My get up and go got up and went. Or maybe his wasn't the attitude that needed changing. "It seems, I don't know, a little shaming," he said.

"Oh cut it out, Stan." Dr. Beha finished his drink, shook the ice in the glass, and sipped again; then put it down. "Come by the office," he said. "I have a passel of free samples. Try it out and see if it's for you."

Stan knew himself to be a hypochondriac, or at least frequently fussed about his health, but his hypochondria consisted mostly not in talking himself into believing he was sick but in obsessive recountings of the good reasons why he surely wasn't. Sort of a glass-half-full hypochondria, Terry thought. The idea of a new pill with sudden major effects and unknown consequences set off his alarms, even as it stirred his hopes. Dr. Beha said—as on an afternoon of the following week he handed over a blister pack of four pills—that he understood porn stars used it, to reliably get wood (their term, good Lord). Dr. Beha had a way of being cheerfully frank, no harm in it really; before he'd done Stan's vasectomy long ago he'd told him that it was usual at this point to give some psychological counseling, but he'd never seen that it made a difference, and so with Stan's permission he'd skip it.

Get wood. Of course Terry couldn't be told; he'd have to keep it from her; she mistrusted any resort to pills, she hadn't wanted the HRT at all until her situation got so bad, and he was sure a sex pill would turn her off entirely, she'd be disgusted with him for falling for it. But then what if he had a bad reaction in her presence, fainted or something, how would he explain? What if he counted on a night's certainty of its working and then it didn't? How much could worry about the pill's effects actually offset the effects? Driving the deeply familiar curling road back up from the valley in the softening light, Stan fell into that late-afternoon flow of word and image, logicless and dreamlike. He pictured himself, or saw someone like him, fired up and eager, grinning as he popped his pill, young wife in a baby-doll so happy for him. Nubile. His old-coot habit of letting something lie where he'd put it down, or putting it carelessly away, on the assumption he'd remember later what he'd done with it—what if he hid his new pills and then forgot where he put them? Yes, hold on a minute, honey, I'll be right there. Stan turned downward onto the village road, feeling like the town would be shocked to know what he had in his pocket, if it could only know it; but why would he think that? Maybe in every old couple's bathroom drawer.

> *Said the old coot on his way to Niagara*
> *To his young wife, "Just can't wait till I shag ya!"*
> *He's sure he'll get wood!*
> *But his memory's no good*
> *And he'll find he forgot the*

Stan swerved a little sharply to avoid an SUV appearing before him at a turning, using up more than its lane. Ugly fatass cars, why were they so selfish, alpha male at the wheel, Stan realized he actually knew the guy. Heart quickened, he settled down and made it home.

The pills were pretty things, kite-shaped and softly rounded, a dull azure. The long microscopically small list of warnings and side effects stirred Stan's fears; he'd need a magnifier to read them, and so didn't. He revolved in his mind the right time to swallow the first of the pills—apparently it took a while to kick in, so to speak, longer in fact than any sex act he was likely to be capable of, hopped up or not, it'd be all over or given up on well before he got the help; he'd have to take it in anticipation, or expectation. Or hope. Would he remember that he'd put them in this old travel shaving kit? Some other place better?

"Hi, babe, you here?"

It was Terry, entering the house on little cat feet; she trod lightly on the earth, disconcerting sometimes actually.

"Yes! Be right there!"

"How was your doctor?" she called, coming closer.

"Oh, fine."

"The thing you were worried about?"

"That? Oh, nothing. He said treating it would be just a bother, it'll pass."

"Oh." Terry at the door of the bathroom regarded him, smiling just barely, her thoughts unreadable. She wore a loose cotton sundress he hadn't seen on her in years; once he'd told her he thought it was sexy, which amazed her. What was sexy about it? It was sexy, he'd said, because it looks like it would come off easily.

The summer solstice had passed but the sky was light till late, by now you were used to it as though it had always been so; the last dim blue at nine o'clock and then stars and then a golden moon appearing in their bedroom window as though taking turns coming on stage.

In the dark of the morning Stan got up to pee, and on an impulse dug out the pills from where he'd put them, and took one. He went back to bed and lay open-eyed on his pillow, waiting. He heard thunder, or thought he did: trucks down on the road? No, there it was again, thunder, a dull far-off throat-clearing. First of the spring. Harry Watroba had told him that in many American Indian languages birds are related to thunder. Because when they go away in the fall the thunder stops; it begins again when they return. Makes sense. Thunderbirds, arising at its rumble, up from the dark mountain's slopes into the red air. You could see, from these ramparts, the lightning dully flaring. No, said Harry: bombs. The bombs are falling out there, see, coming closer, the birds fleeing.

Stan awoke as though shaken, feeling weird, not himself, and couldn't think why. Ill? Fever? None of that.

Oh yes the pill.

He was erect, as often after morning dreams, but good Lord the thing was hard as a broom handle, feeling to his touch to be not his but as though affixed to him. It seemed to be of no mind to go down. Stan felt like giggling. And now what? Tap Terry on the shoulder, make her look?

She rolled over and woke. "Oh God it's late. I have to get up."

"It's Saturday," Stan said.

"Oh right. Oh good." She rolled back, and went back to sleep. Stan waited, sensing an impatience in his magic power, like it might evaporate, but if it worked as promised he could worry about that and it wouldn't have any deflating effect, and so he didn't worry. For a time he lay quietly and listened to her breathe, wondering where she was and what she was doing. She had the most startling and unlikely dreams; sometimes waves of chills would pass over him as he listened to her recount one. *Eldritch*, Harry called those chills. Awaking again from brief unconsciousness he snuggled up to her, and started in. "Oh," she said.

"Hi."

"Hi there." Smiling, a smile clear and open like her son's, just the same. Stan kissed her throat, touched her here and there, tried to assess the response he got. It seemed to be going well. Moist and open. Certainly his own side was good, no problem; he nearly laughed. He bent to her ear, whispered things, then gave attention to the parts of her he could reach, looked into her eyes. He was inside then and she was moving beneath him; she seemed, though, somewhat thoughtful or doubtful; he wondered if it was possible for her to discern a difference, from within. She twisted, grasping his arms in her hands, working. All right, he could probably go on for hours, but it began to be clear she wasn't writhing in delight or the struggle to get off. No, definitely cooling, like molten lava in a nature film ceasing to flow, turning dark and stony. Now she was actually pushing him away, teeth grit and a wild sound in her throat. What? What? She pushed his chest, pulled back her hips, and Stan popped out, astonished, horrified; his knee slipped off the side of the bed and he went over, barely managing not to land on his ass, though ever after when these events passed through his mind it seemed that's just what he'd done.

"What the hell, Terry! What are you, what."

"I hate that," she said, eyes alight with anger. "I hate it when you do all that. You know I hate it."

"All that what?" Stan cried. What had he been doing? Just the stuff, the usual stuff. Sex.

"All this mem-mem-mem," she said, waggling her fingers in the air to suggest the inappropriate or witless or insensitive things he did and had done and done. "All this, all this myeh-myeh-myeh you do." She gave up and fell back against the pillow. "Ack." For a while she only lay staring at nothing.

Her rage and her bareness consorted badly. It was the first time in all the years they'd lived together that she reminded Stan of his first wife.

"I try," he said, "to do what you want."

"You never knew how to do what I want."

"Never?"

She said nothing.

"Why didn't you tell me?" Stan asked. He stooped to pull on his shorts. Tucking in the rejected tool, its head now hanging, but still engorged. "Why?"

"I did tell you."

"You didn't tell me," he said. "You only ever told me—sometimes you let me know what you didn't like. That's different." He waggled his fingers at her, miming her disgust. "No mem-mem-mem. Well, I don't know what you mean by mem-mem-mem," he said. "Myeh-myeh-myeh."

She laughed a little, relenting, and moved within the sheets.

"You can't teach somebody something by negatives," he said. It was a key doctrine of Human Resources, in which he'd worked so long. Terry'd heard him say it before; he wondered now how often. "Can't get somebody to do right by telling them they're wrong. There are too many ways to be wrong. Over against one way to be right."

"I didn't want to teach you," she said. "I wanted you to just know."

Breeze lifted the lace curtain at the window in a gentle arc.

I wanted you to just know. Well, that made a kind of awful sense. She said no more, he sat down on the bed, the two of them in the strange air of having said unsayable things.

"This was all along?" Stan asked.

Terry sighed, covered her eyes with her hands.

"I'm not inside your head," Stan said. "I mean there's always a certain amount of guesswork. I did what I thought you liked. I can't feel the effects of it."

"I'll make coffee," Terry said.

Stan watched her climb from the bed, draw on a pair of sweat pants and yesterday's shirt. She wasn't looking his way.

"I love you, Stan," she said at the bedroom door, but not looking back at him where he sat. "I always will."

He listened to her feet on the stairs, the old stairs crackling faintly as she went down.

What the hell, he thought, now what the hell. What an awful thing to do, no matter what. Wasn't it? A wave of some black cataclysmic kind seemed to rise up behind or before him, then recede, but not vanish, not now or ever after.

He noticed that the daylight growing in the room seemed a strange shade of blue. Just spring advancing? No, couldn't be. He turned on the lamp by the bed, and its bulb burned blue as a Christmas light.

What was he supposed to do, was he supposed to do something, mend his ways somehow? What were his ways? Myeh-myeh-myeh. He clapped his cheeks in his hands and muttered what Terry's books called an imprecation. And then another one.

Once in a college art class that Stan had taken for no real reason, the students were told to hold up their portraits or self-portraits to a mirror; when a portrait was reversed, you could suddenly perceive all its faults, the face hilariously misshapen, wall-eyed, broken-jawed, all wrong. It was hilarious and also mortifying. Also you didn't know what you were supposed to do to fix it, or, if you began again, how to do it better. Just keep trying, the teacher said. Give up your preconceptions and really look.

He didn't want to have to do that. Wasn't he too old to? He sat immobile a long time, the unreal blue day brightening; not thinking, not doing anything. His organ had recovered from its humiliation, and Stan lowered his shorts to look at it. Wood. It rose from its base at an acute angle he hadn't seen since adolescence, as though straining to take off. Big help that is. The odor of coffee arose from below, as it always did, as it would.

Stan worked hard that summer, his busy time. The dot-com bust cut into sales but not as badly as everyone feared; in fact for some reason or reasons that Stan couldn't analyze, house prices around the valley went up, and the eagerness of buyers that drove them up was apparently intensifying. Sometimes Stan felt the unnerving sensation of big engines revving up in preparation for a takeoff, and wondered what he'd got himself into: he hadn't expected his post-retirement job to be a demanding one, full of urgent labor.

Even the house that Terry had come to call the Tragic New England House, the Ancient Wrong House, tall gaunt place divided in half by warring brothers, began to get offers. The cousin who'd inherited it brought in a crew at one point and ripped out all the two-by framing and the plasterboard and Celotex so that potential buyers could at least see what they had to work with. Stan stood within it looking at the unscabbed wounds where ceiling plaster had come down with the divider walls, at the floors tiled or painted to the middle and no farther, a black line of mildew where for years the wall had stood. Forty years of not parting, not reconciling either, getting by, and now the awful makeshift exposed for what it had been. Tragic New England, land of embittered making-do. A living-room window had been split between the halves, rag of curtain on one side, narrow blind on the other; whole now, showing a nice view of the river, actually.

It sold for not a bad price, just as summer was ending.

Through this time Stan took no more of the blue pills; it was obvious what the drawback of these was, which the manufacturers had certainly foreseen, grinning as they watched their sales climb: if worrying about performance is what's diminishing your performance, and the pill fixes that, then worrying about how you'd do without the pill would be enough to cause failure all by itself. So better stock up, take 'em early and often.

No. And for Stan the necessity to keep them secret only increased the impossibility that they'd help in any way with the big process that it seemed he was on, that he and she were on, which couldn't have a secret plot, a concealment, at the heart of it. So it was up and down—as Stan would reply (wry smile) to an imaginary questioner who asked how it was going: up and down. Whatever it was that made them a bad match somehow in bed meant it continued knotty, sudden surprising ardor sometimes that wiped away worry, at other times ambivalence and what-now-ism that produced cascading failure, sometimes worse than that, a sadness never expected, not by him.

Meanwhile Terry went on flourishing, growing younger, wrinkles erased, skin gleaming; watching her undress and hop into bed was like one of those movies where someone's sold her soul to the Devil and been given things she shouldn't have, delighting in her new and luckier self while the audience knows it's going to turn out very badly. Though to say that out loud to her without being able to laugh with her at it too—he couldn't. The HRT regimen might keep her in youthful shape for years (years: like a bell the word struck in his breast) and so they had to work on their marriage, anyway he had to. It was as on your wedding day when you say solemnly that you will take it on, whatever comes, without knowing really what you might be assenting to, but as though all the labor that followed that day now lay once again ahead, all of it to be done as it was done but done differently.

He was trying to change his life. He knew he must. His good beautiful life.

Another bottle of Muscadet, another incipient spring. She was preparing to make nettle soup for the first time, an experiment which Stan was enthusiastic about, anyway he was on her side concerning it. She wore gloves, to keep from stinging herself.

"So the doctor," Terry said. "There's news."

She wasn't looking up from her washing and cutting, which made Stan attentive.

"About HRT," she said. "It seems there are test results."

She moved without haste around the kitchen. It was a talent she had, in tough moments, to keep at work in that calm tea-ceremony concentration, even as she said hard things.

"What results?"

"The HRT increases risk of breast cancer, Stan. Like quite a bit. In fact they had to put an end to this huge study because the number of women getting breast cancer went over the stopping boundary."

"Stopping boundary?"

"That's Doctor Florenz's words. She said: too many. So you stop the study."

"Okay," said Stan cautiously. "And this means . . ."

She turned on him then, ceasing her all-alone-in-a-room mode. "It means I have to stop. Everybody's going to stop, unless they don't care about the risk."

"Well, of course," Stan said. "You have to stop."

Terry went back to cutting nettles. "So that's the answer to the question," she said.

"Which question?"

"Whether you take them your whole life long. Now we know."

Stan made the tsk sound, blew air, drummed his fingers on the tabletop. Complications, well you could have guessed. How strange that medicines could do this, he thought, upend your life, float your boat, overturn it too. He cleared his throat to say something about that, then didn't.

"The cooking takes away the sting," Terry said, as though to herself, gathering the green stuff. "I don't know how."

Stan watched her, her beautiful absorption, and felt a sudden spasm of grief for her, all that youth regained, only to be given up again, maybe, probably. Would that reborn sex drive now evaporate?

Not the time to raise that point either.

He lifted his glass and looked through the pale wine at the pale sky scribbled on by still-leafless branches. Perhaps, without a choice, they'd soon be returned to the calmer waters they'd been sailing on not long ago. Which actually he couldn't think would be so bad. But—this occurred to him—it might seem bad as a place returned to rather than a place arrived at. Returned to with new *baggage* as they said now.

You can't un-know something you have come to know.

For the first time Stan seemed to see that these developments ever-arising in time weren't opening outward the life he would live, he and she, as once they had seemed to do; instead they were filling it in, gradually or abruptly, like discoveries filling in the blank terra incognita in an old map; and they would go on doing so, lands and peoples, until in the end there were no more.

3. Mount Auburn Street

Harry Watroba kept a lookout for signs that he was transitioning into old age. For instance he had come to notice how, like a cheerful oldster, he took increasing satisfaction in tidying, in small-job completion, in preparation and storage, in refreshment of the spaces around him. Shaping up the last redoubt? It didn't seem so, but certainly he was becoming more like the ant than the grasshopper he'd been in youth. Also he was growing more miserly, a sign of age in many cultures, as he knew: the slippered pantaloon counting over his coins. Right now he was scrubbing the accumulated calcium and minerals from an old stainless-steel tea-kettle that had become so coated with thick white stuff the water could hardly come out. He'd had to find a thin sharp thing (an ancient silver nut-pick, in the end) with which to poke down through the stubby spout and clear the holes that the water would, or rather wouldn't, pour out of; scrape with a green scrubbie the interior, and—as long as he was at it—the greasy and water-spotted exterior too. The water in this place he'd come to live in was phenomenally hard. The kettle belonged to the place, not to Harry.

Harry's own kettle, an even older and more battered one, had been lost forever when Harry's house burned down, or up—Harry pondered the difference, what made one preposition preferable to the other. And "lost": the catastrophe had given him many reasons to consider the various and differing occasions for that word. *I lost my wife,* we say, though (excepting the case of a separation at a mall or in a crowd) we know just where she is. The *lost* in *I lost my way* seems to be a rather different word than it is in, say, *I lost my hat,* or in *I lost that fight.*

Another thing Harry had lost in the fire was the nearly complete draft of a major revision and updating of his popular (even briefly best-selling) book *A Rhetoric for Everyone.* He had certainly lost the book even though he knew where the scorched remains of the pages and the sturdy binder that had held them were: they were with his library, down in the wetted ash and blackened lumber of his former office in the nice Colonial Revival house in the hilltown where he had lived for decades. He'd lost the computer on which it was almost done being typed, and the disks on which several drafts were stored, and those also on which it was backed up, and he knew where those were too. Because of the fire he had also lost, different sense, his wife, Mila: she blamed him (justly enough) for the fire, and had moved in with her mother in a nearby city. In various losings then, his home, his book, his occupation, his wife, his way, his future, and his (weirdly longstanding) innocence.

The old tea-kettle now shone, glowing like an athlete after exercise. The dent on one side made it all the more appealing: refreshed and ready, but old and reliable too. *Baraka:* long ago Mila had told him this Arabic word meant "the holiness human things acquire through long use." Only recently had it occurred to him to look this up and confirm she was right, and she wasn't. Which left a gap in the language, for surely a word for the condition he'd thought *baraka* described was necessary and gratifying.

He put the kettle back on the stove-top where it resided.

———

For a couple of months after the conflagration Harry'd moved in with his daughter Hope and her daughter Muriel, in the spare room, feeling a weird sense of privileged stasis, like a soul in the quiet forecourt of a not-yet-determined afterlife. That couldn't continue, and without making an actual decision, or to avoid making one, Harry had rented this small and uncertain-looking little house beside a stretch of highway, a town away from his old home.

Despite doing not much of anything, he had somehow managed to accumulate a large number of belongings in the time he lived with Hope and Muriel. Clothes, of course, to replace the lost contents of his closets; Old Navy mostly, as he felt guilty about spending more than necessary of the diminishing savings that were both his and Mila's. Sales at Old Navy astonished him: jeans and shirts and cotton sweaters with prices that seemed to hark back to Harry's youth, thence reduced to next to nothing, buy one get one free. Hope had at length loaded all this and the rescued books and papers and winter boots, the laundry, and a little radio into the Subaru and trucked it up on a sunny Tuesday when she had a late shift at the hospital and Muriel was in school.

She stood on the threshold now looking in. "Why didn't you go the whole distance and just move into a damn trailer?"

"Actually I looked at a few," Harry said. "Immobile homes."

She crossed her arms before her.

"Furnished," Harry pointed out. "A deck." He was able to show her the whole place from the doorway, which she seemed reluctant to pass through. "A river. Just there."

Hope went to her car and pulled stuff out, shopping bags and boxes; Harry came to help. "How long's this supposed to last you?"

"I can't say how long," Harry said. "The insurance company is havering." Good old Scots word, related to *hovering*, meaning something between pausing in uncertainty and dithering. The insurance company had been alerted to the presence of possibly flammable materials stored in the basement, the proximate cause of the fire, and no funds from the policy had yet been seen. Harry and Mila were still paying the mortgage on the place, which didn't leave much for alternate digs.

Flammable things had formerly been called *inflammable*, till warnings and tags became so common in the world that the ambiguity in that prefix became a problem. (Harry'd discussed it in Section 20 of his book, "Affix a Prefix.") The opposite of the old *inflammable* had been *uninflammable;* it was uncertain, now, what the opposite of flammable could be—*nonflammable*, probably. But really, who needed a warning that something would not catch fire?

"So are you going to get a new computer? Can you get online here?"

"Dial-up," Harry said, with a smile that he could tell from Hope's face was deeply annoying to her. A large truck just then going past the house on the road could be felt as well as heard. That was a drawback; Hope indicated it with a thumb, saying nothing. Harry shrugged, nodded in assent.

"All right," she said, fishing for her keys. "I gotta go."

"Tell Muriel I live by a river."

"She misses you." She kissed her father's cheek.

That had been a dreary day in late autumn. The place was a little nicer now, due mostly to the melting of the filthy snow around it and the soft pour of sun throughout a longer day, but not much. Harry didn't mind it, could stand even the mildewed davenport and finger-grimed television and all the other signs of terminal impoverishment. He did, though, find himself tucking his arms and knees in a fetal ball in the lumpy bed at night, child or pup trying to comfort itself. And when he was here all day, nothing to do, he had to go out, every hour or two through the day, and sit in the aluminum lawn chair a while and look at the little river or stream or creek (he hadn't learned its name, or even if it had one). On this mild April day wearing a beret and overcoat, his gloved hands crossed.

Inconceivable as it seemed, he would have to bestir himself. He might cease moving altogether if he didn't.

It wasn't quite true that Harry had lost everything connected to the new draft of *A Rhetoric for Everyone*. He possessed a large folder of notes and scraps of paper with queries to follow up on, photocopied book and magazine pages on which he had circled examples of this or that notion, and many complete pages of early drafts, a heap of disordered stuff that had tended to travel with him in his old shoulder bag; that's where it was the day of the fire, in the bag on the passenger seat of his Oldsmobile station wagon, when he'd come up the hill to his house smelling the awful wet-cigarette-butt smell of a fire just put out. That it was all he now had of the book made it worse, in some ways, than nothing; but he did have it. He planned to start in on transposing it to a single document, and cutting and pasting that document into the beginning of some sort of draft. He thought of Carlyle rewriting his entire history of the French Revolution after John Stuart Mill's maid used the only manuscript to start fires in the fireplaces. There was no lack of such tales. No one would care to hear his.

What had kept him from beginning was the horror of typing it all into the computer. He could not have dreamed, not in detail, that such a thing as a personal computer with word processor would come into being when as a young man he had hunched sweating and swearing over his Royal Standard, punching at keys with two fingers (the index of the left, the medicus of the right, for no reason he knew). His machine had forever needed and never got a cleaning and oiling, which would have reduced his toil somewhat. No more than most men of his age and time, even those who earned their living by writing, had Harry ever tried to learn to type for real, any more than he'd learned to sew. What he could imagine was one day being rich enough to deliver his work, typed on smudgy erasable paper, interlined, overwritten, cut up and taped together, to a real typist, to be returned to him perfect and clean.

But then that modern miracle had come to pass, and now typing was a world easier though still not exactly swift or pleasant, not for him, and the luxury of that long-imagined typist was unjustifiable. After much indecision he had brought to this place a computer to replace the deformed and dead one at the old house. Unlike that one, this one came to him used, or pre-owned, but like a good but aging servant dismissed and thrown on the job market it was surely capable of handling the new additions to or *upgrade* of his book, as the agreed-upon term was. It'd come from the shop to which the University students and their thriftier or more poorly paid instructors went, where ancient and less-ancient drives, monitors, laptops, and printers were piled like old clothes at the Salvation Army. Harry actually loved computers, and knew enough about them to pick the correct components, but he had to fight a tendency toward nostalgia and not buy a system redolent of his first encounters with the phenomenon. A final choice had taken him several visits, but now it was set up and awaiting him in his front room, before it a maple kitchen chair with a knitted seat-cover. Two years before, all machines made such as this one was, from grand data centers on windswept prairies to the innards of digital clocks, had been thought to be at risk of stopping dead—their systems could not, it was said, understand dates past 1999. *Y2K* was the neat designation for this catastrophe, which had passed with no harm done, as Harry out of an inherent optimism had supposed it would.

Faced with typing up the mass of notes and snippets of printouts and loose papers, WordPerfect or no, Harry had been driven to an additional purchase he thought he might regret. And now from the back deck where he sat he heard the arrival of the UPS truck, and the drop of a delivery onto his miniature front porch. He knew what it was. It wasn't a gift. It wasn't a master-key or an arcanum. It was one of those conveniences that promise you can increase your work output for no increase in effort, and present this as an opportunity, even a delight.

Dragon Naturally Speaking it was called. How had it come by such a name? Harry was reminded of the weird literal translations that used to appear on old Chinese menus. Why not Dragon Speaking Naturally? Harry the Dragon collected the package from the porch, opened it, and drew out the product within. He smelled the sharp odor of its newness, and touched the sheen of the cellophane that covered its box, which was likely not actual cellophane but a modern successor.

The usual stack of floppy disks, which held the program, were half the size of the old floppies and encased in stiff plastic, but still and likely forever to be called "floppy." A pleasant half-hour was spent installing these. A headset, like those used by telemarketers and 911 operators, went over the head and pointed a small microphone at the mouth. Feeling faintly silly, Harry pressed the wire loop into his grizzled hair, and discovered that there was on his new old computer a place to plug it in, naturally.

Things got curiouser: in order to train the program to understand his peculiar, that is particular, speech ("Adjectives on the Move," Section 21 of his *Rhetoric*), the training manual instructed him to read passages from *Alice in Wonderland* in a distinct yet relaxed and natural voice as they appeared before him on the screen. Fine. When that process was done, the promise was that he would be able to read aloud the notes, bits, examples, vocabulary, hints, wonderments, and fun facts from his notebooks as effortlessly as a lawyer reading a will to a roomful of descendants.

Having at length (his computer proved less trainable than Harry had expected) been certified, his particularities processed, Harry tried out a few simple sentences of his own. "Perfection of form is the most perfect content," he said aloud to program-and-computer—a phrase he'd actually once written in his nicest hand on the bathroom wall of some john somewhere. He watched as it produced a sentence not resembling his very much. He tried again. *Defection affirms the nosed turf at contend.* He tried again, and then again. *Puff action of form is the mows Purvis condemned.* There was of course a way to tidy up the natural errors the poor thing made, but having to do that made the speaking not a bit more easeful than simply typing as fast and as well as he could. Harry thought of Henry James dictating his serpentine sentences to a typist, who probably did far better than the Dragon. She had been, of course, a human.

Harry disengaged from the headset and went to take a nap.

Like a toddler in a talkative family, the Dragon did learn, and on a rising curve—getting better faster every day. The nonsense that persisted, like a toddler's, could be amusing: the program always took a guess, no matter how odd; it never just ran a line of question marks or X's. Harry decided that it, or he, had passed the tests, pulling a C+ or B- anyway, and on a bright and hopeful summer morning he chose a section from his notebook pages to dictate.

These were some little puzzles that would go into the section "Text and Context," showing that dictionaries could not finally settle questions of meaning, that words were simply too cunning for that, and without losing the definiteness of their definitions, could alter to match their surroundings in the same way the fabled chameleon does. Two related stories were presented, and the reader was to come up with two words to fill the two blanks in the summation that followed each story, in one order after the first story, and the reverse order after the second.

Harry began reading the first of the puzzles aloud. Headings and explications he'd add later, when he'd composed them.

I owned a pair of rare Bugatti Type 57s roadsters, he read aloud. *They cost a fortune. One of them I never drove. But in the second one I tooled around the neighborhood, enjoying the stares—until I flew through a stop sign and tangled with a lowly SUV. The Bugatti was totalled.*

Well done, Dragon! Harry had only a few corrections (*boo got he*) to make. He inserted the fill-in-the-blanks sentence by hand:

My _____ car was no longer _____.

Then the second story:

The other Type 57s lived in my heated garage after that, and I watched its market value rise—that is, until the latest market downturn. It rapidly become nearly worthless, as did the garage, the heavily mortgaged house, and the stocks I had bought on margin. In order to avoid bankruptcy I had to sell everything at fire-sale prices, and the Bugatti, no less precious than it had been, went for a song.

My _____ car was no longer _____.

Mila had shown no interest in this riddle, as she had in some other games that he produced for the book. Why did he want to write stories about expensive sports cars, especially imaginary ones? A lawyer, she was invested in the ways in which words had power and did things in the world; toying with them just for the fun of it, or even to uncover their interesting innards, was to her a habit of Harry's not much different from his constant sing-humming bits from classical music or jazz standards.

"You never finish," she said once in impatience. "You just do your little diddle-diddle-doo and then nothing. There's no conclusion. No closure."

"I do the theme," Harry'd replied. "I can't whistle-hum the whole symphony."

"Just don't do it then," she said. "Do something with a payoff. Or don't do it."

Mila. God how long he'd loved her.

As he thought this, sitting in a house where she was not, a new switch-the-words puzzle occurred to him. Unwilling to draft it in speech (though that was advertised on the Dragon box as possible), he removed his headset and turned away from the screen, took a pencil and a pad, and balanced it on his knee to scribble.

My place of residence, he wrote at speed, *where I have lived for many years, has been terribly damaged in a fire, and all my books, cherished memorabilia, old kitchenware, and inherited furniture, lost. It could be rebuilt perhaps, but to me it could not ever be the same.*

My _____ is no longer a _____ .

Then:

I sought shelter, and eventually found a space under a bridge. I have been welcomed and taken in by the others there, who are very kind. I have laid out blankets and set up a camp stove. I never would have thought I could live this way, but I find I can, and have not lately thought of moving on.

My _____ is no longer a _____ .

For a moment, pen in hand, Harry felt a shame so profound and thoroughgoing that it seemed to draw into his soul all the embarrassments and lacks of his life, his cowardice, his unwarranted self-reliance, his pride.

He turned back to the screen. There was a word typed there that he had not entered.

woman

He regarded it in bafflement. He lifted a finger to erase it, or to type something else, as a test; but felt suddenly immobilized. Another word typed itself as he looked:

womb

What glitch in the program could possibly. He reached to turn it off. Another word appearing on the screen stopped him:

woe

A shiver passed over Harry. If his wife, or his dead mother, were speaking arcane words to him through the machine, or over the dial-up Web, should he reply? What could he say? He laughed aloud in mystified awe. For a time he waited to see if further messages would be sent. None came.

He ought to get out now, he thought, staring, and go for a walk. Yes he should.

He nearly tipped over his chair as he rose. Sought his jacket and hat, thinking *What on earth,* and also that maybe he should save his work, and its work also. He might need the evidence. Pausing before the computer, jacket half on: yes, the words were there, none added, none erased. He powered down, but not off. Let it be.

The otherwise rather charmless small town where Harry had rented his house was blessed with Wordsworthian walks, climbs, views. Like all such New England places its old fields and farms were becoming reforested (were reforesting?), but still there were broad meadows and hedgerows, ponds and wetlands; grand old maples on their last legs marched along the quiet roads, left alone by the first settlers so as to shade the way after they had cut and sold or used the others. Harry, walking upward through the dense pools of shadow these cast, looking out to far hills pale with sun, thought not for the first time that landscape painters must be the happiest of people, with a job that could only bring peace and delight. He felt a vast gratitude that he had been allowed to experience this, all this, the world, the air, the wonderful gatherings of five senses.

He hadn't reached the top of the rise when he had to stop. A pain across his breastbone, or maybe his back, hard to say. This familiar pain he attributed to a pulled muscle in the chest area caused by moving things into and out of his rental.

Certainly it would get better, he told his daughter and wife, and both urged him to just go get it checked out; but Harry, as a doctor's son, had an antipathy to bringing trivial complaints to Dr. Beha, a good man but (like Harry's father) seeming to enjoy being cheerfully dismissive. *It's not a pulled muscle, Harry,* Mila told him over the phone. *It's angina! My mother just got diagnosed with it! Will you please just listen?* And he said he would.

The pain had sharply worsened. The top of the rise seemed far away suddenly, and Harry had broken out in sweat. Nausea flooded him. He stopped by a mailbox, and put his hand on it to stay standing. After a moment the door of the house to which the mailbox belonged opened and a woman hurried toward him, wiping her hands on her jeans, a gesture somehow betokening help and mercy.

His good neighbor, whose husband had died of—but there she'd stopped her relation—took him in her truck to the ER at the nearest hospital, Harry alternately trying to breathe and to read the colorful prayer stuck to the dashboard. Though doubtful, at his insistence she dropped him off at the wide doors, still walking at least, waving her goodbye.

First an EKG was done, inconclusive but not good. Blood tests showed he had not had a heart attack, not precisely anyway. A stress test, quickly aborted when Harry began to exhibit danger signs. An angiogram, showing multiple blockages in Harry's coronary arteries. But, but (he complained to no one, there being no one to complain to) he'd taken his statins faithfully, he'd cut down on fats, he walked often. Pretty often. His carotid artery when last tested was clean as a whistle—that was the term used. But like characters in

Wonderland, the doctors and staff behaved as though there was nothing surprising at all about Harry's having fallen into this hole and down among them, and went on talking sense to him that sounded as strange to him as nonsense. He was put to bed and scheduled for a double bypass as soon as a room opened up. Mila was called, Dr. Beha (who had privileges here) looked in on him and made mild jokes, his insurance thank God was in force, Mila and Hope arrived and stayed by him. And clothed in a backless johnny printed with violets, holding their warm hands, before nightfall Harry went meekly into oblivion.

What meaning relates anesthetic to aesthetic? His Greek professor had long ago posed that question, which ended up in Harry's burned book. What relates cosmic to cosmetic? Mila told him that these were his first muddied remarks after arising from the depths. He didn't believe her. Sitting with him in his semi-private room (that is, non-exclusive or shared; Harry made a mental note he soon would lose) she related this funny positively true fact to the man in the other bed, who made no reply.

When she was gone, though, he lifted his unshaven face to Harry.

"Anesthetics," he said.

"Yes," Harry said,

"There's horror stories," his roommate whispered, seeming to be one himself, as yet untold. "People waking up in the middle of their operations, not enough gas, looking up at this crew with their hands in your innards."

"Not possible," Harry said. Speech hurt.

"I'm telling you," the other said. "It's because the gas is so toxic that they want to use as little as possible. They take a chance on the minimum. So people are waking up, experiencing their operations, all the pain, but just unable to speak. Frozen."

"We'd know," Harry said. "They'd tell."

"They give you this stuff so if it happens you won't remember. Sometimes it's called Versed. Other names. Wipes the memory. But here's the problem: you do remember. If you try. It's like remembering a dream. One little hint, and it all comes back."

Versed. Pronounced as two syllables. The anesthetician had explained it to him and to Mila, and Hope restated it. Drug names fascinated Harry; they were Joycean mashups or Lewis Carroll portmanteau words, sometimes suggestive of their claimed effects (Librium) and sometimes merely pretty or forceful-sounding, but often retaining some vestige of their chemical composition. The path to the right name, he knew, was fraught. A doctor had told him of a tranquilizer named with the common -ol ending that came near to being marketed before somebody finally said it aloud. It was called Damitol.

Versed was also called something less handy, what was it, lovely and mysterious, the doctor had said the name. Bedazzling. Midazolam! Me bedazzled, sawn open, safe from self-knowing.

There arose then, like a warning or truth swimming up from the dark pool within the Magic 8 Ball, a memory. A memory he should not have been able to make. Not of the surgical table, the bloodstained gowns, but after, as he lay blind and immobile on the respirator in a no-world. He had heard a voice—Mila's. Speaking to someone, who, his doctor or some doctor or nurse. They were talking about *shutting him down:* Were those the words? *Well, he wouldn't want to live if he wasn't fully okay.* She was prepared, he had heard her say; he'd had a good life and she was ready to say goodbye. And she was—he heard this clearly—his health-care proxy.

He sprang to alertness, eyes wide in the semi-dark, beside his harshly breathing roommate. A dream? Opiate hallucination? He didn't know. For a long while he lay still, experiencing it again and again, with a deep thrill of horror each time. His monitor surveyed him, unalarmed. At last he slept.

"Harry," Mila said to him when next day he asked her, tell me the truth, had she said those things to the doctor? "Harry, how could I have. How could you think it. You weren't even in that much trouble."

"Well, I thought. I mean I thought I remembered."

She leaned over him where he lay, and smoothed his unkempt hair. "I love you, Harry, you dope. Maybe I also can't stand you. But I don't want you dead."

"Good to know," he said, all he could say.

He was only in the hospital a couple of days, which amazed him. They wanted him up, they wanted him walking, they wanted him out. His roomie remained in bed, suffering something worse than he had. Harry, resting from a mandated trudge around the ward, exchanged a few words with him; they named their residences, this man's in Boston originally.

"Here's a Boston riddle," Harry said. "Why is life like Mount Auburn Street?"

"I know this," the other said. "I've heard it."

"Because," Harry said, unwilling to leave it unsaid, "it begins at a hospital and ends at a cemetery."

The man mulled, lips moving as though tasting a tidbit. "Funny," he said. "It's not true, though."

"Not true?" Harry turned carefully to look at him. "That life doesn't begin in a cemetery, or end in a, I mean the other way around?"

"No no," said his friend. "It's not true of Mount Auburn Street."

"No?"

"One end is up way past the Mount Auburn Hospital, toward Harvard Square. Mount Auburn Cemetery's not far down. A few blocks. The street goes on after that."

"And where does it end?"

The man gazed upward, his pain seeming for a moment mitigated by the effort of speculation. "A long ways," he said. "I think it goes as far as the river, and ends there. The Charles. I think. I bet."

Harry seemed to see dark water flowing, stone riparian works, a far side where maybe lights were lit. He was near sleep. "So life isn't like Mount Auburn Street," he said. "But still, is Mount Auburn Street like life?"

But his roommate was now once again actually asleep, or dead, and answer came there none.

Harry, discharged, couldn't return to his shack by the river: his wife and daughter were clear about that. For one thing, he wasn't allowed to drive for several weeks, and for the first of those weeks even had to sit in the backseat of whatever car ferried him here and there. But why? Well, said the Physician's Assistant—a new healthcare-provider role which Harry confused with the similar but different Nurse Practitioner—just suppose you were to get into an accident. Your airbag might deploy, and smack you right in the chest, and break your breastbone open again, which would be . . . well, it would be very bad.

Mila took him to her mother's huge old house in the city, smelling of cleaning products and boiled vegetables, the home she'd escaped from years before and from which her mother refused to move now when she was at last alone in possession. Harry through the calm of painkillers could feel clearly Mila's sense of purgatorial impatience at being there and with them.

When his awful wound had healed sufficiently, Harry was signed up for cardiac rehab. It wasn't optional. He was to report every other morning at a space in the large city hospital with other heart-procedure survivors, better or worse off than he, and walk treadmills and do other things while hooked up to recording devices that would track heart rate and blood pressure, with nurses or overseers ready to take him off if he began to fail or fibrillate. Fine. There was no place Harry hated more than a gym, which this sounded very much like, where he would take his place amid a crowd of wounded or fading old men, what fun.

"Fun," he said to Hope on the phone.

"Fun!" he heard Muriel cry from Hope's side.

"She's so affirmative," Hope said. "It's amazing. Dad, just tell me you'll go."

"It's fun!" Muriel shouted into the receiver, her mother laughing and trying to retain the phone, Harry could hear it.

"Not fun," Harry said. "Toiling in the Devil's pit is fun. Being drafted into the Soviet Army and doing jumping jacks for years is fun. This is not fun." But he went. The hospital was only blocks from his (incipiently, putatively) ex-mother-in-law's house.

The first morning was Intake. Harry waited for his turn on a long bench outside the door, able to observe the walkers to nowhere, slow and slower, hung with recording devices, underarms of their athletic wear gray with sweat.

His turn was called. He entered Intake's miniature office and sat.

"So let's see, Watroba?"

"Yes."

Intake shuffled files, opened one, then another. "And let's see, you're here after an incident where your pants caught on fire?" He regarded Harry without judgment. A strange moment of immobile silence fell, in which Harry doubted reality.

"What? No," he said. "No, not."

Intake looked again at the file he held. "Watroba," he said. "Stanley. Fifty-nine years old. SS number—"

"No," said Harry. "Harold. Not Stanley. Sixty-one."

"Oh right." He put down the folder and picked up another without apology. "Here we are. Double bypass."

"Yes."

"It's a common enough name," Intake said. "Around here."

"Around here," Harry said.

Intake went on talking, explaining things about hearts and arteries that Harry knew, and describing his own healthy outdoor practices (tracking, though not in any way harming, game and other animals). Harry, caught in an ontological twist, could listen and respond well enough, while also being elsewhere and otherwhen.

Pants on fire. It had been in D.C., where he'd gone with Mila, who was to be interviewed for a government job. He was proud of her even if he didn't very much want her to want a government job. Strong legs in glossy stockings, a real attache case and a smart black suit. They'd got off the train and Harry was hunting for something in a pants pocket, not finding it and giving up just when a pointing passerby cried out and then Mila too. Harry's pocket was smoking. In fact, as he later remembered it—though he couldn't now be sure the physics would work—his pocket was showing pale yellow flame. He beat it out in a moment. But Mila's look in that moment he couldn't extinguish: wonder, horror, disbelief, and then less nameable faces too, coming and going as Harry checked for burns and attempted nonchalance.

Liar liar.

"So you understand the regimen," Intake said.

He brought himself around, reviewed what he remembered of what had just been said, and said yes he understood. He didn't however understand the mystically unlikely coincidence that put his namesake and fellow pants-burner both here. It seemed another puzzle set him, whose terms he couldn't grasp, whose answer didn't exist.

It turned out Stanley wasn't in cardiac rehab, not anyway in Harry's class. Once having been wired up each morning and gotten underway with the others, walking steadily to nowhere all covered in dots like Lazarus's sores, he thought about it. Which one would be taken, suddenly, at the machine, and be hustled away by the attendants? Would the rest of them walk on and on?

Harry hadn't ever been particularly afraid of death, and now he was. Not all the time and not seriously so far, but alone in the dark of night sometimes sharply. What exactly does that mean, "afraid of death?" It didn't mean afraid of being dead, or afraid of Judgment or what would happen next, the strangely named Afterlife (Hugo's *peut-être*, the Big Maybe.) None of that did he find alarming. No, it was the process itself, the approach to the big door, the feeling as of being unwillingly put on the scariest ride at the fun-fair. Would he funk? He was afraid of being afraid, afraid of an unseaming fear gripping him at the arrival of it. He worried about being taken suddenly by unmistakable symptoms in a public place, knowing he was doomed and seized by terror while blank-faced bystanders looked on, glad it wasn't them. He didn't know if he was brave enough to die, solid enough as a soul or as a man to face it.

And instead it had only snuck up beside him and whispered in his ear. The doctor knew what it was, though. The Fellow in the Bright Nightgown, as W. C. Fields named him. Harry had simply come upon a flaw or trap, a *gin* they'd have said long ago, that had been lying in wait within him, growing more dangerous as the years passed, while he went on in ignorance, willed ignorance or at least an unwillingness to look deeply. He had been thinking of his cardiac event and all that had succeeded it as a portal that he had come to and passed through in some agony and much doubt. But it hadn't been a portal, certainly not a portal to somewhere new. It was where he'd been all along, only he hadn't known it. The technical medical term, Harry supposed, was *fool's paradise.*

"Harry," Mila said to him. He was propped up on pillows in the living room, on a large plush sofa. "The insurance agent called. They've decided to pay. Just about the settlement I expected."

"Oh God."

"It took some maneuvering," Mila said, almost tenderly. She pushed Harry's pillow up behind him, and moved a coffee cup out of danger. Wife, nurse, handmaid, lawyer. A dense rush of painful gratitude possessed him.

"So you've got to start thinking about what next," Mila said.

"Yes."

"I mean really thinking."

"Are you thinking?" Harry asked. "I mean, I'd like to know what you're thinking."

Mila regarded him, seeming to be thinking many things. Following the fire she had announced (if that could be the word for her rageful flinging of reproach) that she wanted a divorce. He remembered how she had talked to the doctor about pulling the plug. No that had been a false memory.

"Let's start small," she said. That was a tactic learned from his Pay Attention! program, and passed to her. "What are you gong to do right now?"

"Go back to my house, I mean the place there you saw."

"I've never seen it."

That must be true, Harry thought. Her face at the window, her hand shielding the sunlight to peer through the dirt? Not true.

"But Harry. You can't live there. You have to think."

When at last he was allowed to drive the Oldsmobile by himself summer was nearly over. He almost drove past his place by the river; it seemed enfeebled, invisible. The door resisted him, swollen like an old joint. Inside, mouse turds littered the drainboard; a lovely bloom of white mold covered the unremoved food scraps. Harry flung open the windows, cleaned up what could be cleaned—the place had long since reached that point of equanimity between old dirt and new cleansing that could not now be altered.

The computer sat where it had, the stack of floppies still beside it. It hadn't actually been shut off on the summer day when Harry never returned. He pressed its start button. Even as he was remembering what he would see—the mystic information he had left there—it swam into focus. *Woman. Womb. Woe.*

He had been to the other side, had returned alive and chastened, and this problem was still set for him. Very carefully he sat on the kitchen chair, not taking his eyes from the screen. He moved to take up, but then didn't touch, the Dragon headset still plugged in. There was a tiny light on it, he saw now, amber when he noticed it, then turning green. On.

One of the day's number of gravel trucks approached—Harry could tell by now that's what it was—and rushed past, its sound cresting as it passed, then falling to low and soft as it went away. The Doppler effect, wasn't that the name?

A new word had appeared on the screen:

wound

Harry pressed his hand to his chest, as he did now a hundred times a day, querying or comforting. Wound. He would have long pondered this word too in spooked ignorance, but it was just then, in a moment of transformed understanding—as though his shirt had been put on backward and now was suddenly righted—that Harry got it. He picked up the Dragon headset and pointed it toward the open window and the road. Another truck went by the house. Another word:

well

He laughed aloud. Two other trucks rolled by in quick succession. *Well well* averred the Dragon.

What it was—if only every miracle were so suscepti-
ble of explanation!—was the whoosh of a truck's going by
being picked up by the microphone; and because, as Harry
had learned, the program was incapable of displaying a sound
except as an English word, it produced the best one it could.

He sat a long time before the screen. "Well," he said. All
will be well. All manner of thing will be well. Was it only his
imagination (of course it was only his imagination) that the
computer looked a little diminished, abashed and apologetic?

He would have to remove his fractious Dragon friend and
put it away; it hadn't really done nor ever would do what it
promised. He unplugged the mike. He should call Mila, he
thought, and tell her this story, how he had been spoken to as
by a Ouija board, spoken to about her, and himself. *Mila, we
have to talk.*

He turned off the machine, matter unsaved, and went into
the sad sitting room with its ragged rag rug and its humble
linoleum. Yet the day was beautiful, darling September, his
favorite month, and smiling so sweetly. For a time yet the windows could remain still open; smell of sun-heated hay, or dried
leaves, from somewhere. All will be well. On an impulse—an
impulse he'd remember, looking back—Harry picked up the
remote and turned on the television.

Conversation Hearts

On the day before Valentine's Day the snow advancing from the west suddenly became a storm; the snow would cover them and then deepen rapidly (the radio weather said) toward the east as evening came. Perry and Lily (she in first, he in third grade) were sent home early from school, the telephone tree reaching the Nutting's house just as John Nutting was about to pick up the phone to call the Astra Literary Agency in Boston, to tell his wife that she should probably start for home as soon as she could. When he got the office, he was told that Ann-Marie, his wife's agent, was actually meeting Meg in a restaurant in Brookline. John considered calling the restaurant and paging her, but that seemed somehow too alarmist, and he sat and waited instead for the kids to get home.

The snow was already a couple of inches deep by the time the bus stopped in front of the house, so John lifted Lily off and carried her. Perry followed after with Lily's crutches. John set Lily down in the hall and helped with her coat.

"Now we can make valentines," Lily said, who had wanted to the night before, but John had got out the box of lace doilies and red hearts and glue and stickers too late, and Meg had said no, time for bed, causing something of an uproar for which John felt himself still in the doghouse all around. So now he said yes they'd make valentines, and Perry sagged and groaned in a fine display of weary disgust, though John knew he actually liked making paper things of any kind and was (John thought) actually highly gifted, in a way; and all talking and thinking and disputing, they went into the kitchen and got going.

"Are you going to make valentines, Daddy?"

"I'm going to make one. For Mom."

"Is she your valentine?"

"I think so."

"Me too?"

"You too."

"Did Mom go to see Anne-Marie?" Perry asked.

"Yes, that's why she went. She wants to talk about her new book. The kid's book."

"Is it a chapter book?" Lily asked.

"Yes." John considered. "As I remember, it is a chapter book."

"I could read it," Perry said, with an air of negligent competence.

"I'm sure you could."

"What's the story about?" Lily asked. She actually knew, but liked to hear it again.

"It's about," John said, "a little girl who has no fur."

Lily laughed. "Girls don't have fur."

"You don't have fur?"

"No, Daddy."

"Well then maybe this book's about you."

"I doubt it," she said, grinning, which made Perry laugh aloud.

[FIRST CHAPTER]

When you look up into the sky at night, all the stars you can see are really suns, like the sun that shines on Earth. Some stars are bigger suns than our sun, and some are smaller; some are hotter, and some are not as hot. Some stars have planets going around them, just as Earth goes around our sun.

Maybe one star you can see on a clear dark night has a planet going around it that is like Earth, only different.

Maybe there are animals and people living on this planet who are like the people who live on Earth— only different.

Say the people are like us, and have hands and feet and two eyes (one eye on each side of their nose) and a mouth underneath; and two ears, one for each side of their heads. And heads too.

Only say that instead of plain skin they have beautiful thick soft fur all over, from head to foot, even on the backs of their hands and the tops of their feet.

And say that the bottoms of their feet are thick and tough as shoe soles.

And say that the name of this planet is Brxx.

A woman named Qxx and man named Fxx lay awake late at night in their house on the planet Brxx. It was a cold night, but the windows of their house were open.

Actually the house didn't have any windows, only big open spaces in the walls through which the wind came in. Qxx and Fxx didn't mind, because they were both covered from head to foot in their own beautiful thick soft fur. Qxx's fur was red.

Qxx and Fxx were awake because they were thinking about the new baby that Qxx was soon to have. They were also awake because Qxx was so big with the new baby that she couldn't get comfortable in bed. (Actually they didn't have a bed; they slept together on a wide flat rock, but they didn't mind because their thick fur was as good as a mattress and a blanket together.)

Since they couldn't sleep, they were talking about what they would name the new baby.

"I've always liked the name Trxx," said Qxx.

"I've always liked that name too," said Fxx. "But it's a girl's name. What if this baby is another boy?"

Qxx and Fxx already had a baby boy, named Pxx, who was curled up cozy and asleep in his own room, on the stone floor.

"It's not a boy," said Qxx. "I know."

"How do you know?" asked Fxx.

"I know," said Qxx.

The new baby was a girl. But as soon as Fxx and Qxx saw her, they knew she was different from other babies.

Trxx was pink and smooth. Her eight tiny fingers were pink and her eight tiny toes were pink too. Her knees were wrinkled and so were her elbows. On top of her head there were a few strands of dark hair—but except for those, Trxx was naked all over.

Trxx had no fur.

"Oh dear," said Fxx. "Oh my stars."

"Oh," said Qxx. "Oh my baby." She was almost afraid to hold the newborn baby, she looked so strange.

"I'm sorry," said the doctor who had helped Trxx get born, whose name was Nxx. "It happens sometimes. Not very often. But it can happen. I'm so sorry," she said again, and she really was sorry.

Trxx didn't look like her brother, Pxx, when he was born; when Pxx was born he already had thick fur, over all his body, and on his feet he already had the beginnings of the thick tough pads that would protect his feet when he grew up and learned to walk. So did all the other babies born in the town that day, just as they had thick warm fur, red or brown or blue.

But Trxx didn't.

She didn't look like a baby of the planet Brxx at all. She looked a lot more like a baby of planet Earth. She looked like you and I looked when we were first born.

"Will she ever change?" asked Qxx. Her eyes filled with tears. "Will she ever grow fur and be like other people?"

"No," said Dr. Nxx, and her eyes filled with tears too. "No, she never will."

"Oh, my poor baby," said Qxx. She started to cry.

Fxx started to cry too. So did little Pxx.

The only one who didn't cry was baby Trxx.

"All right," said Fxx, and he wiped his eyes with the fur of his hands. "All right, no more crying for a while.

Not having fur is too bad. It's a bad deal, and it's going to be a lot of trouble for us, and a lot of trouble for Trxx. But she's our baby. And we love her."

"Just the way she is," said her brother Pxx.

"Yes," said her mother Qxx. "Just the way she is. And that's what matters most."

✿ ✿ ✿

"Look, Dad," Perry said. "Lily's jumping for joy."

Lily had recently figured out how to lift her whole body up off the floor with her crutches, like someone on a pogo stick; she lifted, dropped, lifted, dropped, in delight. Meg called it Jumping for Joy. Lily called it dancing. Sometimes she could turn herself around as she came down, so that she could actually jump in circles. She stopped after a while—it was surely pretty exhausting—and came to study what her father was doing.

"Is that the pin for Mom?" she said. He took it from its little box, out from its white blankets of cotton batting.

"Yes. Do you like it?"

Lily shrugged elaborately, who am I to say, but with a smirk of delight, in herself or the gesture or the day or the gift. The pin was dark steel, a pin for a coat lapel say, that was an arrow, made in such a way as to look when it was worn as though it pierced the fabric through, though it didn't really, it was an illusion; and on the arrow's top instead of an arrowhead was a hand, open, with a little garnet heart held in it.

"How are you going to wrap it? Is it going to be a surprise? Will she be surprised?"

"She's going to be so surprised."

"Do you know how to wrap it, Daddy?"

"Sure he knows," said Perry.

"Sure," John said. "I've got a plan. I can see it all."

It was John Nutting's strength and his weakness, as he had come to know: that seeing a thing as it might be or as he wanted it to be was to him what *having a plan* meant; that thought and care lavished on the picture of the thing that would come to be was the refining of the plan. What he'd thought of now, what he saw, was a heart, a full heart, a swollen heart, that could be opened and spill its contents—*what he had in his heart* was his idea. He had found a padded envelope of the kind you put fragile or special things in, that had a red stripe or tab or thread that the addressee was to pull to open. He wanted to somehow cut a heart shape out of this package in such a way that the pull-to-open stripe would run right down the center of the heart.

"Then see, Mom pulls the string thing, and the stuff inside comes out."

They looked at the parts of the project, what he had to put in, not themselves sure about this idea.

"You'll see," John said.

Inside the heart shape, before he sealed its edges with red tape (the dull brown color of the package was the downer part of the idea, but he couldn't see painting or coloring it), he was going to put a handful of candy hearts Along with these there was a long narrow strip of paper, folded accordion style, on which he had written these words:

> *Come on and TAKE A*
> *Take another little piece of my heart, now, baby—*
> *You know you got it, if it makes you feel good*

So what he hoped, or saw, was that when the package was opened the little hearts would spill out, and the long folded strip spring forth a little to be taken hold of and pulled out and read, and the steel pin with the garnet heart appear last shyly among all this show. She'd laugh and she'd see and know. The little hearts were the pastel candy kind with little remarks printed on them in pink. He told the kids that they were called *conversation hearts.*

"Oh you kid," Perry read, from a blue one.

"They're candy, right?" asked Lily.

"Well, sort of," John said. "I don't really know how good they are. I don't remember them being so hot. Not the point, in a way." Raggedy Ann and Andy had each had, under their rags and hidden within their stuffing, a conversation heart. It said *I love you* (as he remembered), and it was what animated them, brother and sister, made them live and talk. His own sister's Raggedy Ann doll was asserted to have one, but there was no way to be certain except to rip open her bosom and find it: his suggestion as to this was rejected.

"Cutie pie," read Perry. "Go girl. Get real."

He held that one out to Lily, who leaned forward, eyes closed and tongue out like a communicant, that same pious expectation too, and Perry put the heart on her tongue. He and John waited for her reaction. She let it melt, small smile on her face, then crushed it with open mouth. John then remembered the chalky tasteless sweetness.

"Be mine," Perry said. "New you. Howzat? Page me." He put on his Puzzlement face at that one, a comical screw.

"It means call me," John said. "Don't eat them all."

"Why not," said Perry, but this was another heart's message. He didn't seem tempted by them. His sister's reaction had not been enthusiastic. He often used her to test new edibles.

They'd thought, John and Meg, of getting a car phone: enough emergencies were now possible that it might be justified. Thinking, though, was all they'd done so far. Outside it was now all dark, and the falling snow was mounting without his monitoring its depth and intensity, which seemed to lessen his control of it, which was nil, then and now. If Meg left the meeting at five, she should be home by seven.

"Home soon," Perry said, and showed his father the yellow heart that said so.

[NEXT CHAPTER]

Soon Trxx went home with her mother and father and brother, wrapped in a soft blanket Dr. Nxx gave her.

She ate and slept and cried and made noises. She grew a little every day, and every day she saw new things and touched new things and heard new things. Everything in the world was new to Trxx, including Trxx herself.

She found out she had fingers and toes and learned to wiggle them. Soon she learned to smile and laugh. She laughed when her brother Pxx made faces at her, and when her mother tickled her, and when her father tossed her in the air and caught her.

She loved her mother and father and brother, and they loved her too, just the way she was. The hair on her head grew thicker and longer, but she never grew fur. She stayed just as she was when she was born.

Her mother and father learned to wrap Trxx up carefully in her warm blanket, and when it was cold at night they put her in between them on their bed to keep her warm. But when she learned to crawl she'd get out of her blanket and out from between her sleeping parents, and cry from the cold.

"If only we could figure out a way to keep this 'blanket' stuck on her, like fur," said Fxx.

They asked Dr. Nxx what to do. "What she needs is 'clothes,'" said Dr. Nxx.

"'Clothes?'" said Fxx and Qxx together.

"'Clothes' are like a blanket that fits over you and won't come off. All over. Nice and warm."

"All over?" said Qxx. "What about going to the bathroom?"

"Then you take them off."

"Every time?" said Qxx.

"Not all of them," the doctor said. "Don't worry. It's not as hard as it seems. You'll get used to it."

"And where," Fxx asked," do we get these 'clothes?'"

"I'll give you a prescription," said Dr. Nxx.

There was a shirt, and pants, and booties, and a little warm hat, and a warmer shirt to go over it all. The clothes cost a lot of flappers (that's what they call dollars on the planet Brxx), but at least they didn't come off every time Trxx wiggled, and leave her cold.

"How do you like it?" Qxx asked her daughter. "How do you like these clothes?"

Trxx just smiled and giggled. Her mother had never seen a baby that looked like Trxx with her clothes on, and she didn't know whether to laugh or cry.

Trxx grew fast, and needed more clothes all the time. They got dirty and had to be cleaned. They ripped and split as Trxx got bigger. The buttons fell off and rolled away and got lost.

"You'll need more buttons," Dr. Nxx said. "And some of this 'thread' and a 'needle.' Then you can sew the buttons on again when they come off."

"Hm," said Fxx. He took the tiny needle in his big hands. He'd never seen anything so impossible. "And where do we . . ."

"I'll give you a prescription," said Dr. Nxx.

Winter came, and the weather got warm and the sun shone brightly. (On the planet Brxx it's warm in the winter and cold in the summer.) At last Trxx didn't need to get wrapped up in her shirt and pants and her socks and her other shirt and her little warm hat every day. She could go out with nothing on.

On a hot winter day Trxx's mother took her to the park to play without her clothes in the sun.

"Nice?" asked her mother.

"Nice," said Trxx. It was her first word.

But the other people in the park didn't think it was so nice. Some of them looked at Trxx all naked and furless, and their mouths would curl up in a way that seemed to mean they thought seeing Trxx all naked was creepy, or sad, or too bad. Other kids stopped what they were doing and stared at her.

"Does it hurt?" one person asked Qxx.

"No," said Qxx. "It doesn't hurt."

"Is she sick?" another person asked.

"No," Qxx said. "She's not sick."

"What happened to her?"

"She was born this way," said Qxx. "She's fine."

Trxx didn't know what the people were saying, and when they stared at her she stared back at them, and smiled.

But her brother Pxx hated the questions people asked.

"Why can't they mind their own business?" he said.

"They're curious," said Qxx.

"Well, they should butt out," Pxx said.

"Why don't you go play whackball with those boys?" said Qxx.

But Pxx didn't want to leave his sister. He was bored and wanted to do something else, but he was afraid that if he left, something bad would happen to Trxx, even though he couldn't imagine what it would be. He didn't like the way people looked at her, and he didn't want her to be different.

"I wish I could give her my fur," he said. "If I could, I would."

"Fine," said his mother. "Then we'd have to buy clothes for *you*."

And then she put her arm around her son's shoulder and hugged him hard.

✳ ✳ ✳

"So how are the kids?" Anne-Marie asked Meg. "I never asked." Meg would have liked to order a great gleaming bowl of scarlet wine like the one Anne-Marie now lifted and sampled; but Anne-Marie was going home by cab, and Meg had a couple of hours of driving between here and home. The snow had just begun to show itself as something more than a bother out the windows.

"The kids are good. No bad news."

Anne-Marie laughed a little. "The only person I know who'd answer that question that way."

"Well, they're fine. They do the things. They knock you out. They . . . I don't know. They're like the weather."

Anne-Marie's eyes, which could be beautiful when wide, were somewhat reptilian when hooded in doubt, if doubt was what she felt as she regarded Meg.

"So you got a chance to read that kid's book thing," Meg asked.

"I did. I liked it. It was fascinating. You know I love your things."

Meg waited for more.

"I gave it to someone who knows this market," Anne-Marie said. "I got a report and I made some notes." She plunged into her bag and did some business with papers that seemed to have come from a phone pad. "Did you know they have people at publishers of children's books who analyze the vocabulary, to see if the words used match the intended age of the readers?"

"Well, I can imagine."

"They do."

"So what did this person think?"

"Well, there's problems. Of course she liked it and wanted you to know that."

Meg said nothing.

Anne-Marie glanced at her notes. "She says. It's too short for a chapter book, but the words and sentences are too hard for an I-can-read-it-myself book, and the subject matter is too hard for a picture book."

"Really."

"Another thing," Anne-Marie said, putting the notes away. "In a kid's book, as she sees it, and I believe this, you can't go switching the point of view too often. It's best to stick to one point of view, one kid or one animal or one grandma or whatever. I think you especially can't have parents' point of view overwhelming the child's point of view. I think that happens in this."

"I didn't realize there were so many rules," Meg said. "In fact, actually I don't think there *are* so many. I know the books Perry and Lily love. There's not always . . ." She stopped then, though, because she saw she had come up on a crux that arises between writer and agent, or writer and publisher, or writer and reader finally: they see something wrong, something that fails, and they don't really know how to say what it is, something in the toils of the story, sometimes in its core, but what is it? They think they know, and they say "The plot's not involving" or "The characters aren't sympathetic" or "The point of view is wrong," which sound like objective errors being pinned down, but which, *a*, aren't that at all but only a way of saying I don't like it, and *b*, are therefore impossible to counter with reasonable arguments, and *c*, no good at all to you as the writer. The only thing worse than leaving it as it is, wounded and feeble, would be to try to fix it by the formulas they give you.

"Listen," Anne-Marie said. "I know how important this is to you. I know what you're trying to do with this, to write about the prejudice, the prejudice against people who are different. I get that, and I of course understand. But I just don't think it's going to fly in the children's book world. Something that's so, you know, directly instructional. They just shy away from stuff like that."

"Uh-huh."

"I wonder if there's some way to get it out under the sponsorship of some group."

"Some group?"

"Well, you know, a group that has an educational purpose. Like a group that deals with the problem this is addressing."

Meg could see the kind of book or booklet Anne-Marie meant. Such things were in every waiting room she went to with Lily, every office. "Okay," she said. "Never mind. It was just a thing. Thanks for checking it out."

"It's not going to go to waste," Anne-Marie said.

"No. I know. Look, Anne-Marie, I appreciate your trying."

Anne-Marie drank. "So to get back to your prenatal diagnosis piece."

"Sure."

"They're very interested in it, but you know how it is. If they don't get involved they think they aren't important and don't really have a job."

"Okay." A weariness had begun to spread upward from her feet or her knees toward her heart and head. She'd only wanted to do an article, a think piece, but Anne-Marie thought she could get a book deal, and Meg hadn't said no yet.

"First there's what you want to call it—'*A New Delphic Oracle*'? Isn't that a little, I don't know, remote?"

"Well, you know what the Delphic oracle was, right?"

"Darling, of course I know, but will your readers and book-buyers know? What are you hoping they'll get from this title?"

"Well, I thought it was good because of the ambiguity. Oracles are true, but you don't know in what sense, until they've come true. They can be true and yet turn out not to mean at all what you thought they meant. And you have to beware of bringing into being the thing you first thought the oracle meant, usually by trying to avoid it."

"Like Oedipus."

"Right."

"So this relates how?"

Meg crossed her hands as in prayer and bent toward her agent, the only agent she'd ever had. "You get a prenatal diagnosis. Your child has some anomaly. It's there; it has a name, a prognosis. You try to understand what it means, for the child's life, for your life. The doctors think they know. You do your best to act on what you think it means, and what the docs think it means. But maybe you also start to *bring about* that outcome by how you interpret the information. Maybe all of us do, the parents, teachers, docs, grandparents. And maybe you bring about a good outcome. Or not. Maybe not as good as it could be."

Anne-Marie was one of the first to know about the ultrasound that showed Lily would have problems. It was just a routine scan, and done in Boston; she and Meg had planned on lunch after. "Okay," she said.

"Then at the far end, you look back and say Yes, it was predicted to be this way. This was what the oracle said, this is what was there all along. But it wasn't. Not necessarily; not all of it; not what it's *like.* What you hope is that you'll learn better as you go, learn that the possibilities are greater than they seemed."

"So the oracle can bring about what it predicts. That's a responsibility. Because the oracle might be wrong."

"The oracle isn't wrong," Meg said. "It just isn't determining. *You* determine. You and the gods. The Greeks knew."

"They knew everything." Anne-Marie lit a cigarette, this restaurant being one that let her, which is why she came here. "Except the book business."

Meg reached for the gloves that lay beside her plate. The sense of hopeless incapacity got a little higher: the book business, other people, the weather; the things her life had come to be about, the fight against prediction. "Anne-Marie I've got to go. I'm getting scared. It's been coming down heavier ever since we got here."

"Weatherman said only a couple of inches."

"Yeah?" Meg said. "That's what he predicted?"

They both laughed. "We'll do this," Anne-Marie, said. "I feel it'll work out."

"Sure," Meg said. "What's that thing the Chinese say? Tell me again, Auntie Anne-Marie."

"The Chinese say," Anne-Marie said, her favorite catch-phrase, "'When we reach the mountain, the road upward will appear.'"

[CHAPTER AFTER THE ONE BEFORE]

Trxx grew up. She learned to talk. She was angry sometimes and cried sometimes and sometimes she wanted everything in the world and she wanted it *right now* and really screamed. But most of the time she was happy. "As happy as the day is long," said Qxx.

"What does that mean?" Trxx asked her.

"I don't know what it means. But it's what you are. Now where's your shirt?"

"Shirt! I don't want to!"

"Here it is!" said Pxx.

Pxx had learned to help his mother put on Trxx's clothes and take them off and even wash and dry them. But Trxx took a lot of time to get dressed, and changed; she couldn't run out of the house every morning like Pxx could, because she had to get dressed first.

And sometimes she didn't want to get dressed at all.

"Shirt!"

"I don't want to!" said Trxx, and started to run.

"Shirt!" said Pxx, and chased after her,

"Trxx!" said her mother, and chased after her too.

Imagine: Trxx was nearly six, and she was smart and handy, and she still couldn't put on her own clothes! But that was because she didn't know she was supposed to be able to, and neither did her mother or her father. Nobody said to her: "Oh, everybody who's six can put their own shirt on! Everybody who's six can tie their own shoes!"

Because nobody else could.

Of course all the other kids in the neighborhood where Trxx grew up had thick fur, black or blue or red, and thick pads on the soles of their feet, just like her brother Pxx. Some were older than Trxx, and were mostly her brother's friends; and some were just her age.

Mostly the kids in the neighborhood liked Trxx and played with her and didn't think all the time that she was the Girl Who Had No Fur.

But sometimes her friends talked to her as though she were a baby, and sometimes they treated her as though she were a doll or a pet. Sometimes they wanted to be best friends, and sometimes they told her to go away, because she couldn't play the same games as other people.

They weren't really being mean. They just forgot, sometimes, that—except for having no fur—Trxx was just like them.

"So are you going to go to school?" they asked her one cold day of summer, when everybody was thinking about school starting. All of Trxx's friends were going to be in the first grade.

"Sure," said Trxx.

"You are?"

"Sure. Why not?"

All of Trxx's friends stared at Trxx, and looked at each other as though they knew something she didn't know.

When Trxx came in from playing, she had a blister on her ankle.

"Trxx!" her mother said. "You have to wear a *sock* with your *shoe* or you get a blister. You know that!"

"Mom," Trxx said. "Am I really going to go to school?"

"You bet you are, my darling dear," her mother said. "You bet you are."

"But," Trxx said. "What if the teacher doesn't like people with no fur?"

"She does. You met her, Trxx. She likes you."

"What if the kids don't like people with no fur?"

"They'll like you. Some of them are your own friends, Trxx."

Her mom was trying to clean Trxx's ankle and get a bandage on. It took her a long time, because she had only done it once before. *Your* mom does it very quickly, because she's put bandages on blisters ever since she was a little kid herself.

"What if my shoes come untied?" Trxx said. "Who will tie them?"

"I'll come to school at lunchtime," her mother said. "Just to check." She helped Trxx put on one shoe. "And pretty soon, Trxx, you'll be able to tie them yourself."

"I can't!"

"You'll learn. I learned. Watch."

Qxx tied Trxx's shoes again. While she tried to tie the lace, her tongue came out and curled up. Her furry fingers got stuck in the laces. You could have tied Trxx's shoes in a minute, but Trxx's mother took a long time.

One day Qxx found about another child in town who had also been born with no fur.

"Is it a girl?" Trxx asked. "Like me?"

"No, a boy," said her mother. "His name is Jaxx."

"How old is he?" Trxx wanted to know. "Six, like me?"

"He's eight," said her mother. "But I think he's very nice."

Trxx and her mother got ready to go visit the boy with no fur. It was a cold day in summer, and they had to put on almost every piece of clothes Trxx had.

"Someday," said Qxx to her daughter, "you are going to have to learn to do all these things for yourself!" She was a little impatient and tugged and pulled Trxx's clothes on.

"I will," Trxx said. "Someday."

"*And* tie your shoes."

"I will," Trxx said. "Someday."

"Someday *soon*," said her mother.

Trxx watched her mother and thought: *I'll never learn.*

But she would.

The boy who had no fur lived on the other side of town, and Qxx and Trxx took the buxx to see him. On the buxx, a woman with bright orange fur kept staring at Trxx. Trxx stared back, and smiled. When Trxx smiled, she saw a little tear well up in the lady's eye.

"Brave little thing!" the woman said. "Brave little tyke, putting up with so much!"

"Oh good grief," Qxx said, so only Trxx could hear. She looked down at her daughter and rolled her eyes so only Trxx could see. Trxx laughed, because that was what her mother always did when people said that Trxx was brave. She said *Oh good grief* and rolled her eyes.

Trxx wondered why people thought she was brave to have no fur. She was brave when she climbed tall trees and brave when she went to sleep with no night light and brave when she got a shot without freaking out. But what was so brave about having no fur and having to wear clothes?

"I don't understand people sometimes, Mom," she said.

"Neither do I, darling," said her mother. "But then I think a lot of people don't understand us, either."

Jaxx and his mother were glad to see Trxx and Qxx. *They* could understand one another just fine.

"Having no fur sort of runs in our family," Jaxx's mother said. She showed them a funny old picture. "My great-uncle Braxx had the same condition. He used to travel with a circus, along with the sword-swallower and the fire-eater. He was called 'Braxx the All-Bare, The Amazing Furless Man.' He had some clothes made that looked just like most people's fur. He would slowly pull them off, until he had nothing on. Just skin. Some people would faint."

"Wasn't he embarrassed?" Trxx asked. "With all those people looking at him?"

"Well, not after a while. He said he loved show business. And people did pay a flapper apiece to see him."

———

While Qxx and Jaxx's mother sat in the kitchen and drank hot gurgle and talked about where to get clothes made cheap, Jaxx and Trxx played together.

They talked while they played, about everything in the world. About clothes and how awful they were. About what it would be like if it were hot in the summer and cold in the winter, instead of the other way around the way it is on the planet Brxx. They talked about getting sunburned (nobody else knew what that felt like) and going swimming naked (nobody else knew what that felt like, either).

Jaxx called other people "the furballs" and made Trxx laugh.

"Jaxx," she said. "I have a question."

"What's the question?" said Jaxx.

"What do you say when a little kid or somebody comes up to you and stares at you and goes *What's the matter with you?*"

"That's easy," Jaxx said. "I tell them I'm from another planet." He stood up and stuck out his chest. "I tell them I came here to Brxx from another planet, and I tell them that on *my* planet *nobody* has fur and everybody looks like me. And that on my planet I have super-powers so they better watch out."

Trxx laughed. Trxx's mother laughed too, and Jaxx's mother smiled and shook her head.

"And," said Jaxx, "I tell them that if any *furballs* ever ended up on my planet, we'd probably put them in the zoo."

Trxx laughed so hard she almost fell down. She didn't think Jaxx really said that to people who asked him *What's wrong with you?* or *What happened to you?* But ever after, when somebody asked her a question like that, she would think of Jaxx, and laugh.

* * *

A week or two after the ultrasound had shown them Lily wound palely inside Meg, her flawed spine traceable like the spine of a translucent guppy, a snowstorm like this one had fallen over their house. It was one of those spring snowstorms that come down in big sodden flakes and layer the trees as though with thick pudding or wet wash, comical-seeming snow that's not funny in fact; it began in the night and when morning came and John went out to the porch it was grievous. The tall arbor-vitae cedars that stood in pairs on the corners of the lot were so heavy-headed that they had bent nearly double, and the low branches of the big firs in the back were laid down into the mounting heap as though consumed. As soon as the fall of it subsided, John pulled on boots and took a broom and a long-handled plastic rake and labored out through it to the cedars, to try to knock off enough snow to release them, so they wouldn't break; he beat at the branches and combed with the plastic rake, and some of the branches did lift away like arms freed from shackles, and the tree raised its head a little, but some of the branches, some of the biggest too and not the small springy ones, didn't snap free. Broken. One whole secondary trunk of the smaller of the pair, broken, unresponsive. When he had done all he could, throat seared with cold and boots filled with snow, he made his way to the firs, going down on his knees once as he waded forward. God damn it, he breathed. God damn it. It was so unfair, a snow so heavy, so wrong that spring could come so close and then do this. He reached the firs and it was the same: he beat at the bound limbs to knock away their burden and some lifted free and grateful, amazing resilience, flinging snow in his face as they went up, but some not, inert, unable to rise, broken, you couldn't see beneath the smothering snow which was hurt and which wasn't. He tugged at them with icy hands to pull them free, but some wouldn't come up when he had loosened them, couldn't spring.

He sat back at last exhausted. He was weeping in anger and hurt. God damn it, he said again and again. God damn New England. Cruel, cruel New England.

Perry and Lily had grown tired of valentines; they piled theirs in two piles and John hid away the valentine for Meg to put with her breakfast next day. Then he made popcorn for dinner, something Meg sometimes did on nights of emergency or hurry or many urgent claims, which this seemed somehow to be even though they couldn't do anything but sit. When a car came close and stopped—they could only see its lights and hear the slow milling of its tires out on the road—it turned out to be the newspaper deliverer, hero or dope out on his rounds in his ancient Chevy Malibu. Perry pulled on boots and coat and went out to the box at the driveway's end to get their paper, and then sat eating popcorn and turning big pages one by one, reading the headlines aloud, letting Lily and John know the news. The high school was putting on *A Midsummer Night's Dream* and there were to be real flying fairies in it.

"It's a play by Shakespeare," John said. "There are fairies in it."

"Real flying fairies?"

"Well, actually it says with wires," John said, looking over Perry's shoulder.

Perry studied the text, brows knit with effort to decode the false claims. Kids from middle school were being recruited to be Peaseblossom and Cobweb. Flying. Perry wondered if he envied them.

"Usually the fairies don't fly in this play," John said. "They just well sort of trip."

"They *trip?*" asked Lily. That smile of wonder she had at things, at things she didn't get, as though they tickled her by their weirdness. Always. When she'd started to talk, her first complete sentence was *Where'd come from?* About some object that she hadn't suspected would be produced before her, what was it, a bar of Castile soap, a rubber duck, a bunch of flowers. *Where'd come from?* In delight and confusion.

"I mean they sort of dance along. Tripping." He did some tripping, little steps, winglike arms fluttering delicately. "Where the bee sucks, there suck I," he sang in falsetto. "In the cowslip's bell I lie."

Perry danced too, flying; then pretended to trip and fall, flail to stay upright, trip again, regain balance. Lily jumped and spun. The phone rang and stilled them.

"How is it there?" Meg asked.

"It's not good. They're saying six to eight inches. But you know how it is. Every county's different. It could be okay all the way till you start up the hills."

"Well, I'm coming," Meg said. "We're done here."

"How did it go?"

"I'll explain," she said. "What are you guys doing?"

"Tripping," said John.

[NEXT-TO-LAST CHAPTER]

Every weekmiddle, Fxx, Trxx's father, went to play whackball with his friends. (On the planet Brxx, they don't have weekends, but they do take two days off in the middle of the week, and that's called the weekmiddle.)

Fxx was an excellent whackball player, and over time he had practiced and got better and better. Almost every time he played, he beat his friends easily.

One weekmiddle day after they had finished a game and Fxx had won again, he said with a grin: "Well, this isn't much fun."

His friends agreed. They decided the only way to make the game fun again was to give Fxx a *handicap*. That means they made it harder for Fxx to play, so that the game would be more even. What they did was to make Fxx tie one hand behind his back.

With the handicap, one hand tied behind his back, Fxx had to try much harder. He had to think carefully at every stroke. His friends got way ahead at first, and though Fxx did well, considering his handicap, one of his friends won that game.

As they were all laughing together at the end of the game, Fxx suddenly had a thought:

This must be what it's like for Trxx, he thought. Trxx is playing with a handicap. She's just like everybody else, but with something taken away. Like my hand tied behind my back.

When he came home that night he told Qxx what he had thought of. "Trxx is playing with a handicap," he said. "She's just like everybody else, but with something missing."

"Hmm," said Qxx.

"That means she has to try harder, but if she does, she can do anything she wants."

"Hmm," said Qxx. "I don't know. I have to think about that." She didn't like thinking that Trxx was like everybody else, except with something missing. But maybe Fxx was right.

That night Qxx dreamed that there really was a planet like the one Jaxx pretended he came from. She dreamed she went there in a spaceship.

On this planet everyone was like Trxx and Jaxx: they had no fur at all, only a little hair on the tops of their heads or on their faces. All of them, every one, had to wear clothes all the time, and shoes too.

She saw them, in her dream, going up and down the streets, in and out of the stores and houses, every one of them in their clothes: shoes and socks and pants and coats and hats and scarfs and mittens.

Some of the stores they went in sold nothing but clothes. Of course! If everyone needed them, they would be for sale everywhere! No wondering where to get them, no prescription from the doctor! Store after store with clothes for men and women, little clothes for boys and girls, whole stores with nothing but tiny clothes for babies! Qxx almost cried in her dream to see them.

In their houses, these people had special little rooms to put all their different clothes in, and special hangers to hang them on. They had long mirrors in their bedrooms to look at themselves in and see if their clothes were straight and neat. People didn't have just one set of clothes or two sets, they had many different sets, dozens of different shirts and socks and scarves and hats. They had clothes to go swimming in. They had clothes to go to bed in.

They even had clothes for their beds!

And the most amazing thing of all was that nobody thought that wearing clothes was strange.

Qxx laughed in her dream as she sailed over this amazing impossible planet. She thought: If nobody has fur, then not having fur is normal.

The people of this planet didn't think it was brave to wear clothes; they didn't think it was dreadful, and they didn't think it was special. They didn't mind wearing them, or buying them, or keeping them clean. No little tear welled up in people's eyes when they saw children in their funny clothes; nobody made the creepy mouth to see other people without their clothes on and their bare skin showing; nobody made fun of them, either.

Wearing clothes was normal.

Qxx dreamed that she landed her spaceship and stepped out. And in her dream, Qxx saw the people of the planet turn to look at her. And she looked down at herself to see the bright red fur that clothed her from head to foot.

Qxx understood, just then, how Trxx felt when people stared at her and tried to figure her out. It was very uncomfortable.

The people of the planet in their clothes and hats and shoes came closer, with expressions of amazement and even fear on their bare faces. Qxx thought some of them might faint, as the people did who came to see Braxx the All-Bare.

"Hey," said Qxx. She held out her arms to show herself, furry as could be. "Hey! It's normal for me!" Then she woke up.

* * *

This prejudice against people who are different. Meg pondered that, Anne-Marie's summary of what her probably foolish little book had been about, and wondered how she'd got that idea. Was there something in it that would push a reader toward that, or was it just what the reader expected to see there and so saw it anyway? Anne-Marie was probably right that it wasn't really a children's book at all, only sort of seemed like one, but what it was *about* ought to have been clear. If everybody could fly (Meg explained to no one), then anyone who couldn't would be at a disadvantage: even though they'd be just as able as they are now. Because everything would be arranged for people who could fly. That's all. "That's all," she said aloud, and just then realized she had been carelessly turning out of her lane into a less-plowed one to pass a truck. She felt her heart in her mouth (one of those phrases that make no sense until you've felt it) and fell back with care into the safer lane, her wipers wiping furiously at the snow flung up by the truck.

Pay attention, she said within. I'll pay attention.

It was a long time, but she was now in sight of what she thought of as the half way mark, the stacks of a chemical plant of some kind, lit luridly, hard to apprehend from a distance, its floodlit smoke rising into the blowing snow, like a Turner storm done in black and white. Half way. But now along the road she began to see cars on the margins, in the breakdown lane, sometimes askew or otherwise seeming not to be there on purpose; sometimes a dome-light on, shining within a car rapidly coming to be covered with snow, a lamp lit in an igloo. It was bad. It was evidently and obviously really not good. She began to think that it was stupid, she'd been stupid, should have stayed over, found a hotel, she was almost beginning to think she should pull off now into the streets of Sturbridge or Brimfield and find a motel: she could envision the streets she would have to get through, the quick-falling snow veiling the streetlights, the local plows maybe not out, no it was hopeless: she told herself so, told herself it wasn't the way you do this, considering hopeless alternatives, visualizing hopeless escapes. You just keep on: you keep on and cover every mile, one at a time, not in advance or in hope but only by doing it, and only counting it as done when it was done. Just keep on, she thought. Just keep on steady.

John thought of her thinking these things, envisioned her seeing these things, both the cars she saw along the highway margins and the streets and roads of villages that she pictured; he thought of her going on, telling herself how to go on. So often had they both traveled that stretch of Interstate, going to or from things that had been hard or impossible to imagine in advance or carrying home consequences that couldn't be calculated: operations and consultations and examinations. Prognoses. He could see her, the seat snugged up tightly to the steering wheel the way she liked it, both her hands at the top of the wheel and her head slightly forward, as though to see a little farther into what was coming.

[LAST CHAPTER]

When Qxx woke up she remembered: today is the first day of school.

"Mom!" Trxx called. "Help!"

Qxx jumped up. Outside the cold wind blew and the rain fell. It was a cold summer day. Trxx was trying to get her shirt on, and her head was stuck in the head hole, and her left arm was stuck in the right arm hole.

She was learning to put on her own clothes, but sometimes she got confused.

Trxx was up especially early, because her mother knew it would take her longer than most kids to get ready for school. After all, if you're covered with thick fur, and you don't wear jammies and you don't wear clothes, all you have to do is get up, eat your crackles and drink your slurp, brush your teeth, and go. You don't even have to make your bed!

But Trxx took longer. Even when everybody helped.

"Shoes," said Fxx. "On."

"No no," said Qxx. "Socks first, remember?"

"Ah," said Fxx. Socks."

"Pants," said Pxx.

"No no," said Trxx. "Underpants first!"

"Oh yeah," said Pxx.

"Mittens!" Qxx said to Trxx. "Hat!"

When Trxx was all ready, and her hair was brushed (and Pxx's fur was brushed) and her hat was tied on and her scarf was knotted around her neck, the others stood for a minute and looked at her.

"Hey," said Fxx. "First grader!"

Trxx was all ready to go when she decided to have one more bite of crackles and one more sip of slurp to give her strength. But when she picked up her big cup in her mitten hand, it slipped. It started to slip and kept on slipping faster while everybody stared in horror and couldn't move.

Then Pxx jumped and tried to catch the cup. Too late!

"Oh no! Trxx!"

"Oops," said Trxx. "Oh no."

Trxx was covered from scarf to shoes with sticky brown slurp. Ugh!

Her coat was wet, and so they took that off. Underneath, her shirt was wet, so they took that off too, and her pants. Underneath her pants her underpants were wet, so they took them off.

The stuff had even got into her shoes. Her socks were wet, and she had to take them off too.

Then they had to start all over again.

"I can't do this," Trxx moaned. "I'll never be able to."

"You can do anything you want," said Qxx. "You can do what you want to do. It just takes you a little longer."

"A *lot* longer," Trxx said angrily.

"Sometimes a lot longer," said Qxx.

"Like hours."

"Then we'll get up earlier," said Qxx.

"Then I'll be tired."

"We'll go to sleep earlier."

"Oop, there they go," said Pxx.

He pointed out the window.

Across the field the other kids were running and tumbling and yelling and chasing after each other on their way to school. The wind howled and the cold rain fell, but the kids laughed at it. In school they would sit in their seats in their warm coats and the smell of drying fur would fill the room.

Trxx looked after them. They were getting farther and farther away. She was going to be last.

Of course.

For a minute, just for a minute, Trxx decided that she would never put on her stupid clothes ever again, and never go outside again, just stay inside and cover herself up with her mother and father the way she had when she was a baby, and sleep forever.

That made her sad.

And then she got mad.

Suddenly she jumped up. "Okay!" she said. "Underpants!"

"Underpants," Qxx said. "Right." She found underpants.

"Socks!" Trxx shouted. "One for each foot!" She struggled into her underpants while her parents and Pxx looked for her only other pair of socks.

Fxx brought the socks. Trxx pulled them on.

"Shoes!" Trxx shouted, like a general in a war. "Shirt! Pants! Coat!"

Pxx and Fxx found a sort-of clean shirt and the shoes and her old pants. Trxx pulled her shoes on.

Then she tied them.

"Trxx!" said her mother. "You tied your shoes!"

Everybody looked down at Trxx's shoes.

"You did it," said Pxx. "Wow."

Trxx looked down at her shoes too, and they seemed a little bit farther away than they had been the day before. Maybe she was getting taller.

"You did it," said her father.

"Sure," she said. "Mom, I'm late!"

She grabbed her bag and Pxx grabbed his bag and they ran out (they didn't need to open the door, because there wasn't any door) and ran across the field.

Qxx and Fxx stood in the doorway waving to their children.

"I forgot to get a kiss," said Fxx. "Shucks."

Qxx saw Trxx stop and bend down to tie her shoe again. When she bent over her hat fell off. She picked it up and jammed it on her head, and then ran after Pxx.

Qxx thought of the dream she had dreamed, where everyone in the world had no fur, and wore clothes.

If *everybody* had to get dressed every morning, Trxx wouldn't be last: not every time. Somebody else would forget their socks or their hat or forget how to tie their shoes.

"Tough job," said Fxx.

"You're wrong," Qxx said.

"It's not a tough job?"

"I mean what you said yesterday. About Trxx."

"Oh?"

"It's not true."

"What did I say?" Fxx asked

Fxx had said that Trxx was the same as everyone else, except that she had a *handicap*—something taken away or held back from her, something normal people had but she didn't have, something she had to get along without.

But that wasn't true.

Trxx *wasn't* the same as everyone else.

No one is the same as everyone else.

Trxx was Trxx, and the way Trxx was was normal for Trxx.

"Life isn't whackball," she said to Fxx.

Fxx looked surprised. "I never said it was," he said.

"Well don't forget it," said Qxx. "Trxx isn't a normal person with something missing. Trxx is Trxx. She's being all she can be, and that's as much as you or me or Pxx or anyone on this planet can be."

Qxx put her furry arm through Fxx's furry arm. She watched her daughter as she ran out of sight.

"It's all that anyone can be," she said. "On any planet anywhere."

* * *

"There she is," said John. "There she is."

"There she is," the kids said, who had never doubted she would come, did not yet need to wonder whether she might not. Silently she'd entered the driveway, the car's sound swallowed with all other sound by the snow, but the searching lights sweeping over the dark lawn as she turned in to the driveway and then illuminating the closed door of the garage, they could see the light from the kitchen, sign of homecoming. Once, you left a light burning for the returning one; now the returning one's own lights brought her home, announced her arrival.

O You Kid. I Love You. Way to Go. What A Babe. Love Life. Page Me. U R Mine. Lily and Perry followed him to the door out to the garage, welcoming committee; Lily watched her father and Perry go to pull up the door, watched the car creep forward through the drift by now as high as the bumpers, chewing the snow as it came forward, coming breathing hotly into the bright space.

"Hi, hi."

"God, some night."

"Yes. We were worried."

"I'm all right," Meg said, climbing out. The car's underparts were thick with clotted snow like a wintering buffalo's.

"Did Anne-Marie like your book?" Perry asked.

"Not much," Meg said.

"Uh-oh," Perry said.

Of course she was all right. She was all right all along, or at least now it was evident that all along she had been all right. John Nutting felt a spasm of recapitulatory relief of a kind he was becoming familiar with, though he hadn't known it in his life, or at least he hadn't noticed it—until the day Lily first got out of the hospital.

"Mom!" Lily cried to her from the door. "Come see what we made! Dad made a heart! We made valentines!"

"I'm coming, hon, I'm coming."

It had been snowing that day too on their planet, the day Lily got out, but only a few flakes blown around out of an iron sky, almost too cold for snow. Lily was nearly a month old and had yet to see outdoors, yet to be outside the hospital where she'd been born. Meg had gone to the parking garage to get the car and told John to bring Lily out to the curb and watch for it. So it was he who took her out. He lifted her from the hospital bassinet at the exit door and wrapped her in her own blanket, bought for her by her grandmother before she was born, hope against hope, and he tugged her hat down; made her a papoose inside the blanket, pressed her to him, and (tugging down his own hat) he just walked out into the day, a con walking free after having finished his sentence, or con-man having pulled off his scam. Don't look back. Lucky, he'd felt so damn lucky, knew they were all lucky, though what he and she and Meg from now on would mean by "lucky" might not be what everyone else meant. They weren't the same as everyone else: no one is. *You're out* he'd said in exalted won-derment to her small face. *You got out, Lily. You got out.* And of course she had, because here she now was, Jumping for Joy as her mother came into the house on a gust of cold air. That's how it is, how it would be, for them all: when they had come through all right, it would be seen that of course, all along they must have: all along.

Flint and Mirror

[*Editor's note: The following pages were recently discovered among uncatalogued papers of the novelist Fellowes Kraft (1897-1964) that came to the Rasmussen Foundation by bequest following his death. They comprise thirty-four typewritten sheets of yellow copy paper (Sphinx brand) edited lightly in pencil, apparently intended to be a part of Kraft's second novel, A Passage at Arms (1941), now long out of print and unavailable. In the end these pages were rejected by the author, perhaps because the work had evolved into a more conventional historical fiction. The mathematician and spiritual adventurer John Dee would appear in later Kraft works, both finished and unfinished, in rather different character than he does here.*]

Blind O'Mahon the poet said: "In Ireland there are five king-doms, one in each of the five directions. There was a time when each of the kingdoms had her king, and a court, and a castle-seat with lime-washed towers; battlements of spears, and armies young and laughing."

"There was a high king then too," said Hugh O'Neill, ten years old, seated at O'Mahon's feet in the grass, still green at Hallowtide. From the hill where they sat the Great Lake could just be seen, turning from silver to gold as the light went. The roving herds of cattle—Ulster's wealth—moved over the folded land. All this is O'Neill territory, and always forever has been.

"There was indeed a high king," O'Mahon said.

"And will be again."

The wind stirred the poet's white hair. O'Mahon could not see Hugh, his cousin, but—he said—he could see the wind. "Now cousin," he said. "See how well the world is made. Each kingdom of Ireland has its own renown: Connaught in the west for learning and for magic, the writing of books and annals, and the dwelling-places of saints. In the north, Ulster"—he swept his hand over lands he couldn't see—"for courage, battles, and warriors. Leinster in the east for hospitality, for open doors and feasting, cauldrons never empty. Munster in the south for labor, for kerns and ploughmen, weaving and droving, birth and death."

Hugh looking over the long view, the winding of the river where clouds were gathered now, asked: "Which is the greatest?"

"Which," O'Mahon said, pretending to ponder this. "Which do you think?"

"Ulster," said Hugh O'Neill of Ulster. "Because of the warriors. Cuchulain was of Ulster, who beat them all."

"Ah."

"Wisdom and magic are good," Hugh conceded. "Hosting is good. But warriors can beat them."

O'Mahon nodded to no one. "The greatest kingdom," he said, "is Munster."

Hugh said nothing to that. O'Mahon's hand sought for his shoulder and rested upon it, and Hugh knew he meant to explain. "In every kingdom," he said, "the North, the South, the East, and the West, there is also a north, a south, an east, a west. Isn't that so?"

"Yes," Hugh said. He could point to them: left, right, ahead, behind. Ulster is in the north, and yet in Ulster there is also a north, the north of the north: that's where his mad, bad uncle Shane ruled. And so in that north, Shane's north, there must be again a north and a south, an east and a west. And then again . . .

"Listen," O'Mahon said. "Into each kingdom comes wisdom from the west, about what the world is and how it came to be. Courage from the north, to defend the world from what would swallow it up. Hospitality from the east to praise both learning and courage, and reward the kings who keep the world as it is. But before all these things, there is a world at all: a world to learn about, to defend, to praise, to keep. It is from Munster at first that the world comes to be."

"Oh," Hugh said, no wiser though. "But you said that there were five kingdoms."

"So I did. And so it is said."

Connaught, Ulster, Leinster, Munster. "What is the fifth kingdom?"

"Well, cousin," O'Mahon said, "what is it then?"

"Meath," Hugh guessed. "Where Tara is, where the kings were crowned."

"That's fine country. Not north or south or east or west but in the middle."

He said no more about that, and Hugh felt sure that the answer might be otherwise. "Where else could it be?" he asked.

O'Mahon only smiled. Hugh wondered if, blind as he was, he knew when he smiled and that others saw it. A kind of shudder fled along his spine, cold in the low sun. "But then," he said, "it might be far away."

"It might," O'Mahon said. "It might be far away, or it might be close." He chewed on nothing for a moment, and then he said: "Tell me this, cousin: Where is the center of the world?"

That was an old riddle; even boy Hugh knew the answer to it, his uncle Phelim's brehon had asked it of him. There are five directions to the world: four of them are north, south, east and west, and where is the fifth? He knew the answer, but just at that moment, sitting with bare legs crossed in the ferns in sight of the tower of Dungannon, he did not want to give it.

It was in the spring that his fosterers the O'Hagans had brought Hugh O'Neill to the castle at Dungannon. It was a great progress in the boy Hugh's eyes, twenty or thirty horses jingling with brass trappings, carts bearing gifts for his O'Neill uncles at Dungannon, red cattle lowing in the van, spearmen and bowmen and women in bright scarves, O'Hagans and O'Quinns and their dependents. And he knew himself, but ten years old, to be the center of that progress, on a dappled pony, with a new mantle wrapped around his skinny body and a new ring on his finger.

He kept seeming to recognize the environs of the castle, and scanned the horizon for it, and questioned his cousin Phelim, who had come to fetch him to Dungannon, how far it was every hour until Phelim grew annoyed and told him to ask next when he saw it. When at last he did see it, a fugitive sun was just then looking out, and sunshine glanced off the wet, lime-washed walls of its wooden palisades and made it seem bright and near and dim and far at once, heart-catching, for to Hugh the wooden tower and its clay and thatch outbuildings were all the castles he had ever heard of in songs. He kicked his pony hard, and though Phelim and the laughing women called to him and reached out to keep him, he raced on, up the long muddy track that rose up to a knoll where now a knot of riders were gathering, their leaf-bladed spears high and slim and black against the sun: his uncles and cousins O'Neill, who when they saw the pony called and cheered him on.

Through the next weeks he was made much of, and it excited him; he ran everywhere, an undersized, red-headed imp, his stringy legs pink with cold and his high voice too loud. Everywhere the big hands of his uncles touched him and petted him, and they laughed at his extravagances and his stories, and when he killed a rabbit they praised him and held him aloft among them as though it had been twenty stags. At night he slept among them, rolled in among their great odorous shaggy shapes where they lay around the open turf fire that burned in the center of the hall. Sleepless and alert long into the night he watched the smoke ascend to the opening in the roof and listened to his uncles and cousins snoring and talking and breaking wind after their ale.

That there was a reason, perhaps not a good one and kept secret from him, why on this visit he should be put first ahead of older cousins, given first choice from the thick stews in which lumps of butter dissolved, and listened to when he spoke, Hugh felt but could not have said; but now and again he caught one or another of the men regarding him steadily, sadly, as though he were to be pitied; and again, a woman would sometimes, in the middle of some brag he was making, fold him in her arms and hug him hard. He was in a story whose plot he didn't know, and it made him the more restless and wild. There was a time when, running into the hall, he caught his uncle Phelim Turlough and a woman of his having an argument, he shouting at her to leave these matters to men; when she saw Hugh, the woman came to him, pulled his mantle around him and brushed leaves and burrs from it. "Will they have him dressed up in an English suit then for the rest of his life?" she said over her shoulder to Turlough Luineach, who was drinking angrily by the fire.

"His grandfather Conn had a suit of clothes," Phelim said into his cup. "A fine suit of black velvet with gold buttons and a black velvet hat. With a white plume in it!" he shouted, and Hugh couldn't tell if he was angry at the woman, or Conn, or himself. The woman began crying; she drew her scarf over her face and left the hall. Phelim glanced once at Hugh, and spat into the fire.

Nights they sat in the light of the fire and the great reeking candle of reeds and butter, drinking ale and Spanish wine and talking. Their talk was one subject only: the O'Neills. Whatever else came up in conversation or song related to that long history, whether it was the strangeness—stupidity or guile, either could be argued—of the English colonials; or the raids and counter-raids of neighboring families; or stories out of the far past. Hugh couldn't always tell, and perhaps his elders weren't always sure, what of the story had happened a thousand years ago and what of it was happening now. Heroes rose up and raided, slew their enemies and carried off their cattle and their women; some were crowned high king at Tara. There was mention of Niall of the Nine Hostages and the high king Julius Caesar; of Brian Boru and Cuchulain; of Shane O'Neill and his fierce Scots redlegs, of the sons of Shane and the King of Spain's son. His grandfather Conn had been the O'Neill, but had let the English call him Earl of Tyrone. There had always been an O'Neill, invested at the crowning stone at Tullyhogue to the sound of St. Patrick's bell; but Conn O'Neill, Earl of Tyrone, had seen King Harry over the sea, and had promised to plant corn, and learn English. And when he lay dying he said that a man was a fool to trust the English.

Within the tangled histories, each strand bright and clear and beaded with unforgotten incident but inextricably bound up with every other, Hugh could perceive his own story: how his grandfather had never settled the succession of his title of the O'Neill; how Hugh's uncle Shane had risen up and slain his brother Matthew, Hugh's father, and now called himself the O'Neill and claimed all Ulster for his own, and raided his cousins' lands when he chose with his six fierce sons; how he, Hugh, had true claim to what Shane had usurped. Sometimes all this was as clear to him as the multifarious branchings of a winter-naked tree against the sky; sometimes not. The English . . . there was the confusion. Like a cinder in his eye, they baffled his clear sight.

Phelim tells with relish: "Then comes up Sir Henry Sidney with all his power, and Shane? Can Shane stand against him? He cannot! It's as much as he can do to save his own skin. And that only by leaping into the Great River and swimming away. I'll drink the Lord Deputy's health for that, a good friend to Conn's true heir . . ."

Or, "What do they ask?" a brehon, a lawgiver, asks. "You bend a knee to the Queen, and offer all your lands. She takes them and gives you the title Earl—and all your lands back again. You are her urragh, but nothing has changed . . ."

"And they are sworn then to help you against your enemies."

"No," says another, "you against theirs, even if it be a man sworn to you or your own kinsman whom they've taken a hatred to. Conn was right: a man is a fool to trust them."

"Think of Desmond, in prison in London these many years, who trusted them."

"Desmond is a thing of theirs. He is a Norman, he has their blood. Not the O'Neills."

"Fubun," says the blind poet O'Mahon in a quiet high voice that stills them all:

> *Fubun* on the gray foreign gun,
> *Fubun* on the golden chain;
> *Fubun* on the court that talks English,
> *Fubun* on the denial of Mary's son.

Hugh listens, turning from one speaker to the other, and frightened by the poet's potent curse. He feels the attention of the O'Neills on him.

In Easter week there appeared out of a silvery morning mist from the South a slow procession of horse and men on foot. Even if Hugh watching from the tower had not seen the red and gold banner of the Lord Deputy of Ireland shaken out suddenly by the rainy breeze, he would have known that these were English and not Irish, for the men were a neat, dark cross moving together smartly: a van, the flag in the center where the Lord Deputy rode flanked by men with long guns over their shoulders, and a rear guard with a shambling ox-drawn cart.

He climbed monkey-like down from the tower calling out the news, but the visitors had been seen already, and his uncle O'Quinn and the O'Hagan and Phelim were already mounting in the courtyard to ride and meet them. Hugh shouted at the horse-boys to bring his pony.

"You stay," Phelim said, pulling on his gloves of English leather.

"I won't," Hugh said, and pushed the horse-boy: "Go on!"

Phelim's horse began shaking his head and dancing away, and Phelim, pulling angrily at his bridle, commanded Hugh to obey; between the horse and Hugh disobeying him, he was getting red in the face, and Hugh was on the pony's back, laughing, before Phelim could take any action against him. Turlough had watched all this without speaking; now he raised a hand to silence Phelim and drew Hugh to his side.

"They might as well see him now as later," he said, and brushed back Hugh's hair with an oddly gentle gesture.

The two groups, English and Irish, stood for a time some distance apart with a marshy stream running between them, while heralds met formally in the middle and carried greetings back and forth. Then the Lord Deputy, in a gesture of condescension, rode forward with only his standard-bearer, splashing across the water and waving a gloved hand to Phelim McTurlough; at that, McTurlough rode down to meet him half way, and leapt off his horse to take the Lord Deputy's bridle and shake his hand.

Hugh, watching these careful approaches, began to feel less forward. He moved his pony back behind O'Quinn's snorting bay. Sir Henry Sidney was huge: his mouth full of white teeth opened in a black beard that reached up nearly to his eyes, which were small and also black; his great thighs, in hose and high boots, made the slim sword that hung from his baldric look as harmless as a toy. His broad chest was enclosed in a breastplate like a tun; Hugh didn't know its deep stomach was partly false, in the current fashion, but it looked big enough to hold him whole. Sir Henry raised an arm encased in a sleeve more dagged and gathered and complex than any garment Hugh had ever seen, and the squadron behind began to move up, and just then the Lord Deputy's black eyes found Hugh.

In later years Hugh O'Neill would come to feel that there was within him a kind of treasure-chest or strong-box where were kept certain moments in his life, whole: some of them grand, some terrible, some oddly trivial, all perfect and complete with every sensation and feeling they had contained. Among the oldest which the box would hold was this one, when Phelim leading the Deputy's horse brought him to Hugh, and the Deputy reached down a massive hand and took Hugh's arm like a twig he might break, and spoke to him in English. All preserved: the huge black laughing head, the jingle of the horses' trappings and the sharp odor of their fresh droppings, even the soft glitter of condensing dewdrops on the silver surface of Sir Henry's armor. Dreaming or awake, in London, in Rome, this moment would now and again be taken out and shown him, and he would look into it as into a green and silver opal, and wonder.

The negotiations leading to Sir Henry's taking Hugh O'Neill away with him to England as his ward went on for some days. Sir Henry was patient and careful: patient, while the O'Neills rehearsed again the long story of their wrongs at Shane's hands; careful not to commit himself to more than he directly promised: that he would be a good friend to the Baron Dungannon, as he called Hugh, while at the same time intimating that large honors could come of it, chiefly the earldom of Tyrone, which since Conn's death had remained in the Queen's gift, unbestowed.

He gave to Hugh a little sheath knife with a small emerald of peculiar hue set in the ivory hilt; he told Hugh that the gem was taken from a Spanish treasure-ship sailing from Peru on the other side of the world. Hugh, excluded from their negotiations, would sit with the women and turn the little knife in his hands, wondering what could possibly be meant by the other side of the world. When it began to grow clear to him that he was meant to go to England with Sir Henry, he grew shy and silent, not daring even to ask what it would be like there. He tried to imagine England: he thought of a vast stone place, like the cathedral of Armagh multiplied over and over, where the sun did not shine.

At dinner one night Sir Henry saw him loitering at the door of the hall, peeking in. He raised his cup and called to him. "Come, my young lord," he said, and the Irish smiled and laughed at the compliment, though Hugh, whose English was uncertain, wasn't sure they weren't mocking him. Hands urged him forward, and rather than be pushed before Sir Henry, Hugh stood as tall as he could, his hand on the little knife at his belt, and walked up before the vast man.

"My lord, are you content to go to England with me?"

"I am, if my uncles send me."

"Well, so they do. You will see the Queen there." Hugh answered nothing to this, quite unable to picture the Queen. Sir Henry put a huge hand on Hugh's shoulder, where it lay like a stone weight. "I have a son near you in age. Well, something younger. His name is Philip."

"Phelim?"

"Philip. Philip is an English name. Come, shall we go tomorrow?" Sir Henry looked around, his black eyes smiling at his hosts. Hugh was being teased: tomorrow was fixed.

"Tomorrow is too soon," Hugh said, attempting a big voice of Phelim's but feeling only sudden terror. Laughter around him made him snap his head around to see who mocked him.

Shame overcame terror. "If it please your lordship, we will go. Tomorrow. To England." They cheered at that, and Sir Henry's head bobbed slowly up and down like an ox's.

Hugh bowed and turned away, suppressing until he reached the door of the hall a desire to run. Once past the door, though, he fled, out of the castle, down the muddy street between the outbuildings, past the lounging guards, out into the gray night fields over which slow banks of mist lay undulating. Without stopping he ran along a beaten way up through the damp hissing grass to where a riven oak thrust up, had thrust up for as long as anyone knew, like a tensed black arm and gnarled hand.

Near the oak, almost hidden in the grass, were broken straight lines of worn mossy stones that marked where once a monastic house had stood; a hummocky sunken place had been its cellar. It was here that Hugh had killed, almost by accident, his first rabbit. He had not been thinking, that day, about hunting, but only sitting on a stone with his face tilted upward into the sun thinking of nothing, his javelin across his lap. When he opened his eyes, the sunlit ground was a coruscating darkness, except for the brown shape of the rabbit in the center of vision, near enough almost to touch. Since then he had felt the place was lucky for him, though he wouldn't have ventured there at night; now he found himself there, almost before he had decided on it, almost before the voices and faces in the hall had settled out of consciousness. He had nearly reached the oak when he saw that someone sat on the old stones.

"Who is it there?" said the man, without turning to look. "Is it Hugh O'Neill?"

"It is," said Hugh, wondering how blind O'Mahon nearly always knew who was approaching him.

"Come up, then, Hugh." Still not turning to him—why should he? and yet it was unsettling—O'Mahon touched the stone beside him. "Sit. Do you have iron about you, cousin?"

"I have a knife."

"Take it off, will you? And put it a distance away."

He did as he was told, sticking the little knife in a spiky tree-stump some paces off; somehow the poet's gentle tone brooked neither resistance nor reply.

"Tomorrow," O'Mahon said when Hugh sat next to him again, "you go to England."

"Yes." Hugh felt ashamed here to admit it, even though it had been in no sense his choice; he didn't even like to hear the poet say the place's name.

"It's well you came here, then. For there are certain . . . personages who wished to say farewell to you. And give you a commandment. And a promise."

The poet wasn't smiling; his face was lean and composed behind a thin fair beard nearly transparent. His bald eyes, as though filled with milk and water, looked not so much blind as simply unused: baby's eyes. "Behind you," he went on, and Hugh looked quickly around, "in the old cellar there, lives one who will come forth in a moment, only you ought not to speak to him."

The cellar-place was obscure; any of its humps, which seemed to shift vaguely in the darkness, might have been someone.

"And beyond, from that rath"—O'Mahon pointed with certainty, though he didn't look, toward the broad ancient tumulus riding blackly like a whale above the white shoals of mist—"now comes out a certain prince, and to him also you should not speak."

Hugh's heart had turned small and hard and beat painfully. He tried to say *Sidhe* but the word would not be said. He looked from the cellar to the rath to the cellar again— and there a certain tussock darker than the rest grew arms and hands and began with slow patience to pull itself out of the earth. Then a sound as of a great stamping animal came from ahead of him, and, turning, he saw that out of the dark featureless rath something was proceeding toward him, something like a huge windblown cloak or a quickly oaring boat with a black luffing sail or a stampeding caparisoned horse. He felt a chill shiver up his back. At a sound behind him he turned again, to see a little thick black man, now fully out of the earth, glaring dourly at him (the glints of his eyes all that could be seen of his face) and staggering toward him under the weight of a black chest he carried in his stringy, rooty arms.

An owl hooted, quite near Hugh; he flung his head around and saw it, all white, gliding silently ahead of the Prince who proceeded toward Hugh, of whom and whose steed Hugh could still make nothing but that they were vast, and were perhaps one being, except that now he perceived gray hands holding reins or a bridle, and a circlet of gold where a brow might be. The white owl swept near Hugh's head, and with a silent wingbeat climbed to a perch in the riven oak.

There was a clap as of thunder behind him. The little black man had set down his chest. Now he glared up at the Prince before him and shook his head slowly, truculently; his huge black hat was like a tussock of grass, but there nodded in it, Hugh saw, a white feather delicate as snow. Beside Hugh, O'Mahon sat unchanged, his hands resting on his knees; but then he raised his head, for the Prince had drawn a sword.

It was as though an unseen hand manipulated a bright bar of moonlight; it had neither hilt nor point, but it was doubtless a sword. The Prince who bore it was furious, that was certain too: he thrust the sword down imperiously at the little man, who cried out with a shriek like gale-tormented branches rubbing, and stamped his feet; but, though resisting, his hands pulled open the lid of his chest. Hugh could see that there was nothing inside but limitless darkness. The little man thrust an arm deep inside and drew out something; then, approaching with deep reluctance only as near as he had to, he held it out to Hugh.

Hugh took it; it was deathly cold. There was the sound of a heavy cape snapped, and when Hugh turned to look, the Prince was already away down the dark air, gathering in his stormy hugeness as he went. The owl sailed after him. As it went away, a white feather fell, and floated zigzag down toward Hugh.

Behind Hugh, a dark hummock in the cellar place had for a moment beneath it the glint of angry eyes, and then did not anymore.

Ahead of him, across the fields, a brown mousing owl swept low over the silvery grass.

Hugh had in his hands a rudely carven flint, growing warm from his hand's heat, and a white owl's feather.

"The flint is the commandment," O'Mahon said, as if nothing extraordinary at all had happened, "and the feather is the promise."

"What does the commandment mean?"

"I don't know."

They sat a time in silence. The moon, amber as old whiskey, appeared between the white-fringed hem of the clouds and the gray heads of the eastern mountains. "Will I ever return?" Hugh asked, though he could almost not speak for the painful stone in his throat.

"Yes."

Hugh was shivering now. If Sir Henry had known how late into the night he had sat out of doors, he would have been alarmed; the night air, especially in Ireland, was well known to be pernicious.

"Goodbye, then, cousin," Hugh said.

"Goodbye, Hugh O'Neill." O'Mahon smiled. "If they give you a velvet hat to wear, in England, your white feather will look fine in it."

Sir Henry Sidney, though he would not have said it to the Irish, was quite clear in his dispatches to the Council why he took up Hugh O'Neill. Not only was it policy for the English to support the weaker man in any quarrel between Irish dynasts, and thus prevent the growth of any overmighty subject; it also seemed to Sir Henry that, like an eyas falcon, a young Irish lord if taken early enough might later come more willingly to the English wrist. Said otherwise: he was bringing Hugh to England as he might the cub of a beast to a bright and well-ordered menagerie, to tame him.

For that reason, and despite his wife's doubts, he set Hugh O'Neill companion to his own son Philip; and for the same reason he requested his son-in-law, the Earl of Leicester, to be Hugh's patron at court. "A boy poor in goods," he wrote Leicester, "and full feebly friended."

The Earl of Leicester, in conversation with the Queen, turned a nice simile, comparing his new Irish client to the grafted fruit-trees the Earl's gardeners made: by care and close binding, the hardy Irish apple might be given English roots, though born in Irish soil; and once having them, could not then be separated from them.

"Pray sir, then," the Queen said smiling, "his fruits be good."

"With good husbandry, Madame," Leicester said, "his fruits will be to your Majesty's taste." And he brought forward the boy, ten years old, his proud hair deep red, almost the color of the morocco-leather binding of a little prayer-book the Queen held in her left hand. Across his pale face and upturned nose the freckles were thick, and faintly green; his eyes were emeralds. Two things the Queen loved were red hair and jewels; she put out her long ringed hand and brushed Hugh's hair.

"Our cousin of Ireland," she said.

He didn't dare raise his red-lashed eyes to her after he had made the courtesy that the Earl had carefully instructed him in; while they talked about him above his head in a courtly southern English he couldn't follow, he looked at the Queen's dress.

She seemed in fact to be wearing several. As though she were some fabulous many-walled fort, mined and breached, through the slashings and partings of her outer dress another could be seen, and where that was opened there was another, and lace beneath that. The outer wall was all jeweled, beaded with tiny seed-pearls as though with dew, worked and embroidered in many patterns of leaf, vine, flower. On her petticoat were pictured monsters of the sea, snorting seahorses and leviathans with mouths like portcullises. And on the outer garment's inner side, turned out to reveal them, were a hundred disembodied eyes and ears. Hugh could believe that with those eyes and ears the Queen could see and hear, so that even as he looked at her clothing, her clothing observed him. He raised his eyes to her white face framed in stiff lace, her hair dressed in pearls and silver.

Hugh saw then that the power of the Queen resided in her dress. She was bound up in it as magically as the children of Lir were bound up in the forms of swans. The willowy, long-legged courtiers, gartered and wearing slim English swords, moved as in a dance in circles and waves around her when she moved. When she left the chamber (she did not speak to Hugh again, but her quick, bird eye lighted on him once), she drew her ladies-in-waiting after her as though she caught up rustling fallen leaves in her train.

Later the Earl told Hugh that the Queen had a thousand such gowns and petticoats and farthingales, each more elaborate than the last.

A screen carved with figures in relief—nymphs and satyrs, grape-clusters, incongruous armorial bearings picked out in gold leaf—had concealed the Queen's chief counselor, Sir William Cecil, Lord Burghley, and Doctor John Dee, her consulting physician and astrologer, from the chamber where the Queen had held audience. But through the piercings of the screen they could see and hear.

"That boy," Burghley had said softly. "The red-headed one."

"Yes," Doctor Dee replied. "The Irish boy."

"Sir Henry Sidney is his patron. He has been brought to be schooled in English ways. There have been others. Her gracious majesty believes she can win their hearts and their loyalty. They do learn manners and graces, but they return to their island, and their brutish natures well up again. There is no way to keep them bound to us in those fastnesses."

"I know not for certain," said Doctor Dee, combing his great beard with his fingers, "but it may be that there are ways."

"*Doctissime vir,*" said Burghley. "If there are ways let us use them."

A light snow lay on the roads and cottages when Philip Sidney, Sir Henry's son, and Hugh O'Neill went from the Sidneys' house of Penshurst in Kent up to Mortlake to visit John Dee. There was a jouncing, canopied cart filled with rugs and cushions but the boys preferred to ride with the attendants, until the cold pinched them too deeply through the fine thin gloves and hose they wore. Hugh, careful now in matters of dress, would not have said that his English clothes were useless for keeping out cold compared to a shaggy Waterford mantle with a fur hood; but he seemed to be always cold and comfortless, somehow naked, in breeches and short cloaks.

Philip dismounted and threw his reins to the attendant, rubbing his hands, his narrow blue-clad buttocks clenched. When Hugh had climbed in too they pulled shut the curtains and huddled together under the rugs, each laughing at the other's shivers. They talked of the Doctor, as they called Dee, with whom Philip already studied Latin and Greek and mathematics—Hugh, though the older of the two, had had no lessons as yet, though they'd been promised him. They talked of what they would do when they were grown up and were knights, reweaving with themselves as the heroes the stories of Arthur and Guy of Warwick and the rest.

When the two of them played at heroes on their ponies in the fields of Penshurst, Hugh could never bully Philip into taking the lesser part: *I will be a wandering knight, and you must be my esquire.* Philip Sidney knew the tales, and he knew (almost before he knew anything else of the world) that the son of an Irish chieftain could not have ascendancy even in play over the son of an English knight.

But whenever Philip had Hugh at stick-sword's-point in a combat, utterly defeated, Hugh would leap up and summon from the hills and forests a sudden host of helpers who slew Philip's merely mortal companions. Or he postulated a Crow who was a great princess he had long ago aided, whose feet he could grasp and be carried to safety, or an oak tree that would open and hide him away.

It wasn't fair, Philip would cry, these sudden hosts that Hugh sang forth in harsh unmusical Irish. They didn't fit any rules, they had nothing to do with the triumph of good knights over evil ones, and why anyway did they only help Hugh?

"Because my family once did them a great service," Hugh said to Philip in the rocking wagon. The matter was never going to be resolved.

"Suppose my family had."

"Guy of Warwick hasn't any family."

"I say now that he does, and so he does."

"And there aren't . . . fairy-folk in England." That term carefully chosen.

"For sure there are."

"No, there are not, and if there were how could you summon them? Do you think they understand English at all?"

"I will summon them in Latin. *Veni, venite, spiritus sylvani, dives fluminarum . . .*"

Hugh kicked at the covers and at Philip, laughing. Latin!

Once they'd taken the issue to the wisest man they knew, excepting Doctor Dee himself, whom they didn't dare to ask: Buckle the Penshurst gamekeeper.

"There was fairies here," he said to them. His enormous gnarled hands honed a long knife back and forth, back and forth on a whetstone. "But that was before King Harry's time, when I was a boy and said the Ave-Mary."

"See there!" said Philip.

"Gone," said Hugh.

"My grandam saw them," said Buckle. "Saw one sucking on the goat's pap like any kid, and so the goat was dry when she came to milk it. But not now in this new age." Back and forth went the blade, and Buckle tested it on the dark and ridgy pad of his thumb.

"Where did they go?" Philip asked.

"Away," Buckle said. "Gone away with the friars and the Mass and the Holy Blood of Hailes."

"But where?" Hugh said.

A smile altered all the deep crags and lines of Buckle's face. "Tell me," he said, "young master, where your lap goes when you stand up."

Doctor Dee's wife Jane gave the boys a posset of ale and hot milk to warm them, and when they had drunk it he offered them a choice: they might read in whatever books of his they liked, or work with his mathematical tools and study his maps, which he had unrolled on a long table, with compass and square laid on them. Philip chose a book, a rhymed romance that Doctor Dee chuckled at; the boy nested himself in cushions, opened his book, and was soon asleep "like a mouse in cotton-wool" Jane Dee said. Hugh bent over the maps with the Doctor, whose round spectacles enlarged his eyes weirdly, his long beard nearly trailing across the sheets.

What Hugh had first to learn was that the maps showed the world, not as a man walking in it sees it, but as a bird flying high over it. High, high: Doctor Dee showed him on a map of England the length of the journey from Penshurst to Mortlake, and it was no longer than the joint of his thumb. And then England and Ireland too grew small and insignificant when Doctor Dee unrolled a map of the whole wide world. Or half of it: the world, he told Hugh, is round as a ball, and this was a picture of but one half. A ball! Hung by God in the middle of the firmament, the great stars going around it in their spheres and the fixed stars in theirs.

"This," the Doctor said, "is the Irish island, across St. George's Channel. Birds may fly across from there to here in the half-part of a day."

Hugh thought: the children of Lir.

"All these lands of Ireland, Wales, and Scotland"—his long finger showed them—"are the estate of the British Crown, of our Imperial Queen, whose sworn servant you are." He smiled warmly, looking down upon Hugh.

"So also am I," said Philip, who'd awakened and come behind them.

"And so you are." He turned again to his maps. "But look you. It is not only these Isles Britannicae that belong to her. In right, these lands to the North, of the Danes and the Norwayans, they are hers too, by virtue of their old kings her ancestors—though it were inadvisable to lay claim to them now. And farther too, beyond the ocean sea."

He began to tell them of the lands far to the west, of Estotiland and Groenland, of Atlantis. He talked of King Malgo and King Arthur, of Lord Madoc and Saint Brendan the Great; of Sebastian Caboto and John Caboto, who reached the shores of Atlantis a hundred years before Columbus sailed. They, and others long before, had set foot upon those lands and claimed them for kings from whom Elizabeth descended; and so they adhere to the British Crown. And to resume them under her rule the Queen need ask no leave of Spaniard or of Portingale.

"I will find new lands too, for the Queen," Philip said. "And you shall come too, to guide me. And Hugh shall be my esquire!"

Hugh O'Neill was silent, thinking: the kings of Ireland did not yield their lands to the English. The Irish lands were held by other kings, and other peoples altogether, from time before time. And if a new true king could be crowned at Tara, that king would win those lands again.

It was time now for the boys to return to Kent. Outside, the serving men could be heard mounting up, their spurs and trappings jingling.

"Now give my love and duty to your father," Doctor Dee said to Philip, "and take this gift from me, to guide you when you are grown, and set out upon those adventures you seek." He took from his table a small book, unbound and sewn with heavy thread. It was not printed but written in the Doctor's own fine hand, and the title said *General and Rare Memorials Pertayning to the Perfect Arte of Navigation.* Philip took it in his hands with a sort of baffled awe, aware of the honor, uncertain of the use.

"And for my new friend of Hibernia," he said. "Come with me." He took Hugh away to a corner of his astonishingly crowded room, pushed aside a glowing globe of pale brown crystal in a stand, lifted a dish of gems, and with an *Ah!* he picked up something that Hugh did not at first see.

"This," Doctor Dee said, "I will give you as my gift, in memorial of this day, if you will but promise me one thing. That you will keep it, always, on your person, and part with it never nor to no one." Hugh didn't know what to say to this, but the Doctor went on speaking as though Hugh had indeed promised. "This, young master, is a thing of which there is but one in the world. The uses of it will be borne in upon you when the need for them is great."

What he then put into Hugh's hand was an oval of black glass, glass more black than any he had ever seen, black too black to look right at, yet he could see that it reflected back to him his own face, as though he had come upon a stranger in the dark. It was bound in gold, and hung from a gold chain. On the back the surface of the gold was marked with a sign Hugh had never seen before: he touched the engraved lines with a finger.

"*Monas hieroglyphica,*" said Doctor Dee. He lifted the little obsidian mirror from Hugh's hand by its brittle chain, hung it around the boy's neck. When Hugh again looked into the black sheen of it he saw neither himself nor any other thing; but his skin burned and his heart was hot. He looked to the Doctor, who only tucked the thing away within Hugh's doublet.

When he was at Penshurst again and alone—it was not an easy thing to be alone in the Sidney house, with the lords and ladies and officers of the Queen coming and going, and Philip's beautiful sister teasing, and the servants coming and passing—Hugh opened his shirt and took in his fingers the thing the Doctor had given him. The privy (where he sat) was cold and dim. He touched the raised figure in the gold of the back, which looked a little like a crowned mannikin but likely was not, and turned it over. In the mirror was a face, but now not his own; for it wasn't like looking into a mirror at all, but like looking through a spy-hole and into another place, a spy-hole through which someone in that place looked back at him. The person looking at him was the Queen of England.

On the Impregnation of Mirrors was not a book or a treatise or a Work; it wouldn't survive the wandering life that John Dee was to embark upon as the times and the heavens turned. It was just a few sheets, folded octavo and written in the Doctor's scribble hand, and no one not the Doctor would have been able to practice what it laid out, for certain necessary elements and motions went unwritten except in the Doctor's breast. It exists now but as name in a list of his papers and goods drawn up for an application to her Majesty's government for recompense, after his library and workshop had been despoiled by his enemies at court during his long absence abroad. Only one mirror of those that he had worked the art upon had succeeded entirely, only one had drawn the lines of time and space together so as to transmit the spirit of the owner to the eye of the possessor.

The making of it began with a paradox. If the impregnation of a mirror required that the one who first looked into it be its owner, then no other could ever have looked into it before, not he who silvered the glass, not she who polished the steel. How could the maker not be the owner? John Dee had seen the solution. There was one perfect mirror that needed no silvering, no polishing: it needed only to be discovered, detected, its smooth side inferred, then taken from the ground and secreted before even the finder's eye fell upon its face. He knew of many such, taken from the lava fields of Greece or the Turkish lands, first found, as Pliny saith, by the traveler Obsius; his own he'd found in a lesser field in Scotland. He remembered the cold hill, the fragments sharp as knives, keeping his eyes steadily on the fast-flying clouds above while his fingers felt for the perfectest one, pocketing it unlooked-at.

He had placed it in the Queen's hand himself. Slipping it from where it hid in a purse of kidskin, feeling for its smooth side, which he held up to her face for a long moment, as long a moment as he dared, before giving it to her to examine. She seemed dazzled by it, amazed, though she had seen similar obsidian chips before. None like this one: Doctor Dee had bestirred its latent powers by prayer—and by means he had learned from helpers he would not name, not in the hearing of this court.

And then forever there was the Queen's face within, and more than her face, her very self: her thought, her command, her power to entrance, how well the Doctor knew of it. She had not asked to keep it—the one danger he had feared. No, she had given it back to him with a gracious nod, and turned to other matters, for it was his. And now it was not his. For having taken its owner's face and nature it could be handled, and the Doctor had milled it and framed it in gold and given it to the Irish boy.

It may be there are ways.

Doctor Dee stood on a Welsh headland from where on a clear day the Irish coast could just be seen across St. George's Channel. The sun was setting behind the inland hills of the other island, making them seem large and near with the golden brightness. There where the sun set Hugh O'Neill was one day to become a great chief; the Doctor's informants had let him know of it. The little Irish kings and the old Irish lords would press him in the years to come to make a single kingdom out of the island that had never been one before, and to push out the English and the Scots for good. But Hugh O'Neill—whether he knew it or did not—was as though tethered by a long leash, the one end about his neck, the other held in the Queen's hand, though she might never know of it; and the tug of it, of her thought and will and desire and need, would keep the man in check. She could turn to other matters, the greater world, more dangers.

And to himself as well.

He turned from the sea. A single cloud like a great beast streaked with blood went away to the north with the wind, changing as it went.

After seven years had passed, Hugh O'Neill was returned to Ulster. He was not yet the O'Neill, he was not Earl of Tyrone, but nor was he any other man. By the English designations, in which the Irish only half believed, he was mere Baron Dungannon. The quiet boy had grown into a quiet man. His father, Shane's rebel son Matthew, had been killed by Hugh's uncle Phelim McTurlough, for which act the English had favored him—whatever that might mean for Phelim's benefit, to which the English would never commit: the rich earldom, an empty name, letters patent, loans of money, or nothing at all.

Hugh on Irish soil again, with English soldiers in his train and around his neck an English engine that he did not yet know the uses of, rode through Dublin and was not hailed or cheered. Who was on his side, whom could he count on? There were the O'Hagans, who were poor, and the O'Donnells, the sons of the fierce Scots pirate Ineen Duv (the "dark girl"). And Englishmen: the Queen's men, Burghley and Walsingham, who had taken his hand and smiled. They'd known Conn O'Neill, and remarked on the white feather Hugh wore always in his cap. He'd learned more than courtly English from them. Their eyes were colder than their hands.

The castle-tower of Dungannon still stood, but the old chiefs and their adherents who had feasted and quarreled here were scattered now, fighting each other, or gone south to fight for the heirs of Desmond. But even as he came to the place with his little train they had begun returning, more every day: poor men, ill equipped, not well fed. There were women still there in the castle, and from them he learned that his mother had died in the house of the O'Hagans.

"It is ill times," said blind O'Mahon, who had remained.

"It is."

"Well, you have grown, cousin. And in many ways too."

"I am the one I was," Hugh said, and the poet did not answer him.

"Tell me," he said. "Once in a place nearby, up that track to the crest of the hill, where a holy house once stood . . ."

"I remember," Hugh said.

"I thing was given you."

"Yes."

A man may keep a thing about him, in one pocket or purse or another, and forget he has it; thinks to toss it away now and then and yet never does so—not because it's of value but only because it's his, a bit of himself, and has long been. So the little carven flint had lain here and there throughout his growing up, getting lost and then turning up again. It had ceased to be what for a moment here in this place and long ago it seemed to be: a thing of cold power, with a purpose of its own, too heavy for its size. It had become a small old stone, scratched with the figure of a man that a child might draw.

He felt here and there in his clothes and came upon it: felt it leap into his hand as soon as it could. He drew it out and for a foolish moment thought to display it to the blind man. "I have it still," he said.

A commandment, O'Mahon had called the stone. But not what it commanded. He closed his hand on it. "I will soon build a house here," he said. "A house such as the English make, of bricks and timber, with windows of glass, and chimneys, and a key to lock the door."

"Will you go with me now, up to the place I spoke of?"

"If you like, cousin."

O'Mahon took O'Neill's arm, and Hugh led him where O'Mahon guided; the poet knew very well where he went but wanted help so as not to stumble on the way. They climbed the low hill that Hugh had known in youth, when he had first come to this country with his O'Hagan fosterers, but then there had been tall trees now cut, and beyond the trees to the river fields of corn and pasture where cattle moved. Now fallow and bare.

"Day goes," the poet said, as though he saw it. Past the riven oak, amid the low rolling of the hills there was the one hill taller and of a shape not made by wind and water, but by hands—it was easy to tell. A thousand rods or more in length, but smaller somehow now than when he had seen it as a boy. "This hour is the border of day and night, as the river is the border of here and there. What cannot be known by day or night shows itself at twilight."

"You know these things, who can't see them?"

"My eyes are a border too, cousin. At which I forever stand."

They stood in silence there while the sky turned black above and to a pale, red-streaked green in the west. A mist gathered in the hollows. Hugh O'Neill would not later remember the moment, if there was a moment, when the host came forth, if it did, and stood there against the rath, hard to see but seemingly there. Growing in numbers, mounted and afoot.

"The foreign queen you love and serve," O'Mahon said. "She cares nothing for you but this: that you keep this Isle in subjection for her sake, until and when she can fill it with her hungry subjects and poor relations, to take of it what they will."

The ghost warriors were clearer now. Hugh could almost hear the rustle they made and the rattle of their arms. The Old Ones, the *Sidhe*.

"They command you to fight, Hugh O'Neill of the O'Neills. The O'Neill you are, and what you will be you do not know. But you are not unfriended."

They formed and reformed in the dark, their steeds turning in place, their lances like saplings in wind: as though impatient for him to cry out to them in supplication, or call them to his side.

The commandment, Hugh thought. But he could say nothing to them, not with his voice, not in his heart; and soon the border of night and day was closed, and he could see them no more.

In Munster where the world began the old Norman earls of Desmond and Kildare and Ormond had risen again, resisting the English adventurers whose papers and patents said they owned the lands that those families had held for time out of mind. The earls acknowledged no power higher than themselves except the Pope. Hugh O'Neill kept as far from the quarrel in the south as he could; he told himself that his work was to make himself pre-eminent here, Lord of the North.

But the obsidian mirror judged him and found him wanting. *You are a cold friend to her who loves you and will soon do you great good:* the Queen looked out at him, her white face framed in a stiff ruff. Eyes he saw in dreams too. When the English gathered an army at Dublin under old and weary Henry Sidney, Hugh rode south with him, bringing fighters of his own, feeding them from the plunder of Desmond villages and fields. Any town or village that Sidney invested and would not surrender was put to the sword, the leaders beheaded and their heads impaled on stakes across the land. The earls and their followers burned the standing grain in the fields to keep Sidney's army from the provender, and then in the spring Sidney's soldiers burned it as it sprung green, to keep it from them. The people ate cresses, and when they had none they died, and others ate their flesh, and the flesh of their dead babes. And the Queen spoke to O'Neill's heart and said *Look not on their suffering but on me.*

But the flint in his pocket had its say as well.

He kept on with Sir Henry—but he went his own way. He avoided pitched battles and retributions; he largely occupied himself in Munster not with fighting but with . . . hunting. He brought along with him on his hunts men with guns (*Fubun on the grey foreign gun* O'Mahon had said long ago, but this was now, not then). Wherever he went, wherever men had lost their lands, he would ask the men and boys what weapons they were good at using, and after they named spears and bows and the pike he would bring out a gun, and explain the use of it, and let one or another of them take it and try it. The handiest of them he'd reward with a coin or other gift, and perhaps even the gun itself. Keep it safe he'd say, smiling.

That was wisdom the mirror would never give him and the flint could not know: When the time came for him to lead men against English soldiers—if it did come—he would not lead hordes of screaming gallowglass against trained infantry with guns. His army would wheel on command, and march in step, and lay fire. When the time came.

In Dungannon again he began to build himself that fine house in the English style, where wardrobes held his velvet English suits and hats, his rugs and bedclothes made from who knew what. When he could get no lead for the roofs of his house, Burghley saw to it that a shipment of many tons of sheet lead were sent to him; it lay for years in the pine woods at Dungannon until a different use for it was found, in a different world. He fell in love, not for the first or the last time, but this time providentially: she was Mabel Bagenal, daughter of Sir Nicholas Bagenal, officer of the Queen's Council in Dublin— Bagenal resisted the match, not wanting an Irish chieftain for a son-in-law and thinking Mabel could do better: but when Hugh O'Neill rode into Dublin in his velvets and his lined cloak with a hundred retainers around him, her heart was won. And the power in the black mirror was glad of it.

The morning after the wedding night Mabel discovered it on its gold chain on his breast and tried to take it off, but he wouldn't let her; he only turned it to her and asked her what she saw. The third soul ever to look in. She studied it, brow knit, and said she saw herself, but dimly.

Himself was never what Hugh O'Neill saw there. "It was a gift," he said. "From a wise man in England. To keep me safe, he said."

Mabel Bagenal looked into her husband's face, which seemed to seek itself in the black mirror, though she was wrong about that; and she said, "May God will that it do so."

In the same spring Doctor John Dee and his wife, Jane, and their many children left for the Continent with trunkloads of books, an astronomer's staff, bottles of remedy for every ill, a cradleboard for the newest, and in a velvet bag a small orb of quartz crystal with a flaw like a lost star not quite at its center. In a cold room in a high tower in the golden city in the middle of the Emperor's land of Bohemia he placed the stone in its frame carved with the names and sigilla that his angelic informants had given to him.

There was war in heaven, and therefore war under the earth, and soon enough on the lands and seas of all the empires and kingdoms of men.

It would engulf the States and Empires of Europe; even the Sultan might be drawn in. If Spain claimed Great Atlantis for her own, then Atlantis too would be in play, and Francis Drake's license as a privateer would be traded for the chain of an Admiral of the Ocean Sea, and Walter Raleigh given one too. The heavenly powers that aid the true Christian faith, the armed angelic hosts, would go into battle. They would be opposed by other powers great and small, powers that take the side of the old faith. The creatures of the middle realm, of earth and water, hills and trees, shy and self-protective, would surely fight with the old religion: not because they loved the

Pope or even knew of him, but only because they hated change. There was little harm they could do, though much annoyance. But in the contested Irish Isle where Spain would be welcomed, there were other powers: warriors who appeared and disappeared after sudden slaughter, bright swords and spears that made no sound. Were they men, had they once been men, were they but empty casques and breastplates? They could be captured, sometimes, imprisoned if you knew the spells, but never for long. *It is useless to hang us,* they would say to their jailers, *we cannot die.*

Look now: the swirl of winds within the stone, the sense (not the sound) of heavenly laughter, and the clouds parted to show as though from a sea-bird's eye the western coast of Ireland, and on the sea little dots that were big-bellied ships, the great red crosses on their sails.

A flotilla in the North Sea, and in St. George's Channel, come to make Philip King of England. And to make the Virgin Queen his bride, old now and barren though she be. In the stone the tiny ships rocked on the main like mock ships in a masque or a children's show. An angel finger pointed to them, and John Dee heard a whisper: *That is not far off from now.*

Hugh O'Neill had passed almost without noticing from his twenties to his thirties; one by one the endless line of enemies and false friends and mad fools that he faced in the claiming of his heritage were bought off, or befriended, or exiled, or hanged. The black mirror was his adviser and his ruler in these contests. When he contested with the mirror itself, he might deny it, and later be sorry he had. Sometimes when he looked in it would say *Strike now or lose all* and sometimes it would only look upon him; sometimes it wept or smiled, or said *Power springs from the mind and the heart.* But never was any sound heard, and it was as though Hugh thought or said these things in his own mind, which made them not the less true or potent. If he could discern the meaning of what was said and act on it, it would come out as predicted, and he would win. And in the spring of 1587 he returned to London to be invested at last by the Queen with the title Earl of Tyrone.

He knelt before her, sweeping his hat and its white feather from his head. "Cousin," the Queen said, and held out her ringed hand for him to kiss.

The face Hugh saw in the black mirror had never changed—at least it would seem always unchanged to him, white and small and bejewelled—but the woman of flesh was not young. The paint couldn't cover the fine lines etched all around her eyes, nor the lines in the great bare skull above. Torn between love and shame Hugh put his lips near to the proffered hand without touching it, and when he raised his eyes again she was young again and serenely lovely. "My cousin," she said. "My lord of Tyrone."

At the dock when he came home again, with more gifts and purchases in his English ship than twenty ox-carts could bear, he saw, among the O'Neill and O'Donnell men-at-arms and their brehons and wives come to greet him, the poet O'Mahon, like a withered leaf, leaning on a staff. Hugh O'Neill went to him, knelt and kissed the white hand the poet held out to him. O'Mahon raised him, felt his big face and broad shoulders, the figured steel breastplate upon him.

"That promise given you was kept," said O'Mahon.

"How, cousin?"

"You are the O'Neill, inaugurated at Tullahogue as your ancestors have ever been. You are Earl of Tyrone too, by the grant of the English: you gave them all your lands and they gave them back to you just as though the lands were theirs to give, and added on a title, Earl."

"How is that the keeping of a promise?" O'Neill asked.

"That is for them to know; yours to act and learn." He touched Hugh's arm and said: "Will you go on progress in this summer, cousin? The lands that owe you are wide."

"I may do so. The weather looks to be fine."

"I would be happy to go along with you, if I might. As far at least as to the old fort at Dungannon."

"Well, then you shall. You will have a litter to carry you, if you like."

"I can still ride," the poet said with a smile. "And my own horse knows the way there."

"What shall we do there?"

"I? Not a thing. But you: you will meet again your allies there, or perhaps their messenger or herald; and see what now they will say. And they will tell you of the others, some greater than they, who are now waking from sleep, and their pale horses too."

The streets that had been silent and empty when, some years before, a young Irishman came home from that other island to which he had been carried away—they were not still now: from street to street and house to house the news went that Hugh O'Neill was home again, and they came around his horse to touch his boot and lift their babes to see him; and now and then he must acknowledge them, and doff the black velvet cap he wore, with the white owl's feather in its band.

Two enemies, the Queen of England and the old ones under the hills, had acted to make Hugh O'Neill great. He had become what they had conspired to make him, and what now was he to do? When he tried to take the black mirror from around his neck he found that he could not: he had the strength, it was a flimsy chain that carried it, he could snap it with a thumb and finger, but he couldn't do it.

Hugh O'Neill, Lord of the North, stood at the center of time, which was not different from the time of his own span. There are five directions to the world around: there is North, and South, and East, and West. And the fifth direction lies amid them. It points to the fifth kingdom, the only realm where he or any man ever stands: Here.

Well, let it be. What was he but a battleground where armies and their generals tore him in two for their own reasons? There was no knowing how the world would roll from here where he stood. Let it be.

The Queen was dead, and John Dee was dying. His books and alchemical ware and even the gifts that the Queen had given him had been sold for bread: his long toil for her meant nothing to the new Scots king, who feared magic above all things. It was all gone but this small stone of moleskin-colored quartz, that had come to have a spiritual creature caught in it: an angel, he had long believed, but now he doubted. The war she had shown him had paused, like a storm's eye passing, and a calm had fallen over the half part of the world: it would not last.

What he saw now wasn't what he had seen, the armies of emperors and kings, nor the towers of Heaven and their hosts. He saw only long stony beaches, and knew it was the western coast of Ireland; and there where the Spanish ships had once been shivered on the rocks, other ships were being built, like no ships men sailed, ships made out of the time of another age, silvered like driftwood, with sails as of cobweb; and the ones building and now boarding and pushing them out to sea were as silvery, and as fine. Defeated; in flight. They sailed to the West, to the Fortunate Isles, to coasts and faraway hills they had never seen. The voice at John Dee's inner ear said, *This is to come. We know not when. Well, let it be.* And as he bent over the glowing stone the empowered soul within him spoke to him in vatic mode, and told him that when the end did come, and after it had long passed, the real powers that had fought these wars would be forgotten, and so would he, and only the merely human kings and queens and halberdiers and priests and townsmen remembered.

Anosognosia

for Paul Park

CLOV: Do you believe in the life to come?
HAMM: Mine was always that.
    —Samuel Beckett, *Endgame*

In the last week of May in 1959, a high-school student, John C., made a misstep at the top of the stairs of the family house on Ponader Drive in South Bend, Indiana. Perhaps it was a yellow Ticonderoga pencil that caused it, lying crosswise on the floor at the top of the steps, and perhaps he stepped on it in such a way that it rolled under his foot and threw his leg out over the first step or over the first and the second steps, whereupon he fell turning head over heels, or more exactly heels over head, to the bottom. He must have struck his head very hard at some place on the way down—on a step, on a banister, on the floor at the bottom of the stairs—for he lay there inert, his legs twisted on the lowest stairs, shoulders and head on the floor.

His initial cry of amazement and horror, and the noise of his falling, brought his mother from the kitchen, where she had been pondering dinner and sipping a glass of inexpensive sherry. According to her later account she tried to wake him, listened to his heart—which seemed to be beating in normal fashion, unlike her own—and then, being a doctor's wife and knowing the basics of first aid, did not attempt to move him but called the operator (dropping the new Princess phone that sat on a table in the hall at first and fumbling the earpiece in desperate hurry) and asked for an ambulance. Then she called her husband at the college infirmary where he worked, and knelt on the floor beside her son and held his hand, which she thought surely couldn't count as moving the patient. He had a pulse, fast but not wild or irregular. They two were alone in the house.

John C. was still unconscious when the ambulance arrived, and when his father arrived very soon after. He remained unconscious—a state that was described as a coma but which didn't meet all the criteria for such a diagnosis—for three days; he was given intravenous fluids, and his temperature, heart rate, and blood pressure were monitored. Whatever injury he had suffered internally didn't appear outwardly; a scratch on his cheek from something, a bump on the back of his head that soon resolved. His parents sat with him, singly or together; his four sisters came from school to sit in turn by his bed, and the eldest and most pious of them got them all to say the rosary there for his recovery.

It was his mother who was beside him when he opened his eyes, took a huge breath, and lifted his hands from the bedclothes as though they stung, or perhaps in preparation to arise. He didn't do that, though, only looked around cautiously and then at his stricken mother, sitting forward in her chair waiting in awful suspense for what he'd say, if he could say anything at all.

Are you all right? she said, conscious of the fatuity.

I am, he said. I am all right. Then he closed his eyes again.

Within the hour he was alert again and speaking almost normally, with what appeared to be a great and deliberate caution but making perfect sense; he observed his mother's face with an intensity of attention that was unsettling—as though he were trying to remember who she was, she said later, but actually it seemed to her that he knew very well who she was and it was himself he didn't quite recognize.

What could only be understood as lingering side effects of his apparent coma remained for weeks. Though he recognized his house and his room, they seemed at the same time strange to him; he'd touch in wonderment or curiosity the surfaces of his books, the tools in the kitchen, the clothes in his closet (being the only boy in the family he had a room of his own). Sometimes he'd laugh aloud coming upon some ordinary item, as though astonished to find it existed, or as though an old acquaintance unseen for years had suddenly appeared before him. He didn't talk much, though he had been the most voluble person in a talkative and lively household; he sat among them in silence but obviously enjoying their company and their attention, the extravagant jokes they made about an event that it was now all right to laugh about. At times he could be overcome by a sort of vertigo or paralysis, apparently overwhelmed by the sensation of the world entering his consciousness, and have to lie down alone for a time. Once, standing over a pile of his many drawings for imaginary productions of classic plays—he aimed, or had aimed, to be a stage designer—he actually fainted, slumped will-less to the floor; but he recovered quickly.

Yet it couldn't be denied that almost all the time he was well. A kind of wonderful elation, even, seemed sometimes to possess him; he gazed at the world with open eyes and swallowed it all down. He was happy. It was evident; very happy, divinely happy.

As the small oddities that accompanied his return diminished, a larger change in him appeared. He was, or was rapidly becoming, a different person than he had been. Not only was his way of speaking odd, his way of thinking was also. Dreamy, inventive, intensely inward, sometimes goofily cheerful; bookish, a show-off where literature and arcane knowledge were the matter; careless of his person (as the sort of books he chose to read might put it), vague and clumsy outside the realms where he felt secure but alone: that was how he had been. Now he was not describable in those terms. If he'd gone off on a journey to another world during his days unconscious, he'd returned, estranged, but with gifts and weapons he hadn't had before.

The school year—John was a junior at St. Joseph's High School—was now almost over. He'd been excused from classes for as long as he needed, though there was some discussion of his having to repeat a class or take a summer-school makeup. In the school he seemed more lost than at home; he recognized only a few of his classmates, had no memory of where his classes were held or what the general rules of school life were. He'd lost much of his Latin. Organic chemistry was a blank. Boys he didn't know would joke to him about his having water on the brain, or allude to the personality and role he had apparently possessed in their eyes, but which he couldn't quite remember. With surprising directness and aplomb, though, he managed to negotiate with the Brothers various projects and papers he could do outside of class that would assure him at least passing grades for his junior year. When he described the deal to his father at supper, his father regarded him with a mild bewilderment that resembled John's own in the previous weeks. Who are you?

But Dad, he said. There's something else I want to talk about.

His father waited, eyebrows raised.

I don't want to go back to that school next year.

I think you're doing fine, his father said. I think you can handle it. You've got the whole summer to rest up, get back to yourself.

That's not it. It's a terrible school, Dad. You know it is. And it must be horribly expensive.

Dad began to laugh, astonished. What are you talking about? It's your school. You don't want to graduate? You want to rest for life?

I don't. Of course I want to graduate. I just want to go somewhere else.

Oho. Like for instance.

I'd go to Central.

A silence had fallen around the table during this exchange. John's sisters, from the one older than he to the three younger ones, ought to have been at once alarmed and scandalized—not go to Catholic school?—but he was well aware that at least the two older sisters, one graduated from and the other now attending St. Joe's, knew why he'd want to. His father was silenced too: never had he been spoken to in this fashion by a child, as though from equal to equal, on a matter of importance. Likely his father thought now: so the fall, or the coma, *did* do some damage.

Could you even do that? John's mother put in, somewhat timidly. Would the credits and all that match? Could you really go for only one year?

His older sister Martha snorted at that. I did, she said. (That had been when they'd moved to Indiana from Kentucky, Martha with only two years left of high school. She'd graduated the year John had entered.)

He told his mother he didn't know, that he'd have to go and ask, or write a letter; anyway he'd find out.

How would you get there? his sister Kathy asked. It's way far away. Downtown.

Well, John said, with a big warm smile for all of them, that's another thing.

John C. had always been unconscious of having a future, beyond a dreamy sense of distant fame and gratification; when he had been a young child he'd imagined that one day he would be pictured on the cover of *Time* magazine as Man of the Year, without being able to imagine for what. When a classmate had described his own goal of getting into pharmacy school by doing well in science and chemistry courses, earning a degree, moving to Los Angeles where the weather was always perfect, and there starting a family, John could only marvel; he supposed the making of such firm plans was unusual, even rare. His own this-world planning (as opposed to otherworld imagining) had been rudimentary, reaching only as far as learning to drive and getting a license, which so far he had not accomplished.

That minimal ambition was now extended to actually possessing a car, and soon. It would be necessary to the idea he'd proposed, about not returning to St. Joseph's in the fall. He didn't think that his father's objections were a real obstacle—he hadn't actually made any, beyond his expressions of affronted surprise. Of course Catholic families stood under an obligation to send their children to Catholic schools, but it wasn't a sin not to, and John didn't think his school—it resembled a big new-ish public school building, made of yellow brick, and run and staffed by an order of brothers, something like male nuns, who were third-rate intellects mostly and full of bizarre notions about the world—this school could hardly retain anyone's allegiance. John had only to cross the barrier between his standing in the family and his father's, address Dad with grown-up reasonableness on the subject (as he had begun to already), and solve all the lesser practical problems, and then even if his father was in a mood to put his foot down, John was prepared to be intransigent too—for the first time. Evasion, restive acceptance, resentment, inertia: no more.

He laughed that rich laugh, alone but heard down the hall and in the kitchen: a laugh of amusement or amazement or both.

So the practical problems. These included the research about transferring schools, and the driver's license, and the car.

All these would depend on solving a forestanding problem: money.

He'd been told, upon reaching the age when he could legally drive, that in order even to get a beginner's license he would have to raise the money to pay for the additional premium that the insurance company demanded to cover a teenage male driver, whose risks were higher than any other's. His sisters would not be charged this extra premium. It was a big number—more than sixty dollars, payable at every quarter—and the John C. that he had formerly been was incapable of imagining how to raise a sum like that. He had used to scan the *South Bend Tribune* for part-time jobs, and for a time worked downtown at the Colefax Theater as an afternoon usher, but at fifty cents an hour, most of it used up taking the bus back and forth from town to where his mother could pick him up, the proceeds couldn't accumulate fast enough. He also bravely committed himself to try to sell water softeners door to door—no experience required, the ad said, just get-up-and-go. He was to show possible customers how hard their water was with simple chemical tests and display glossy pamphlets about the machine. Not only had he shrunk from the impertinence of doing such things—start with your neighbors, the sales manager told him and the other trainees—but intuited, without actually understanding, how unlikely it was that anyone would buy a large item of household machinery from him or anyone like him: slight, shy, slovenly, and profoundly uninterested. He didn't in the end make a single pitch.

But he now knew a way to solve those two problems (car, insurance premium) at a stroke. It would take a little time, but it was summer now and he had plenty of that.

There was at that time a television program, rather groundbreaking (it took very little to break the ground of network television programming then) and widely popular. John C.'s family watched it every week: the saturnine man in black with his eternal cigarette coming out of the darkness to propose some possibility, or impossibility; raise a profound-seeming question about life or time. And a story would follow that illustrated it.

Where does he get these ideas, Mom wondered.

They're not mostly his, John said. Writers send them in. I read that. Stories and scripts. Some of them are from stories in magazines.

Well, I don't know how anyone can think up these weird things.

I bet, John said, crossing his legs and taking his knee in his hands, I could think of one. He cast his eyes upward then as though pondering a notion. His family were laughing now, at his brag, at the histrionic pose of meditation, which he continued by rubbing his chin and contorting his features into a parody of intense thought. I bet I could.

The Christmas before, his older sister had been given a pretty little portable typewriter, for her school papers and so on. John had borrowed it frequently—using it perhaps more than she did—and now that school was out he could sequester it in his own room for the work he had in hand. At the top of the first sheet of "erasable" style typewriter paper he rolled into the machine he typed this, in capitals:

THE BUREAU OF SECOND CHANCES

—and below this his name, including his middle name (Michael). Then he began.

He tried at first to write his story as a screenplay—he could see vividly the scenes he planned, the stark black-and-white images, could hear the curt and pointed dialogue—but the mechanics of the typewriter were clumsy and trying; he got impatient attempting to put characters' names in the center of the page and their dialogue in a shapely square below, and he made so many typos that the typewriter roller became coated in pink eraser dust. He cleaned it out and started again with a plain story, though in a very filmic style.

Joe Noakes is a lucky man, it began. (This would, on television, be among the host's minatory opening remarks.) *He has a beautiful wife, and he'd come into a lot of money. His whole life's ahead of him. So why should Joe be sitting in a dark bar in a dark part of town with nobody but the bartender to tell his story to?*

The story continued with Joe and the bartender—John C. tried to figure out how to communicate in words that looming angle at which movie scenes filled with foreboding are shot. *Sure,* Joe tells the bartender, *I had a lucky break—or so I thought. . . .* Joe's story, with Joe's telling heard "over," returns to its beginning: Joe walks a city street, buys a paper, pops a mint in his mouth, strolls on, turns right into an avenue and stops at a bus stop. A woman—a good-looking woman (John C. strove for the usual adjectives) in obvious distress stands at the stop. Spotting Joe, she runs to him, takes his arm as though she knows him. She's in big trouble, needs a friend, pleads for his help. She puts a satchel into his hands, whispers the address of a meeting place, and hastens away—but not before planting a kiss on his cheek and looking long into his eyes.

Sure I went to meet her, Joe tells the barkeep. *For a couple of reasons. First of all, she was a stunner, the most gorgeous animal that's ever licked my face. And something else: that bag she was carrying turned out to be full of US currency, high denominations. Where she got it, I guess I really didn't want to know. And anyway we never spent much time talking.*

Joe tells his tale, and the scenes of his life with the woman continue. She presses him to quit his job, move to another city. She's demanding, then unfaithful; she tortures him with her beauty, mocks him as a weakling. It's clear she's been using people since she was a kid, and Joe's just the latest of her catches. When the money starts to run out she needles him to get more. When he tries to break free she lets him know she can turn him over to the cops—after all, he received stolen money, her accomplice, her sucker.

I can't break with her, he tells the bartender. *I can't live with her.*

Tough, the bartender says.

If there was only a way out . . . If only I could start again, knowing what I know now.

Yeah? What would you do?

Just one thing. If I could relive that day, when I got to that corner I'd turn the other way: left, not right. That's all I'd ask.

The bartender studies him thoughtfully (John C. had in his conception already cast the man—a heavy-set seen-it-all actor who appeared in many shows) and then from the corner of the bar mirror he plucks a card that's stuck there and hands it to Joe. In closeup (as on TV it would be) he reads it: *Bureau of Second Chances,* and an address.

Take it, says the bartender. *You're just the kind of guy they might help.*

The story follows Joe to the address on the card, a standard office building, and to a high floor and a door with the name lettered on the glass. The office within is plain and grim: a desk, a gooseneck lamp, a filing cabinet, a telephone. The dour man in the swivel chair seems to have expected him, and when Joe proffers the card, shows him a chair.

The next bit of dialogue took John the longest—Joe negotiates for his second chance, the power to return to where he started, and at that fateful corner turn left, not right, into the good, simple life he should have had. What reason can Joe give that he and not another should get this chance? What evidence that the Bureau has the power to produce it? In the end John got it pretty right (after many pages, both written and typed, had been crumpled and discarded).

Then the ending, which he'd known all along.

Then the writing of a letter of introduction, and mailing it and the story to the Los Angeles office of the production company, whose address took some library work to find.

The strange thing was that from the first time the television show made from his story aired—he was gone from home by then—and then every time down through the years when he happened to see it again, when the weekly program he wrote it for had become a perfect example of a certain era of popular entertainment and the childhood of television, when people would gather to watch ancient reruns of the degraded kinescopes, when the one made from John C.'s initial story turned up on rerun channels (to ironic cheers among his friends and colleagues), he would every time be seized with an inexpressible dread or loathing, a heart-sickness that he couldn't admit and couldn't relieve: felt it most intensely in watching Joe, in the final moments of the show, walk down the street (a street in Santa Monica, as by then he knew), stop at the kiosk for the paper, pop a mint in his mouth, come to the corner, and at the light turn left not right.

And walk—inevitably, forever, each time—right into the bank robbery, the heist from which the dame he'd made his wife, in the life he's just escaped, has got away with the take. She passes him with a curious look, he stands dumbfounded; the rest of the gang barrel out of the bank chased by the bank guard, who shoots *bang bang* at their fleeing backs, and hits—

Joe.

The last shot of the show—excepting the hosts's grim setting of the moral—is Joe dying on the pavement. His POV, looking up at the faces of bystanders looking down (a trick shot John C. couldn't himself have thought of in the writing of it). And among them one who mouths, *Poor dope. He never had a chance.*

———

John C.'s typescript of the story came back to South Bend from the production company with a brief printed rejection notice, on which someone had written in ball-point pen *This is good. Get an agent.* John C. found it fairly easy to do that: an agent he found in a directory at the library, who had sold more than one story to the show as well as many stories to the drugstore mystery and science fiction magazines that John never read, responded quickly to his letter of inquiry and the (by now rather weary-looking) typed pages.

With six hundred dollars the agent got him for publication and TV rights to the story—by then it was late summer and things were getting urgent—he could make a case for driving lessons, being now able to afford not only the extra insurance premium for a couple of years to come but also the car itself. His father drove an Oldsmobile, having progressed upward over the years as many men did from one General Motors model to another—from Chevrolet to Pontiac to Olds, though it was unlikely that a doctor at a college student infirmary would ever arrive at a Buick or a Cadillac. For a first-time driver the choices were more limited, and John C.'s would come from the great pool of used Studebakers available at every price, any year and condition, there in the town where they were made. The family's second car, driven by Mrs. C. and now also by John C.'s older sister—who was charged no additional insurance premium—was a 1949 Studebaker two-door coupe, one of the oddest cars ever produced by a major American manufacturer. "Can't tell whether it's coming or going," a wag once remarked about its styling. The car for me, John C. said.

First, though, he needed to learn to drive, and in that car he did.

His father didn't elect to do that work, so (having been taken to the bureau of motor vehicles and obtained a beginner's license) he asked first his sister Martha, and when she begged off, his mother. She took him out to empty parking lots and back roads, and was amazed at his swift progress; it was almost (she said) as though it were in his blood. After a little practice, laughing at himself and the big car and its heavy pedals and huge steering wheel and column-mounted gearshift, he could get around easily; learned to parallel-park in minutes (after a period of smiling self-doubt); did three-point turns faultlessly. Maybe I should be a race-car driver, he said.

Within a couple of weeks it was apparent he was ready to take a driver's test, though he insisted he felt still uncertain, and needed more days. But he passed the driving test with ease—he told his mother (who sat in the backseat in a state between unease and hilarity) that it was because he'd worn a tie; an American young man in a tie qualifies for a license, he said, just by reason of those qualities. He'd never be a race-car driver, but not long after inheriting the Studebaker (his mother and sister moved a step up to a 1950 Chevy paid for in large part by John C.) he took it to a motor-parts shop that sold and installed racing equipment, and had a seat belt installed. It may have been the only Studie sedan in the city, perhaps the world, that had one.

The remainder of the money he received from the sale of his story he divided between his father, for the insurance, and a brand-new savings account. Then he settled down to meet St. Joe's requirements and complete his junior year, driving himself to the Notre Dame library each day with a long yellow legal pad and a Scripto ball-point pen made in two lovely shades of gray-green plastic, a red button like a mocking tongue projecting from the top to press: of all the things he recognized newly after his return, this was among the most touching to him; he almost wept to see and use it. He sat at a long table in the library, a place he knew well, or he walked under the old trees of the campus, thinking about other things than the subjects of his papers or the facts about American government or organic chemistry he was committing to, or recalling from, memory. Nuns in the habits of many orders, attending summer school classes, strolled or hurried along the paths in twos and threes, books under their arms, veils lifted by the summer airs. In the cool basement of the Student Center he put dimes in the red machine for small pale-green bottles of Coca-Cola, again thinking of many things, and in the late afternoon drove home with dreamy slowness along the road past the old and humble Little Flower Church where he'd been an altar boy not so long ago, past the road down which lived his beloved Miriam, schoolmate in eighth grade, turning on Ironwood past the new and unlovely Little Flower Church, and down the long hill to Ponader Drive. In his room after dinner he continued to write, volumes of the family Britannica next to him and papers on *Macbeth* and the Bicameral System growing longer while the laughter of TV audiences, mixed with his family's, came in from the living room. A remarkable thing his family had noticed, resulting (presumably) from his accident and his coma, was that his handwriting had changed. It looked like the hand of someone else entirely: someone long out of school.

John C. enrolled at Central High School for the fall semester of 1959, having convinced his father and the principal and the director of studies that he had enough credits to transfer, and that with enough effort he could graduate in June of 1960. He was helped to select courses that would be applicable, and was allowed to take typing as an elective. When the semester began he found, without surprise, that he was the only male in the typing class. He loved it, loved the girls in their skirts and dresses, their beehive hairdos and flips, their Capezios and their tennis shoes. St. Joseph's had been divided into wings, one for the males taught by brothers, the other for females taught by nuns; the two connected nowhere. Now he sat amid the upright backs and lifted hands, the unearthly clatter of all the Remingtons going at once like an enfilade, and could hardly keep from laughing aloud in delight.

That month his agent sold a new story of his to a science fiction magazine for twenty-seven dollars and fifty cents. On a Saturday he went to Robertson's department store and bought new clothes: soft pleated grey flannel slacks, narrow at the ankle; white shirts, to be worn with the sleeves rolled up two turns; patterned sweaters in cashmere and merino. The cuffed slacks broke prettily over penny loafers (also new) and showed a bit of bright white sock. John C. had before been a poor dresser, mostly content with what his mother brought home from sales. In October he was ready to start dating, which the school he'd previously attended, and his lack of wheels, and his timidity, had made difficult. His parents, who had never before seen any reason to give him a curfew, told him he must be in by ten on school nights, and by midnight on weekends. He never violated the rule.

With a car and a daily drive to Central, and soon the trips to Barbara's house in Sunnymede, a middle-class development off Wayne Street, or later on to Phyllis's in the similarly named but very different Sunnyside Apartments on Jefferson Boulevard, he learned more about South Bend in this year than he had in all his isolated years on Ponader Drive. He had always had an odd disability, a nearly absent sense of spatial orientation that for a long time he hadn't actually perceived, just as people who have no color vision sometimes don't perceive their lack until it's proven to them. Now he knew about it, and knew he had to take it into account. He acquired a city map at a drugstore and marked it in colored pencils, the way to this place, the way to that, the houses of girls, the diners and carhop places, the drive-in movie theaters. At the drive-ins, the Western Theater on Peppermint Drive, the Moonlite on Chippewa, he sat with Phyllis resting in his arm and watched fox-eyed Natalie Wood and James Garner in *Cash McCall*, admiring Garner's beautiful suits of blue and black. You'd look so sharp in that, Phyllis murmured, and John thought, yes, he would. When the second feature, *The Electronic Monster*, started he talked to Phyllis about Phyllis, looking with genuine delight and sympathy into her eyes, which strangely resembled Natalie Woods's. Then no talking for a long time while the great beams of light from the projector played over the screen, producing the illusion of motion. The cones of her white stitched bra were stiff; the sleek sateen of her underpants, which he found beneath the gingham skirt, grew damp beneath his hand: but he'd go no farther.

Amazing how it was that he could now know, as though granted a new sense or instinct, what he hadn't known, what other boys growing up elsewhere might have known but he never had: that the girls he was drawn to were just as drawn to him, some of them at least, and more than that: that their desires were as intense as his own, however muffled or tied down; and if you did know that, how easily released they were, right up to the last barriers. What trust they placed in him, what hope: that he'd be good, that he'd know them, know their hearts. And he was, and he did. And he'd bring them home and they'd straighten themselves in the odorous front seat and do their lipstick in the rear-view mirror, eyes soft in the street-light. In no way would he *get in trouble,* as the phrase was, the trouble that haunted parents, and no way he would get girls in trouble, wake up little Suzy. He broke no hearts; he made clear to them he would not, but neither would he would pledge his own. And he'd drift in at his front door at the appointed hour and his mother would look up from her mystery novel and look at him with interest and some kind of knowledge of her own that he had not suspected, not before; and in his narrow bed, night after night, he'd lie in the grip of a lust more potent and unceasing than he had ever felt—or rather than he had felt since he had last left this point in time behind and gone on into the life he was to lead. He'd relieve the pressure twice in a night and then sometimes wake from thrilling dreams anointed again, and turn his face to the wall in wonder, and he'd laugh: remembering, and at the same time being, what he once had been.

La Brea Medical Transcription Service • 1419 La Brea Avenue • Los Angeles CA 90019
For: Dr. Carla Young PhD
9/23/92 Initial Session

CY Notes: John C. White male in good physical health, employed as a screen-writer, age 49. Presenting with undefined anxiety and midlife crisis.

Transcript begins at 05:00:02

CY:—and record our conversations, purely for my own uses. If you object—

JC: No, no. It's all right. I'm sure it will be useful. A record.

CY: So how are you today? How can I help?

JC: I'm fine, thank you, Doctor. I'm in trouble. I am at . . . an impasse, I guess would be the word.

CY: Well, all right. Good enough to start with, I suppose. Do you have any questions for me before we—

JC: Several questions. Just deciding to make this appointment made me question myself.

CY: Can you say what sort of questions?

JC: Questions of how much I want to tell you, and whether what I tell you will be believed, and what good it would do me if you did believe me. Or didn't.

CY: Those are extremely important self-queries, but I think we'd need a lot more groundwork before it would be useful to address them. For us to address them together, or for you yourself to do so.

JC: All right then.

CY: Can we perhaps begin with the problem you named on the form?

JC: The one I came in with, or maybe you'd say "presented" with?

CY: Your creative block, or what you experience as one. We can begin with that, if that's where you now feel comfortable.

JC: I no longer feel comfortable anytime. But thank you, okay. The film. It's an idea I've been working on for a long time. Years, actually. Now the situation seems right. Rocco Sisto has committed to the concept—you remember he got Best Actor last year for *Midsummer,* the Shakespeare adaptation. Terence Malick has expressed interest.

CY: And?

JC: And I—well—I can't, I can't conclude it.

CY: You can't imagine an ending for it.

JC: No. I know how it has to end. It's just that the story, as a film story, can't end.

CY: I'm lost. You'd better try to explain.

JC: All right. This won't be easy for me.

CY: I'm patient.

JC: Okay. The film story—or maybe better to call it the *situation*, because the story or what might be called the plot is the problem—is this. A man, a man about my age, learns that he can begin his life again, starting from a point in his past that he chooses, and can make it different: he can choose a different way of life, fulfill different ambitions, meet different people. And just as important avoid the choices he did make, the life he did lead, the people he did meet and get involved with.

CY: Hm. And what earns him this chance?

JC: Well, nothing. It just suddenly appears to him to be possible. That the world holds that possibility.

CY: No magic ring, no djinni, no three wishes?

JC: No. Anyway none will be revealed. But there's one limit, or not a limit but a condition, or an *out* you might say, depending on how things work out for him. He is given a way to return to a point in his youth or childhood and then to mature and grow older again in a new life that he makes through new choices. But when that day comes around again, the date on which he first found he could go back and do everything differently, he can—no, he *must*— decide whether to continue the new-made life, or return to the first life, and take it up again at exactly the place and moment he made the choice to leave it. And begin there at that moment again.

CY: A sweet deal. He gets to make a whole new lifetime of

mistakes and surprises and, I guess, gratifications, and then annul it. Is that what he does?

JC: Well. That's the problem. He's approaching that day, and can't decide. Or *I* can't. The audience will have seen both lives, quite different in lots of ways but neither one clearly better or worse—crises or big moments from each life are shown in the year the character reaches them. Until, in fact, he reaches the age I am, or he is, when this chance was given him. And he has to choose.

CY: I see. I think I see.

JC: It's an aesthetic problem. If a character in a story is presented with two distinct things or paths or outcomes, and the story makes it possible that he might choose either—that is, in the story as it unfolds, neither possibility vanishes or becomes obviously wrong—then there is no right way to end the story.

CY: Why is that?

JC: Because audiences will perceive that *either* choice is arbitrary, is imposed by the creators, isn't compelled. It could just as well have been the other. Neither choice can be a satisfactory ending.

CY: Okay.

JC: Like love stories, where a character has to make a choice between two people, neither of which is clearly Mr. Right. Or Ms. Right.

CY: Okay.

JC: Well. The commonest solution—and this is such a general problem in storytelling that it does have a common solution—is the Third Thing. The Third Thing is something, or someone, that has been in the story all along, little noticed or maybe misunderstood, but whose real nature is suddenly brought out at the end and negates the other two false choices.

CY: As for instance . . .

JC: For instance a woman's first pulled to A, who's nice, then to B, who's different but flawed, then back to A, who turns out to have a nasty secret. And all along she's talking to her gay male friend about it all. And in the last minutes it's revealed that the friend isn't gay at all, that what she thought she knew about him was wrong, and he's the right choice. The third thing. You get it, right?

CY: Right. I pretty much got it when you began. So this third-thing solution—is finding that third thing what you are stuck on?

JC: I'm stuck because there is no third thing. There can be no third thing in this story. And whichever choice the character makes is at once neither the right nor the wrong one, and likewise the choice that he doesn't make. And not to make a choice, to remain in the state he's in, well, that's to make a choice as well, and is unsatisfactory in the same way.

CY: It's Buridan's ass.

JC: It's *what?*

CY: Buridan's ass. An ancient philosophical problem posed in, I don't know, the 12th century maybe? A problem of choice. An ass—you know, a donkey—is standing equidistant from two piles of hay. Each pile is the same size, the same tastiness or whatever it is that makes some hay more appealing than other hay, all of that exactly equal. And so the donkey can't make a choice. Has no rational basis on which to make a choice. And so . . .

JC: He starves to death.

CY: Right. Actually there's a different and in a way more interesting version, where the donkey is equidistant between two *different* things, a pile of hay and a bucket of water, and he's exactly as hungry as he is thirsty, and so . . .

JC: So he . . . he . . . Yes.

CY: Is that what your story is? A philosophical problem play? A problem you want to work out by creating a character who faces it?

JC: No, no.

CY: It would seem to be at least metaphorical, wouldn't you say? Is that the difficulty? To get the story to reflect what you want to say about your own life. You seek to grasp what it is in your life that seems insufficient or disappointing . . .

JC: It's not metaphorical. It's . . . autobiographical in nature.

CY: Autobiographical.

JC: Yes.

CY: You mean that the events that happen to the character in the first life you describe resemble the facts of your own life? Or do you mean that the events and people in the other, the *imagined* life, are autobiographical—

JC: No. Not either of those.

CY: Maybe "metaphorical" wasn't the right word. But it's sort of well known that people who come to therapists with some very particular reason or problem they want to work on—their suffering actually comes from some other source. Even if the initial reason is real enough to them. But in order for me to help—

JC: Doctor. What I need from you is not any of that . . . argumentation.

CY: Then what?

jc: What I've come for is to ask for help in making this deci-
    sion. You have to listen. You have to listen first to all that
    happened, and then you have to help me to decide.

Transcript ends 58:32:02

In his first semester at Central, John C. began to visit the Student Counseling office for help with his post-high school
plans. It's possible that there had been some sort of student
counseling at St. Joseph's, but he had never asked about it, nor
even considered the possibility.

He already had an offer from Notre Dame, via his father
and his father's associates there, to attend the college tuition-
free; and since he could easily live at home and commute, he'd
save himself and his family a lot of money that way. Though
he hadn't yet explicitly rejected it, in no world past or future
was this an invitation he would accept, and he believed he
would never have to. He could certainly go instead to Indiana
University, which by law had to admit any person who graduated from high school in the state, but that also was not in
his plans. He would instead do what no teacher in his former
high school had suggested and no one at home knew how to
do: he would *apply* to universities elsewhere, and in his appli-
cations give his reasons for selecting each of them, listing his
interests, his achievements, his honors, and his publications.
At the Office of Student Counseling he got the addresses of
the universities he'd selected, so that he could send away for
their particular forms and requirements, which upon receipt
("What's all this?" his father asked, starting a brief but touchy
conversation) he filled out, with advice from Counseling; and

with the application fee of two or four dollars of his own money in the form of a postal money order, he put them in envelopes, addressed them in his new grownup hand, and lastly added multiple 4¢ First Class stamps (some commemorating the Boy Scouts, some the VIII Winter Olympics) plus one plain blue 1¢ Abe Lincoln after another until the postmistress nodded assent. When he received letters of acceptance from those schools, including their offers of decreased tuition or other inducements, he would choose among them.

The University of Southern California. The University of California at Los Angeles. The University of California, Berkeley. Not Harvard, nor Yale, universities where (like Notre Dame) only boys were admitted; he hadn't applied to those. John C. had a general aversion to boys. He liked girls. It was something that had long been noted by his father, who had of course surrounded him with sisters.

When the acceptances began to come in, and the colorful brochures showing happy students and wide lawns and earnest professors, he decided after brief study (his sisters leaning over his shoulder and marveling and choosing for him) on the University of Southern California.

And the worlds he would occupy and the world he had occupied began to divide irremediably.

In that world he had never played sports of any kind. Though he certainly could have taken one up, track or tennis, but not football or basketball (the ones that mattered), he did nothing about it, and only at his father's insistence would he go with him to the golf course to caddy, or at least pull the golf-bag trolley behind him from hole to hole.

In this world he asked his father to take him golfing, teach him the basics, and he took up the game his father was devoted to, and proved to be at least basically competent; he was a good putter but his long game was weak. He asked his father for pointers.

In that world he had found himself often unable to sit alone comfortably in the same room as his father, though he could never understand why he felt that way. If the rest of the family or his siblings or his mother were there, he could share the space, but not alone with his father (feet up, reading the paper; watching television; leafing through a medical journal). He'd work to overcome it but mostly he'd just leave.

In *this* world he sat contentedly with his father, asked him questions, tried to elicit his opinions or his history, just by the way; they talked about McCarthy and the Communists, about Ike and Nixon, about his father's father and his grandfather. John C. talked about himself too: what he hoped to do—make movies, direct plays, write poetry—and his father had to assent to listen. Sometimes he'd bring his sewing—capes and vestments and robes for his tall rod puppets.

Don't worry, Dad, he said one evening as his father observed the work. I'm not queer. Just artsy.

La Brea Medical Transcription Service • 1419 La Brea Avenue • Los Angeles CA 90019
For: Dr. Carla Young PhD
10/06/92
<u>*Subject:*</u> *John C.*
Second Session
CY: *Notes. Second session, the presenting problem was set aside and at my suggestion a general life story was begun. In the course of that session a string of odd beliefs or magical thinking influencing behavior appeared. Unusual*

perceptual experiences, including bodily illusions. Inappropriate or constricted affect. This is a very odd duck.

Transcript begins at 02:07:00

CY: John, we haven't got a lot of time left in this hour. I want to be very clear as to how you yourself understand this story you are telling me.

JC: The *story* I'm telling?

CY: Well, your account. I meant it in no prejudicial sense.

JC: Though of course you have in fact prejudged it.

CY: I try not to prejudge. I may make tentative hypotheses.

JC: It's okay that you prejudge. I would completely understand.

CY: Let's continue with the account of your past you began with, and see where that leads us, from then to now.

JC: All right. But which account?

CY: John, you're the one who believes there is more than a single account. I can only accept the one that brings you here to this office in this city in this year. The other is what you want to relate, which is fine, but it doesn't have the same . . .

JC: The same ontological standing.

CY: That's a rather chilly way to describe it. It doesn't have the same claims, not in this room. I'd call it something more like a *doppelganger*, or perhaps it's a sort of incubus, a creature and creator of dreams who rides you.

JC: There's your prejudgment.

CY: Very well. Tell me whatever you like, and perhaps my judgment will surprise you by changing too.

JC: And what's your judgment now? At this moment?

CY: What I think is that you have developed a sort of private mythology. A mythology in which you have become entrapped. One that limits you as a person even though it seems to you to be an enlargement.

JC: For a long time it did feel like an enlargement. An enormous, an indescribable enlargement. It doesn't now.

CY: Exactly. Now you wish to escape from it, to free yourself to be . . . well, ordinary. To join the rest of us, from whom you've become so estranged.

JC: Doctor. I want help. But escape isn't possible at all. Even the choice I face, which can change everything, doesn't have escape in it as a component.

CY: Of course it does. I'd use the word "freedom" instead of "escape," because there's nothing to escape *from.* There is no actual evidence for it but your own fabulation. This idea that you alone can actually, physically, remake the past and make other choices—

JC: But what if, Dr. Young, I'm *not* alone? If the universe can divide once, it can divide many times. There may be vast populations by now that have done what I did, learned what I learned . . . You're laughing.

CY: I can't conceive what evidence could be collected that it's possible, much less that it's the case, that it's common.

JC: Well, there couldn't actually be any *evidence* except for the stories people tell. And just because no one before has ever told you theirs—

CY: No. I have heard stories in many, many forms. I have heard about worlds that people believe they inhabit but that can't be found in the physical universe. I've also helped to uncover stories that I came to believe are true—stories of abuse and trauma—that persons in deep travail refused to allow themselves to know, and who were freed to some degree by coming to know them as true. All of it without physical evidence. Stories are your business. Mine too.

JC: Of course.

CY: And were you so unhappy in that supposed other life that you were able to conceive of this radical remaking? So desperate that you needed to believe this strongly in the possibility?

JC: No, no. I wasn't desperate. I was living a pretty good life.

CY: But it wasn't enough.

JC: It was enough, but the whole range of alternate possibilities haunted me, haunted me day and night. Haunted is wrong. Intrigued and tempted.

CY: How can you be tempted by something impossible? That's harmless daydreaming; everybody does it. What was it you felt you didn't have that made this daydreaming so . . . importunate, I guess? Did you feel you hadn't got recognition enough, or fame enough?

JC: I would have liked more recognition. It wasn't that I'd had none.

CY: For your screenwriting and film-making.

JC: No. I wasn't making films. I was writing novels. I was living in New England and I had a family and I wrote novels and stories. I wasn't dissatisfied. I just wanted to know what would have happened to me if I had made different choices. Choices that I couldn't have made because I didn't know they were possible, and I wouldn't have known how to make them possible.

CY: So you returned from maturity—age what now, fifty? . . .

JC: Forty-nine.

CY: . . . to the point in time when it seemed you had the greatest chance to make a wholly different life. You were in the body you then possessed but with a consciousness that had been created later, in a different life. Is that right? How did you bring that off? I mean by what mechanism, what—

JC: Well, by no mechanism. I guess . . . I just understood that I could.

CY: And did the whole of this new-to-you other West Coast world come to be around you as you lived in it? The one I'd call "this world"? Did it day by day replace the one you had lived in all your life, begin to be changed for you, and not only for you but for everyone?

JC: Of course not. It's a world that has existed from the beginning. At least now it does. All I did was to enter it.

CY: And what became of the world you departed from, the one where you went to the state school, lived in New York, wrote novels, all that?

JC: Here's what I know: Both those states of the world exist until one is chosen. When one is chosen the other ceases to be. Ceases to have ever been. I don't want to bring up the name Heisenberg here. It might be an utter misdirection.

CY: From what I'm hearing, John, this is *all* misdirection. Your task should be to learn that. Do you know the term "anosognosia"?

JC: Of course. A condition where a person is incapable of recognizing an illness, even a paralysis that seems impossible to ignore or deny. It might be you are thinking I am such a person.

CY: Well?

JC: If I am, of course, I wouldn't be able to know it. And if I'm delusional—as I know you believe me to be—I'd deny it even if I was anosognosic.

CY: Yes, well. How anyway do you come to know about this condition? It's quite rare.

JC: The first film I wrote and directed was about it. A short film. It's actually called *Anosognosia*, a title that was almost designed to keep people from wanting to see it. But it also won awards. You've heard of it?

CY: No.

JC: It actually turns on *two* neurological conditions: that one, and one I heard about from a professor of neurology at USC: one where certain kinds of brain damage can cause people to fail to recognize common objects, including the alphabet. My film was about a viral plague that causes this condition, spreading among the story's characters, eventually including an investigator of the plague, who continues to write his accounts though he can no longer read what he has written.

CY: I see.

JC: It was all done in still photographs, with his narration over. He can increasingly not recognize the various items he is studying as possible disease vectors, but he continues to make his notes. *A sort of fruit I cannot put a name to—perhaps it's foreign or tropical—I seem to recognize the shape—totally unknown to me though . . .* We can see it's an apple.

CY: And because of his anosognosia he can't realize that he is suffering from the condition of being unable to recognize common things, the condition he's seeking to find a cure for.

JC: Exactly.

CY: That is unbelievably cruel.

JC: Yes. It was also very funny. I was sort of unable to make such distinctions back then. It was . . . *witty,* and a few people still remember it for being witty. It's on cassette, if you'd like to see it. A good transfer.

CY: Maybe. I think we have enough levels of illusion here to deal with already.

JC: In that regard. There's something I haven't explained clearly why I have come to you, something about this . . . story.

CY: Not about a writing block.

JC: I came because the terms of my . . . good fortune, superpower, mad illusion, whatever it is, are very specific and have become urgent. I have to make the choice I must make—whether to stay in this world or return to the world I began in—before the end of my fiftieth year. On my fiftieth birthday, in effect.

CY: And that would be when?

JC: The first day of December of this year. A month from now.

CY: Well, John. Let's hope that we can relieve you of the anxiety that must come with that rule, or condition. Let's assume that we can—together—help you to see it as it really is.

JC: And to choose correctly.

CY: Not to choose at all, and stay in the real world with the rest of us.

Transcript ends 51:36:00

At USC John C. was a theater and art major, though many of his classes were in the film department. The making of student films at that time was so constrained by the equipment that John C. felt that he could get more experience in the things most important to a director from theater work—directing actors, conceiving approaches to plays, building and slowing tension in a scene. He had used to believe that he couldn't succeed as an *auteur* in film or theater because the real medium of both those arts was the same: not words, or actors, or camera movement, or "light," or anything but *other people.* The medium of theater and film is other people: people who have to be cajoled, encouraged, bullied, subjected to the demands of the project. The contributions of these others—actors, designers, lighting technicians, animators, editors, costume designers, musicians and composers—have to be all put in service of an overarching vision, the director's. That vision can be modified and even upended by brilliant work contributed by others, but only as the director perceives that work; the director has to be able to refuse any work that doesn't meet what he sees in his head or heart. John C., who had never been assertive, who was small, easygoing, open, and afraid of hurting others, even the inadequate and the clueless—he could, he had believed, never be that imperial central point around which everything moved.

At USC he aimed to be. And learned that he could be. All that stood in his way was the past he had shed.

His mode had to be soft-spoken; it had to depend on the projection of a calm certitude, as though resulting from a long career in collaborative creation, though of course it couldn't and didn't. When he took modern-dance classes, when he did animation projects in art, he entered into them and spoke about them to others as though these were simply parts of a mastery he aimed for and in some sense therefore already possessed, and the others who must be his medium accepted and acknowledged that. By the time he was a senior he had taken on several independent projects, some with fairly large casts. His senior piece in directing was a chamber *Hamlet*, the text reduced to an hour's playing time. A woman who had taken two acting classes with him was his inspiration: she was lean, fierce, disputatious, always challenging her teachers, constantly pissed off in a deep part of her; she wore her thick black hair in a boyish mop, she had a single thick eyebrow above her deep black eyes and a nose like a predator's beak. She dressed in beatnik jeans and sloppy T-shirts, and it was clear to everyone—certainly to John C.—that she was what was called in those days, without censure in the circles in which she and John C. moved, a dyke. He wanted her for his Hamlet. Her first response to the invitation was swift and angry, as at an insult. *Oh yeah right.* He kept after her. It had long seemed to John C. that *rage* was what possesses Hamlet, fury, fury at his own inadequacy, at his opposers and the clueless: and few actors ever got that, not the ones John C. had seen. He and she tussled and argued over scenes and speeches, she yelled at him and he coldly demanded more and she mocked him and her obdurate lines and gave more, as though devouring herself to feed her Hamlet.

He staged the play on a small platform, the whole cast on stage all the time, getting up from their chairs or stools or the floor to enter the action. The characters were afraid of this Hamlet, and so were the actors. She was exalted at moments, face fuliginous, wrath unleashed and purified in beautiful sense: and it showed. No one had ever seen a Hamlet like this. They played the play in schools, in the park, in the rain, got into the papers, the news shows. Of course it was sensational that a woman, or a girl as most of the notices called her, was playing Hamlet; there were mentions of Bernhardt and Asta Nielsen (John C. had taken her to the film archive and retrieved a silent reel of Nielsen's performance, which she watched with supernatural intensity and then said *Bullshit*), but whatever anyone imagined a woman playing Hamlet would be like, it wasn't this. When Horatio challenged her actions— *Why, what a king is this?*—she rounded on him, the only loyal friend she has, grasping his lapel, almost unable to spit out the lines:

> *Does it not, think'st thee, stand me now upon—*
> *He that hath kill'd my king and whored my mother,*
> *Popp'd in between the election and my hopes,*
> *Thrown out his angle for my proper life,*
> *And with such cozenage—is't not perfect conscience,*
> *To quit him with this arm? and is't not to be damn'd,*
> *To let this canker of our nature come*
> *In further evil?*

For her, it proved to be a one-time thing, as though in doing it she'd spent her lifetime's store of black energy. John C. couldn't get her to do more work, take on different things, some he'd written himself for her. His desire for her, the impossibility of it, how he and she had transmuted impossibility and need into shared power in art, made it seem she would have to go on giving and getting with him, but after graduation she went into biology, got a degree, set off on months-long collecting trips to the Costa Rican rain forest, sent him postcards and curt letters almost indecipherable, and then stopped.

Even a self-designed life has doors that won't open, or won't stay shut.

Becalmed, he stayed at USC, going to movies, acting in the movies people he knew were making, jokey or earnest or outlandish; he enrolled in graduate school just to keep working. He would forget, now and then, just how young he was, no matter how old the soul was that inhabited him, whose sour faults he still came up against. Classes he skipped, assignments he skimped, but his master's thesis production of Webster's *The Duchess of Malfi* attracted actors and designers and techies who would come and go in his later life. The *eclat* he'd earned with his *Hamlet* won him resources and scope for a larger and richer production. He set the old dark play, a horror story at bottom, in present-day Italy, in modern dress: the factor Bosola was dressed in a soft Italian black leather jacket and dark glasses, his hair in a razor cut, a cigarette often in the corner of his mouth; the Duchess was sexual and fierce as certainly no college lead had ever been, in loose dressing-gowns and slips—John C. modeled the look, and the lust, on Elizabeth Taylor in *Cat on a Hot Tin Roof*, or on his memory of it—here, the play hadn't, apparently, been filmed. He took the cast—the leads, anyway—to see *Eclipse*, with Alan Delon and Monica Vitti, Marcello Mastroianni in *La Dolce Vita*. Ennui, intrigue, a sense of entitlement smashed in jealousy and death. *Rome is a city of young men waiting to have their shoes shined. Since God has decided to bestow upon us the Papacy, then let us enjoy it.* He wanted to create a modern Italy as sinful and passionate and burdened by history as it had seemed to the Elizabethans: the story, after all, was a true one. The flashbulbs popping at the end as the police arrive to find the Duchess dead gave Bosola's famed line more point: *Cover her face,* he tells the servants. *Mine eyes dazzle. She died young.*

All that certainly caught people's attention. But what he really did that was innovative was to teach his actors how to speak Elizabethan verse in the present moment, what his dyke Hamlet had had as an instinct. For most actors it was still the age of the British greats; college kids unable to do what the Oliviers and the Gielguds did ended up instead reciting the verse in a singsong lilt with a sort of pious or elevated expression. This is what John C. combated, astonishing himself with the toughness he could muster before them, all of them looking at him with awe, or at least as much awe as Californians could then produce. *You have to find a way to say these lines as if you just now thought to say them, as though they came right from your heart and out your mouth. It's you who's saying this stuff. Say it as yourself. But say it as if you weren't you but this person. Bosola. The Cardinal. The Duchess. When you have to say antique words your audience might not know, say them just the way you'd say the modern equivalent, they'll get it because you—you the Cardinal—you know what it means and always have.* He pushed them together, faces fiercely close; he made them take pauses impossibly long before huge shouted admissions or desperate, whispered fealty.

Some of his actors confused his instruction with what they knew of method acting—finding the character they are playing within themselves and their experience, bringing up emotions as in a therapeutic session which they could then attach to the imaginary people they instantiated. *No, that's not it,* he told them. *All this is happening to someone else, the person you are being; it's all on the outside, it only seems to be on the inside.* A couple of them quit in disgust; authenticity was their touchstone, this all seemed hypocrisy or artificiality. But not his Duchess. He told her that the Duchess knows, of *course* she knows, she's doomed; but she's going to fight right to the end with every trick and every power she has. You have to be both, he told her: both doomed and fighting. And sexy. Sex is power, sex is proof of love, sex is everything. Her damn *brother* is in love with her. In a motel room on Alvarado he drew still more out of her, and she gripped his shoulders fiercely in the dark.

And later that night sat alone in a bright bar, filled with a subtle and pervasive nausea, the Sartrean kind he did not need to read about again in Sartre: a profound embarrassment at the fact of existence.

La Brea Medical Transcription Service • 1419 La Brea Avenue • Los Angeles CA 90019
For: Dr. Carla Young PhD
10/06/92
<u>*Subject*</u>*: John C.*
Third Session

CY Notes. This is the most thoroughgoing delusion I have ever encountered, and it is maintained with a calm and certainty that is remarkable. An icy calm I would say except that he does not seem frozen in the way that a paranoid schizophrenic can seem. He can recount the contents of long novels he wrote (and was writing) in his "other existence" as a novelist. Asked if he could write out one of those novels now—his answer was Why would he? A check of the arpanet shows that no such titles as he puts forward are in existence. It's clear that he has invented the other life because of unhappiness in this one: desire for marriage and children, for real love which he can't feel in the disconnected, perhaps alienated, LA life he has led. It's a mental illness that he can't acknowledge: that he has invented the other life as a repository for his unacknowledged and inadmissible disease. I wonder if I can help him at all. I wonder if he'll be back.

Transcription begins at 06:09:00

CY: . . . Now it's turned on. I'm always forgetting to push the button. We were saying—well, I was—that it must have taken you some courage to make this leap from one life to another. With the knowledge that as many limiting and disappointing things would be likely to happen, despite all this careful planning you say you did. Life itself. Can't be controlled, can it?

JC: Well—Doctor—I think that you are like everyone in this respect: you're sure that anyone given the chance to remake his or her life is going to make just as much of a mess of it the second time. Isn't that what all the stories tell, the stories about second chances, about getting a do-over? Isn't that the moral?

CY: It was, in that TV show you wrote.

JC: You think, don't you, that it would have to turn out that way, the way it does in all the stories about such possibilities. That it would turn to the bad, in retribution for doing the forbidden, taking the fruit. That it will lead to a *worse* life than before, at least no better.

CY: Since I don't believe it's possible in fact, I'll have to remain silent on the question. You alone know how it differs, what the changes amount to.

JC: I'd have liked it to change more than it did. The private history too—the history of private life, you might say—that too I'd like to have been more different. I'd like to have been taken by surprise more often. But that great sweep of change that occurred in my twenties and thirties—both times—well, having experienced it once, I could marvel at its coming to be, and at the same time be irritated at how little it knew itself—if self-knowledge can be ascribed to history, as Hegel almost says it can be. I didn't know whether to be bored or elated half the time.

CY: And the other half?

JC: I exploited what I knew. I was on the curl of the wave.

I knew what to say before others could get their heads around it, as the phrase then was. The films I wrote, the television series, were breakthroughs, or seemed to everyone else to be breakthroughs. I'd gone to school with the people who would become the most important and potent in the field I wanted to work in, and I knew I would when I applied to go there. And I knew what they couldn't know: what would become of them, which of them would fail or die, which would survive and grow. My faith in them—which of course wasn't faith but knowledge—earned me their loyalty too, and I've profited from it. I attracted women. Many women. It was like knowing every bet you placed would win, a little or a lot, no matter which horse you played.

CY: Horse? You seem to be saying that remaking your sexual experiences was the real reason for your restarting your life from adolescence, to avoid commitments and enjoy a sort of movable harem. Can that really be so? Wouldn't your disposition and the limits of your, what'll we say, your charms, come along with you into the new life? I'm sorry to find this just a little amusing. It just seems a bit adolescent.

JC: Yes, I counted on it, the many women. I looked forward to it. *It* never got old, but somehow the life I lived turned out . . . more chaste than I would have thought.

CY: You've been celibate?

JC: I said chaste, not celibate. I've never understood why. Something about the physicality of sex, of nakedness, of heat, so intense, made me more aware that it was in a sense manufactured. It was abashing. I'll tell you how I thought of it. It was like being in an exquisite museum, all alone and free among priceless works of art. You wouldn't steal them, would you? You could, but you can't *have* them really, even if you did steal them; they'd never be yours, and possession isn't the point anyway. So you admire, and maybe touch, and are gratified just to be there, with all of it around you.

CY: You've never married. Did you never want a family? Children?

JC: I've been married. Had children. Two daughters. Just not in this time-stream.

CY: And what was that like, when you think about it now? Did it seem a burden?

JC: Oh, sometimes it was. Mostly it was a delight and a wonder.

CY: Strange how easy to was for you to abandon them.

JC: See, but I *didn't*. I . . . sort of took a vacation. A years-long vacation. They're still there, where and when I left them. In two days I might be with them again. Might well.

CY: Ah yes. I've been thinking about this crux you believe you face, and I have a question.

JC: Yes?

CY: You said that the film you were writing couldn't have an ending, that the choice of either ending for the character would be a disappointment. But what prevents your character from simply doing it all again, starting again from the same place or from a different place? If he believes he can. Wouldn't that be a Third Thing, in effect?

JC: Well, yes, I suppose it would be.

CY: Have you thought that it would be possible for you?

JC: I couldn't do it. I can't.

CY: Because you feel you'd find yourself disappointed again, disappointed in the world?

JC: No. I haven't been disappointed. I can't do it again for the same reason that I *could* do it in the first place. You can't see it, Dr. Young, but you and I are of the same kind, and so are all the other persons that have appeared in my world and that appear to you in yours. Any one of you might be granted the power I was granted. To be granted it you just need to know you have it. And at that point the world grows transparent, and you can walk through it, and do as you like. But only once. This one time. After this time, it closes up. Those are the conditions.

CY: And who set these conditions? God?

JC: The God of this world, maybe.

CY: I can only think that it was you yourself.

JC: You think I've constructed this whole, this dilemma, this ontological problem . . . You think I'm anosognosic, that I can't see I'm delusional.

CY: I'm far from making such a diagnosis.

JC: But do you think, Doctor, that I . . . that someone with this condition, this sickness that he can't know he has, might perceive or . . . well, *account* for the way he is, by supposing that he is, for example, a fiction? A character in a story, whose fate is being written rather than just appearing to him day by day out of the chances of the universe. That his life now is a kind of second draft. Wouldn't that make a kind of sense? That that's the reason why he—

CY: Yes. Of course. There are examples of such negation.

JC: Is it what you want me to see, something like that? What I should confess to, if ever I can see that it's so?

CY: I want nothing from you, John. Honestly. You came to me for help. I think you're in need of help, and I believe help is available. Whatever you now believe you are, whatever you think you can choose tomorrow, whatever you think you

have chosen, I hope and expect to see you back here next
week at your usual time.

JC: God willing, Doctor. God willing.

Transcript ends at 49:43:13

From the beginning, from the time of his re-arriving in the
world, John C. watched with anxiety, knowing how the things
arriving endlessly from up ahead in the time-stream could turn
out on arrival, knowing also that they could turn out better, or
not so good, or far worse than they ever had in the world he
had left. He was sure of what he had told Dr. Young, because
he'd seen it: in the short space of thirty or forty years the general pressure of forward-moving time in all its infinite parts
could not be deflected in huge ways, though in small ways it
could. But what would count as huge? What as small?

He was in his third year at USC when the bombs almost
did fall, but—once again—didn't. *Toe to toe with the Russkies.*
He knew they wouldn't—*almost* knew. Would it be more or
less likely in this here-and-now, that it hadn't happened in the
there-and-then he had come from? That was incalculable; it
was as though the worst lay hidden and unchanged within the
world even as, day by day, it didn't come about. John C. had
known immediately that what had not happened in Dallas
would alter what did happen thereafter, but not how.

He dropped out of grad school, he began making a living
in films and television, did some acting, courted women, and
watched the world dream its unending dream of possibilities,
the descendants of other dreams. The escape from fate that in
this reality kept the President from the telescopic sight of a

Mannlicher-Carcano, though he hadn't in the reality John C. came from (a story John C. had decided not to tell to Carla Young). John C. once tried to write that story, to write it just as it had not happened, until he found himself one late night before his little green Hermes typewriter in such a bath of cold sweat his fingers kept slipping from the keys, seeing inwardly napalm and Hueys, in a hellish film that would never be made.

Yes, that great whore History changed her mind, and the course of events in Southeast Asia was deflected. In November Kennedy experienced a crisis because of his Addison's disease—the thing that would kill him at 60—and lay for days in a coma. He awoke a different man. When American commitments in South Vietnam were withdrawn after the Catholic Diem family was murdered, Kennedy was able to let go of the domino theory. The South Vietnamese army unraveled, a new plebiscite was enforced by the United Nations. About the year 1972 John C. sat on the terrace of a grand old colonial Saigon hotel reading his *Paris Herald Tribune*, drinking an iced artichoke tea and watching the people, small beautifully formed men and women, the most graceful he'd encountered in a year's travel in these parts. A Viet Minh veteran sat impassive at the next table, smoking a cigarette Russian-style; he nodded, and John C. nodded in return, maybe a little more deeply, acknowledging the winning side.

The *Trib* he returned to reading on that day, like the news he watched and read back in the USA, had articles about people and events that were shadow-play versions of the ones he'd known in these years as he lived through them before. About the Hidden: growing numbers of American young people living in remote places in America, tribes of the golden west, placid, inventive, self-righteous or anarchic, almost illiterate. John C. imagined joining one of the beautiful and secret ones (there were fragmenting and slovenly ones too) and living out of time, beyond the reach of a strangeness and difference that sometimes made him dizzy. They were still there now, still a force; larger than ever, quietist, immune to history for now. But he never went beyond the imagining.

He stayed in LA, and did things that assumed the world would go on about as it had or better, and did other things that assumed it would be engulfed soon in mad destruction. He thought of buying gold to hoard with the money he made from his story sales and screenplay options, and people he'd gone to school with and were already much richer than he was urged him to do it, but in the end the absurdity prevented him; instead he bought shares in young companies that he could expect would do as well as they had done, or were doing, in the world he had exited from, and so they did. It was enough. He acquired a lovely British-green Jaguar and had it restored; once the restoration was done it would last for decades, a century. As he had his old Studebaker, he had it equipped with seat belts. He'd met Ernie Kovacs; he remembered James Dean. He got himself a house in Topanga up above the killing smog, not fancy but comfortable: good *feng-shui*, those few who knew the concept then told him. He was immune to nostalgia—it seemed to him inevitable that he would be—and yet the Canyon and its denizens, the scent of eucalyptus, the rock musicians and the folk musicians, the filmmakers with their Nagras and Eclairs, the photographers following them with their Leicas and Hasselblads, all filled him as though with memories, memories of a place he had never been but had known he wanted to be. He had a big stone-lined pool on the

edge of the cliff at the edge of his place, from where bath-
ers could look out over the lower reaches of the canyon and
glimpse the Pacific. An old stone farmhouse or shelter with a
roof of still-odorous cedar, dating from the previous century:
the photographers liked to pose people there. Canyon people
liked the pool and the place, and John C. liked having them
there; they understood there was something isolated or evanescent about him, that he never smoked dope or took drugs, but
with the women and certain young boys who were drawn to
him he was quite open: a spectrum shift that was profoundly
attractive to certain wilder natures or hearts more aflame than
his was. Often enough he slept alone.

And the world just rolled forward, or gave the illusion of
doing so, no longer able to be guessed at; he gave up guessing,
practiced Zen in the morning, he himself a *koan* that could be
pondered but not solved. *Things exist,* his wrinkled little guru
said, *but they aren't real.* This baffled some friends who came to
sit with him, made them laugh or fall silent. But John C. knew
it was simply so: he lived in a world falsified by the continued
existence of another in his own unreal heart and mind.

At about the time his life here outstripped his power to
control it—when the world as he had made it for himself
seemed to be wholly subsumed in the world that everybody
all together made, and would have made even if he had never
been part of it—he realized that he would still have to go
through all the events from the first life that would not or
could not be changed. His father's death, at a relatively young
age, burst aneurysm in the hospital to which in that time he'd
gone for a CAT scan and where in this time, soon, he would
go again, and the same thing would happen, for there was
nothing John C. could do about it and nothing in this life

would be likely to deflect it; he would have to wait for his mother's call, the same call he had got in this year in a different place. And there would be all the other griefs, his sisters', the nation's, to pass through: a few of them avoided by luck or a clinamen accounted for by nothing, but that were mostly just the ones he knew were to come because they *had* come and he had experienced them once already. He began to feel monstrously old.

And now it's the day before his birthday, seven o'clock in the evening, a sweet LA winter day. Five hours till midnight. What should he do, this night that is different from all other nights? Should he be Socrates, gather around him the wise and the young who love him (there are a few) to pass the last hours? Drive the Jag out to the desert, sit alone and watch dawn and judgment come? He can't know if the whole of his birthday is allowed to him to make his decision, or if it has to be made on the stroke of midnight or be moot. He decides that he will spend the hours exactly as he would if he didn't have destiny's coin to flip. He'll go to a party.

When was it that he began to find himself, even in the midst of the memorable and lovely things he earned in the second life, missing the small things of the first life? It didn't surprise him really, anyone with a shred of consciousness would have known at the start that such would be possible; it wasn't as if he escaped from a life in hell or prison or from poverty or hideous abuse, no, it was a good life, and the remembered moments are mostly sweet. He can even feel shame that he abandoned wife and children, friends and associates, career and home—but of course he has abandoned nothing, it all remains there for him to rejoin it if he chooses to. Whereupon the other life, this life he now inhabited, will—if he understands the rules—simply and entirely vanish away, never actually having existed.

If it were possible that he could be returned to the other, the first, life and once returned have no memory at all of this life; that if he did choose that life, which just because it *was* the original had ontological status different from the made life, then might he somehow contrive to be reconstituted in it at some commonplace moment, a moment that had arrived just at the point of his vanishment, or rather of his duplication or his revision, whatever the word might be; a moment anyway in which real life would tomorrow commence or recommence for him seamlessly, he himself oblivious that decades of otherness elsewhere had ever passed?

What if that could be, what if all along, from the beginning, it was *meant* to be? With a soft moan, a child's cry of longing or amazement, he sees himself beside the old Toyota wagon, ignorant of all of this world he looks out upon. A thundery summer evening, nineteen ninety-one, he inserting his exclaiming daughters into the backseat; the New England maples, smell of rain coming, and over him the swallows that nested in his barn flashing in the electric air.

No, it is not going to be so. It is not like that.

He takes the Jaguar down the Old Topanga Canyon road to the Santa Monica beach, because he may never see it again in his lifespan: the water blue satin, lifting like a veil with graceful gestures, the sun going down in a clear winter sky. It's longer this way, but he'll go along broad Sunset, glimpses of old mansions behind high walls and shaggy overgrown trees; up Hollywood Boulevard into the Hills.

Perhaps he does suffer from anosognosia, as Carla Young seemed to believe. It would make everything simpler. Can you suffer from a condition of ignorance that you don't know you have? Of course you can. If it's true that a neurological condition prevents his understanding that he has simply *invented* another life, a life wherein he graduates from a Catholic high school and goes on to Indiana University and then New York and all that thereafter happened, the life that (so he believes) he was living when he was given the chance to return to an early key point in that life and deflect it consciously and deliberately to make a life he'd rather live, *this* life—well, if he invented all that then it doesn't matter what choice he makes, because he will awaken tomorrow to find himself still here, in the only actual life he has ever had.

No. No. He did, he really did make that new life for himself starting at sixteen, in delight and a rage of creation, meeting and overcoming obstacles because he knew now what obstacles are and how to overcome them, which he learned only as he grew to maturity in *that* life, before he was given the choice to begin again. And he did win for himself what he wanted, taking every well-thought-out step in turn, from adolescence through early creative development and on.

He was offered a choice, the choice a hundred fools and heroes and maidens in tales are offered, but his choice was a choice he offered to himself. He understands at last now, though, that it wasn't in fact a choice at all: choice, and even possibility in some weird but absolute sense, has been drained out of the arrangement he made and the world he entered, and the world also that he left. He supposed at the beginning, in a vague way, that there would be a lesson and that he would have to learn it, about choice, about life, about desire, and that learning it would make the ultimate and mandated choice-making easier, hard but also easy, or clearer at least, because he would have learned in the course of his second life to choose the right one in the end. But he has learned nothing, and there is no choice. There is not one thing and another thing, one pile of hay and another pile. It's a single indivisible soup of possibilities and memories. If he returns to the first way, he will return imbued with three decades' worth of memories of another world; if he remains in this path or place he will swim always in the past he exited from, a world that has ceased to exist: which is dreadful to imagine.

He belongs in no place. It's just as though he has been exiled from the land of his birth, the land that was his, because of what he did: his hubris. He is that folklore figure who at a moment in his life laughed at Jesus on the Cross and so was cursed to wander forever, in lands and times he could never inhabit but only pass through in embarrassment, empty-handed.

The house in the Hills he comes to is one of those built up here in the late 1940s, Modernist masterpieces made of vast windows divided by slim columns, stone patios, wide stairs, jutting beams, and nothing else. As calm and open as a Greek temple empty for a thousand years. He stops the Jaguar where the parking service waits. His door is opened for him and he climbs out, takes the proffered ticket, and feels a sharp pang as he turns away, as though he is abandoning a friend, nevermore to see him. He climbs the broad shallow steps.

Maybe this was a mistake. Too many people, too many he knows well or superficially. But no, he can make no mistake now, no more than a skier on a fast downhill run: it's all go. He feels evanescent already, but calm enough. Takes a glass of champagne—something fizzing anyway—from the tray of a passing waiter. Is hailed, returns the wave. Is carried forward. Seconds continue to come and die.

Hours later. On the deck cantilevered over the rubble of rocks that seem to be frozen in their fall down the canyon he stands alone; a screening has been scheduled, and he has slipped away. He has decided that the limit set for decision won't be midnight, first seconds of the day. Dawn, he thinks, will be the moment. He's always felt, and on this deepening night feels intensely, "the always coming on/The always rising of the sun." He was born about dawn.

Below him on the lower level is the azure pool, where now naked boys and girls, bodies as hairless and gleaming as dolphins', are climbing out and taking towels; he knows they laugh, but he can't hear them. Something about their aliveness, and how they vanish two by two, leaving the water empty, the golden lights endlessly chasing, returns a thought to him that he once had but set aside.

He made it clear to Carla Young that in the story as he has lived it there could be no Third Thing: but of course there could be a Third Thing. Even now, at the very end, the unexpected resolution appears to him, the *anagnorisis.* How can it be that he has not ever considered it?

Death. Death as meta-stability, causing a permanent system crash in both worlds.

Maybe it's why he chose to come here, why he stands looking down from this height; maybe he knows, maybe he knew, that this is why. A step up onto that corner of this low concrete wall, a brief flight outward. *Put out the light, and then put out the light.* For the first time in years he remembers his dyke Hamlet on stage, thrusting a pistol, bare bodkin, into her mouth, desperate to do it, unable to. Barking out all those makes-cowards-of-us-all qualifications as though (*Yeah right*) she knew she was lying to herself, and to us. Not conscience but consciousness, and its inconceivable extinguishing.

No. Even if he was allowed to he wouldn't, and it's clear to him he is not.

He glances at his watch, or rather turns his wrist to see it, but doesn't comprehend the hour it shows. It's hard to tell, in the dull coming-on of the city lights and the smog that thickens above and resists them, whether the sun is near rising. He feels at last no anxiety, no urgency; he will make a decision or he will not; if it doesn't arise within him, it will be borne in upon him, and it will be made; and it will make no difference at all. Either he has invented all this, or he is himself invented: and these are not two contradictory things but one thing.

Yes: he can see it now: the sky in the east is really lightening, and clouds are taking shape, lit by the sun just under the horizon.

About the Author

John Crowley's novels include *Little, Big,* the *Ægypt* series, *Ka: Dar Oakley in the Ruin of Ymr,* and a new edition of *The Chemical Wedding, by Christian Rosenkreutz.* Recently retired after teaching creative writing at Yale for twenty-five years. He has received the Award in Literature from the American Academy and Institute of Arts and Letters, the Grand Prix de l'Imaginaire, and the Mythopoeic, Locus, and World Fantasy awards, including a Lifetime Achievement award. His website is johncrowleyauthor.com.

Publication History

"The Girlhood of Shakespeare's Heroines" (*Conjunctions* 39, 2002)

"In the Tom Mix Museum" (This Land Press, 2013)

"And Go Like This" (*Naked City*, 2011)

"Spring Break" (*New Haven Noir*, 2017)

"The Million Monkeys of M. Borel" (*Conjunctions* 67, 2016)

"This Is Our Town" (*Totalitopia*, 2017)

"Mount Auburn Street"

    "Little Yeses, Little Nos" (*Yale Review*, Vol. 93, 2005)

    "Glow Little Glow-Worm" (*Conjunctions* 59, 2012)

    "Mount Auburn Street" (*Yale Review*, Vol. 105, 2017)

"Conversation Hearts" (Subterranean Press, 2008)

"Flint and Mirror" (*The Book of Magic*, 2018)

"Anosognosia" is published here for the first time.